GREENRIDGE

to Jo

Patrick Bentley

Stay Safe

WITH FUNDING FROM
Comhairle Contae Fhine Gall
Fingal County Council

Cover design by Michael McGuinness, Bernie Sexton, Shauna Woods

This book is dedicated to my lovely brother Alex.

1962-2018

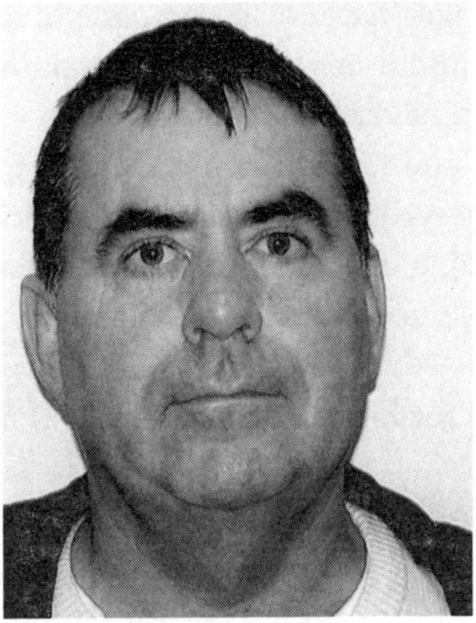

When I die
I want to die
not in a home built for
the unknown.
When I sing
I want to sing
sing like a lark as dawn beats the dark
That sweet melody set me free.
The battlefield
it rages on,
heart against mind
the mean versus the kind,
Small stones cause huge waves

By Damien Dempsey.

ACKNOWLEDGEMENTS

There are many people I would like to thank for their support and encouragement in the writing of this novel.

My wife Sharon – I cannot thank her enough. She's done so much to help, advise and encourage me with what proved to be the book that was hardest to complete, due to our personal family losses. Without her love, wisdom and sense of humour, Greenridge would never have been possible.

To my editor and friend Kevin O'Malley for all his wisdom and advice that paved the way yet again. Less is more.

To John Manning of Fingal Independent and Gerry Kelly of LMFM for their support and great interview skills. Always a pleasure.

To Don Baker for his encouragement and influence. Thanks for the texts.

To Rory O'Brien and Fingal Arts for their support of Greenridge.

To Paddy at Skerries Bookshop, for all the years of support and encouragement.

To Paul Carson, for a lifetime of inspired creativity.

To you, the readers, who support me at the doors and elsewhere. Thanks for sticking by me. I'm forever in debt to every one of you and wouldn't have been able to keep going as a writer were it not for your generous support.

Over and above everyone is my personal relationship with the Lord Jesus. In seven years at the doors selling my books, he's always been with me on this journey, and not once in all that time have I ever gone home discouraged or defeated . . .

with love
Patrick Bentley

patrick.bentley@yahoo.com
086 3363992
www.patrickbentley.ie

What you lose in the fire,
you will find amongst the ashes.

CONTENTS

Chapter 1

In a Split Second

I sat shivering in my wedding dress, staring intently at myself in the mirror. I did my best to pile on extra makeup, attempting to cover the thin, lined scar to the right-hand side of my face. *Everything's going to be okay,* I nervously repeated over and over in my fragile mind. *I've never been this happy, have I? So keep smiling, Amy Watts. You're only 27 and you have your whole life back on track.*

Another deep painful intake of breath, slowly exhaling with a nervous quiver. *Okay, okay,* I sighed as I felt a lump in my throat. *Remember Rob's strong words: 'Time to let the past go and move on to a bright future. Our bright new future together!'*

But it was impossible to stop glancing to my right at the photo on the dressing table of myself and my mother. Her amazing warm smile as she held me so close, so proud of her daughter after I had passed my Leaving Cert. with six A's. The bond between us so clear in both our faces.

That sharp, painful memory again invaded the moment. Another unwanted flashback to that awful day, now as real as if it was only yesterday. The visual memory as graphic as it was when the horrifying nightmare unfolded three years ago.

Another one of those unwanted flashes: I could see myself texting one of the girls as I threw my jacket on and headed out the door, all ready to jump into the car that morning, all smiles as Ma joked away about getting her hair done blonde for a change.

'And why not?' I laughed. I gave Dad a sly wink as he walked out behind us to bring in the black bin. I remembered I may have said something like 'Oh, Ma, he'll be all over you like a bad rash for the weekend if you return as a blonde!'

My memory has never been 100 percent clear about all that transpired that morning, or other aspects of my past life before that day. I just get flashes of hearing myself laughing and turning the key and carefully driving out our driveway in Hampton Cove in Balbriggan in County Dublin. Then nothing till we're past Skerries and parked in the town of Rush to pick up our weekly regular box of fresh veg from Buttery's stall next to the garage in the main street. The next stop was supposed to be Rachel's Hairdressers in Swords.

Then, in a split second, everything stopped. My life changed forever.

I hate the memories and have tried so hard to erase them from my thoughts. But it's impossible. I let out a painful sigh. The memory partially unclear, but the main horrific facts somehow are. I see the blood running down my face. The smell of oil and freshly-dug clay and grass. Even the overpowering smell of smoke and rubber. I was informed that the car had landed down a bank at the side of a field after hitting the side of a small stone wall on the right-hand side of the road, bouncing us back across to the other side, just missing a telegraph pole, before finally coming to stop with the car on its side in a ditch.

I could hear my mother moaning in discomfort. I turned my head slowly, painfully. The shock of the crash made it impossible to take in the horrible reality. We both just lay there, seemingly trapped, as time seemed to stand still.

'Is everyone okay?' I heard a frantic voice yelling. 'Help is coming!'

It was only then I realised to some degree that we had been involved in a serious car accident.

I tried to edge across towards my mother, but it was almost impossible to move my body correctly. I tried to wipe the blood from my own face to help myself see her properly. 'Ma, can you hear me?' I gasped, trying to reach my right hand across to touch her. It was only then to my horror I realised that my hand seemed to have been ripped open down the middle and looked like it was partially hanging off.

'Stop . . . stop this right now, Amy!' I screeched under my breath as I tried to banish the dreaded painful memory from my mind. 'No, stop. Rob's right. I've come so, so far in the last year. Time to do exactly what he keeps drumming into my head to do. *'Take your future back, Amy, take it in both those lovely hands of yours. And leave this nasty nightmare and depression where it belongs – in the past! In the past, love. Okay? Pull yourself together and do what you've been doing, and move onwards and upwards.'*

Another deep, nervous intake of breath. *Right, Amy! Wipe those tears away and let's put the final bit of makeup on and let's show off this beautiful wedding dress to my friends.*

In the next room, Claire Roberts exhaled a deep, fed-up sigh. 'Bit early to be trying on a wedding dress, don't you think?' she whispered, throwing her eyes up to heaven.

'Will you stop with the face, Claire?' snapped Sue. 'Nine months isn't that far away to the wedding. Anyway, once she's happy. My god, after that painful court case with that horrible heartless gas company crowd! God, that experience placed her close to death's door . . . then that frightening overdose . . . her depressed and heartbroken, on a bucket-load of anti-depressants . . . Will you at least look happy for her, Claire!'

'I know, but . . .'

'Then a big miracle unfolds,' continued Sue as she expressed a sense of frustration. 'She meets Rob. And now look at her. Deeply in love with the best-looking guy on God's own earth, who's not only taken her out of a dark hole, but has, almost single-handed, restored her to her old amazing self. So what's it matter if she buys her dress early and wants to show it off to her friends? So please, will you just lighten the hell up!'

Sue Walker, who wore her blonde hair short, was a slim, good-looking girl, unlike Claire, who wore her long black hair to shoulder-length and, since she was a kid, struggled with her weight, which played havoc with her own personal self-esteem. But as far as her personality was concerned, most people got on reasonably well with her. Plus, in spite of her struggles, at 28 years of age she was able to maintain a long-term relationship with her boyfriend, Colm Blake. But it was common knowledge that this relationship was anything but stable.

'Look,' said Claire in her now jealous tone, 'all I'm saying is this: it's supposed to be very bad luck to show off your wedding dress before the big day. Well, that's what my ma told me when I–'

'Oh, my dear god!' said Sue, throwing her arms up in the air. 'Will you listen to yourselves! Sheila Roberts lives in the bloody dark ages. Tell her to get with the times, Claire. It's 2009 and this is the happiest I've seen Amy in three long, painful, dark years. And you and your mother are worrying about some stupid, old-fashioned wives' tale about it being bad luck to wear a dress? Will everyone feckin' wake up!'

'Okay,' said Claire. 'I'm just a little bit nervous for her, Sue. She's so happy, I just don't want anything to spoil it. That's all I'm saying,' she muttered in an even less sincere tone.

'Look at me, Claire. What can go wrong? She's met Mr Hot-Hot-Hot-Sex-On-Legs-Colin-Farrell-Lookalike, as you keep whispering to me when we're out in the pub with them. Admit it yourself that like every other girl around town you go weak in the knees when he walks into the room!'

'Well, I do admit I go a little faint when I get a prolonged hug from him. I'm like a big lump of wobbly jelly when he gives me two minutes of his attention. And those big, brown come-to-bed eyes of his and his low, soft voice! I feel weak just thinking about it!'

'Will you keep your bloody voice down?' hissed Sue. 'Looks aren't everything. What's commendable is the fact he could have had his pick of any girl he wanted, yet he picked our Amy. And will you look at the time, the energy he's put into helping her get back on her feet. The hours of listening to her cry over her mother and having to give up the job that she loved so much. I mean, the understanding about her depression and restricted disabled hand. And not once have you ever seen him try to make her jealous when the girls flock around him. Not once. Always holding her hand and kissing her in public. Admit it, Claire. What other guy would have taken all that on? God, I just hope it all works out for them both.'

'I hear you, I hear you. Rob definitely has the whole package deal to offer our Amy,' she confessed, trying to hide her increased jealousy. 'The rest of us have to settle with the big beer bellies of this world, Tom and my Colm . . .'

'Hey! My Tom hasn't got a bi–'

Suddenly the door burst open and Amy breezed in. 'Well, girls,' she laughed. 'What do you both think of me now?' She swung around full circle.

'Oh, my good god!' gasped Sue.

'You look out of this world!' said Claire, putting her hand up to her open mouth.

Amy gave them another couple of twirls.

'Oh, wow,' beamed Sue. 'Rob is going to pass out on the spot. Gosh, you look absolutely stunning, girl.'

'What about my face, girls? Can you notice the scar?' A hint of insecurity, and uncertainty, suddenly took the glow from my incredibly warm smile.

'No, no, you'd hardly notice,' said Claire. 'You look absolutely radiant, Amy Watts.'

Sue assured me that I was the most beautiful bride ever. She placed a hand on both sides of my small face. Looking deep into my eyes she said, 'When Rob Cooper looks at you, he sees who you are. He sees your amazing eyes, your warm heart. He sees *you*, Amy, and that's all you need to focus on right now. He loves you! Listen to me, Amy. He loves you to bits.'

'You think so? Really? You both think I look okay?' My bright smile returned. 'Okay . . . Time to get out of this dress and hide it real fast. Rob texted me saying he'll be down later – and I think he's staying over,' I grinned.

They both helped me clean up and hang the dress away before sitting down to a coffee and a long girly chat.

'Seeing it's Friday, why don't we all meet for a drink later in Raff's?' smiled Sue.

We all agreed for around 9pm.

Amy rang her Dad later in the day while she went about making a chicken curry for dinner. 'Hi, Dad. How did the appointment go? Was expecting your call all morning. You're running a bit late. Thought you'd be home hours ago. Did they get the test results back?'

'Ah, everything came back clear, Amy. I'm grand, totally forgot to bell you with the news. I'm stopped off here in Skerries for a coffee in the Rockabill Café with Steve.' He winked.

'So did they say what it could be? Have you to do more tests?' I asked, concerned.

'Now, now, no fussing over me, Amy,' he said in a strong voice. 'You know I hate that. Look, they say it's all just probably stress-related after that long drawn-out court case last year. But they took more bloods and put me in for a fresh appointment after the Christmas. 25th January at 10am.'

'Okay . . . Well, look, Rob's coming over to join us for dinner, so don't you let Steve bloody Hill divert you in the Gladstone for pints of cider. Remember what Doctor Bayle said about your drinking and smoking. He said–'

Des hung up. He let out a deep and painful sigh before placing the phone back on the counter in the bar. He paused, and then looked sideways at Steve who was shaking his head in disagreement. He lowered the rest of his pint in one gulp. 'I can't tell her, Steve,' he said, dropping his voice to a whisper. He sighed again, shaking his head and nodding to the young-faced barman for two fresh pints. 'Not now, anyway. She's doing so well. She's even off all medication. Her doctor rang me two weeks ago saying he's very confident that she may be permanently out of the dark woods from this horrible depression.'

'And how the hell would he know that for sure!' snapped Steve. 'No one knows when or how depression really works, Des. It comes, it goes, it hits, it goes, then it creeps, it slithers back again – like a feckin' uninvited nightmare. My own sister Kate, remember? She suffered for 25 long years with the cursed illness. Anyway, as your best mate, I don't think you'll be able to hide the truth from her for long. What about when you start the chemo and you start losin' your hair?'

'What hair?'

They both laughed in spite of the seriousness of the situation.

'Look, I'll keep it hidden as long as I can. I just need to make sure she never finds out the full picture of my health. Well, not till after the wedding. As you know, I signed the house over to her months ago, so she'll have that as her security if the worst comes to the worst. Plus, if she can't return to work, she has the 270 grand from the claim to keep her going. Anyway, from what Rob told me, they're going to be financially okay.'

He let out another painful sigh, placing both hands over his face before continuing. 'The bloody truth is, Steve, I've never been able to properly mourn Tina's passing. All my time has been spent taking care of Amy's issues – the head injury that still affects her memory no end, the leg procedure for burns, her hand . . . then I had her depression to deal with daily, not to mention the . . . ye know . . . the suicide attempt last year. It's just worn me out, mate. All the hospitals, all the appointments. Then to top it all off, every time the phone rang when I was working, I jumped. God, hope it's not bad news. I never told you, but I'm getting this recurring nightmare of late, that I walk in and find her . . . dead. hanging in the hall way. I wake up in some sweat and have to remind myself that she's in a much better place now.'

'Jay, Des, that's . . .'

'Anyway, I need to just remain positive. Rob did a fantastic job getting her back from the brink, so in truth I should be very grateful for that. I just have to plan around everything so she never knows anything about my cancer. As far as everyone knows, I'm just run down, stressed out. That's all we tell anyone for now.'

'Well, fair play,' said Steve as he downed a fresh mouthful of cider. 'You have it all worked out.' He paused, placed his hand on his friend's shoulder and looked him straight in the eye. 'Now look at me, mate. We're going to fight this illness, you hear me? At 59 I think you have more than a few years left in that big tank belly of yours.' They both smiled as they lifted their glasses in agreement.

*

I jumped when the doorbell went. I checked one last time in the hall mirror and fixed the hair. Taking a deep breath, I opened the door to a smiling Rob holding two bunches of flowers and a box of chocolates. He almost fell over the hall step trying to lean forward to hug me. We both burst out laughing as he dropped everything there on the spot in the hall and grabbed me in his arms as we kissed passionately.

'Stop!' I giggled. 'Dad's on the way home. My god, you look so great. Did you get your hair cut? It looks shorter.' *Try to catch your breath.*

'Nah, it's just an added bit of gel. But enough about my hair. What about you? You're looking sexier every time I see you!'

I blushed, holding my good hand up nervously to brush some hair from the side of my head to partially cover the thin facial scarring, a nervous insecure reaction that was pointed out to me by a counsellor. But Rob lifted his hand and brushed my hair back in place. Then he ran a gentle, caressing finger down the scar to reassure me how loved, how accepted I was in his eyes.

I paused and stood looking into his deep brown eyes for ages before nervously laughing aloud to break the tension. 'Okay, so what's the story with the two bunches of flowers, dummy? Don't tell me you fancy my dad as well!'

We both giggled.

'Well,' he said, picking them back up off the hall floor, 'the roses are for you and the others, the big bunch, are for . . . your mother. You told me her anniversary is December the 2nd. That's Tuesday, so look: why can't we both go hand in hand to her graveside? Now I know before you start giving out to me for bringing it up, I know you keep saying you can't go there. *Never, ever,* as you put it. But at least try to face this.' He was trying his best not to ruin the happy smiley moment.

'Eh, not . . . right now,' I managed as the smiled disappeared.

'But look, thanks very much for remembering the date. What a lovely, kind and thoughtful thing to do.' I let out a sigh as he took me in his arms.

'Look,' he went to continue. 'I smell burning.'

'Oh, shit! The dinner!' I raced down the hall but thankfully it was just the water from the rice that had boiled over and was giving off a burning aroma.

Rob followed, now laughing. 'Jay, now I have to have a serious rethink. Do I really want to go marrying a woman that burns a man's dinner?'

'Will you stop it!' I laughed, throwing the kitchen towel across at him. 'By the way, you're on bloody wash up. Here, give me those chocolates till I have one before dinner.'

'No, no!' he protested as he held them up over his head.

'Oh, just one caramel. Please!'

Just then, the key turned in the front door. Dad.

Rob threw the box on the table and put his head out into the hall. 'Des!'

'Give me one sec, Rob. Need to take a big leak.' He looked intently at the flowers in the hallway as he struggled to take his jacket off after the feed of pints. 'Who's the flowers for?' he mumbled.

'Rob's taking the big bunch to Mammy's grave,' I called as I turned my back and put the plates out on the table. 'He brought them up just now. Hope you're hungry.'

'Hope . . . What's hope?' he muttered under his breath as he finally got the jacket off. 'Hope me arse!' He cleared his throat. 'Right, right. I'll be down in a few minutes. Clear the runway!' he sniggered to himself as he trudged upstairs.

After half an hour Rob tiptoed up the stairs and found him on the bed with his eyes closed. 'Hey, Des, up you get,' he ordered. 'Dinner's gone cold.'

Des opened his eyes slowly. 'Sit down for a minute, Rob, but close the door first. Need to tell you something. But you're not to breathe a word about it to anyone. You have to promise me not to tell Amy.'

'Hey, big man,' smiled Rob as he closed the door quietly. 'You know you can trust me with anything.' He sat at the end of the bed. 'Is everything alright?'

Des went on to explain to him about the cancer. 'But those doctors did explain that a few treatments of chemotherapy should blast it away,' he heaved, trying his best to make it sound non-life-threatening.

Rob gulped and stood up. 'What cancer? God. Where?'

'Right lung. They found a spot – well, a very small lump. But said it hasn't spread. But look, you have to make sure that if and when I start losing the small bit of hair I still have, if Amy gets at all suspicious, you'll step in and tell her I'm grand. Lie through your teeth if you have to, Rob. I just don't want my girl getting that horrible depression back. Not now, not with her doing so well.' He closed his eyes again.

Rob sat back down. Moving up closer, he placed his right hand on Des's shoulder. 'I'll do anything. Anything at all. And I can't tell you how sorry I am that you have this sickness. But Des, don't ask me to lie to Amy. Please, no lying. We both promised each other faithfully from the start that we would never lie or have big secrets. We both sat down one evening in my apartment in Swords we had a real heart to heart. *No secrets,* we said. So if you're asking me to hide something from Amy, I'm afraid I can't do that. I'll say nothing about this talk, but if it starts to look too obvious about your health, I think then you need to sit her down and tell her yourself.'

He stood up and let out a deep sympathetic sigh before turning to the door. 'I think you underestimate just how far Amy has come along in the last year, Des. She's not that broken-down little girl you saw almost at death's door last year. She may even surprise you one day as to how strong she's become.'

Des slowly opened his eyes and stared. 'I know I've a few beers on me but I've said this to you before when I was sober. Thanks for everything you've done to help her and this family. You've been a . . . a godsend.'

Rob smiled back. 'Ah, will ye stop! It works both ways.

You've been like a father to me in the past year.' He smiled, extending his hand to help him up.

*

After a lovely relaxed dinner, Rob and I headed out to Raff's pub in Skerries town. Claire and Sue, along with Sue's boyfriend Tom Carroll were already in and had a table over to the right-hand side of the pub.

'Oh, my god!' Claire whispered, 'Here comes Sex-on-Legs!' She downed another mouthful of beer trying not to make it to noticeable that she was staring.

Every girl's head turned as Rob passed by the main bar holding Amy's hand firmly.

'What a butt!' gasped a blonde girl sitting with her friends.

'Wouldn't be my type, I have to say,' said one of her friends. 'He just loves himself no end.'

'Right,' said Rob as he pulled a chair out for Amy. 'A round of drinks on me.' He nodded to Tom. 'You help me carry them.'

I went to stand up to offer to help but Rob insisted I relax as Tom finally dragged himself up from his chair.

Up at the bar Tom checked that no one was in earshot. 'Listen, Rob,' he said in a low tone. 'Sorry I haven't been around to add my support to Amy and yourself. My job has me tied up in bloody knots. Whatever you do, mate, don't take up driving lorries around Europe. Anyway, I was going to ring you last Friday as I was thinking more about what you were saying about investing money in small developments. I mean, not a word to Sue, but I've a good few grand saved. And if you're as confident as you sounded five weeks ago, I'd be willing.'

'Stop, Tom,' hissed Rob as he paid the girl for the drinks. 'I wasn't trying to get people to come in with me on some kind of deals. I was just explaining what I do for a living. I'd never let you or the gang risk your savings.'

'But you said there were no real risks.'

'Everything has risks, bud. So not on my life, Tom, would I

want it on my conscience that one of Amy's best friends went and invested his life savings with me, and somehow it went pear-shaped and he lost everything. I'm rather new to this game myself and still kind of finding my feet with the way it all works out. A lot of stress involved. Plus if Sue found out she would kill you stone dead, but that's after cutting my head off for getting you involved. Come on. Help me with the drinks.'

As they approached the table Rob could hear Amy tell the gang the extra bit of good news.

'Yeah, that's right. I'm starting back at my old job in child care in January. Well, three days a week to just see how I get on. Can you all believe that!' she beamed. 'After three long painful years I'm going back to the job I love!'

'Excellent!' Tom yelled as he placed the drinks neatly on the table.

Everyone gave Rob the thumbs up, for it was clear he had yet again played a hand in this latest development in Amy's recovery.

'Well!' shouted Claire. 'Let's raise our glasses to this!'

Everyone clinked glasses. 'To Amy!'

'To Rob and Amy!' yelled Sue.

Claire's phone went, spoiling the moment just a tad. It was Colm. She placed her glass back down and headed to the smoke room. She lit up and rang him back. *Take a deep breath and don't lose the head.* 'So are you coming down? Everyone's here for them, but yet again you're not. It's bloody embarrassing. We're supposed to be her best friends.'

'Will you slow down, Claire. I'm in the Millrace pub, waiting on a taxi. Be there in ten minutes.'

'Hurry up. She was asking where you were.'

When Claire returned, Rob was telling all the gang that the plan was to have the wedding reception close to home. 'The Bracken Court Hotel seems the obvious spot according to Amy,' he smiled.

'Perfect!' laughed Tom. 'Not far to fall after the big feed of pints!' 'This has to be a story for your man, Mark Cagney at Ireland

AM,' said Sue. 'My god, I'm close to tears, Amy!' she confessed as she leaned over and hugged them both.

*

The night ended with everyone crashing late into the local Balbriggan 'Home' night club.

I stood alone in the corner wrapped around Rob as the gang danced away. 'I think God sent you,' I slurred in his ear. 'some kind of angel is what you are! Everything about you I love. You saved my life.'

Rob brought my face around gently, looking intently into my eyes and smiled. 'Do you remember the first time we met?'

'Of course. Outside Joe May's pub, 2.45pm, 21st of September. It was an unusual sunny Sunday. You walked across the road. I thought you were heading past me to the girls behind me. But to my amazement it was me you wanted to chat to. I remember saying that I thought you were following me as the week before I'd seen you in The Harvest Pub in Balbriggan and the week before that in Raff's.'

'Do you remember what I kept saying after we started dating?' he asked, before landing another warm kiss on my lips.

'Yes, that I should be taking the credit for my progress.'

'Bang on. See, I exhaust a bit when people slap me on the back. You're the one that's got yourself to where you are. I'm just the guy who's had a small hand in encouraging and witnessing this astonishing miracle unfold. You and your friends all think I'm some kind of messenger sent to you, but I'm just an ordinary guy. And everything that's got you to where you are is down to you alone. Now listen, Amy. There's just one thing left for you to do before we set off to live our lives together.' He paused. 'This isn't the greatest place to say it, but here goes.'

I nodded for him to continue.

'Tuesday morning you need to take the flowers and go to your mother's graveside and make your peace about the car crash. You have to face her, Amy. You cannot expect to hide from this past forever. Then – look at me, love, look at me – and then you'll be free to live your life. Otherwise this journey you and I are on will always have a dark cloud hanging over it.'

I stepped back but he took my hand and drew me closer into his arms.

'It's time to move on, Amy. Time to move on.'

Moments later Sue raced over, pulling us both out onto the dance floor to join the rest of the gang in dancing the night away.

*

Next morning at 9.05am, four miles from the Naul in a remote part of County Dublin, a patient attacked Nurse Peters in the main hallway of Greenridge Psychiatric Hospital.

Chapter 2

Greenridge

51-year-old Nurse Peters screamed in terror when Frank Crosby, a long-term mental patient at Greenridge, attacked her as she was taking another patient into one of the main bathrooms. Crosby, a big man, grabbed her aggressively from behind and dragged her out of her standing onto the stone-cold marble tiled floor in the main hallway as she repeatedly screamed out for backup. Within seconds, two well-built male nurses were on the scene and tackled Crosby to the ground as he shouted and fought to free himself. They seemed to be losing their struggle to restrain him when his right arm got loose, allowing him to punch one of them in the face, sending him flying back through the main dining room doors with a loud bang. The second male nurse was himself unfortunate as he lost his footing in the struggle and went crashing to the floor. Crosby, now loose again, re-seized Nurse Peters by the throat.

Suddenly 56-year-old Christy Boyle came rushing from the main hall doorway shouting for calm. He was a short, half-bald man, but built like a tank. His only disadvantage in such circumstances was the bad limp he carried.

Yet again he astonished everyone with his surprising ability to defuse a risk in situations such as this. He took one of Frank's arms and in a split second freed up Nurse Peters from his left-hand grip. He then calmly pinned Crosby to the wall, pleading to the patient in a gentle yet firm voice. 'It's over, Frank. Please, let Nurse Peters go,' he reasoned. 'Everything is okay. I'm here. '

Frank was breathing heavily with perspiration running down his haggard, frail face. He finally released his right-hand hold on the terrified nurse as his anger seemed to slowly drain away as he fixed his eyes intently on Christy's kind, non-intimidating gaze.

'No one's going to hurt anyone today, isn't that right, Frank? Not today,' said Christy before backing away to let the two male nurses restrain Frank as one administered a sedative injection. 'Easy with him,' gasped Christy in an anxious voice as he stood back looking around as if he detected staff wanted to applaud him for his efforts. He wiped the sweat off his face with his sleeve. 'Please, lads,' he stressed again as he put his glasses back on.

Just then the main hall door swung open again and in came the top man himself, Dr Grimes, with Nurse Bridie Whelan in tow. Frustration now written all over his face when he saw Nurse Peters struggling to get up off the floor, her dress badly torn at the side, as one of the staff nurses attended to her.

'I'm going to be okay,' she fumed as she held her neck. There was blood everywhere from the male nurse's bloodied nose.

'Get the hell back to work!' Dr Grimes barked as more staff workers stopped and stood observing the unfolding drama. Even some of kitchen staff came out for a nose. 'We have a hospital to run, in case you've short on memory!'

He turned and pointed to Frank Crosby who was by now starting to ease from the injection that had been administered. 'You've hurt one of my staff for the last time, Crosby,' he hissed through gritted teeth. 'The bloody size of you, hitting a defenceless women like that!' He leaned across to Nurse Whelan. 'Take him out of my sight, down to B Ward.'

'Nooo! . . . She hit *meeeee!*' Frank bellowed as he was hauled away.

Christy stepped in. 'Randy or I mean Dr Grimes, if I could have a small word, Sir. Mr Crosby has been doing so well of late and –'

'Don't, Christy. Don't you ever or anyone ever address me by my first name. How many times do I have to remind staff, It's *Doctor Grimes* or just *Doctor*. That's it. Now don't you dare question my instructions in front of my staff!' he hissed again. He turned to Nurse Whelan, lowering his voice further. 'What the hell is wrong with everyone around here? Is everyone going soft in the head or what? In case you're forgetting,' he snapped back at Christy, 'this is a bloody psychiatric hospital with very dangerous patients at large. Not some kids' playground, or babies' crèche where a small slap on the arse sorts everything out.'

Now with index finger stabbing accusingly in the air he upped his voice to the remaining staff that were still standing around within earshot. 'Some members of this staff aren't doing their job right around here of late, and that's why, every single day, half the patients in this hospital are going around under-medicated.' He pointed at Christy. 'That, in turn, enables them to become not only violent to one another, but extremely dangerous to my staff. And, as I have to remind you yet again, my number one priority as the big dog of this hospital is for the everyday safety of my staff.'

He walked away but turned again, beckoning Christy to follow him to his office.

'Right away, Doctor. Right away,' gasped Christy, now with an air of insecurity.

Grimes closed the door and asked Christy to take a seat. 'What you did may be what you observed others doing down the years, and I must acknowledge it was brave. You may have saved someone from serious injury, at the risk of getting yourself hurt.' His voice was now calm and relaxed. 'As you already know from our staff meetings, I'm fighting hard to establish and maintain calm here at Greenridge. Now from what I hear and see, you seem to be very obliging at stepping in to try calm the more dangerous of patients down. But my own professional opinion is you seem to fall into the deadly illusion that you're some kind of top trained nurse, a saviour to patients like Crosby and others. But look at me. Don't for a single moment think that patients like him aren't capable of ending your life. A split second, that's all it may take. Never turn your back on them, Christy, because one day they may go in a split second from as innocent as a child to a wild murderous animal and you'll end up badly injured, if not killed. Anyway,' he sighed, 'that's all for now.'

He picked up his pen and started writing.

Christy paused for a moment, then stood up and headed towards the door. He turned and gulped. 'Em, thanks for the reminder, but I was initially trained by my own father Oliver for some of the smaller duties. At the time he was one of the best carers ever to grace the profession here at Greenridge. You can check the records – it should state all the facts. He communicated to me very forcefully that each sick patient at Greenridge was once some mother's child, and we must love and respect them as we would our own friends, even our own family. Help them recover and be sane again. But I hear your warning. Believe me, I'm very aware of the dangers, and as you know I'm fully insured to help in such dangerous situations. With 39 years as active maintenance man plus helper here in the hospital, that's a lifetime of experience.'

'But not a trained nurse,' came the calm, cutting reminder.

Christy paused then looked directly at Dr Grimes who had stood up walked over to gazed out the window. 'Maybe not, but I would have given everything to be one. It was my one dream growing up to be head nurse here. But my father said that,' he paused. 'Anyway, if you don't mind me speaking my mind, we need more staff like the new young Nurse Wendy Collins if we're going to get back to some kind of stability around here,' he continued. 'And I don't think I'm overstressing the situation one bit by saying that, in my humble opinion, Miss Collins has the attitude and ability to make the world of difference here at Greenridge. The woman has love, and vision, and from what I have seen, she, like me, is horrified that we're back using shock treatment as a means of dealing with some patients, when it's clearly not necessary. She's told me in private that it was her understanding from her last training post that this procedure is well outdated. Done away with, years ago. And that we have many other modern forms of medication to deal with extreme situations, like today.'

Dr Grimes dropped his head turned and observed Christy over the frames of his glasses. He was a small, chubby, odd-faced character, mid-to-late forties, who always wore a white shirt under his black suit that complemented his black hair combed neatly back. The only flaw in his rather strange appearance was a dodgy-looking bend in his nose, a result from a belt of a hurley stick in his school days. 'Not true. Some doctors like me still see a place for electroconvulsive therapy in our practices, but only in extreme cases – like today.'

He went back to writing notes pointing out in a stern tone that what Christy was stating was none of his business. Not part of his job to even be asking about such procedures. Then in a lower, more direct tone he asked, 'Has Miss Collins been asking anything else about the way I handle my hospital since taken over? You yourself more than once seem to be somewhat frustrated at the new way I run things around here. Am I up against a little secret sect?'

He sat back down and picked up a file and then glanced up with a look of annoyance at Christy. 'This is . . . what? . . . the fourth time you have made reference to my handling of issues at Greenridge. Not to mention those complaints that have been handed in by you under every other doctor that graced the halls of Greenridge.'

'Well, no. Well, yes . . . First, Miss Collins does seem, like me, to be observing with some displeasure how other staff nurses handle patients. And yes, it's no big secret around here that I myself am more than concerned at how Nurse Whelan and others handle some of the more disabled patients. And yes, there is a file the width of your arm full of concerns I aired about patient treatment over the years.' Christy gave Dr Grimes a look that meant he was now attempting to challenge his authority on the way things were being run at Greenridge since he took up the post.

'That will be all for now,' Dr Grimes sighed, going back to his writing as Christy made his way again towards the door. 'On that very subject, changes at Greenridge,' he continued, without looking up, 'there is a small matter that's been kind of a concern for me of late, Christy. Your age. You're what . . . 56? Almost 57?

That's actually very close to retirement age, is it not?' he said in a condescending tone. 'Have you ever thought about getting out early?' He paused, then with a smirk continued, 'Well, maybe I shouldn't say this, but it's been coming up a lot of late. Well, what's the most sensitive way of saying this without sounding offensive? Right, here goes. It's been reported to me a number of times that some visitors who drop in at the weekends to see family members and see you out and about: well . . . it's your size. Your dress code, it's not a pretty sight, totally at odds with the new image I'm trying to create. Plus other factors, etc., etc. Well, it's your whole appearance, Christy, if you can understand.'

He stood up and looked out the window again. 'One visitor openly confided in me that it made their first visit here very uncomfortable. I don't mean to sound cruel when I say this, but there has been instances of late where two, maybe three visitors saw you doing some gardening, wielding that large hedge clippers you use, as they drove into the main car park they became terrified to get out of their cars at first. You see, they were convinced you were someone from the hospital. An actual *patient*. Do you get my gist? My concern?' he now sneered. 'Look: bottom line, Christy, I could certainly pull a few strings to make certain you get the best possible retirement deal.'

Christy tried his best to hide his hurt at the insensitive remarks. 'I love my work and I'm very determined to see out my full term here,' he said, 'and stay on in my staff digs here at Greenridge as part of my retirement deal. But thanks for the offer.' He composed himself and kept his cool.

Just as he was opening the door Dr Grimes muttered under his breath for him to hear, 'Of course, I could have you transferred.'

But Christy decided not to respond.

'Oh, one last little matter that I forgot to mention,' Grimes called out. 'There was one other notable complaint put in by members of female nurses regarding your appearance. Could you see to it that you wear a proper belt on those trousers or jeans? The top half of your . . . arse . . . is hanging out all over the place for all to see. Very unprofessional, don't you think?'

Christy's face went bright red with embarrassment, as he tried not to show his anger. He closed the door behind him with a loud, angry bang.

After taking two strong painkillers in a glass of water, Grimes made his way to down to B Ward, but bumped straight back into Christy who was struggling, with a helper, to carry a big heavy door down the last few steps.

'Over to the left, Alan,' puffed Christy. 'Okay, just lean it up against the wall. Thanks very much. I'll take it from here.'

'And what's all this?' asked Grimes.

'Well, it's the soundproof door for B Ward. You did ask me to order it,' explained Christy, trying his very best to hide his anger from earlier.

'I never ordered a soundproof door! Let me see those papers.' He checked the invoice and looked back at Christy.

'You asked for the best possible door as part of our upgrading of Greenridge,' stressed Christy.

'Yes, yes, of course. I remember now. But didn't I sign off for just a plain door? Not this big expensive-looking thing!'

'Well, I have to confess,' sighed Christy. 'This is my mistake. I'll have it returned straightaway. It's just the guy on the phone who we deal with pointed out that if it's for the most dangerous wing, the noisy guys as he put it, then why not get a soundproof door as it will drown out the eerie echoes like loud howling and crying at night? That in turn will remove the ongoing problem of other patients in C Ward who are being disturbed at all hours of the night when they're trying to sleep. I thought he made perfect sense. But sure, look. I'll ring him and get him to change it straightaway.'

Dr Grimes paused for thought. 'No, actually. Now that you say it, that does make sense. We'll keep it.'

He walked past into the corridor. Just off to the right was the small room where they administered the EST. They already had Frank Crosby strapped down.

Christy in the meantime was feet away at the top of the hallway as he placed the new door next to the old steel one.

Dr Grimes gazed around at what was once just a plain open ward, but now had been split into twenty small padded rooms with just a single bed to each. The doors were locked at night, but each had a small, plastic, unbreakable window so that the night nurses could check without actually entering the rooms. B Ward was of course used for the worse, the most dangerous patients – individuals that posed a threat not only to themselves but to others.

Dr Grimes remained composed. Then he nodded to Christy to leave the door till after lunch. With a hint of irritation in his eyes Christy returned upstairs without a word.

Dr Grimes slammed the steel door closed. 'Right. Who was responsible for this latest disaster? Who administered the medication this morning, Nurse Whelan? *Who?*' he shouted at the top of his voice, startling the other patients no end. 'I could have lost a member of staff, which again would leave me looking like a very incompetent doctor. Since I took over, I've lost count of the number of times someone's been attacked. Miss Whelan, please step into the hall and check this chart.' He handed her the morning's medication checklist.

'I . . . don't understand what happened on this occasion, Doctor,' she said. 'There was just me, Nurse Peters, two care staff. Christy was at hand and well, the new girl, Nurse Wendy Collins.'

Dr Grimes looked down the hall, remembering Christy's words. 'Of course, the new girl, Nurse Collins!' 'Right, okay. We'll come back to the matter later today. But first . . .' He nodded to one of the male nurses, Noel Jennings. Jennings was formerly from London and had worked in a hospital in the Brixton area for many years before moving to Ireland with his wife and family. He was highly regarded by everyone as the strongest minded staff member that ever graced this difficult line of work. Everyone in the profession turned to him for advice and council when things got too much for them to handle.

'Got ye, Doc,' said Noel as he showed little or no emotion by instantly letting fly and slapping Frank across the face ordering him to shut the hell up. He then placed the gum guard in Frank's mouth and proceeded to set him up for the treatment.

'And when you're all done, Miss Whelan,' continued Dr Grimes, 'tell Nurse Collins I want a word with her in my office.'

'I'll see to that,' she smirked as she gave a strong sense that she didn't rate her at all.

Miss Whelan was known to most patients as just Maggie. Dark rumours had it that for years she tended to have an evil reputation as one who singled out certain poor frail elderly patients for horrifying sadistic abuse. Life would be one of pure hell if you were one of her unfortunate victims. Incidentally, she got the nickname Maggie some years back from patient Fredrick Bowels as she bore a gloomy resemblance to Margaret Thatcher. She even had the same scary hairstyle and talked like her. But bear in mind she was always extremely clever not to unleash the darker side of her cruelty in front of the younger staff members or even patients, bar maybe one or two like her colleague, Nurse Peters.

As Grimes walked back up the stairway, he could hear Crosby's shrieks and restricted moans echo out. 'We need that soundproof door in today!' he roared back down the stairs. '*Today!*'

'Well, Nurse Collins. You're working here . . . what? Three short weeks?' Dr Grimes said through a smirking grin as he closed the office door with another loud bang. 'Sit down, sit down. You're what . . .? 21 years of age? And with little or no experience at how a place like this is run? And already you're going around complaining about how we do things around here. Oh, yes, I hear everything. Miss Judge-and-Jury from Sligo comes down to Dublin and in no time thinks she knows everything about how places like this is run. Over and above me and Nurse Whelan who's in her 50s and who's worked here for 25 long, painful years.'

'Dr Grimes . . .' started Nurse Collins in a strong un-intimidated voice, 'the other staff may seem somewhat scared by the powers-that-be around here, but not me. Firstly, I'd like to make a complaint about what I witnessed with my own eyes here yesterday at 10.40am. Yes, I'm making an official complaint against Nurse Peters, who was bathing Mr Frank Crosby – *in cold water*. Yes, I was so, so shocked myself, Dr Grimes. The man was crying with the cold, and then she left him unattended for a good ten minutes. He then started to cry again. She came back, and from where I was standing, she seemed to place his head under the water as if she was about to drown the man. Nurse Whelan seemed to think that it was hilarious and screamed the place down laughing before Peters said, 'Why not drown him as you would a rat!' Now that is nothing but plain torture, Dr Grimes. Cold-hearted torture. And when I tried to intervene, she . . . well, she effed and blinded me to mind my own effin' business. In front of everyone. And people wonder why poor Mr Crosby attacked her this morning in the hall? Well, there's your bloody answer!'

'Oh, pipe down, Miss Collins, and listen to me very carefully.' He turned his voice to a low, gentle tone. 'You and others assume a lot of things. This isn't any normal hospital. We have very disruptive patients to deal with. Some are very physically deformed, who cry and scream at the drop of a hat. Then as you know we have our hands full with very dangerous, criminally insane patients who need very careful attention. And to top the problem, we've had cutbacks which have left us way understaffed. Now listen. If a little crying and cold water is a concern to you, then you may hand in your notice right now, Miss Collins. Right now, this is hardball. Not everyone's cut out for the harsh realities of Greenridge, but may I end with a word of warning: be very careful about making wild accusations about other staff members. I will certainly do a follow-up to your concerns and do out a report. I see great things here for you at Greenridge. But you need to learn to understand a little more about this line of work. Is that okay?' He hoped he was giving the strong impression he was well in control of his hospital.

'Yes, that seems fair enough, I suppose,' said Nurse Collins, now looking somewhat less sure and less confident in her own statements.

'Oh and be more careful about administering the medications in the mornings nurse. There was a small notable complaint sent in by a staff member that you may have given Crosby a slightly lower quantity of medication. Not a hanging offence but after this morning's episode you may need to be more attentive while handing out the tablets. You can close the door on the way out.' He ended with Nurse Collins heading out the door trying actually to remember.

Only three days later she was in the dining room where other members of staff were busy feeding breakfast to the more disabled patients. One of the staff gave her a bowl and spoon and she began feeding a girl who was strapped into a chair. Five minutes into the feeding she found herself continually stopping to halt the girl from pulling the spoon out of her hand and partially spitting her food back out.

After a couple more unsuccessful attempts to fed her she snapped. 'Stop grabbin' my feckin' arm!' she shouted. She slapped the girl across the back of hand. 'I said stop it – now!'

Suddenly everything went silent as Nurse Collins looked around in shock at her own mindless action. Nurse Whelan stared at her with a spiteful grin.

Christy had just walked in from the kitchen and saw the tail end of the incident.

But most importantly, over at the opposite side of the main dining room door, there was Dr Grimes, scrunching his bent nose as the situation unfolded, chart in hand doing his early morning rounds. He smirked. *Welcome, Nurse Collins. Welcome to Greenridge.*

*

The morning after the night out clubbing, I sat on the side of the bed with coffee in hand. Thankfully my hangover wasn't bad, as I didn't seem go as mad as the girls with the late-night shots at the club. But something was obvious to me since I woke up. Something had changed in the middle of my conversations with Rob that went on into the early morning hours. I stared across the bed at him as he slept soundly. For a long time now I'd been trying to get that last breath of confidence to race down that runway and take off with him into our future. But so many big events had kept me from taking off and flying up, up, flying above the dark clouds of my past. Big events like my mother's death, the crash, the guilt, the blame. Then the obvious stuff like the side effects to my head injury, the facial scar, and this horrible disabled hand I had to carry around. These just added tons to my own crippling insecurities when we were out, seeing all those good-looking girls giving Rob the eye. Every time we went out socialising, they seemed to flock over almost in a queue waiting to chat, even flirt with him, all of them far more attractive than me, so I thought. Yet in truth Rob never gave them his full attention. He always turned around in his polite manner and involved me in the conversations.

So today is the day to take off into our future. No more holding back. If Rob wants all of me as he stated over and over last night, then I must give him my heart, my soul, my all. This was my second chance at a happy life, and this is the time to race down that runway and take off.

'I love you so much, Robert,' I whispered, before heading down to make him a big Saturday fry-up.

Dad was up and had already got breakfast started. I went straight over and put my arms around him as he put another rasher on the pan.

'Oh, Dad, everything's going to work out, isn't it?' I smiled, hugging him from behind.

'Not so fast!' he laughed as he almost dropped the eggs on the floor. He turned and eyed his girl. He paused in thought before. 'It's been a long journey for us both, Amy,' he said, looking somewhat surprised at my early morning emotional statement. 'I lost count of the times I earnestly prayed we'd see light at the end of these three years of darkness. And to see you smile all the time like you are now after everything is simply just brilliant .

. . Now I know you've going to kill me for putting a dampener on this little moment, but have you put any more thought into facing a visit to your mother's grave? You know that counsellor said it's a step you have to –'

'Strange that you mention that,' I interrupted. 'Because Rob was talking to me again last night about exactly this, Dad. And I've already made up my mind to visit Ma's grave, not Tuesday, but today. Yes, that's right. Today. I'm going to say what I need to say to her.' I was filling up with emotion as I spoke. 'Dad, I'm going to move on with my life. Everyone is so right. And this is the time. This is something I have to do, not tomorrow, but today.'

He grabbed me and hugged me. 'God, I'm so happy to hear you say that, Amy,' he said, his voice beginning to catch in his throat, 'and I know your mother is smiling down right now from Heaven as we speak.'

Tears appeared in his eyes. My god, I knew deep inside Dad was still hurting so much over losing Ma in such a horrific way. They were so in love, so close and with all my issues, I wasn't able to be there for him. I felt so guilty in that moment about things I cannot talk about or admit even to myself. Something I hid from everyone about the accident, a hurt, a horrible guilt, a dark secret, from Dad and even Rob. But to survive I had to keep this one thing to myself. Here was I moving onto a happy conclusion with Robert. But Dad was never going to move on, was he? And yet there he stood, beaming, so pleased that I was making this final step out of the past into my new future.

'You're so blessed to have that man upstairs,' he went on to say as he turned his head back, feeling slightly embarrassed at crying openly in front of me. He dried his tears with a bit of kitchen roll, then nervously laughed. 'My god, what are we both like!' he said, blowing his nose, turning around with a smile. 'Ha, a pair of walking soap operas. Your mother would be throwing her eyes up in the air laughing at me!'

My phone went. Claire.

'Go on, take it. I'll sort out these rashers and eggs.'

'Oh, my god, Amy!' confessed Claire as I sat on the sitting room sofa. 'My bloody head. Feels like someone's after hitting my brain with a big bloody hammer. I'm never, ever drinking those shots again. Never, Amy. Do you know what me and Colm bloody ended up doing? We fell in the doors of Deli Burger at 3.30am and got a big large feckin' family chicken box meal between us. Then we got a taxi up the road to Pinewood Green Road to his mother's house, and then he ate nothing, I don't know if you noticed anything odd with him last night. He seems slightly withdrawn and saying very little of late, he said he was okay but he has something on his mind – I can tell a mile away. I'll get it out of him today. Anyway, we woke up at 9am dying a death, with chips and half-eaten chicken all over the floor.

I heard Rob upstairs moving around in the bathroom.

'I have to stop eating crap food. My arse is getting so big. Anyway, enough about me. How are you? You looked so extra happy last night with heartthrob Rob. Ha, ha, everyone was watching you both dance. Everyone is thrilled to bits for you, with marriage around the corner and now going back to your old job next year.'

'Heartthrob Rob!' I laughed. 'I'm grand. As you noticed, I didn't go as mad with the drink last night. Stayed up drinking a glass of wine for ages when we got home, just talking about stuff. Just making breakfast now with Dad, and then, wait for it . . .' I took in a deep, emotional breath before saying it. '. . . I'm going to my mother's grave. Yeah, I know. I can't believe it myself, Claire.' I went on and on about how Rob and Dad finally made me see sense.

'Wow that's great for you.' She checked herself in the mirror and threw a bit of make up on. 'I cannot believe it, that's great. Everything has certainly fallen into place for you.'

'All things are happening lately for a reason, Claire. And I have both you and Sue and others to thank for all the amazing support.'

'No problem, Amy. Look, I've got to sort my head out and get home to my own house. I'll drop around for a coffee after dinner.

Say hi to Rob.'

I went back in to help Dad. As I entered the kitchen, he was in the middle of downing a mouthful of water.

'What're those tablets you're taking?' I asked as he tried to stuff them back into the press.

'These? Ah, they're for, you know . . . mild lung infection, which came up in one of my blood tests yesterday.' He handed me a plate full of greasy rashers, egg, beans and black and white pudding. Here. Take this up to Robert.'

'Right, so is everything okay with you?' I prompted him, glancing up to the kitchen press. 'Lung infection? You never mentioned that. You said everything was clear.'

'Well, I'd hardly tell you about a mild infection, now would I? Look, I'm fine, Amy. One week on this stuff and I'll be back to work.' He smiled persuasively.

'Okay,' I kind of half-smiled.

As I came to the top of the stairs I could hear Rob in the middle of a phone call.

'Yes, it looks like Tuesday at the latest, Peter. I've fingers and legs crossed all week. Even have me granny saying a few prayers!' he laughed heartily. 'The Manager himself rang yesterday morning and I stressed to him about next week's deadline on the investment. He said he'll do everything to push it through for me. No panic.' He laughed again down the phone as I pushed open the door. He winked at me warmly as I entered the room and sat on the bed. 'Right, Peter. The minute I hear, you'll be the first to know. Bye.'

He hung up. 'Right,' he smiled. 'What's this? Are you trying to keep me in bed all day?' He threw one arm around me, almost knocking the breakfast out of my hands.

'So, what's this about granny praying, and legs crossed?' I said, putting on my detective nosey face. 'Is everything okay?'

'God, yeah . . . Everything is fine, love. It's just the investment deal closes next Friday. The other four investors have sorted out their cash end of things. But the bank are a little late getting back to me on my loan. Peter – my partner, as you know – who you only met briefly, well, he's the brains behind what is turning out to be a major investment, biggest I've ever been involved in. His main job is researching everything, right down to the smallest little detail, to make sure there's as little risk as possible. Then he does the whole money end of it. Anyway, it's all a bit complicated, to be honest, and still something I'm still learning. So much paperwork and small print involved.'

'Would you trust people like him just like that with your money?' I asked.

Rob laughed. 'He's sound, like a close family member. I knew his father who was in that kind of work all his life. Then me and Peter got chatting at a bar and the conversation turned to investments he had done. Anyway, we're friends ever since. He's got me involved in a number of deals to date. Smaller investments, mind, but he's bang on. No issues whatsoever. Incredible guy.'

'Right . . . Once you're being careful. That's all I care about.' I snatched a rasher off his plate and snuggled down beside him on the bed.

Right, here goes, I braced myself.

'Rob, I've something to tell you,' I smiled. 'I'm going to my Ma's grave today.'

The words hung in the air for a moment before Rob almost shouted with delight.

'Brilliant! It won't be easy, but this is just brilliant!' He threw his plate to one side and grabbed me in both arms to hold me. 'This is the beginning. The real beginning,' he said with extreme delight.

Meanwhile over in Greenridge Nurse Collins sat in the locker room crying after another tense meeting with Doctor Grimes.

Chapter 3

Maybe

'Please, don't, don't cry,' offered Christy as he walked in, closing the door quickly behind him.

But Nurse Collins was inconsolable. 'Oh, Christy, I can't believe what happened,' she sobbed. 'I'm still in shock. How could I . . . me . . . hit such a vulnerable person like that? Everything I was taught, all my training, everything is now gone out the window.'

She went on and on before she composed herself somewhat and dried her eyes as Christy got her some more toilet tissue from the bathroom before sitting down to listen.

'Doctor Crooked-Nose Grimes made me look like a bloody Hitler in the meeting just now,' she continued. 'He sneered and said, 'Now finally your eyes are open, Miss Collins. You're not so different to any other nurse here at Greenridge, are you now?' Then, with that horrible grin of his, he told me that on this occasion I was only getting a verbal warning, but that he'd be watching my progress very closely. I was lost for words and stood there feeling like the biggest hypocrite in the entire world. My god, after all I said to him last week!'

'Now, now,' said a soft-spoken Christy. 'Don't you go beating yourself up like this,' he stressed. 'You're not laughing your head off at what happened like the rest of them do when they mistreat patients. Not that you did mistreat anyone. Okay, now listen to me. You're a damn good nurse, and I for one know how deeply remorseful you are, okay? So you made a mistake this morning. You're young. You'll learn and move on from this,' he said in a deep, forgiving tone.

Nurse Collins wiped her tears and collected her thoughts best she could. 'Doctor Grimes isn't acting like a doctor, not a real one anyway, is he? He's strange, so cold-hearted. How have you been able to work here for so long, Christy? How can anyone? I think I should just go back into him and give in my notice. What's the point?' She started crying again.

Christy took a chair and sat next to her. 'Look at me, Nurse Collins. Some 41 years ago,' he began in a sobering tone, 'I was just starting out here, helping my father, doing the teas and helping with bathing the elderly on Saturday mornings. Anyway, one day a patient grabbed my hair in a joking kind of way and I snapped and screamed abuse at him. Almost struck out and hit the man. Like you, I was so shocked at my own behaviour and wanted, like you, to walk away, but my dad sat me down and told me stories of others who'd made little mistakes and went on to become the best staff workers here at Greenridge. Told me I'd learn from that one bad experience, and I did. I never lost my temper to that level again.' He sighed. 'This can be the hardest job on the planet, Miss Collins. But listen to me: if you and I give up, what hope will there be for people like Frank Crosby in a place like this? Who's left here if we give up? Who'll lead by example? Bottom line, we need people like you to make the changes that are needed here at Greenridge. So wipe those tears away and look at me. Don't you dare give up. Don't you dare! We need folk like you like a pair of lungs need air to breathe.' He stressed his words in the most convincing manner possible.

'God, thanks so much for that,' she sniffed. 'You give so much hope, Christy. You're so, so kind and soft-hearted. How have you kept it all together, kept so calm in a dark, crazy, eerie hospital like this? And remain so sane?'

Christy burst into laughter, which broke the tension no end. 'My father used to say,' he chuckled, 'maybe I'm the insane person and everyone else is perfectly normal!' Oldest joke in the book, I know.'

He stood up and took some teabags from his locker and stuck the kettle on. 'A nice cup of tea and a chocolate biscuit will get your energy levels back up,' he assured her.

Nurse Collins stood up and composed herself before asking, 'What were the other doctors like? God, they wouldn't have turned a blind eye and let patients like Frank suffer like this, would they?'

'Well, Mr O'Brien was in charge here for a good ten years and from what I saw he never turned a blind eye. But before him a lot of abuse did go on from time to time. I saw so much of it, but as one doctor said, 'What do you expect, Christy? Law and order in a place like Greenridge?''

He dropped two teabags into cups and poured the boiling water in.

'But sadly, the payback for reporting abuse comes at a price. I got awful things said and done to me down the years.' He sighed with a sudden downcast expression. 'The names I was called. 'The big fat-arse rat of Greenridge' was the popular one, but never to my face. Oh, God, they wouldn't be that brave. Stuff stolen out of my locker. On another occasion my favourite photo of my dad was pinned to my mirror with 'Burn in Hell Boyle!' written across it with a red marker. On another occasion, I even found a dead mouse in my cup of tea that I'd left unattended while painting the main hall. That made me sick to my stomach. On and on it went. Silent attacks, I call it. You see no one; no one says a word but they're there, watching, waiting, to try and push you over the edge, drive you insane and out of Greenridge or into bloody B Ward for the rest of your days.'

'Oh, my god, that's so sick and so disturbing. I'm so sorry that you were treated like that, Christy. God, I hope they don't start doing stuff like that to me,' she gulped. 'I absolutely hate feckin' mice.'

'Not everyone's like that,' he continued with a cheerful smile. 'I've friends here at Greenridge. Good-hearted staff who want everything we want. But as I've told you, they're not strong-minded enough. They live in continuous fear for their jobs, fearful of Grimes and others. Making complaints like you did last week is very rare, and people like Grimes and Nurse Whelan and the male nurses will try everything to push people like us out. But if we stay close, stick as a team, in the end I feel we will win. We will beat them down bit by bit with our love for the patients. And in the end we will conquer and have what my father once dreamed and never stopped talking about.'

'Which is?'

'A *sane* Greenridge, Nurse Collins. The perfect hospital.' He beamed with delight as he remembered his father's words. 'Can you imagine proving every doctor on the planet wrong and going forward to save every patient from all forms of illness, Miss Collins? See them all happy-clappy and free from all this suffering and pain? Can you? We will do it!' he said with a new air of childlike excitement. 'We may be the heroes in the storyline that completely changes the face of this hospital forever. Imagine that!' he beamed. 'As John Lennon sang so beautifully: Imagine all the people living life in peace!' After a prolonged silence and a sip from her tea Wendy processed Christy's words with more than a tad of concern as he sat eating away at the chocolate digestives.

'Well,' she confessed. 'That all sounds great but a little extreme, don't you think? But sure, look, we need dreamers like you, Christy. I feel like you've given me back so much of my own hope today. You're just so encouraging and courageous and brave. And from now on I'm standing up with you.'

He smiled back at her.

'The ironman of Greenridge!' she then yelled with arms in the air as she jumped up and walked over and gave him a big hug and a warm peck on the side of the face. 'You're like an angel! My angel, Christy Boyle!' she beamed. 'Thank you for listening to me today. I'm not giving up. I'm going to keep at it, stay focused and push onwards. Sorry I can't stay for the rest of my tea, I'm already late to get back on duty. Don't want to give Grimes and others an excuse to drag me back into his office for another disciplinary hearing.'

She smiled as she dried her eyes, grabbed her hat and was gone, leaving him stunned and red-faced.

No one ever kissed me before, he thought. *No one.* He put the cups of tea down but not before spilling tea on the floor. His body shivered. A warm shiver. He ducked his head out the door and looked down the long corridor after her in total bewilderment. *Maybe . . .?* he thought as he wandered back into the room, placing his hand up to touch the spot on his face where she had kissed him. He was almost beside himself from the whole experience when back in the door raced an out-of-breath Nurse Collins, startling him.

'I forgot my pullover!' she gasped as she grabbed it off the back of the chair. Now with a new sense of confidence she turned to race back out the door. But suddenly turned one last time and said, with a bright cheerful smile, 'You don't have to call me Miss or Nurse Collins anymore, Christy. Name's Wendy.'

She was gone, running down the corridor before Christy had a chance to change his facial expression. Tall, blonde and incredibly beautiful. She waved back. 'See you at tea break!'

Christy staggered back. His heart was spinning around in circles as he tried to gather his thoughts. *I think I'm going to pass bloody out!* he thought as he pushed open the door of his locker once again and anxiously went about checking himself in the mirror. He grabbed his ancient hairbrush and did his best to make his small bit of hair look fuller and somewhat attractive. He buttoned his tea-stained shirt up to his neck before grabbing his bottle of Old Spice and splashing half its contents all over his face and neck. He took a deep breath and stood with the biggest smile ever spreading out across his face. *I'm going to up my gym training from three to six days a week,* he thought as he looked at his set of boxing gloves. Hanging proudly beside them was his Irish boxing Under 21 runners-up medal. With his smile disappearing for a moment he thought, *I shoulda won that feckin' fight . . .*

Suddenly there was a gentle knock on the locker room door. Christy turned with a huge smile. 'Wendy!'

'Is there anyone changin' or exposed in there?' It was oul' Carmel Barnes, the old, grey-haired cleaning lady, pulling a bucket of dirty water and mop behind her. With hardly a tooth left in her head and her gums half receding away from the drink and smoking, she coughed, then eyed him up and down. 'Hi, Christy!' she grinned.

Christy's beaming smile swiftly disappeared.

'Oh, I thought you'd want to know,' she said as she walked in with that familiar nosy look about her. She went to say something but suddenly stopped and started sniffing the air. 'My god, did you or somebody blow up the chemist at Boots? That's some whiff of perfume or men's odour!' She paused, blew her nose, then looked up and peered at Christy with a suspicious eye. 'Where was I? Oh, yes. I came in to tell you that Frank Crosby – the big lad who's mentally ill? – Well, between you and me and the four walls, apparently the poor man was transferred to the hospital wing this morning, no one saying a word, all hush hush. But I got information from across there that he was found in a pool of his own blood this morning. Battered to bits isn't the word!'

*

'Right!' shouted Doctor Grimes across his office desk as two top male nurses stood trying to display little or no emotion. 'I know,' he said, now lowering his voice to an angry whisper, 'one of you, or maybe the two of you, took a little walk at some stage yesterday evening to B Ward and finished the job off by beating the living daylights out of Frank Crosby. Somebody did, I'm thinking revenge for one of the staff's broken nose. Oh, I know all about it, Noel. He's got two, maybe more, broken bloody ribs, a cracked jaw, black eye, etc., etc.'

'That's a very serious accusation you're makin',' said Noel in his strong Cockney accent. Being the taller of the two male nurses he let rip. 'As everyone knows, patients are been found in different parts of this hospital with injuries, some attacking each other, most self-inflected. Some we self-restrain physically, like yesterday when I hit Crosby myself to calm him down a little. We all do it from time to time. But never this extreme. Never. And any way I was off duty at 6pm. Rex here signed out at 6.30pm. He was hardly able to manage to drop back in the middle of the night and not be seen on CCTV. Or by staff.'

'Well, okay, sorry. But who did it then? Nurse Whelan? Peters? The cook? The priest? Who?' He took a deep breath and calmed himself down. 'I know. I know why you have a face on you, Rex, so stop the smirking.' He poured a glass of water and dropped two more painkillers in and continued, 'Me, the big hypocrite allowing certain patients to be given severe treatments and a few thumps here and there. But I'm trying so hard, as you can see, and with all the strength I can muster up, I'm trying to bring him and the more violent here at Greenridge under some lasting control. That's a bloody hard job for anyone.'

Rex Read, the smaller-built of the two nurses, was a good-looking guy who was nicknamed Speedy for his fast driving and fast moves in courting just about every good-looking nurse in the place. He stepped forward and calmly handed over a written report of the incident that morning. 'It states here in the report that two of the room doors were not properly locked last night. And that blood was found on patient Myles Power's hands and trousers this morning. Maybe it's all these new experimental drugs this hospital is dishing out, giving all sorts of new medication that in my opinion are having dangerous side effects, resulting in some of the patients becoming violent. Plus, it's not the first time doors have been left open after lights out down there.' He said this with a strong expression that he himself was now just a tad bit concerned at the growing risks to his own welfare. 'I mean, this is what? The sixth attack in the past six weeks.'

Doctor Grimes reached over and took the report sheet. 'How come I wasn't given the full information?' he politely asked trying his best to now display his own professionalism.

'I tried my best just now in the hall, Doctor, to say I had the full report, but you were in such a rage that I –'

'Right, right maybe I . . .' He paused to read it, searching his thoughts.

'Is that all for now, then?' asked Noel in his usual strong, calm tone.

'He got loose while being brought to the toilet and . . . fell down the stairs,' muttered Dr Grimes. 'It was a complete accident. Rewrite the report. That's all for now and I'll sign it off.'

The two male nurses threw a grin at each other before quietly opening the door and letting themselves out.

'Oh, one last thing,' whispered Dr Grimes. 'Watch what you say to others as I'm sure big fat-arse Christy will have his big detective nose all over this.'

*

Rob had a quick shower and dressed and seemed eager to get this over with in case I changed my mind about going. He raced downstairs to have a few words with Des while I kept myself composed by putting on some makeup.

My heart started to jump. Unwanted flashes, dark memories of my mother's moans as I sat in the crashed car with the distant sounds of sirens approaching.

'Mammy, can you hear me? Everything's going be okay,' I managed to slur as the dark realities was drowned out by shock.

'Amy . . .?' she painfully muttered. 'Jesus . . .' She let out a deep slow moan then a painful slur from the back of her throat before her head went sluggishly forward and then slumped against the dashboard. She was gone.

'Oh, good Jesus help, no! Ma, talk to me! Say something to me, anything, No, Ma! Jesus, please, I beg you! God, no! Help my mammy, help her. I'm begging you. Please, Maaaaaaa . . .!' My mother was dead and I couldn't even reach over and touch her, be there with her, hold her hand. I must have blanked out as my next memory was seeing flickers of light, then flames, as the car started to go on fire. I continued screaming hysterically. Everything went dark as a paramedic person came down, leaned in the window and started to cut me free from my seatbelt. I remember nothing after that until I came out of a coma days later.

'You okay up there, Amy?' Rob shouted up the stairs. I held a pillow up to my face, soaking up the last few deep, painful tears. *Deep breaths,* I told myself. *Deep breaths.* I gasped and shivered a bit before I finally stopped shaking like a leaf. Only then had I sufficient air in my lungs to shout down. 'Grand. Just putting bit of eyeliner on. Won't be a sec.'

Dad had a nervous smile for me as I arrived down the stairs.

But there was no turning back this time.

Dad opened the hall door and nodded that he was going, but, like Rob, he too would stay in the car.

As we drove out of the Hampton Cove estate and down towards the turn over the county bridge, I spotted Claire in the front of a taxi arriving into Fancourt Heights, the estate which is next to mine. She saw me and waved like crazy, giving the thumbs up to encourage me on.

Suddenly Dad cleared his throat, went to say something, but then seemed to have second thoughts.

I wanted to say so much but somehow kept my own lips sealed. I just sat back in the seat as Rob placed one hand on my shoulder in support. We pulled into the side road opposite the main gates of the graveyard.

I didn't want to prolong it anymore. I jumped out without a word, but then I felt so stupid when I had to lean back into the car and face Dad to ask where exactly Mammy's grave was.

'Up to the left on the main pathway,' he said, pointing. 'You can't miss it. Her photo is on the headstone.' He forced a smile.

I moved off without another word. my knees becoming weak as I made my way towards the spot. Her face, her smile. There it was, a big white gravestone. Her eyes, her face radiant as ever.

Rob sat back in his seat, eyeballing Des in the rear-view mirror. 'This must bring it all back,' he said in a soft, caring tone.

'It never goes away, mate,' came the painful sigh. 'Never. I remember that morning so well.' He paused, holding back the emotion. 'Tina had a lovely warm smile and this big infectious laugh that everyone loved. Her last words were, 'You clean up after breakfast, Sleepyhead, and bring the bins around to the back, don't leave them at the side.' I remember walking them out to the car and started to drag the bins. Amy had her head down, busy on her phone. Tina turned her head in the car with the window down and we both smiled, then turned away and back again and said, 'See you, love.'

'We did everything together, never apart. My mates slagged me no end about it. Was rare to see us without each other.' His voice was breaking. 'My god, Rob, that day will haunt me for the rest of my entire life. That sickening phone call that we all fear, that we all dread. Then in a split second you kind of go into survival mode, shock, whatever they call the bloody thing. And before you know, the funeral is over, and everyone is gone. People stop calling around, the phone stops ringing, people just get on with their lives as normal. Almost as if nothing has changed. Then you get into bed at night, turn off the light, and darkness is everywhere. I remember them first few nights turning to look for her, expecting just by a huge divine miracle she'd be there resting her head looking across at me in the dark with that smile of hers. Then one night it hit me. *Tina's gone, never coming back, ever.* The pain hits you, and it's a pain you wouldn't wish on your worst enemy. Some of my family say I had a little bit of a breakdown shortly after as I did hit the drink a bit harder.'

He took a moment to compose himself and wipe the tears away.

'But I had Amy to look after. As you know, we almost lost her as well. She was out for days. The head injury was the main problem. As you know, she can remember almost all the accident, but a whole lot was lost about her life before the crash, and her hand was so seriously injured, at one stage they were going to amputate. Then when she came out of it all, the screams out of her, Rob, it would frighten you to death to hear them cries for her mother, who we had laid to rest the previous day. Well, she was never the same girl again. When she woke up, something was amiss. Something gone. The doctors told me the bang to the head did it and that we were blessed to still have her. Over time she'll come back and remember more, they said. But to be truthful, she's still not the same Amy I knew before the crash. She's still a bit lost or changed in some ways. Anyway, let's not look at this as a bad day. Let's look at the positives.' He took a moment to fully compose himself. 'You can't imagine what you've done for this family, Rob. I know I keep rambling on and on but if it wasn't for you . . .'

Suddenly Rob noticed Amy wandering through the graveyard in floods of tears. He reacted fast and jumped out of the car, leaving the door open. Des sat back in his seat and put both hands up to face to keep his own emotions in check.

'I got you,' he said as he grabbed me in his arms. 'You did it, Amy. Everything's done now. You're so brave for doing this!'

'Maybe I should go back, say more . . . I've so much more to say. Maybe . . .' I sobbed. 'I'm so sorry! I told her how much I miss her, how sorry I am over what happened.' I turned and shouted, 'I love you so much, Mammy. I miss you so much!' I twisted as Rob wrestled to calm me down.

'No, don't,' he offered as I slid down on my knees.

'I just want her back so, so much!' I pleaded with my face in my hands. 'Please come back to me, Ma! I beg you!'

An elderly woman was walking on the pathway outside. She put her head down in a respectful gesture, then blessed herself and hurried on.

I regained some focus and could see Dad's face as Rob held on to me. He was in tears as he looked on from the car window. It was the first time I had seen the full pain of his own loss, all raw and visible as if the mournful day of the funeral was taking place all over again. I stood up and raced towards him. He jumped out of the car and grabbed me in his arms and held me for ages.

'Ahhh, Daddy! Hold me.'

There was a prolonged agonizing silence before Rob walked slowly up the pathway, giving us as much time as he thought we needed before putting his arm around the both of us.

As we drove home I kept muttering thought the tears, 'Maybe we should turn back. Stay longer . . .'

'Everything is going to be just fine now, Amy!' affirmed Dad now in a strong, fatherly tone as he threw Rob a wink in gratitude.

When we arrived home and settled into the evening, a strange calm came over me. I felt a first step had been taken that would lead to being emotionally healed from all the hurt and grief that was unlocked.

We both sat up chatting while Dad went to the Millrace pub for a few late pints with Steve.

Rob searched me with smiles and encouragement, asking me had I any more fears or issues.

I turned the question on him. 'Why don't *you* tell me about *your* fear issues? I've cried and imposed enough on you for a week today.'

'Ah, I don't have many issues.' He paused in thought before admitting he had one very strange yet real crippling fear. He hesitated again for moment. 'Well, I'd have to confess, it's . . . the horrible reality of ageing. It's my only fear in the world.' He went on to explain to me how this fear had haunted him since he was old enough to understand it. 'Oh, my god, I hate the thought of being old. It's always frightened the hell out of me to the point that some years ago I went to counselling to try and deal with the overwhelming dread of the problem. It still haunts me to the point that I must confess I don't like being around old people at all, don't like even seeing them. I admit it. In the past I've avoided my grandparents like the plague. Well, bar when I needed prayer for my investments deals,' he said with a smile. But I could still sense the fear, the dread in his voice.

'Ah, would you stop', I joked. 'You're only 35 and the best-looking man in Ireland! It'll be years before you see even one little grey hair or wrinkle.'

He smiled and leaned across and held me as we lay on the floor before a roaring log fire.

'Well, you know my two big fears in life. Losing you and this relationship – that, and spiders!'

'Spiders! You never mention that to me before.' he quizzed.

'Did I not? Oh my god, Rob, you have no idea how much I hate and fear them. As I've told everyone many times over, apparently one got into my bed when I was only two years of age.'

He smiled and held me and assured that we were, as he put

it, lifers. 'Stuck together with superglue. And don't worry, I'll protect you from any big spiders who try to invade our bed!'

We both giggled.

But unknown to Rob when I popped over to Jimmy's shop in Pinewood Green to get milk, I decided to get a lovely *Thank You* card that I just knew Rob would like. I wrote how much he meant to me and how thankful I was for all he'd put up with relating to my list of hang ups. I ended by saying how much I looked forward to us being man and wife. I picked my moment and placed the card in the inside pocket of his jacket when he was up in the bathroom.

We kissed at the door after my fourth failed attempt to get him to stay another night.

'Please, pretty please!' I begged, grabbing his arm as he walked down the driveway, laughing.

'Work, Amy. Lots of unfinished work to get sorted. As you heard today with my boss Peter Bradley, big, big deal going through this week. Our future!' he winked. 'But I'll have everything sorted by Tuesday. Then the rest of the week I'm all yours,' he smiled.

I gave in, but not till I landed him with another prolonged kiss.

I waved at him as he drove away. Then closed the door and crashed peacefully onto the sofa and just stared with a smile into the open fire before finally falling asleep.

An hour later Dad woke me up as he turned the key in the door. We sat up for ages chatting about everything, from Ma to the wedding.

Then I told him that there was just one issue that I really needed his full approval on. He sat back and listened carefully. 'Dad, I've put a lot of thought into this. Okay, here goes. I want to give every cent of the claim we got from the accident to some kids' charity. I know that sounds so crazy but please will you agree with this? I can't spend a cent of that on myself, and I can't do this till you approve of it. Please. Then I can truly move on with my life with Rob.'

Des sat up, took a long thoughtful sigh and with a puzzled

expression said, 'Well, I'd give that some more thought if I was you.' He paused. 'But, okay, look, whatever makes you happy, that's all I care about. But have you thought in depth about the injuries you have? What if the attempt to go back to work fails and in six months' time the depression returns? What if –?'

'Dad, listen to me. I can't spend this money. I've made my mind up a long time ago. I just need you to stand by me on it. Rob is doing very well financially. Please trust me with this one decision.'

He sat looking at me in two minds for ages before that big smile of his spread across his face. 'Look, I think you should give that some further thought. Give *some* to a charity but good God, not the whole lot! But then again, you jumped a big hurdle today, and if spending that money on yourself isn't something you want to do, well who am I to argue? Once you send it to the right charity and not some dodgy group who'll pocket the half of it.'

'I'll be extra careful, I promise,' I smiled and hugged him.

*

Rob drove into Applewood estate in Swords. But he wasn't in the door of his apartment five minutes before his phone rang. Peter Bradley.

'Go ahead, Peter.'

'I don't want a row,' he said in a controlled yet annoyed tone. 'But It's been three weeks, so where's my feckin' three grand? And why haven't you been man enough to answer my calls or even return my texts?'

'Calm bloody down,' snapped Rob. 'I can explain.'

'Why didn't you ask your buddies Karl Wilson and Co. for a loan to pay back your debts? The so-called big boy investors, who disappeared into the night, never to be seen again! Who you mouthed off to everyone about being the best of the best! Where are they now? Where's all the investment money them fools promised everyone? Then, like a –'

'Look, can I get a word in?'

'Don't interrupt me! Then, like a fool, I give in to your begging notes, felt sorry for you and handed you three grand. Then when I ask for half of it back, nothing. Not even a return call to say you'll part pay me at least a grand. Maybe the person I talked to is right, maybe you are nothing but a lowlife con man, a loser and a –'

'I'll have all your three grand next week, but please stop going on and on about Karl bloody Wilson. Every time I see or hear from you, it's Wilson this or Wilson that. Okay, so you were right all along about him. Let's just leave it in the past. But –'

'No buts, Rob!' stated Peter in a low, firm tone. 'We did a string of small deals and never once did l let you or the rest of my investors down. I was 100% honest with you and the others and certainly paid you every cent from every deal. But of course, the greed got to you. All of sudden, you thought you were the big man on the up, and even as I stood in your apartment pleading with you to stay with my future projects, that I needed you, that I was building my way up the ladder slowly, being very careful, making sure not to lose anyone's cash, always looking out for your best interests, watching your back against assholes like Wilson . . . Go on, remind me what did I say to you? Go on, tell me!'

'Don't invest a cent with that fool. Stay with me, and slowly and safely we'll make it to the top as a team.' They were your exact words,' Rob sighed as he tried his best to sound like he had truly repented.

'And what did you say?'

The painful reply. 'I need to get with the big organization, the big boys, and invest for the future.' They were the stupid words I used.' He closed his eyes and sighed as he remembered his stupidity.

'Correct,' snapped Peter. 'Now you can't even pay your stupid mortgage, from what I hear.'

'Look, I was pulled in, deluded by that big thick redneck Wilson. My one big mistake in life. But look. I didn't murder anyone! Everything is about to change, as I told you two weeks ago in a text. Everything is on the up.'

'You're skint, Rob. My God, admit that much.'

'Listen to me, I'm coming into big money next week, and if you just –'

Peter broke into a loud laugh. 'You haven't two euro coins to rub together, ye fool!' He paused after he caught his breath from laughing. 'And hey, are you still with that chick, what's-her-name? The one that I heard you were seen with a few times of late? The one with the scar, oh or is it true you're kind of back dating that other one, Gina Watson? Or is it Jill?'

'Close it, Peter,' he hissed. 'My personal life is no one's business. For one second will you listen up? This time next week I'm going to have enough of a cash flow to come in with an offer to invest with this deal you're trying to get off the ground for two years or more. Now listen to me just this once. If we can just put the past behind us and start afresh, I promise on my life nothing like what transpired in the past will occur again.'

There was an even bigger burst of laughter. 'Where in the name of God would you get the cash I'm looking for to invest?' he sneered. 'You're on handouts and now you're suddenly pulling 175,000 out of some kid's lucky bag? Give me a feckin' break here!'

The line went dead. Rob texted him after a number of failed attempts at calling him back. *If I get the cash will you consider me? Rob.*

An hour later Peter replied. *You're broke Robert . . . FACT.*

Rob stood fuming in the middle of the floor before heading into the bathroom and throwing water on his face. His eyes widened when he saw what looked like a grey hair at the side of his head. He panicked and looked closer before realising to his horror that there was not one but three little small grey hairs. He carefully plucked them out with a gulp. While walking slowly back into the sitting room he felt something in his inside jacket pocket. He slowly pulled out the *Thank You* card left by Amy.

He put his phone down and looked at the front of the

envelope. *To the greatest man ever*. He sighed and proceeded to rip it open. He glanced at what Amy had written inside. *Thanks, Rob, for everything. I really appreciate what you've . . .* Without finishing it he tore it in half, lit his lighter and burned it in the sink.

He stood for a few seconds thinking before he unleashed, letting fly with his fist and leaving a sizeable mark on the sitting room door.

I've got to get that cash from her bloody bank account, or I'm finished!

Chapter 4

Blind Love

I awoke to a lovely heartfelt text from Rob thanking me for the card. 'I'm speechless', it read. He ended the text with: 'I've changed a few plans around as I want to spend today with you. I'm meeting Des for a coffee first. I'll be up to see you around 2. Love you so much Amy xxxx'

I jumped up and got out of bed, showered, ran downstairs and grabbed a slice of toast and started to prepare the Sunday dinner. I stuck on the music – which irritated Dad no end as he tried to concentrate on reading the Sunday papers. I then danced in and out from the kitchen peeling the spuds as he watched, shaking his head and half-smiling.

'Right, I'm out of here.' He jumped up and folded the paper.

'Hey!' I shouted after him. 'When you're done chatting with Rob, will you bring back some frozen peas.'

'May go on the beer!' he laughed back as he raced out the front door.

'You bring my Rob back here drunk, you're dead!' I shouted, waving the spud knife in the air, but he was gone.

*

Rob parked his car and took up a table with Des in the local Coffeepot Café in Balbriggan, famous for its fries. He ordered for both and insisted on paying. 'No, no, this is my treat, Des,' he smiled as the lady took the orders.

'You're great, thanks. I'll get you next time,' he said as he ordered a medium breakfast.

'Make it a large for me,' said Rob with a greedy smile. 'I'd eat a horse.'

'Right,' sighed Des. 'I've something I need to confirm about the wedding.' But Rob asked could he just run a couple of things past him first. 'Sure, fire away.'

The waitress returned with a pot of tea. 'Be just a few minutes with the breakfast,' she smiled. 'If you need a fresh pot of tea, just ask.'

Rob sat back and poured two teas and with the other hand he drew an envelope out of his inside jacket pocket and handed it to Des. 'I know, minutes before we went to the graveyard yesterday you stressed you wanted to pay for the whole wedding bill, but as I said, this was something I strongly felt I should do.'

Des opened it and saw it was a receipt for the Bracken Court Hotel for the full wedding payment of €7,050, dated that day. He went to speak. 'But –'

Rob signalled with his hand. 'I know you were keen on paying, seeing it's Amy's big day and she's your only child, but you have more than enough financial worries, with medical costs and more to follow. So last night I put extra thought into it and looked at the long guest list and, well, half an hour ago I took it upon myself to pay the full whack, with all the trimmings, two doves in cage included. If it makes you feel better, you can pay for a nice honeymoon. Amy would love that. But there's no point trying to talk me out of it. It's a done deal.'

Des sat looking somewhat annoyed that Rob had gone against his wishes, but he didn't want to bring any tension to bear after all he'd done for Amy's situation. He took a deep breath of resignation. 'You shouldn't have done this,' he frowned. 'That's a bloody lot of cash for you to pay out in one go. But sure, if you're that keen, I'll agree, but only if you let me pay at least two grand off it, plus a two weeks' honeymoon. I had New York in mind. But whatever suits you both.'

'Here you go, gentlemen,' said the waitress as she placed the two breakfasts on the table. 'If there's anything else, just give us a yell.'

'Ah, with Christmas just three weeks away you could say this is a weight of responsibility off me. It's just . . .' whispered Des.

'Don't,' said Rob as he felt his phone vibrate with a text. 'Leave everything as it is, Des.' He glanced at the message. Peter Bradley.

Get me 1500 by Friday and we call it quits. Then I'm deleting your number. And you will do likewise. Peter.

'Bad news?' asked Des as he cut into his rasher and took a mouthful.

'Feck, no. Good news for a change. Best mate texting me to confirm he has some cash for me that he borrowed weeks ago. Anyway, enough about money matters,' he sighed. 'How's your health? How're you feeling today?'

'Grand, grand, I'll live,' he nodded, forcing a smile before then eyeing Rob up with his serious face again. 'Look, my apologies for changing back to the subject of money, but the reason I rang to see you this morning was to do with another financial matter that came up that has me very concerned.'

Rob nervously buttered two slices of toast and placed an egg and rasher between then. 'Fire away,' he said.

'It's this bloody claim money Amy has had lying in the EBS for over a year. Well just out of the blue last night she started talking seriously about giving the lot to a kid's charity.'

The words hung in the air as Rob almost choked his food back up before grabbing his tea in time to wash it down. 'Yeah?' he managed as his eyes widened and intensely bulged out of their sockets. 'Bloody rashers! Continue, Des.'

'Yeah. I kind of agreed with her last night. Ah, feck it, Rob, she's doing so well and after all the tears at the graveyard yesterday I couldn't go start an argument with her, could I now? But after giving it proper thought, I'm anything but pleased. As you may know, she's always felt the claim was nothing but bad luck money, that she would never see herself spend a cent on herself or anyone else. But oh, she's willing to hand the whole lot to some likely dodgy charity. Contradiction in there somewhere, don't you think?'

Rob's face was turning pink and looked like it was swelling ready to explode, but he checked himself and quickly gathered his thoughts. 'Yeah? She said that?' he just managed. 'And . . . has she a particular charity in mind?'

'Well,' confessed Des, 'once stupid me here went and gave her my full-hearted support last night she went straight online to look up everything from local charities to a string of hospitals. She said she would tell you all about it today. She's not thinking straight at all, Rob.' He took a mouthful of tea and threw his fork onto the plate. 'The only one thinking with a clear head in all this is you, so will you please just suss her out on this one and give her some sound guidance.'

'I hear you, Des,' he managed before pausing. 'Can you excuse me for a moment?' He walked calmly to the bathroom as Des poured two fresh cups of tea.

He closed the door firmly then started totally freaking out. He punched the toilet door in anger. What in the hell is going on now? He stood with his back to wall, mumbling. *You bloody idiot, Rob. You almost lost it out there right in front of her father. Oh, my good God, she's givin' the money away! Maybe she has already!* He staggered forward and gasped. I'm going to be sick. He paused with hand up to mouth. *Right. Stop. Deep breaths. In, out, in, out. Okay, Robert, calm feckin' down, man, and fast. Get your head in gear or you'll end up blowing this whole thing apart.* He splashed water on his face and finally composed himself. *Just unwind and get a bleedin' grip on your emotions and you'll have that money safely in your own account by Tuesday. Right. Change the plan around and stay with her tonight. You're nearly home and dry, man. Relax and keep the charm and strategy progressing.* He went to open the toilet door, paused, took a deep breath before swinging it open and stepped out with a big smile.

He went on to explain to Des that at the end of the day he himself was doing well financially, but he'd do his best to make her rethink. Maybe I can advise her to invest in one of my secure deals, if she accepts that. But listen Des everyone had to accept that if Amy wished to give it all away that's her choice, nobody had the right to stand in her way with this incredibly kind gesture. 'She's thinking better than ever, admit that much,' he added.

Des took a good ten minutes before he kind of came around to Rob's point of view. He pushed his chair back. 'Oh, the frozen peas. I nearly forgot.' He handed them over to Rob. 'Right, at least ask her to keep some cash by for the cosmetic facial surgery that I'm always pushing her to get done. At least that much, for feck's sake.'

Rob stood up to leave. As he approached the main door he froze on the spot. Right in his eyeline was an elderly man trying unsuccessfully to push open the door to let himself in. From nowhere all Rob's dreads of ageing kicked in.

'Come on, I'll get that for you,' smiled Des as he opened the door for the older man, who was well into his eighties and hardly able to walk.

Rob gathered his thoughts as fast as he could, but then gave the old man a glare as he hurried out past him. The old man looked out after him before muttering to himself, 'What's that dopes problem?Little asshole!'

*

I was watching at the window and tried not to make it look too obvious by rushing out to the door, but I did. 'Oh, Rob, I have loads to tell you!' I gasped as we grabbed each other for a deep embrace. 'I went back to the graveyard all on my own!' I beamed. I pulled him in the door, closing it. 'I'm totally free, Rob. I can move on now. There was a load more I wanted to say to my mother yesterday but couldn't, but it's all out. Things I've never told anyone! But it's all said now.' The tears began to well up.

'Okay, okay, calm down,' smiled Rob, as he pulled me back into his warm arms. 'This is amazing news, and if things get any better, we'll have to start bottling this joy of yours and sell it online as one of my new investments,' he laughed. 'Now sit down and I'll make us both a coffee. I've a couple of things that will add to your joy.'

I sat on the sofa as he busied himself in the kitchen. He arrived back in, plonked himself beside me, and pulled out the receipt for the wedding reception.

'What's this?'

'Read it,' he smiled as he took a mouthful of coffee. He went on to tell me that as he was the man I was marrying, he felt it was essential he paid for everything, all the trimmings, right down to cars, rooms for all family and bridesmaid. 'Nothing is left out, Amy. Your dad wanted to pay, but look.'

I jumped up and grabbed him. 'You're the most amazing man ever, Robert!' I paused for thought. 'But Dad was kind of . . .'

'Don't worry. We came to an agreement this morning. Des is paying for a small holiday.' He grinned as he leaned in and kissed me. 'Now . . . another little matter that came up in my chat with your dad. He said you'd tell me the full –'

'I know what you're going to say,' I nervously cut across. 'My decision to give away all the claim money in the bank. I was going to . . .'

Rob waved his hands out in a surrender gesture. 'I think it's not only a good idea, it's a great idea. I'm very proud that you're willing to give the lot to a kids' charity,' he smiled. 'However, I think it best you leave giving anything away for a week or two until your mind settles after the emotions of yesterday and we find the right charities. Okay?

'Okay. So you're with me on this? It's just . . . I always knew I'd do this, and last night after you left, I got to thinking about how fast we're moving forward, and anything that has bad luck attached to it, like this money, I needed to let it all go. Anyhow, I have you, this house, plus my job in January. What else does a girl need?' I beamed.

He held me, looking deep into my eyes. 'You have to be the most kind-hearted girl ever, Amy, and if that's your wish, I'm with you 100%.'

My phone rang.

'Take it,' said Rob as he remembered the frozen peas in the bag and brought them into the kitchen.

It was Claire. I told her all about the morning and the added news about the wedding. 'It's all arranged, all the trimmings,' I gushed, placing the wedding receipt behind a framed photo of Ma and Dad. 'How are you?'

'I'm just picking Colm up,' she moaned. 'He's in the feckin' Millstone pub with Tom. Sue and I are fit to literally kill the pair of them as we were all supposed to go up for a nice dinner at 1pm in the Balrothery Inn. They do lovely food as well, and it would have been a nice change. They've been gone all morning and had phones off. Asshole Tom finally answered Sue's call, and bloody slurred, 'Sure why don't we all go now for dinner next door into the lounge of the Millstone! Or will I get take-outs and bring them up in a taxi?' The pair of them are bucketed drunk. I'm telling you, Amy, my temper's boiling over here. I'm going to feckin' kill him.' She let out a deep sigh. 'Anyway, rant over. All good with you, by the sounds? I'll be over to you later for a coffee, that's if I'm not confined to Balbriggan Garda station for first degree murder.'

*

Colm was picked up by Claire after Tom fell into a taxi ten minutes earlier. She tried everything in her power to stop herself leaning across and belting him one. 'Well? Anything to say for yourself?' she finally managed, breaking the tense silence. No reply was given as she pulled into his mother's driveway in Pinewood Green Road.

'Well, givvve me one little seccc,' slurred Colm as he twice failed to open his seatbelt. 'Oh, yes, yes. I had a little few pints with Tom. Tommy Tom Boy. And a bet or two on the horsies. Got a winner, and you won't bel–'

'Ah, just get out of the car,' she snapped. 'You're making everything worse. Why do I even bother anymore?' she barked.

'Okay, don't shout. I'm tryin', as you can see, to open the stupid seatbelt . . . Oh, one other thing before I do bleedin' go.' His tone now as hostile as Claire's 'I'm not goin' to the meet-up Tuesday afternoon with Rob and Amy.' The seatbelt clicked open. 'There we go. Easy in the end.' He fumbled to open the door.

'And what do you mean you're not bloody going?' a fuming Claire asked. 'It's Amy's mother's three-year anniversary. We all agreed this last night. Plus, Amy went to the grave yesterday for the first time, so we're all just meeting to support her and her dad, and the plan is for everyone to meet in Seasons Café in Skerries for a coffee. Everyone's going!'

'You go,' he sniggered, 'you go, but def'ny not me.' He made another attempt to open the door but failed again.

'What the hell has gotten into you of late?'

'I don't like the games you're playin'! There. It's now publicly out in the open what I think.' He turned and eyeballed the announcement to her face, a hint of real anger now appearing in his tone. Then his face changed dramatically from a mild, annoyed stare to a look of extreme rage and he pointed a stern finger up to her face. 'You've got feelin's for the Rob lad!' he whispered into her face with the other finger up to his lips. 'But all hush, hush, yeah?'

The words hung in the air as Claire sat back, totally stunned at the statement. 'What in God's name were you taking besides a few pints? Are you on an Ecstasy tablets? That's the biggest load of crap talk I've ever heard in my life. How feckin' dare you! Ha!'

'Yeah, laugh all you want. I've observed the way your face lights bloody up when he walks into the room. Givin' him them *you're so sexy* glances. Walkin' away from chattin' to me and over to him like a little excited bloody schoolgirl. You think I'm drunk or on something! Hey, I don't take bloody drugs. Just a few pints, right? You want to know something else?' he screeched, 'It's always *Rob this* and *Rob that*. Well as –'

'How feckin' dare you!' Claire sat back, flabbergasted. 'Rob's a lovely guy and he's Amy's, but that –'

'Don't even start with the excuses! You're into him in a big way and I've sat back and watched all this shit unfold before my very eyes for months, expectin' it would stop, seein' would you keep it bloody up. And that's the one reason I don't like bein' around our get-togethers anymore.'

Claire wasn't sure what way to respond. 'Look. My god,

Colm, you never said a word. Eh . . . we have a bit of fun, a laugh, me and Sue, like.' A hint of nervousness was setting in. 'I wasn't trying to make you jealous or playing games with your head.'

'No? Well, you were not only doin' my head in but you've finally pushed me away and left me so bloody insecure about myself. I've been in the pits for ages. And what's so horrible is, I was the one feelin' guilty about the big gap that was appearin' in our relationship, thinkin' yet again that maybe I should try harder, maybe lose a bit of weight, join the gym, while you were up sky high in yourself, full of confidence, smilin', laughin', so carefree as you lapped up all his attention. Don't look at me with that big shocked face!' He pointed his finger at her again. 'You light up like a big Christmas tree when his name is mentioned, then you turn and look at me like I'm just . . . Ahhh, forget it,' he said as he filled up with tears. 'Forget all what I'm sayin'!'

Claire had never seen him get this emotional, even with drink. 'Forget? Don't you just say *forget* after dropping a big bombshell like that! Hey, where are you going?' she asked in a panic as he managed to open the door and stagger out. She jumped out of the car and went to reach out to him. 'You're looking into this too much with the drink and everything. Last night and this morning you seemed fine.' She softened. 'Come here.'

'Don't you dare touch me!' He waved both hands and pushed her away, stepping back onto a neighbour's garden lawn. 'Never, not once did I try to make you feel jealous, Claire. Not once. I wouldn't. Okay, so I'm not as good-lookin' as him. Maybe I've a bit of a belly on me. Anyway, feck the lot of it. I won't be goin' anywhere near him or Seasons Cafe,' he slurred, almost tripping over himself. ''It'ssss all over.'

'Look, let's go inside make a cup of tea and sober up and we'll chat about this more,' Claire pleaded.

Colm laughed as he wiped the tears away. 'No bloody way. I've had enough. Oh, there's more! Oh, yeah. No wonder I'm drinking so much!' he slurred again and finally balanced himself and slammed the car door shut.

'Look, I wasn't playing with your feelings, Colm. I wouldn't.

I . . .' She started filling up with tears herself.

'Well, Claire, here's the bombshell to end all bleedin' bombshells. Mr Simply Glorious isn't as squeaky clean and as wonderful as you and Amy and the stupid world thinks! Oh no! So there . . . Now . . . I'm goin' in.'

'What . . .? Okay, so you're a bit confused. Look, I'm sorry. Let's stop shouting. People are watching. You're making a show.'

Colm's mother Bernie opened the door. 'What the hell is all the shouting out here?'

'Nothin'. Right, Ma? Nothin'. It's over. Everythin' is over from today.' He gave Claire the look as he pushed past his mother and headed up the stairs. Claire stood trying to take it all in.

'What's over?' his confused mother asked. 'What's going on, Claire?'

Claire's phone buzzed. She figured it was best to let him sober up. 'Sorry, Bernie, just another small row. Everything's going to be okay.'

It was Sue, fuming. 'Where are you? I'm after having a row with Tom!'

'What? I'm at Colm's. Look, I need to talk to someone. Talk to you *now*, like.'

'Tom was so drunk, saying crazy shit like Colm was crying in the toilet in the Milestone, saying things about you and Rob . . . Who was flirting with who? I asked him . . . Ah, mad stuff.'

Claire stood completely stunned as her mind raced. Flirting? With Rob? Never! But maybe that one time when . . . No! Her thoughtlessness in a split second becoming now factual.

'Where are you, Sue?' she asked as she jumped in her car. 'Stay there. I'm on my way.'

She drove into Bath Road Estate and before she could take another breath, she was sitting with Sue in her sitting room, Sue's mother handing her a fresh cup of tea.

'I'll leave you both to talk,' she said. 'Bit of extra dinner on, Claire, if you're hungry.' She closed over the door to give them some privacy.

Claire sat back, looking white as a ghost. 'So tell me

everything. 'Don't leave anything out,' she stressed.

Sue took a mouthful of tea and sat up. 'Well, apparently Colm rang him this morning, asking to chat, and after two pints he told Tom he'd been very depressed for a long time and started saying crap stuff like he knew you were way into Rob. In feckin' love, like. I know. It's mad, isn't it? Tom kind of laughed it off but then Colm got real upset and rambled on that he doesn't want to be around the group again, and that he was breaking it off with you.'

Claire stood up. 'Well, that's all a big pile of crap. I wouldn't go falling for my best friend's fella!' She stood in the centre of the room, gobsmacked. 'I mean, if I was doing his head in, why didn't he come out and just say it ages ago? The truth is that you and I are both just . . . well, having a bit of a buzz?' She sat back down with a look of guilt appearing all over her face.

'Well,' said Sue, 'I was waiting for Tom to pull me up about my little bit of flirting, but he said nothing. It was all about you, Claire.'

'Well, thanks very much for that. But at least admit I wasn't alone in this, Sue. You and others had your fair share of drooling over him. My god, my head is now absolutely melted here. What else did Tom say? My god, what are we going to do? I've to go to Amy's later today . . . Hmm . . .' Sue let out a deep sigh. 'Well, there's more, and I have to say this part just made me laugh my head off no end. Seemingly your Colm crossed paths with a delivery guy from Swords who's working with Fastway Couriers. Seemingly he got talking to the guy and seeing he lived in Swords area went on to ask him did he know Rob Cooper. Colm said in passing that he was dating a friend of his. Anyway, this person apparently said that if it's the same Rob, he's always on the take, never has money. Gambling habit, if it's the same guy. Then added that he's always got two, maybe three girls going at any one time! Well, I laughed my head off at that one. I think jealousy has reared its ugly head, don't you think?'

'Ah, look, forget that crap, Sue. Bloody hell, he's after paying for the whole wedding, and if Amy and everyone else gets wind of Colm's crazy notions, where's that going to leave everything?'

Sue took another mouthful of tea, composed herself and in a low, polite voice asked, 'Well, do you have any feelings for him other than friendship, like?'

'Will you close it!' snapped Claire. 'I like him, like you do, like most girls do, but I'm not *in love* with the man. He's very attractive, but in love with him? Come on!' She was then shocked at her choice of words. She sat back, now looking totally bewildered and now completely unsure about the extent of her feelings. 'I have to talk to Colm. My god, the more I think about this, the more complicated it's starting to seem. How come I didn't see what I was doing with Rob? Was I totally blind or just plain stupid?'

With that Claire's phone rang, then Sue's. Amy.

Chapter 5

The Mirror Man

Sue signalled with her hand, then muttered with a frightful expression. 'It's Amy!' Claire instantly checked her own phone and noticed a missed call from Amy and Colm.

'Hi, Amy, we were just . . .' She paused as Claire motioned with her hand not to say she was there.

'Listen,' said Amy in a deep, concerned tone, 'have you seen Colm or Clare? It's just I rang them both, but no answer. I'm just a bit anxious about Colm. I got this strange text from him, a kind of weird message. He sounds drunk, the spelling was all over the place and from what I could make out it read *Sorry I won't be there Tuesday at Seasons Café for get-together, sorry but won't be able to meet again. Heads completely gone here. Be careful. Bye.* I've rang him but no answer, and Claire's not answering. Is everything okay? Have you heard anything? I was only talking to Claire an hour ago. She sounded fine to me then. I laughed it off but then reread the text and . . .'

'Em, ah, I wouldn't mind Colm. He's been drinking and texting everyone,' Sue managed as she signalled with hand and facial expressions to Claire, *What the hell will I say*? Look, Amy. I'll ring Claire and as planned we'll all drop over after dinner. Take no notice of Colm's drunken text. Anyway, how's Rob?'

The very mention of his name made Claire throw her eyes up to heaven.

'We're all grand,' laughed Amy. 'Are you okay? You sound different or something.'

Sue laughed down the phone. 'Nah, I'm in . . . in top form, never better,' she said, stumbling over her words. 'I must try ringing Claire and see what's up with Colm, and then we'll be over to you for coffee later on. Is that okay?'

'Okay. Look, I'm just sorting out dinner here, so text me when you're on the way.'

Sue let out a deep, almost painful gasp as she hung up. 'This is horrible. I'm not going down the road of lying to one of my best friends. No way am I getting wrapped up in that kind of crap, Claire. Bloody hell, you better get up to Colm and nip this whole thing in the bud real fast. Now, like.'

Claire shot up out of the chair looking totally at her wits' end as to how to deal with the increasing tension of the situation. 'I didn't do a thing wrong!' she shouted in her defence. 'I'll explain my end of things to everyone, even Amy. I've nothing to hide.' She sat on the arm of the chair as her own words failed miserably to convince her. 'Okay, so I like Rob a lot, and we had a few small flirts. But it was Rob himself, on a number of occasions, as well you bloody know, Sue. Remember that time in the smoke room in Raff's pub when he kind of kissed my face, then said he liked me a lot? He was the one on that occasion who was leading me towards him. Then another time he leaned over and gave you a kind of kiss on the lips. I bet you remember that occasion! If I remember, Amy was in the loo at the time.' She took a deep, nervous intake of breath. 'Well, one thing is for sure in all this. I'm not losing my Colm over this crap. No way!' she confirm with a definite stance.

'Sue?' Her mother tapped the door. 'Is everything okay in there?'

'Yes, Ma.'

'Well, then, will you both please keep your voices down. You'll wake your father. He's working nights, remember.'

'Sorry, Ma!' whispered Sue as she sat down and composed herself. 'Now don't you go airing our harmless friendship kissing stories involving me and Rob, Claire! No bloody way am I being dragged into a heated situation that may wreck what me and Tom have built up.' She paused. 'As I remember it, maybe on my birthday night out Rob said I was beautiful and gave me a small friendship kiss on the lips, but that was all it was, my end. Just a bit of harmless birthday fun. Look, before you say a word to anyone,' she continued, lowering her voice even more, 'we need to be very careful how everything is worded. Specifically around Amy. My god, everything is going so well for her. The last thing we need at this critical time is her being hurt.'

*

Meanwhile, back over in Greenridge, Christy had everyone's head done in as he pushed the odd staff member a little too far with his detective-style questions about the apparent assault on Frank Crosby.

'Look, Mr Christy,' offered one rather discreet care staff member as she took him to one side, 'Or I mean, Mr Boyle – we all get paid to do a job. We get our wages in the bank every fortnight. We go home to our families and live our lives best we can. But one thing's certain: we don't get paid to worry about Greenridge and all the insane problems, because if we did, we'd end up here in our Pyjamas as patients ourselves!'

'True, but . . .'

'No, Christy. I recognize what a protecting, caring man you are, but you'd be better off getting on with your work around here, and maybe it would be advisable to start realising that you need to find a life for yourself outside the crazy walls of this place. You're too tied up with every little issue that happens at Greenridge. Now that's all I'm saying,' she sighed as she continued on her way towards the bathroom with a disabled male patient.

Suddenly a breathless Nurse Collins came into view down the long hallway and signalled anxiously with her eyes for Christy to meet her off to the right in the TV games room. 'Okay, close the door,' she panted. Christy stared up into her beautiful features, made all the more inviting, he thought, by the sweat running down the sides of her face, her gloss-painted lips. 'My god, I'm sweating! And my heart is pounding in my chest,' she finally managed as Christy struggled to snap himself back to reality from staring her up and down.

'What's up, Wendy?' he said, trying his best to further

compose himself. 'You're in a panic.'

'Okay, sit down,' she gasped, 'and wait till you hear this horrible bit of information. I took some towels over to the hospital wing and kind of hung around a while. Finally, I managed to edge my way unnoticed to poor Frank Crosby's ward. My god, Christy, you'd want to see the mess he's in. Believe me, I'm a trained nurse, and I can tell you right now that was no fall down a feckin' stairs. No way. From what I saw when I passed his bed, he looked like two, maybe three male nurses beat the living daylights out of him. Christy, look at me. This was a planned attack by more than one person. I'm sure of it. He looks like he's been hit by a bloody bus, for cryin' out loud!'

She let out a deep sigh and sat down as Christy listened to every word. 'But that's not all,' she said, now in a frightened tone. 'I found out something that has me even more traumatized. Okay, see what you think of this. I got talking to an old nurse, can't remember her name, I think it was a Nurse Ryan. She's the longest-serving nurse over there. Anyway, I clicked into my detective mode and made her a cup of tea and waited till she felt very comfortable in my company. Then I casually asked her what she thought was happening to people like Mr Crosby.

'That was a very bad fall on the stairs,' I remarked.

She threw both eyes up to heaven and replied, 'Falls don't cause that kind of bruising to the eyes, young lady. That's what I call a punishment beating, dear. Oh, yes. A lot of that goes on around here. Oh yes . . . Are you one of the new girls here?'

I nodded. 'Yes, I'm Wendy. Wendy Collins.'

'Well, Wendy Collins, you'd be a bit naïve concerning the dark realities of a place like this, but in time, you'll awaken.' She dropped her voice to a whisper. 'You think Mr Crosby's beating is bad? Dozens arrive down here in that state – and worse. Oh yes, they always say it was a fall, or a row. Or even self-harm. But there's more frightening stories hiding in the walls of this eerie dwelling.' She looked up and down, making sure no one was in earshot. Then she delivered the bombshell. 'People have been murdered here at Greenridge, Wendy. Oh, yes. Murdered!'

'I gasped with terror.

'Oh, yes. A poor man with no family ties was removed dead from a bath some years ago. Drowned, they said. Suicide while unattended, they said. Heart attack or accident, they said. But I saw the body and there was sufficient bruising to his neck to suggest to me he was forcibly held underwater. Sure signs of a struggle. Oh, yes. No investigation. Just a quick burial. Fred Yates was the poor unfortunate man's name. Nicknamed Gates as he was notorious for trying to escape over the main gates to freedom. Always been confined to that horrible B wing across the way.'

'She lowered her voice even more and looked deep into my eyes, as I stood completely shell-shocked at this added horrific revelation.

'But from what I saw there was at least two-to-six more unexplained deaths. Rumours, all just rumours, they say.'

'She gazed over her shoulder with a gloomy, disturbed stare in her eyes. 'Mr Crosby is fortunate to be still alive, Nurse Collins. He should count himself blessed by our good Lord above to still be breathing. But don't go quoting me to anyone. Won't you not, dear?'

'I just couldn't move my body, Christy. I was in deep shock. I mean, beatings? And now possible murders? All the alarm bells are ringing. Can't you see? My good God, no wonder I'm shaking like a leaf and sweating.'

Christy put one arm around her. 'Calm down now, Wendy,' he said in a gentle, disarming tone. 'What alarm bells? See what?'

'Nurse Peters had Frank's head under the bloody water in the bath, maybe she drowned that poor man Mr Gates, or I mean Yates. Em, hello? Isn't that a coincidence or what? Can't you see? It all fits into place, and to think that there was I some months ago in a pub with my boyfriend – well, *ex*-boyfriend now – but I was saying to him that it's such a great honour to have been considered for a job at Greenridge. I mean what in the name of . . .?'

Ex-boyfriend . . . The words rang in Christy's ears like a piece of music from Mozart. 'Now let's just hold up a second, Wendy. I know of the tragic Fred Yates incident in question. But to my knowledge his sad passing was investigated, and cause of death was clearly down to misadventure. He drowned himself at the back of the hospital, took his own life, I believe. There were slight rumours of foul play. Every premature death in places like this causes raised eyebrows. But like Nurse Ryan, I myself on other occasions have had concerns with the passing of other individuals. But not in this case, Wendy. Did Nurse Ryan explain Fred's history of violent attacks on staff here? Like one horrible one against me some six months prior to his sad passing? Yes. Down a flight of stairs, he pushed me. Fractured my back and hip. That's where I got this limp I carry. Never forget the pain as long as I live. I could actually hear the cracks in my vertebra L5-L6 as I hit the sides of the marble steps on my way down. Agony. My screams were like that of a baby. Anyway, did she mention, by any chance, Fred's several suicide attempts?'

'No . . . she never.'

'No. People telling half-baked lies. Look at me, Wendy. Listen now. You and I will never change the past history of Greenridge. But as I've tried to explain today in our chat, we can save the future of our hospital. If we put our energies, our love into correcting the horrid blunders and wrong strategies others have made, then there's hope. All you need to do for now is trust and follow my approach.'

He paused as his face lit up. 'I still remember my father's very words when I was a boy, Wendy.' At this point, he rose once again to excel in his ability to restore confidence in yet another uncertain situation In Wendy's mind. 'Waving a closed fist, my father would shout across the dinner table, 'Do everything, my son, to free and help and restore the broken-minded here at . . .''

'Real sorry to cut across you, Christy. You said all this today and yes, it sounds brilliant in theory, but did you see Frank's battered face? We're dealing with pure evil people, patients being almost eliminated, dark stories that have me reconsidering what's the best way to handle all this. We need help, Christy!' she stressed, 'help to report what we know to the right authorities or maybe a newspaper reporter from the outside . . .' She started to fill up.

He reached across without thinking and gave her a warm hug, his mind racing. The deep female embrace. His mouth now only a fraction away from her beautiful bare neck.

Suddenly the door opened and there she was. Old grey-hair herself, Carmel Barnes the cleaning lady, pulling her mob and bucket along. 'What's happening? I heard a noise. Crying, you poor girl!' she said in a reassuring tone. 'Come here, my love.' She patted her gently on the back. 'I know, and you're so young. But remember the number one rule regarding male and female staff here at Greenridge.' She pointed a stern finger at Christy. 'Hugs are for home. Yes. Home. Remember the staff meetings? How the doctors always stressed this matter?'

'Oh, of course, Carmel,' sighed Christy through gritted teeth. 'I was just . . .'

'You poor girl!' interrupted Carmel. 'You're so young and innocent to the ugly realities of a kip of a place like this. Come with me and I'll get you a nice fresh cup of tea. Come along now,' she stressed in a soft, motherly tone.

But Wendy pulled softly back and turned and politely thanked the woman for her kind offer, then ushered the raging-faced Carmel Barnes back out the door and closed it before walking back to give Christy that added warm embrace. 'To hell with that,' she said. 'No one's keeping the rules that matter around here, so to hell with the rule book!'

'Leave everything to me, Wendy,' said Christy as he started to sweat. 'No amount of running to the outside authorities will work without hard-core evidence,' he told her. 'I tried all that and it resulted in nothing but a few mild complaints being made known. But without any real proof, all the talking in the world is just useless. Hearsay. And could end with both you and me being sued by someone for defamation of character. You could then go on to lose your job, your career by spreading wild allegations. And we can't have that. We must remain patient, as

I've been trying so hard to clarify. Stay as a team, focus on your job first and foremost, and we'll invent our own ways to help make this hospital safe and great. And one slip-up by the person or persons responsible for the awful Frank beating and other horrible wrongdoings, and we'll pounce.'

'Well, I'm taking photos of Frank's face tomorrow and keeping them. At least that's a start, isn't it?'

'Exactly! Now come here,' he gave her another prolonged hug. 'Now back to work we both go!' he smiled.

Once she was out of sight, Christy let out a huge sigh of satisfaction, his mind on fire with passion, he returned home to his small flat that was a stone's throw from the front doors of Greenridge Hospital.

She's single! He paced up and down the floor. *Oh, my good god, that delightful, warm cuddle . . . that beautiful, perfumed smell from her neck . . . Maybe she wanted me to kiss her there and then . . . No, too soon . . . Maybe she wants me to ask her out. Imagine walking around holding hands with her! The whole hospital staff would be feckin' raging. Eyes full to the brim with green jealousy.* He paused as his insecurities stopped him in his tracks. *I don't know, maybe it's all just in my bloody head, and anyway I've never ever kissed a lady before. A peck on the cheek, but never with full open mouths and lips, all them lovely movements that go with it . . .* he thought long and hard for a good half an hour. Then *Ahhh, yes, I've a brilliant idea!* He grabbed his laptop and went straight to YouTube and typed in the words *How to kiss a woman* and up popped a string of videos. He quickly sat down and composed himself.

'Hi there,' came the professional voice of the rather elderly man in the video. 'I'm Doctor Brian Totty, a recognised relationships counsellor. Now first I want you to relax and follow my instructions carefully. I want you to take a mirror from the bedroom or bathroom. A small one would be ideal, but a hall mirror if that's all that's available. Now sit down and get all comfy . . .'

Christy hit the *Pause* button, raced into the bathroom and returned holding the big wall mirror. He sat down and composed himself.

'Now slowly move your face to about two inches away from the actual mirror itself.'

Christy put his unshaven face up as close as he could.

'Now imagine your mouth is actually her mouth. Now, ever so slowly, start to open your mouth. Not too far. Just enough that your lips are apart . . .'

Christy did precisely as the man told him but was put off slightly due to the fact that he started to dribble down onto the mirror almost immediately and was finding it very hard to concentrate. The close-up made him feel totally ridiculous. *Don't stop,* he told himself.

'Okay, now that you're ready, I want you to look at yourself up close and imagine that the eyes and lips you see in the mirror are actually not yours but that of a woman. That's it, a beautiful woman . . . Don't be shy or feel in any way strange or awkward. This is a perfectly normal kissing exercise that you're engaged in. Okay, now for the final part. Put your lips on the mirror, but make sure to keep your mouth open at all times . . . Now as you touch the mirror, go *Mmmmm . . .!* You can say things like, *Ohhhh, baby!* and *I love you.*'

Christy went for it. All out. He lifted the mirror up a bit, rubbed his mouth and lips awkwardly across and up and all around even, making pleasurable noises as he began to get totally lost in the now erotic exercise. He then took it a step further as he tried to visualise that it was Wendy he was kissing. 'Oh, Wendy baby, I'm soooo into you!' But it was all ruined when he opened his eyes and saw the abnormality of the situation he was involved in, with excessive saliva everywhere. He went red all over. *No, this is not working,* he mumbled as he threw the mirror to one side in total embarrassment.

But the best idea ever flashed immediately in his mind. He shot up out of the chair and raced to the back room that was used to store junk.

Back out he came, smiling, holding a full-size skeleton that Christy bought one Hallowe'en but which was never allowed be used at the hospital. *This feels a bit more realistic,* he thought as he stood and romantically held the skeleton in an old-fashioned dance stance. With one hand he firmly gripped around the waist, the other holding the skeleton's hand upward. He paused, then had a private giggle to himself. *Gosh, I hope this isn't a male skeleton!* Then slowly he pressed his lips awkwardly on the exposed teeth area and tried to block out the strange realities of the event. He imagined Wendy's beautiful face, her mouth, and glossy lips.

'Oh, Wendy, kiss me back!' he muttered as he slowly got overly excited in the moment. 'Mmm, Oh, yes I love you, Wendy! Ooh, baaaby!'

Suddenly he heard what sounded like a soft tapping noise. He looked from the corner of his left eye and to his deep, sickening embarrassment, there was the old Carmel Barnes banging at the window.

'Christy!' she gasped in horror. 'Oh, my dear Lord and all the saints! What the hell are you doin' there?' She peered closer in shock.

'I've a bloody front doorbell!' he shouted as he went bright red and tried as best he could to throw the skeleton across the room towards the open bedroom door.

'Oh, my dear god! What were you doin'? Ahhhh!'

There was a moment of dead silence before finally Christy let rip. 'Mind your own bloody business is what you can do, Carmel Barnes, you oul' nosey bitch!' he yelled. 'Now get the hell away from my window!' He then tried to remain calm and maintain an appearance of innocence as his mind raced.

'Ahhhh, Christy Boyle has lost his mind!' she cried out with a look of pure revulsion before turning in a panic and running back down the small walkway towards the main hospital. 'Stay away from me!' she yelled back.

'Oh, dear God!' he croaked, racing out the door after her. 'I wasn't doing what you bloody think I was doing. Come back to the house for a moment!' *Oh my god,* he thought, *she'll tell everyone!*

Before he reached the main door she shouted back, 'I seen

nothin'! Nothin' at all! Doctor Grimes is lookin' for you. It's urgent.' Then she vanished out of sight down one of the side back corridors to the cleaners' store room.

Christy hauled himself in the main door in a panic.

A male carer raced past with a male nurse in tow. 'Christy, follow us! We have a situation unfolding in the main dining room!'

'Stand back! You hear? Get me a new doctor now! Right now!' It was 43-year-old patient Paddy Blake, holding a knife to a young nurse's neck. Blake had spent most of his life in and out of hospital after suffering a massive breakdown after years of physical and emotional abuse at the hands of his own father, which resulted in him stabbing his father to death at the age of sixteen. Paddy was a thin-framed man, very timid with a constant fearful stare. 'I'll cut her bloody head off! I swear, I'll do it! I want a proper doctor, not bent nose Grimes. And I want to go home to my mother and sister. You all hear me? Today, not tomorrow! I'll cut her real bad. You hear?'

Christy arrived to find Dr Grimes and half the staff from the hospital outside the main dining room door, some shouting, trying to reason with Paddy. 'Drop the knife and we'll talk then!' reasoned Dr Grimes, before adding very unprofessionally, 'You hurt her and your mother will be so upset and never want to see you again.'

The minute he saw Christy he looked relieved. 'Where the hell were you? I had staff searching the whole hospital. One of your 'likeable' patients that thinks the world of you has become psychotic and has Nurse Sara Jeffries at bloody knifepoint. Noel's off today. Can you wave your bloody magic wand and talk him down? We've tried everything for the last twenty minutes.'

'Okay, calm down everyone,' stressed Christy as he made his way past the small army of staff. 'Please give me some room. And will you all just please move back from the door. The last thing he wants is to feel imprisoned and a sense that he's suffocating. My god, where is the professionalism around here?'

He glanced at Nurse Whelan, whose facial expression had guilt written all over it. 'I wonder, just wonder what sparked off this latest situation? He was doing very well of late, from what I observed. He was acting as normal as me or you, but anyway . . .' He peeped in the door at Paddy, then turned to Dr Grimes. 'How in God's name did he manage to get that huge knife?'

'Don't ask,' Grimes mumbled. 'Will you just try disarming the crazy fool before we have a deceased nurse on our hands?'

Christy gently opened the door as everyone stepped back. 'Paddy! It's me, Christy. Can we talk? Just you and me. I'm coming in alone.'

Paddy started crying. 'I'm not able, Christy. I'm not able anymore!'

It took a good ten minutes of deep pleading back and forth from Christy before the breakthrough finally came.

'I want to go home now, Christy. They're giving me them injections and it's making me feel awful. I keep seeing plastic soldiers at night trying to shoot me, and then a small spider with a human face talking to me. My eyes, Christy, my eyes feel like they're swelling out to the point that I think they're going to explode. Plus, I can't seem to sleep. I can't take any more. Please get my mother. I'm much happier when I'm at home.'

'Listen. I need yet again to ask you, if you want to go home today, first thing you need to do is to take the knife away from Nurse Jefferies' throat. She never hurt you or anyone else. Now if you can't do that, I'm walking out that door and you'll never see me again. So give me the knife and then we'll sort out your medications and get your mother.'

It took another good ten minutes , but finally, he relented. 'You promise me?'

'Of course.'

'Okay. I'm standing up now. But only you are allowed to come in, no one else. And will you please promise to keep everyone away from me.' Christy softly agreed the terms as a few concerned staff members threw Nurse Whelan a glare. Finally he let go of his grip of the terrified nurse and stumbled back as the knife fell from his hand to the floor. She lunged forward with tears streaming down her face and let out a scream of relief.

Before Christy had a chance to lean forward and lead Paddy calmly out, several male nurses raced past him and took Paddy clean out of his standing. One staff member dived forward to retrieve the knife.

'Get your abusive hands off me!' roared Paddy as he was dragged away kicking and screaming. 'Help me! You liar!' he shouted back at Christy. 'I want to go home!' His cries were heard all over the hospital as he was taken away down to B Ward.

'Well, another brave effort, Christy,' admitted Dr Grimes. 'Bravo! I'm actually impressed.'

Christy wasted no time and without a word he just walked slowly past Grimes and the remaining staff members.

'Well done,' said one as others muttered likewise.

'You saved Nurse Jeffries' life,' said another.

Christy kept cool, never even blinked.

He took the next two days off work to catch up on a trip to Stamullen to get his hair cut in Dee's Barbers, as well as a long-overdue visit to the dental clinic in Balbriggan.

'Well, well, it's been over a year,' laughed the dentist. 'Open wide till I check those choppers at the back.'

'I just want them cleaned up, Billy. As white as you can get them.'

'Hmm . . . Well, for €150 you can get our new advanced laser whitening. It's on special offer. Normally it's €250. You'll have teeth as white as a movie star's for Christmas.' He showed Christy a photo. 'What do you think?'

'Wow. I'll take that. Will they really look that white? Bloody tea and coffee and the red wine has them stained very badly.' He was embarrassed. 'Never should have let them get into this kind of state.'

'Well, by the time you leave here you'll feel like someone's just put a brand-new set of teeth into your mouth.'

Less than an hour later Christy looked into the mirror held up by the dentist.

'Well? What did I tell you? Are they white or are they white? Ha, ha, ha! You won't need a light at night. They'll brighten up any dark room.'

'Wow!' smiled Christy. 'I can't get over how white they came out!' He handed him the cash.

'That's perfect. And how's Greenridge these days? Have you managed to make it perfect and sane as your poor father dreamed it would be? Ha, ha.'

Christy smiled vanished at Billy's remark. 'I'm just as committed as my father was to working hard to achieve that goal. And I may one day in the future shock the world and bloody land that top male Nurse job. Yes, that's right. Just need people on the outside like you to take what we do a bit more seriously and be supportive rather than making it sound like some kind of joke.' Without another word he stood up and walked out.

'My god, Christy,' Billy called after him, 'I wasn't making a joke. I knew your Dad very well. We . . .'

But Christy was gone.

Your father was actually a bit mad in the head, if truth got out, muttered Billy to himself.

Next stop for Christy was McFadden's clothes shop to get some new shirts and trousers. *Maybe I should start wearing jeans again,* he thought. *Look a bit on the old side of it with the shirt and suit trousers.*

'Well, we have a new brand of jeans just in,' said Jeff, giving Christy a penetrating glance. 'Not sure if they're your type. But if it's a change you're looking for, well then I'd recommend the new style G-star jeans. They're a big hit.'

'I'll have them, Jeff . . . and three white shirts. And will you throw in two extra-large white underpants, please.'

He paused and waited till the previous customer left the shop before whispering, 'Can I ask you something personal, Jeff? A private thing. Between you and me, like.'

'Of course you can, Christy,' he smiled. 'What's up?'

'Well,' he said, going a bit red-faced, 'I was going to ask this beautiful lady out for dinner, but I need to be 100 percent sure she feels the same as I do. I'm nearly sure, but just don't want to go and make a big fool of myself. Anyhow it's just . . . how do you recognize when a woman's in love with you? What's the big signs to watch out for?'

Jeff smiled and went on to outline a few tips and signs that he had picked up over the years.

'It's just . . .' continued Christy as he felt more at ease at opening up, 'I've never been with a woman in my whole life. Not even one kiss. Been so caught up with my work at Greenridge that, well . . . it's never happened for me. Being in love and dating was something my father said was just for movie stars, or rich footballers and singers, that I'd be fooling myself even trying to ask a woman on a date. So as you can imagine this is big-time, new to me. And to be absolutely honest, this is the first time I felt this way. I'm bloody nuts about her. So I'm thinking, this must be the love buzz people talk about. Don't laugh, but I'm now starting to bloody wake up at night with her face flashing in my head. Lying there till daybreak, thinking about her with strange, yet warm butterfly feelings racing around inside me belly. Feeling I want to be sick."

'Right, right . . . Well, that sounds lovely, and sounds to me like you're smitten. But this woman, what age bracket is she, do you mind me asking? Just to add as well, whatever you do, don't get in too deep till you're sure of her feelings towards you. You'll only get hurt, Christy.'

'Of course. I'll be very careful, I'm being real cool about it all and just feeling out the ground, like. She's making all the moves on me so far. Oh, sorry. Her age? Well, she can't be any more than 22 years of age. Or is she 21?' He laughed brightly and then, feeling a deeper sense of confidence, he opened his mouth. 'What you think of me new super white teeth? It's a new thing out, no more of that bloody scraping and polishing crap. No, no. They have all this new stuff now. First they put this gel on . . .'

'Yes, yes. Laser teeth whitening. It's been out a while. 22 years of age! That is . . . very young. Can I be perfectly honest? Don't you think that's a bit . . .?'

'Ah, age has nothing whatsoever to do with it, Jeff. If two people have the same feelings, same love, age is out the window.'

He grabbed his bag. 'I'll be back in a few weeks and I'll update you,' he smiled. 'Thanks for the sound advice.'

'But Christy, you asked me for sound adv–'

He was gone.

After picking up a nice bottle of Hugo Boss aftershave in the chemist's and getting some further advice from the female assistant about what best to get a girl for Christmas, Christy drove back to Greenridge, admiring his teeth in the mirror every two minutes. *Wait till Wendy sees the new Christy Boyle!*

*

The next evening on his second day off, he woke from an hour's nap. A flashback into the past had disturbed his sleep no end. He saw himself running a bath near the back of the hospital. Well out of sight. He closed the bathroom door so quietly. He saw himself hurriedly convincing the medicated Fred Yates to then come with him while most of the other staff were themselves busy doing their Saturday morning duties. The splashes of soapy water as the man struggled in vain for his life as Christy then held his head under the water. 'No, no, no, no noise. Sleep, Fred. Sleep.' He puffed as the struggle ended with the water becoming still, Yates right arm slipping lifelessly back after trying to put up some kind of fight. His unresponsive hand sinking back down under the water with the rest of his body, his face the last image to disappear under.

Christy lay back and rubbed his eyes as the grim memory faded. He stared up and across room at a framed photo of his dad. He held his head as a searing tense pain shot through the centre of his brain.

'That fool Yates almost killed you on the stairs. Never forget it. He was never going to be rehabilitated. Well, get feckin' up! Think of something. Change your tactics, time is running out!' his father's voice ordered him. *'Move your big good for nothing, lazy arse!'*

Christy jumped up at the order and looked in the direction of the clock on the wall. Just after half ten. He took a few heavy breaths, dressed, and dragged himself across to the hospital. Thinking of some quicker way to progress with his father's wishes. Opening his locker with a dark glare in his eyes he continued to think. He glared at his boxing gloves. Finally, he headed around with two black plastic refuge bags to empty the bins in all the hallways. He passed Nurse Jeffries who stopped and began thanking him over and over again.

'You saved my life, Christy. You may not be the kind of man that takes praise easily, but I'm so truly grateful,' she continued.

'It's okay, thank you,' he muttered in a gloomy tone as he moved on down towards the stairway.

'Is everything okay?' she called after him. No reply.

He made his way down the long stairway to B Ward. He slowly unlocked the big soundproof door and let himself in. After closing it behind him he dropped both black bags on the spot. He stood for a good two minutes before turning on the main lights. He then started to unlock the room doors of three of the more heavily-medicated patients.

Then with an aggressive roar he appeared out of one cell, dragging a terrified Paddy Blake by the hair. He flung him violently against the wall before hitting him a full-on punch to the head followed by one to the stomach. Paddy crumpled down in a heap and sobbed like a helpless child before uttering a desperate scream for help.

'Scream! Go ahead! Scream all you want!' Christy turned and screamed aloud in an insane manner before thumping the main door with clenched fists in total frustration. 'It's soundproof. Ha, I got soundproof doors in, so scream for help all you want!' he snarled. He took a deep angry intake of breath before grabbing Paddy by the throat, and yelling, 'I did everything upstairs for you and the rest of the stupid idiots that got sent down here. I stood by you, even nursed you as a loving father. I tried as always to turn this hospital into some peaceful, loving and homely environment where sick people like yourself can develop and grow and enjoy some form of happiness. But again I was made to look like a complete fool in front of everybody for caring for the likes of you.' He took a deep breath and wiped the sweat from his face with his sleeve. 'So again I find myself with no alternative but to defer back to some other possibility of rehabilitation.'

Paddy moaned in pain as Christy grabbed him up close to his own face.

'You took a big kitchen knife to a respectable woman's throat!' he roared before hurling him onto the cold floor. Christy's eyes were wild as he breathed heavily. 'I've done everything by the book in this hospital for the like of you and big fool Frank Crosby.' He cried out with hands aloft. 'I loved and was so sympathetic. My god, I couldn't have been more patient with each one of you.' He pointed a finger at Paddy who was now curled up. 'I cared and protected you just like my own father taught me to. But again and again, you all continued to go against the procedure, the perfect programme, which I remind you took my father and me a lifetime to try and perfect.'

He lost control and kicked Paddy as his temper boiled over again. He then entered another room and dragged another male patient out and began to violently beat the helpless man until blood splashed from his nose and mouth. 'It could have been so different, and we could have proved Dr Grimes and his crew upstairs all wrong. But now we're down here again instead of up there. Nothing I seem to do is working, is it? And that means process has to be changed yet again. No more lovey-dovey!'

He stood in the middle of the floor for a few moments before gathering his thoughts. 'Okay. I'm not going to send anyone else to the hospital like Frank Crosby and others, but we are going to get this sorted out, so right now I'm going to try something different. An idea came to me tonight. My father wants things to move faster. So I've come up with a new programme, another difficult responsibility, to try over time to train you all so that you can return upstairs as healed people. Responsible and reliable. Won't be easy. No point lying and saying it will.'

He stood back and took a moment. 'Over my dead body am I allowing all my father's hard work and dreams die over a few messed up people like you lot. No way. Okay, let's get started. Time is running out fast, so let's begin.'

He pulled his under 21s runners-up medal along with two pairs of boxing gloves from one of the bags. He hung the medal on a door handle. He then proceeded to force one pair onto Paddy Blake.

'Up you get on your feet, man. We will train down here for the next few months if need be, till we get everything fixed. Till you all become normal human beings again. Come on, up on your feet, Blake!' he shouted. 'On your feet.'

He put his own gloves on and started doing the footwork, dancing around. 'Come on, try and beat me, throw a punch!' he shouted. 'Try and hit me. Whoever wins gets the medal and gets another chance to go back upstairs.'

But poor Paddy was so medicated he had little or no idea what was unfolding or who was even hitting him. He finally kind of swung his arm aimlessly, but just to wave away whoever was mistreating him.

Christy sidestepped him and then landed a right hook followed by two hard body blows. 'Bang, bang!' he shouted.

Blake hit the floor with a loud crash.

'Come on, get up, you worthless excuse for a human being. Get up and fight me like a real man!' Christy went wild-eyed and started waving his arms in a victory gesture, as he counted down. '10, 9, 8, 7 . . .' He jumped up almost two feet in the air. 'I won!' He took the medal and placed it round his neck and began to wave his hand in the air. 'I am the winner! Yes! Irish under 21 champion of Ireland with a knockout. Christy Boyle. However, you need to be the champ and get the medal off me. Okay! Next!'

He took a towel and wiped the sweat away.

'Next up! Come on now, on with the gloves. I'll take both of you on once a week, and as God above is my witness, I'll create from every one of you a true champion. A winner! Come on! Round 1!'

Over in the corner in Room 19 with his eye pressed up against the small glass window was lifelong patient Mel Flynn. He just watched with not a hint of emotion and repeated in a low but certain tone:

'Once you don't tell,
No one goes to hell!'

Chapter 6

There are no risks

Claire picked at her dinner before letting out a stressed moan. Swiftly gathering her thoughts, she threw the fork down on the plate and raced out the door with coat, bag and keys in hand. She drove at speed back across to Colm's house to try wake him up to resolve things and get added information and peace of mind about where they both stood, relationship-wise. But the panic button was hit when she couldn't wake him up.

She got on her phone immediately. 'Look, Sue, I couldn't wake him and then his bloody mother asked was everything okay, that Colm told her before passing out asleep that everything was one big mess. She asked what was going on. I said I hadn't a bloody clue. Look, will you come with me now to Amy's and feel out things.'

After picking Sue up, they both drove into Hampton Cove. *I don't have feelings for Rob,* she repeated in her mind as Sue continued to talk her way into a state of total innocence in the growing saga.

'Don't, Sue,' she snapped as they pulled up to Amy's house. 'Don't you dare leave me alone in this mess. I wasn't the only one!'

'Well, hiya, girls!' smiled Rob as he opened the front door, holding a tea towel in one hand and a cup in the other. 'Amy's crashed on the sofa in the front room watching one of them boring soaps,' he grinned as he escorted them into the hallway before giving them both a warm, welcoming hug.

Both girls were red-faced, especially Claire, as she stumbled over her words. 'Hi Rob! Em . . . great to see you,' she managed in what sounded more like an exhausted teenager drooling.

Rob waved them into the sitting room before checking his

watch. 'Bloody hell!' he sighed to Amy. 'Your dad must have forgotten the time. I'll fly down and pick him up.'

I yawned and dragged myself off the sofa and gave the girls a hug, before thanking Rob for going to get Des. 'Must have put a few bets on and lost track of time. You're a star. I'll kill him!"

Once in the car Rob drove out of the estate and checked in the rear-view mirror before pulling over and turning the engine off. He removed a second phone from the glove compartment and switched it on. He sat back and took a deep breath before ringing an number: Jill Watson.

Jill was without a doubt one of the best-looking girls you could ever wish to see. With her dark brown eyes, natural tanned skin and long black hair she stood out everywhere she went. But like other women she was yet another victim that fell foul to Rob's good looks and deceptive charm. 'Well, there you are at last,' she sighed in a noticeably insecure tone. 'How many phones do you have? Six?'

Rob made light of it all with a burst of laughter. 'I've two. This is for work. I've been at a meeting all morning.'

'Big important meeting – on a *Sunday*?' she belted out. 'Yeah, right. Look, why did you just give me your work number and not your personal number? Is it so I don't ring you when you're with her?'

There was a long pause.

'Look,' she continued, 'that part doesn't matter. I just want to know what's happening with you and me. Last week you seemed so sure you wanted to be with me, all over me. Then I let you stay the night again. Next morning it was all promises that it was definitely me you wanted to be with, that you were breaking up with this girl whose name I don't even know yet. But since then you only rang me *once* and two short texts. But stupid me here sent you a load of texts and left voicemails, pouring my heart out about my feelings for you . . .'

'Calm down! My god, I told you I'd be up to my eyes with work and that I'd be breaking up with this girl very soon. This week in fact.'

There was another pause.

'Yeah? So? Did you tell her about us yet? That we slept together. What's the holdup, Rob? When are you telling her it's me you want to be with?'

'Oh, my god. As I've already explained weeks ago, she's a very needy girl, and she's extremely dependent on me for everything, Jill. I have to be very sensitive to her, break the news gently to avoid her being hurt, if that makes sense. I can't just pull the rug right from under her. That would be heartless. But listen to me. No, stop and listen to me for one second, okay? By next weekend I'll be out of that relationship, as promised. Then – listen to me – then you and I can start seeing each other full-time. I'm completely mad about you, Jill.' He paused before continuing in his warm, charming voice. 'I'm just so busy putting this big future investment together this week which is going to set me and –'

'So you've told her you're not into her? Have you stopped sleeping with her? I mean, what the hell are you saying to her? Have I ever even come into any of your conversations?'

'Well, no . . .'

'I don't even know what you saw in her to begin with,' she snapped as her jealousy spilled over. 'I bet she's nothing to look at!'

'Stop! Just stop. Look. Can I take you out Tuesday night into town? We can then go on from there. And Jill, you can ring me on any of the phone numbers from now on. I'll text you my own number. I promise I'll return all your calls from now on.' He continued for a good ten minutes to reassure her that she was the one for him and they had a bright future ahead. 'Yes, and I love you to bits too, sweetie,' he said before he hung up and sat back with a deep stressful sigh. He then gathered his thoughts before driving down to pick up Des.

He parked the car and walked into the Millrace pub where he found Des bent over talking to a guy named Matt Benton who was busy collecting the beer glasses while he gulped down a pint of cider.

When Des spotted Rob he turned to face him eye to eye. 'Bet

you €20 Amy sent you. She's bloody worse than me mother ever was!' he laughed aloud. 'And no, I'm not drunk. I only had two small teeny pints,' he added as he unsteadily reached behind to the back of the chair for his jacket. 'Goodbye, my loveee!' he shouted to the barmaid as he turned and hugged Matt. 'Not many in the world like you,' he slurred. 'You're one in a million, Matty. One in a million.'

Matt gave him a concerned look as he went about picking up a few more empty glasses from the far table. 'Take good care of your health,' he stressed, throwing a suspicious eye in the direction of Rob. 'Hey, and remember what I told you to say to Amy. *Small keys open big doors*.'

Des winked back at him before strolling out the main door with Rob in tow trying to maintain his unruffled and confident smile under the observant eye of Matt.

Matt turned, lifted up his pint of cider and then bent across the bar to the owner of the pub Ken Clooney who was observing everything closely. 'Ken! See that lad, Amy's fella?'

'Yeah, saw him drink in here a few times with Des and Amy. Very nice lad. With a nice manner as well. Why?'

'Ahh you're as thick, Clooney! He's full of shit. Full of shit!'

Once in the car Rob quizzed him on the barman's statement. 'What was your buddy Matt referring to with that announcement about Amy, small and big keys?'

'Ha!' laughed Des as it became more obvious that he had drunk more than two pints. 'Matt is a kind of modern-day philosopher,' he laughed aloud. 'He's very fond of our Amy. Told me today to tell her that a small key will one day open the biggest door to her happiness in this life. I told him: 'Rob Cooper is that key.''

Rob kind of nervously laughed before gathering his thoughts and clearing his throat. He went on to explain that his chat with Amy didn't result in any big change of mind about keeping her claim money. And please Des, for all of us, don't bring any of this up for all our sakes. Just leave it be. 'And I'm sorry to add this news to your otherwise happy, smiley day. I rather agreed if that's what she decides I'd be behind her all the way. She kind of got a little upset when I continued to try press home to her about keeping at least 10k for the surgery to her face,' he lied. 'So I told her maybe as another option she could consider investing in one of my safer investments and maybe then give some money to a needy kid's charity. Best I could do Des. No point dragging her backwards if in the end she has her heart on given it away.' he added with a look of concern.

'Ah, drop it so,' sighed Des as he remembered he wasn't wearing his seat belt. 'Anyways, she's happy, so let's thank God for that positive in her life. I say let's go upwards and onwards with the wedding plans,' he stressed with a smile as he clicked his seatbelt.

Rob raced in his thoughts as he got ready to drop another small piece of his strategy into the frame. He pulled up outside the house and for a moment sneaked a sideways glance at Des to see was he sober enough to take in what he was about to offload. He paused and craftily glanced again. 'Listen, Des. Can I share a deep personal concern with you?' he finally whispered as they both removed their seatbelts.

Des sat back and gave him a long, searching look. 'Feck sake, course you can!' he kind of slurred. 'Are you okay? It's not like you to look worried.'

'Well,' began Rob in a smooth, positive yet deceitful tone. He went into a huge story explaining that over the past two months, putting all his energies into helping Amy back from the brink had finally taken its toll on his own health.

Des looked at him, stunned. 'God, are you joking me or what?' He looked at him again. 'You're messing with me'

'I wish! I tried everything to hide this,' he said, dropping his voice. It started with me finding it hard to sleep. And then I started taking a few sleeping tablets. But I still felt I was kind of sinking. Then I plucked up the courage to chat to a counsellor friend of mine who ended up referring me immediately to see a therapist weekly.

'A therapist? Ah, here – seriously!' Gasped Des with a further stunned expression.

'No, and as it turned out he was a good one. Took him only half an hour to get to the source of my issue. I kind of broke down crying. I know it's hard to believe, as I've always come across as strong-minded. But I am human, Des. Anyway, I told him a good bit about Amy. He listened, then sat up and stopped me in mid-sentence.

'You're not a trained counsellor,' he gently explained to me. 'You may love her, but to try to help any individual at that level of hurt and pain and deep loss without proper training is not only very dangerous to the health and wellbeing of you and her, it's no way to even begin to build a lasting relationship. This girl sounds like she's deeply distressed, and you have brought yourself down trying to pull her back up. And now as a result, *you're* depressed yourself trying to cope with it all."

Des was taking in every word.

'To make matters worse, this is something I've hidden from Amy and you. I told you I don't hide anything from Amy. Well, I'm so sorry, but I kept this hidden. I couldn't tell her, not now. She's soaring too high to upset her.'

Des's mouth hung open as he sat speechless for a good 30 seconds. 'I'm stunned,' he finally muttered, 'and feel now at this moment somewhat embarrassed.' He rambled on with every sentence filled with apologies for not asking him more often how he was. 'Why didn't you at least come to me and say something if things were getting rough on you emotionally? I mean, I was here. You know you can talk to me at any time. I'm a good listener.' He sat back, now looking fully sober.

'Ah, the other day when we were chatting, I was nearly going to open up. But you have your own issues, so I held off. Look, everything is okay. I'm fine. Really I am.' He sighed heavily, then looked away, leaving Des resting back in the seat astonished and realising that everything wasn't going as well as he had thought.

*

Back inside the house, Claire did a good enough job of covering up about Colm's text. 'We're going through another rough patch,' she lied. 'He bloody needs to stop drinking as he's been doing far too much of it of late,' she managed. 'Out again today, home drunk as a skunk and then started texting you and a few mates, talking absolute rubbish. Saying he wasn't hanging out with anyone ever again. To wish everyone Happy Christmas but he won't be around. Be careful over the festive time. Best wishes etc. Nothing but drink talk.'

Sue went red-faced and darted a sharp look in Claire's direction, stating that she wasn't at all impressed with the lies being told.

I studied them both back and forth with a searching eye.

'Right, right,' I finally conceded as I then focused the talk back to the topic of my upcoming marriage, with a bright smile appearing across my face. I whipped the Bracken Court Hotel full payment receipt from the mantelpiece. 'Well? What do you both think of this?' I beamed. 'Have a read! And not a word to anyone about the costs, you both hear me? As Rob insisted on paying the lot and I don't want people knowing his business.'

'Wow,' said Sue as she scrutinised the receipt.

'Hope you didn't let him see the dress, did you?' smiled Claire before the door opened and in walked Des, with Rob all smiles behind him. I quickly placed the receipt back in its place.

Everyone sat around drinking coffee and chatting as Des scoffed his dinner and went for a nap.

As Claire drove out of the driveway, her mood changed from smiles and warm waves to apprehension. Once she got around the corner out of sight of the house she pulled over and took a big nervous intake of breath. 'Oh, my god, Sue. It's undeniable.'

There was prolonged tense silence as flashes of Rob's smiles and eyes turned over and over in her mind. Her heart was still warm and spinning helplessly. She paused. 'Right. Here goes.

I've definitely got feelings for Rob!' she blabbered out. 'In fact, I think I'm actually in love with him.' She started to fill up as Sue sat back in her seat.

'I kind of know,' Sue sighed. 'For whatever reason, I never noticed till now how close you were getting to him. But when he hugged you in the hall, and I saw your expression, suddenly the penny dropped that there were feelings involved. But sure look, it's easy to fall for such a fab-looking guy,' she added, trying her very best to make light of it all. 'It happens, and it's not a crime,' she said in a supportive tone.

'But what's going to happen now? What am I going to do? What if Amy notices! What then? I'm not losing my Colm. No way is my life going down the bloody toilet over feelings that no one but me and you know about, you hear me? No one can know this, you hear, Sue?' She wiped her tears as she indicated to give her a smoke. She lit up as Sue remained calm and focused, giving the sense she was right behind her friend, come what may.

'You explain to Tom in any way you want that this is one big misunderstanding and you keep your mouth bolted. Tell him Colm's got his facts completely wrong.' She took a deep pull from her fag and rolled down the window. With a profound expression of self-centredness, she muttered under her breath: 'At the end of the day it was Rob that started the flirting here and there *with me*. Isn't that right, Sue?'

Sue hesitated. 'Yes.'

'Right. I'll drop you home and I'll fly up to Colm. I'll get this all sorted. And we'll all move on with our lives as if nothing happened.'

She arrived at the door of Colm's house to his dad Paul waving his hands in the air as if he'd got the winning goal in the World Cup.

'Hush!' he said as he punched the air repeatedly in delight. 'Our very own Jacko Barry from up the road in Rush is 3 sets to 1 up against Phil the Power Taylor in the Grand Prix of Darts! Yes!' he shouted as he did a little dance in the hall to the Sky Sports theme music as it came back on after commercials. *'Dah,*

dah-dah, dah, dah-dah, dah, dah-dah da! Hey, hey, hey!' He punched the air each time.

Claire took little or no notice and turned and kept walking towards the kitchen. 'Upstairs,' directed Paul with another wave of the hand and another shout of *'Hey, hey, hey!'* 'He's dying with one serious hangover in his room,' he stated as he danced back into the sitting room to watch the rest of the match.

She dropped her bag into the hallway and raced up the stairs, her heart racing, a complete bag of nerves, but stopping for a pause as she now heard the radio playing from behind his closed door.

'I'm all out love
I'm so lost without you
I know you were right
Believing for so long . . .

'You're listening to Gerry Kelly, LMFM, and that's Earth Supply with *All Out of Love,* going out for Karen out there in Lusk County Dublin, who's deeply in love with Bernie. Sorry, I mean Bernard!'

'Crap,' she gasped, realising he was listening to the Sunday slow set, something they both did for years when they had started dating. She tapped on the door softly. 'Colm? You awake?'

She could hear him jump off the bed and turn the radio to another station.

Claire tapped again.

'Come in. Door's open,' he yawned as he sat up in the bed, all red-faced.

'Well, hi there!' she said, trying to smile while preparing her mind for what she wanted to say. After a prolonged silence and a few awkward glances, she broke the tense atmosphere. 'Look, let's just forget all the silly drink talk from today. You were so drunk and . . .'

Colm waved a hand to stop her mid-sentence. He slowly lifted himself off the bed and took a confident defensive stance and repeated everything from earlier. 'No, no, no! You have some kind of feelings for that scumbag! At least admit that much!'

Claire paused, then tried to hold her own but had to then sit down, fold her arms as she was unable to get a word in as her own made-up story completely deserted her under Colm's bombardment.

'From day one I never feckin' liked him. Always got a bad feeling that he was hiding something. Something in his eyes. Something real sly. But for Amy's sake, I kept my feelings to myself. I may not have his pretty boy looks, but I have a brain, Claire.'

He sat back down on the side of the bed, muttering with an intense mix of hurt and hate in his eyes. 'He stands there,' he continued, 'with that smart arse grin: *I'm God's gift to all the women. Look at me, everyone, I'm so sexy!* Oh, I'd love to punch the face off him right now, and as for that stupid big Garth Brooks Country & Western belt he's always bleedin' wearing! Sitting there in the pubs with his shirt wide open, making bloody sure everyone can see his waxed hairless chest. God it makes me want to puke all over the floor every time. Well, that's it, there's nothing left to say, is there? It's over. I for one won't have to look at his sly face again.'

He stood up again firing two painkillers down with a mouthful of water from a bottle. 'I'm bloody dyin',' he muttered as he stole a sidelong glance at Claire, waiting for a response.

'Well, okay,' Claire said finally as she dropped her eyes and searched deep in her own insecure mind for a storyline that would at least redeem herself and her relationship. 'There has been . . . something . . . going on.' She paused, letting that sink in. 'Okay, it wasn't me. I did nothing wrong. And I don't have feelings for bloody Rob. It's been *him*. I was scared to say in case you got real upset. Yes, he's made some strong unwanted advances, moves towards me, and at least two sexual ones, flirting, with not only me, but even Sue.' She let that lie sink in as Colm stood back and listened intently. 'I got drawn in by him a bit. I admit that part. A bit lost in all this attention he was giving me, but then I realised what was unfolding and wanted to say something to you.' She went on for a good five or six minutes explaining that it was only this week she had noticed she was not focussing on her own relationship and how, unbeknown to her, she was being hoodwinked by Rob. 'It's *you* I love, Colm,' she ended. 'Not him. We go back so far, and I wouldn't dream of playing with your mind, or trying in any way to hurt your feelings or make you jealous. My god, you know me. I'm not that kind of person. It was him, playing these very clever, dangerous mind games.' She filled up and grabbed for a hanky as the tears ran down her face. 'I was a victim in this as well, you know. We both were.'

Colm in a supportive role put his arms around her. 'Okay, calm down, Claire.' He let out a huge sigh of relief as his own massive insecurities subsided. 'At least I now know I'm not going completely mad, that there is something dodgy going on with this creep. Now this is very important,' he stressed as he eyeballed her. 'Tell me every little detail of the sexual advances he's been making towards you and when they occurred. I want dates and times. Leave nothing out.'

Claire took her time and went nervously through the three or four times that stood out in her mind, adding bits to each incident while making doubly sure to seem totally blameless. 'I'm so sorry if I hurt you in any way. I didn't realise any of this. I hope you believe me. I don't want to lose you,' she continued with fresh tears.

'Now, now, we're going to be okay,' he assured her as he kissed the side of her face gently. 'Maybe I pushed it a bit too far by putting the blame on you. Plus, maybe I haven't been giving you the time and attention I should have been. But everything is going to be put back in its place regarding our great relationship. I kind of knew it was him all along trying to come between us both.' He put both arms around her and held her close.

Then slowly he turned and faced her with a deadly serious stare in his eyes. 'Now. What about Amy? What about the fact that we've both recognised Rob's not to be trusted? That he's been lying and trying to cheat with two of her best friends. And with all she's been through, we can't risk her going any deeper into all this. He'll end up hurting her and leaving her absolutely devastated. Listen, Claire. If we're her true friends, we need to protect her. Plus, he's skint. I've heard from a good source that he's basically spoofing about being so well off from some kind of successful investments.'

Fearing he was taking it further than she wanted, Claire selected her words very carefully and went on to express the fact that Rob and Amy were in love in spite of his wandering eyes, and that he did have money to back up everything. 'He's gone and paid for the whole wedding. Today, like. €7,000, Colm. I saw the receipt today up in Amy's. I don't think it's fair to stretch it to the point of assassinating the man's whole character over a few mindless flirting moments with drink. He's not all bad, that wouldn't be fair,' she stressed in a nervous tone, not wanting to seem like she was defending him in any way.

'Yeah? And so?' hissed Colm as he paced the floor, his temper now starting to rise again. 'He probably borrowed it. Who cares about that end of it! Fact is, he flirted with my girlfriend! And who knows? Maybe it's true. Maybe he has other women on the bloody side. But listen, Claire. Bottom line is this: Amy's your best friend and you need to tell her everything you just told me before it's too late. You hear me? You need to warn her. We owe her that much. I want rid of him. Do I have to spell that out to you?'

There was a prolonged silence as Claire struggled enormously in her mind with the horrible idea of hiding the full truth from Colm and the reality of telling Amy half-baked lies. But finally she gave into the safe option to safeguard her own relationship. 'What exactly should I say? God, we need to word this very carefully.'

'Don't have me to repeat myself, Claire. You tell the *truth*. That he's made passes at you. For God's sake, will you wake up! It's Amy's future welfare we have to be now concerned about!'

*

'You said *what?*' screamed Sue down the phone to Claire. 'Why the hell did you mention my bloody name?'

'Will you calm down! You never said not to! Now relax. I told him it was all feckin' Rob, and we were both innocent. He bought the story big-time, and everything is back to normal, thank God. My nerves were nearly at breaking point. I almost got sick and threw up when I got home from the horror of the whole day.'

'Look, Claire. Back up here a bit. You're the one that's got strong feelings for Rob, not me, remember? He made one small harmless move on me. Was a joke, really. Feck's sake, I hope he doesn't go blabbering all this to my Tom. He'll hit the bloody roof. He's not the jealous type but . . .'

'Hey, look. Colm told me he's saying nothing to Tom regarding you. We talked about everything for over two hours. Now all I ask is that you stand with me on this. That's all I'm asking.'

'Okay. So what about Amy?' asked Sue as she settled herself.

With a nervous tone Claire spilled out that Colm couldn't have put it over more forcefully that she herself was to inform Amy that Rob had made a string of sexual advances.

With Sue beginning to tense up again on the other end of the phone Claire continued. 'Look, I'll leave it till midweek, maybe the weekend, and say it. I'm nervous and . . .'

'Are you listening to yourself, Claire? That's the most insane idea I've ever feckin' heard. You can't just now dive right in on Amy's personal life with a statement like that!' she almost shouted. 'Have you gone crazy? You'll not only devastate her, but you'll destroy an almost perfect relationship. My god, Rob made a few drunken gestures, but that's hardly a bloody hanging offence. No, Claire. Ask this question of yourself: has this got anything to do with your own personal jealousy of the love Rob and Amy share? Now I'm getting annoyed so I'm hanging up!'

The line went dead.

'Sue! For crying out loud, if I don't say it, Colm definitely will!' she shouted into the empty phone.

*

I awoke next morning and went to lean over to nestle into Rob but he was already up and happily singing as he cooked everyone breakfast. I grabbed my phone and realised I had slept in till after 10am. I remember everything felt so warm inside as I reflected back on the conversation with Rob from the night before. Laying back on the pillow I recalled word for word how he asked right out of the blue did I want to have children. I was so shocked and somewhat taken aback by the question. It was something I definitely wanted to discuss, but deep down I felt a little insecure about bringing the subject up, thinking it would be better to wait until we were married and settled. I kind of sensed it would naturally come up for discussion at some point, as having a family, wanting children was such a huge part of what I always wanted in life. But I was thrilled by the fact that he was now the one that brought it up and stressed it with such emotion how important having children with me in the future was to him. 'At least two,' he smiled. 'A boy and a girl, if that's okay. Maybe even three.' I filled up and told him it was my dream to have kids, but to have *his* child, a child to the man of my dreams was truly the icing on the cake.

As I lay in dreamland, I heard Dad come in the front door so I jumped up and headed in for a shower, trying to make it appear I was up ages.

Des walked into the kitchen as Rob was busy between getting the table ready while throwing an eye on the full pan of rashers and sausages. 'Hope you're hungry,' he smiled as Des took his jacket off and pulled an envelope out of his arse pocket.

'Before Amy comes down, put this somewhere safe,' he smiled. 'Two grand there towards the wedding – and don't even attempt to debate it with me. Right? Now – what can I do to help?'

Rob smiled, then quickly opened the envelope. He kind of mumbled about giving a grand back. 'Right, right,' he finally conceded as Des gave him a look that ended it.

Minutes later while Des had half a rasher egg sambo eaten, his phone went. 'Yes, yes,' he replied as he put his cup of tea down and walked out to the hall. 'And can you not just tell me over the phone?' he asked as he dropped his voice to a whisper. 'No? . . . No . . . I'll come in now. Okay, thanks very much.' He hung up and walked back into the kitchen. His face said it all.

'Is everything okay?' asked Rob in a deep, serious tone.

'That was the Mater Private Hospital. Doctor Ferguson. He wants to see me right away.' He sat down but stood back up, looking anxious.

'Are they starting your treatment?'

'No, that's not for two weeks. He sounded serious; maybe the results from the other two scans came back showing further trouble. I don't know. He just said it'd be best if I bring a member of the family with me. That's not a good feckin' sign, is it?'

He paused in thought as Rob put his arm around him. 'Look, I'm going to drive in with you right now,' he assured him.

Des started to go pale as he took a mouthful from his tea and put his jacket back on. 'No. God, no. You stay here and look after Amy. If she comes down and finds us both missing and a fresh breakfast smoking on the table, she'll twig something's wrong straight away. No. I'll go myself. Maybe I'll ring Steve and pick him up to go with me.' He raced out the door after another failed attempt by Rob to go with him.

The moment the car pulled out of the driveway Rob realised this was the perfect opportunity. He took a few deep breaths before picking up his phone from the table and putting it on silent. He then put his ear to the stairway to see if Amy was out of the bathroom. He waited a good two minutes as his hands began to break into a sweat, his heart racing. Suddenly he heard the door of her bedroom open as she went back and forth. He placed the phone to his ear and began pacing up and down the hall into the kitchen and back out again, playing it shrewd, keeping his tone low but letting out the slightest of yells, just enough to make sure Amy heard.

'No, I don't understand what you just said! You're talking and not listening to a word *I've* just said! And don't say *calm down*. I *am bloody* calm. I was promised there would be no issues whatsoever with this loan. Yes, I know all about the property bubble bursting and the strain on the banks' lending . But as it's stated very clearly in my loan application that I've had loans before and all have been paid back, with a sea full of interest, let me remind you. Now I've a feckin' deadline which I you know is this Friday. Yes, that's right: Friday. Don't make it sound like you haven't all the facts right in front of you. Now my big hard-earned investment plan will go down the toilet if I haven't got the loan approved and in my account by that date!' he yelled just a little louder. 'Risk? My backside! There are no risks!'

I was now listening to the heated commotion and finally threw a top on and raced to the top of the stairs. Rob motioned with his hand for me to come down. But to stay silent.

'It will be too late to seek this amount of a loan elsewhere!' he shouted into the phone before finally hanging up. His face said it all as he fought back the tears. 'Oh my god, Amy!' he managed.

'My god, what on earth?' I gasped as I put both arms around him. 'You're shaking like a leaf!'

He almost slid out of my arms and slumped onto the bottom step of the stairs, burying his face in his hands. Honest to God, I'd never seen him this upset and for a moment I was at a loss to know what to say or do.

'It's over, Amy. They disapproved the loan at the last minute. I just can't believe they'd do this to me. 260k was too much, they said. Too big an amount, as he put it. And in the end they weren't prepared to take the risk,' he whimpered. 'I mean, 260 grand is nothing in light of what this big investment with Peter would have brought me in. My god, it would have almost guaranteed me up to at least three, maybe four times that in the next year alone. Even more. Everything I've worked so hard towards has been lost. Demolished.' He stopped and ran his hands through his hair and back down across his face in despair.

'Hey come here, Rob. Bloody hell, you're a fighter. We'll figure something out. You'll bounce back.' I bent down and pulled both his hands from his face. Look at me, Rob,' I stressed with a bright smile, trying to encourage him back up. But he just couldn't look up. My mind raced, looking for some way, some other route. We talked back and forth, me showing all the encouragement I could muster.

Finally after trying to console him some more it hit me – and I remember just beaming from ear to ear. 'Look at me, love! Everything isn't lost! Now listen to me very carefully. We're both going over to Skerries, to the EBS bank. Yes, that's right, after breakfast. And you can have that claim money. No, no, listen to me, pet. We're transferring that money straight away. My god look at me will you, It's just sitting there in the account rotten away. Stop putting your head down and look at me. It's going towards this investment you're involved in. No, don't, Rob. You're taking it.'

He shook his head, waved his hands and slowly stood up in protest against any such suggestion.

'Rob, wake up. We're a couple, a team now, and everything we own, we share. What we have belongs to each other now. It's okay!' I laughed, trying everything I knew to lighten the tense situation and get him back to happy-go-lucky Rob. 'But there's just one condition, one commitment. I want you to ring that smart-arse bank official back up and tell him to stuff his money up his backside!'

'No, Amy, I can't. Please don't. Thanks very much for the lovely, kind-hearted offer, but I'll try to ring the senior boss at the branch, to see if I can . . .'

'To see if you can what? Pay a massive interest rate back for the rest of your entire life to that horrible bank? Over my dead body am I having you ringing and begging them for the money. No way, Rob!'

Rob kept his eyes downward, still shaking his head with a sense of uncertainty about the suggestion. 'What about the small risk? I couldn't live with myself if anything did go wrong,' he finally said as he looked into my eyes like a lost little boy.

'Ah, Rob please. Look. I was about to give it to charity. It was never money I was ever going to spend on myself! Look at me. Look! *You're* my future! *You,* Rob!' I smiled.

The words hung in the air and almost like magic it finally seemed to bring a definite ray of light to the situation.

'And if it makes it somewhat easier on you, we'll make a deal that when you get your millions back, we can take some of it and give it to some charity of our choice. Come on! Is that a smile I see turning the corner?'

Finally, after a further struggle that swung backwards and forwards, Rob finally surrendered to the idea with one of his big cheerful smiles. 'But as God is my witness,' he beamed, 'you'll get every cent back when the investment develops into the big bucks. Trust me,' he warmly grinned. 'I'll even add whatever interest is due.'

'Ah will you stop!' I laughed and slapped him on the shoulder, then pulled him up with both arms. 'Now, enough of this unwanted stress and let's get this breakfast into us,' I added as we embraced each other.

After a lovely chatty breakfast, it was so obvious that a big weight had been lifted from Rob's shoulders. In fact, as I washed the dishes, I remember feeling a sense of guilt, that it never even crossed my own mind to offer to give him the money prior to all this.

As we drove over to Skerries to do the transfer I reached over with my hand and gently touched his shoulder. 'Sorry I wasn't awake enough to see your essential need staring me straight in the face,' I stressed in a low *forgive me* tone.

'Jay,' he gasped. 'God, how were you or anyone to realise the complicated ins and outs of such a complex deal? I hardly ever mention it, because I thought it was definitely going to work out with the bank.' He smiled gracefully before leaning over and kissing the side of my face. 'I cannot thank you enough for bailing me out of this situation, Amy.'

Gosh. After everything you did for me! I thought as I kept my eye on the road.

Once we parked the car and walked towards the EBS I asked him had he got his bank account number handy. He gave it to me on a slip of paper from his wallet. He then paused and asked if it was okay if he didn't go in as he felt a bit embarrassed about it all.

I smiled and gave him orders to grab a seat in Seasons Café. 'Order me a latte!' I shouted after him. 'And one of their yummy carrot cakes.'

Once in the bank everything took just a few minutes.

'You do have interest on your €270,000 added over the year,' said the young polite guy attending to me. 'Do you want that to remain in your account with the balance?'

'Yes. Just transfer the 260,000 and leave the remaining 10,000 and whatever interest. Thanks very much.'

'All done! Oh, and don't forget your bank card. People are always leaving them behind!' he smiled.

I grinned as I entered Seasons Café. Rob literally jumped up, almost knocking both coffees over as he embraced me.

After about an hour we headed back to the car. Rob, all smiles and hugs, asked if he could just pop into the Bank of Ireland to inform them to let the branch in Swords know he wouldn't be enquiring any further about the loan as he had tried to ring the Swords branch but their phone rang out.

'Go on! Let them have it.'

Rob quickly approached the counter and asked the girl to check his savings account.

'Yes, Mr Cooper. €260,000 has been logged into that account. Would you like to make a withdrawal?'

'No, no. Okay. . . Listen, can you transfer it out of my savings and into my current account, please?' He tried so hard to remain calm about it all as he knew that once it was taken from the savings account and if, for whatever reason, something backfired, Amy couldn't reverse the transaction.

'Certainly, Mr Cooper . . . There . . . All done!' she smiled. 'Is there anything else I can do for you today?'

Suddenly Rob's phone went. It was Des.

'Is Amy with you?' he asked in an alarmed tone.

'Yes, but she's outside. I'm in . . . in a shop . . . in Skerries.'

The bank clerk gave him a quizzical look after overhearing him.

'Right, right. It's just I thought I saw her standing on her own outside the Bank of Ireland in Skerries. I've arrived outside the Gladstone. I'm going to leave the car parked here and get a taxi home later.'

There was an awkward pause as Rob's mind raced.

'Can you talk?' asked Des.

'Sure, sure. Fire away.' Rob walked back to the counter and whispered to the girl to print off a statement from his current account.

'Sure,' said the girl. Within seconds she handed over the slip of paper.

Rob gave her a cheeky wink, making her blush no end.

'Yeah, Des, I'm still here. Go ahead. What's that you just said?'

'I hate imposing on you again, but couldn't get Steve. He's obviously busy and has his phone off. All I'm getting is his answering machine. I went in on my own.'

Rob stepped to one side to let the next person in the queue past.

There was a further pause. 'I got further bad news. Yeah, It's not good at all, Rob, and I know you've taken on so much as it is, but I had to ring someone who I knew would listen. They got another scan result back.' He paused.

Rob peered at the bank statement in astonishment.

'My god, Rob. They found a shadow on my liver.'

'They found what? Oh, my dear,' said Rob in a deadly serious voice as he smiled and looked up to heaven to thank God as he stared at the bank balance in his account for the second time.

Yesssssss! he thought as he fought so hard to contain his overwhelming sense of intense pleasure and relief. But in a scary switch he was immediately able to make that dark transformation back from his heightened ecstasy to his cold callous self. 'Oh dear, Des. I'm . . . I'm lost for words here. I can't believe this. I thought you had all the test results presented to you last week. And now . . .'

'They're not telling me everything. Using all them feckin' big medical terms that make no sense whatsoever. I've to start treatment as early as next week,' he said as he filled up with tears and rambled on and on like a frightened child. Finally, after taking an emotional pause, he continued. 'I think I'm going to die, Rob. I just feel, *this is it*. Please don't tell Amy. I just couldn't bear that just now.'

Rob assured him there was no way he was dying and that no one was going to tell Amy. 'Now, now. Stop talking like that, Des. Look. I'm walking out of Gerry's shop,' he lied. 'And you're right. I see Amy over at Bank of Ireland. She must be getting money from the ATM. Look, do you want me to come around to you?'

'God, no. You take Amy home and just try and act normal till I find my own way to explain this to her.'

When they arrived home, Rob threw his jacket across the chair and excused himself upstairs to the toilet. He closed the door, put both the taps on full, whipped out the bank statement and stood in a state of complete disbelief as he glared at its details. He gradually sat on the edge of the bath, taking up the bath towel in one hand and then placing it over his mouth in a bizarre effort to drown out the noise. Then like a volcano erupting he released all his frustrations at the countless bad financial choices, the losses, the gambling over the years that had all but ruined his life. The blood vessels in his eyes bulged as he reacted in prolonged, chilling screams. He continued to release all the bottled-up tension and frustrations in a string of deep disturbing cries and screeches. Like a once-trapped animal, he howled. 'I did it! Yesssssss! All the weariness and acting, trying to be so careful not to make a mistake around her and them bloody friends of hers!' he screeched.

After gradually calming down somewhat, a shifty, evil type of smile appeared when he reflected how shrewd he had been in directing himself in this brilliant, well-thought-out and organized plan that steered him cleverly into Amy's life and as a result led him finally to the big golden egg in her bank account. The strategy as he called it had to be carefully operated over months of meticulous nervous planning. But now at last here he was at the wonderful, successful conclusion. 'I feckin' cannot believe it! I'm resurrected!' he screeched again before composing himself and thinking: *All that's needed now is to get myself into Peter's big investment plans – and get bloody rid of her downstairs.*

Chapter 7

Aliens in the Milk

Christy sneakily made his way back to the locker room after taking a shower in the small hospital gym. He was careful to wash any traces of blood from his boxing gloves. Incidentally, the gym had been set up by the HSE after Christy and other staff members pushed home their innovative ideas to help with the further rehabilitation of patients, but within a year the gym was now only used by Christy and a handful of keen, fit-minded staff. He beamed his big, bright, innocent smile to all the night staff before leaving to head back across to his small flat.

But once inside, he couldn't settle. He opened a bottle of red wine and drank a few glasses while pacing up and down, throwing an odd nervous eye at the framed photo of his father that hung over the fireplace. Unexpectedly, for the first time in his life, he found the necessary courage to confront his deepest fear. He stood, then turned and pointed a nervous finger at the photo. 'I am trying very hard with all this!' he stressed. 'I've endured years of you drumming it into my skull. *We must rise above the doctor's failings,* you'd say. *We must carefully and privately rearrange Greenridge into a sane hospital,* you'd say. *Set up our own private discipline procedures to bring in real order,* you'd say. 'But what about me?' he strained with frustration. 'What about *my* lost hopes and dreams? I would have given my life to have qualified as a male nurse. It was my only dream as a kid and on into my teenage years. You know how much I talked about it. Then maybe if you had encourage me to go and study in a college, I'd have met a respectful lady. But oh no. *Christy must help with the painting, the gardening. The stupid hedges, they need cutting again today.* Trim. Trim, trim, trim, all bloody day long. Hate it. *Then when you're finished, start washing the windows. Etc., bloody etc.*

He took a moment to try and calm himself down. He lifted the bottle of wine and downed a greedy gulp before firing the empty bottle into the bin and opening a fresh cold can of beer and necking half of it down in one thirsty gulp. He then dropped his eyes downward and continued. *Well, you're not going to like this. And certainly, you're definitely not going to support what I'm about to tell you, as every little idea to further my own happiness has been met with a string of questions and then disapprovals.*

He took a moment to try to keep his emotions in check as he started to quiver anxiously.

Something so amazing is happening to me on a very deep and personal level. Yes, at last I'm completely, ecstatically happy. I don't know myself. He found himself going bright red as his nerves got the better of him. *Yes, that's right, you guessed it: for the first time in my life I'm in love with the most beautiful and adorable woman God ever created. Ha! What do you bloody think of that, Father?'* He gulped the other half of the can of beer and opened a fresh one as he staggered back into the corner of the room, waiting for some kind of hostile reaction. He resorted to muttering a prayer, asking his father to be lenient, to be sympathetic and above all, to forgive his drunken outburst.

Suddenly Christy rose to his feet.

He thought he heard that distinctive voice in his mind whispering.

No, hardly . . . He listened again.

'Ahhh, go on then, but don't mess this up.'

Christy drank a few sips from his can of beer then slowly stepped out to the middle of the floor. 'You approve? For the first time ever, you actually approve of something that I actually want in life?'

There was quietness before he laughed.

'Don't you worry one bit. I won't mess this relationship up. No feckin' way. And, Dad – about your plan for Greenridge: I'll put everything right. Just you wait and see if I don't. You've approved of Wendy, now nothing on this bloody earth will stop me achieving your dream with the likes of Paddy Blake and others.'

He awoke at 5.30am and was up out of bed with a bounce in his step, despite the hangover. He downed his new healthy diet drink before hobbling over to the gym to train for a good two hours.

18, 19, 20 . . . He strained as he lifted up to 160k. *Look at them muscles expand already,* he smirked. *I'll have the body of a 30-year-old in no time!* He grabbed his towel and headed for a shower.

He sat carefully combing his new-look haircut and even put a bit of gel to try keep it spiked up a wee bit. After putting on a new white shirt, he paused halfway through pulling up his new jeans. *Feck's sake! I need to stop buying and wearing these big oul' lad's white trunks and start buying more up-to-date underpants, like them ones from that guy . . . Cavan what's-his-name . . . Climb.* After belting up his jeans he added the final touches with a splash of his new Hugo Boss aftershave. *No more Old bloody Spice for me.*

He walked over to the hospital, trying to look that bit more normal as flashes of Dr Grimes's insensitive remarks about his appearance flashed in his mind.

'Wow!' gasped one of the much older nurses when he arrived into the dining room with a big smile, making sure to hold the smile that bit longer so everyone could observe his new sparkling white teeth. 'You look like you're off on a date!' she remarked, this time with a rather jeering loud laugh that got a few more women staff giggling.

'Midlife crisis!' laughed another.

'Well, I think Christy looks rather handsome, even with the spiked hair,' remarked a younger female staff as she threw a sly wink around the table to the other staff members.

'Just a few small changes to my overall appearance!' he snapped, trying not to blush.

While everyone was muttering and firing questions at him, Wendy arrived in behind him. Just as he stood up to pour himself a cup of tea, she put her arm around him and gave him a warm hug. 'Make that two teas!' she whispered in his ear.

He almost dropped his cup as he overfilled it and scalded his fingers in the struggle to compose himself. 'Oh, hi, Wendy!' He turned and flashed a big smile making full sure she saw his teeth.

She scanned his face then looked somewhat muddled before taking a step back to look him up and down. 'You look . . .' She paused. '. . . You look dazzling.'

Christy's new sense of confidence soared at the remark. 'Aah, thanks very much! Hey, what you think of me new –?'

Suddenly the doors swung open and in marched Dr Grimes with Nurses Whelan and Peters in tow. 'Are we the only staff members who start work on time in this hospital?' he barked.

Everyone was up off their seats, checking their watches and hurriedly making their way out to start their shifts.

'Stooooppp!' yelled Dr Grimes. 'I didn't tell anyone to make a run for the door.' He turned and pointed a menacing finger before questioning the only remaining night staff member who hadn't left the building. 'Drinking tea all night, is that it?' he questioned with a sense of authority. 'I'm starting to think that it's happening again. Oh, yes. I heard about the two so-called night staff members who were caught drinking more than one glass of wine while on duty around here in the past. Glad to say they are no longer employed here – or by any other top-class hospital.'

Everyone put on a face of innocence.

The night staff worker stood up and grabbed her bag. 'Sorry, we were under-staffed again and . . . Nurse Ryan rang in sick again.'

'Well, before you check out, Nurse Bream, go and take a good look down in B Ward before you slither out the gate and home to bed.' He gestured around. 'Place has traces of blood on the floor. More doors left unlocked. Plus, there is no report of any incident on last night's sheets, so that tells me that the hourly spot checks to B Ward were yet again overlooked. Sluggish, lazy staff members not doing their jobs again!' he yelled as he pointed a finger at everyone. 'One patient was found with a black eye the size of a feckin' tennis ball. Which means only one thing. More unwanted stress and more reports for me to fill out, as if my day wasn't –'

He was stopped mid-sentence as a tall, frail figure of a man with wild, manic eyes and still in his pyjamas appeared, pushing open the door and standing at the entrance as Grimes stood unnoticed behind it, out of view. Holding a closed envelope, he spotted Christy and kind of nervously smiled. 'Ah, Christy!' he waved. 'The letter. I have another letter.' He gave a drawn, paranoid glance around the room at the staring eyes of all who were present.

Doctor Grimes approached, popping his head around. 'And what's all this?' he hissed. 'No letter leaves this hospital without my authorisation, and any staff member trying to smuggle letters out, let me remind you of the terms: they will find themselves in big trouble!' He fired a deadly serious glare in Christy's direction before turning to ask for the patient's name.

'It's Eddie, sir,' he finally mumbled as he held his emotions in check, trying his best to hide the letter behind his back. 'I'll head back to my room?' he stated now with a sense of nervousness.

Dr Grimes without hesitation stepped forward and whipped the letter free from his hand. 'Give that here! Eddie, is it? Eddie who?' he asked as he struggled to get his glasses on.

Eddie stood up straight as he could as he now struggled enormously under Grimes's intimidation. 'Nolan, Doctor. I'm Eddie of the Nolan clan from Leitrim, sir.'

All the staff stretched their necks in a desperate attempt to get a closer look at what was unfolding.

Grimes muttered in a harmless tone as he tried to compose himself and show his professionalism and read who this letter was actually addressed to. 'Was there any specific reason why a Leitrim boy writes letters without giving disclosure of the contents to his doctor?'

Eddie's behaviour changed as he threw back and slapped himself on the head, his eyes widened, then darkened. He pointed his thin finger around the room as he became increasingly agitated. 'That's my personal business! This isn't for other people to see.'

'Now, now,' ordered Nurse Peters as other patients started assembling and showing signs that they were beginning to get upset by the progressively tense situation.

Then all hell broke loose when a tall man with black overly-Brylcreemed hair, neatly combed, stepped unnoticed from behind a pillar and yelled. 'Eddie Nolan was caught digging bodies up from their resting places!' He clamped his hands up to his mouth, snickering, then raced away, jumping up and down like a little bold child down the long hallway as Eddie lost it completely.

'What did you just say about me?' he screeched with red bulging eyes as two nurses made a move to restrain him. 'Maurice Dungan! You big Limerick redneck, barefaced liar!'

Three male nurses seized him and after a huge struggle hauled him away as he protested and shouted to be set free.

'Grimes! You give me my letter back, That's for Miss Mary Harney. You tell her . . .' was his frantic fading howl as the other staff made a swift move to bring things back under some control.

Dr Grimes stood still staring at the letter before angrily asking Christy to see him in his office in five minutes.

'Mary feckin' Harney!' gasped a male staff member.

'Isn't she almost retired as Minister for Health?' whispered another staff member as all eyes fixed on Christy.

'Bringing information to the bloody HSE is what he was at! My god, he'll be suspended!' said Nurse Peters as she headed back to attend a patient.

'That may get him the bloody door for sure. But surely he wouldn't be that stupid,' remarked another member of staff.

Christy walked slowly out into the main hall, reassuring everyone. 'It's not what you all think,' he stressed as everyone looked on with judgmental expressions.

'The fat rat mouthing off yet again!' muttered Rex the male nurse to his colleague Noel as they both looked on.

Suddenly Christy saw Carmel Barnes the cleaner peering from behind the staff locker room door. She crooked a finger, gesturing to call him to come and meet her right now while trying her best to remain unnoticed.

Christy had been waiting for an opportunity to explain to her about his little kissing exercise the day before.

His mind was racing between Dr Grimes and the letter. And now this.

But if he needed encouragement, he got it when Wendy glanced around before whispering in his ear, 'I want to meet you, not in this building, for a coffee or a meal, so we can talk properly, get to know each other. You're not alone in this fight. I slipped my phone number under your locker door.' She gave him a reassuring eye before heading off to attend the patients in C ward.

He smiled back and quivered. 'Right, right, that's a brilliant idea!' he gasped, trying his very best to keep calm and unnoticed.

Carmel hissed at him yet again.

Christy clicked back to reality and raced across the hallway and closed, then locked the door. 'Now listen to me. I can explain my odd behaviour yesterday. It's not what you think. I was . . . I was practising for a part in a play,' but Carmel waved him to stop.

'Don't even try!' she whispered in a hearty giggling tone. 'I recognized afterwards what was goin' on with you. Now forget all that and close your eyes. I've a present for you. Don't keep askin' why, and just close them eyes for two seconds.'

'Close my . . .? What present? I've a lot on my plate right now so please make this fast.'

'Close them. I've a little gift that will help you.' She sniggered as she kept one hand hidden behind her back. Christy finally gave in. 'That's it. Keep them closed!' she ordered.

Suddenly Christy felt something warm and wet on his lips with a revolting taste of cigarettes and coffee. His eyes shot open and to his horror there was Carmel engrossed in a full-on open mouth kiss with him. The shock froze him to the floor for a moment and as he tried to pull himself away she grabbed a firm hold of him with her bony fingers that clutched on to him like hooks. It gave her sufficient time to stop for air and go at it for another prolonged kiss.

'Mmmmmmm!' she moaned with delight. 'So, you've never been with a woman before? Well, a few free practice sessions with me will sort you out. Yummm! Come on, put somethin' into it!'

Christy let out a horrified screech as he pulled her up off her feet and away from him. His face turned green and distorted as he felt his stomach ready to throw up. 'How bloody dare you!' he screamed as he raced over to the sink, grabbing a wet towel. He went about washing his mouth and repeatedly spat into the sink. 'My god, you're in your feckin' 70s, you horrible oul' –' He went to continue as his face twisted and turned with a sickening queasiness.

'Oh stop! You've never been with a woman! I know. I notice little men-things like that, stop blushin'!' gasped Carmel as she caught her own breath. 'I'm widowed five years and I see no reason why two lonely grownups can't have a bit of late-life romance.' She smirked. 'We could get a bottle of red wine and a take-out. Oh yes, and then you can have me all to yourself!' She then gave an insane laugh as she did a little twirl and untied her long, greasy, grey hair, then tossing it with her fingers she sensually smirked before placing both hands firmly on her hips and breaking into a slow, inviting, model-style walk towards the horrified Christy who couldn't believe what was unfolding. 'Love the white shirt, jeans. You've certainly caught Carmel's eye of late!'

'Don't you dare! Get the hell away from me now, right now, you hear me!' he gasped. 'You're feckin' mad!' He raced past and tried to unlock the door as fast as he could. But just as he had it opened, she raced across and jumped on his back, forcing him out to the middle of the floor, swinging back and forth, then around in circles, trying to wriggle himself free.

'Wheeeeeeeee! Round we go!' she laughed as Christy whirled full circle, yelling at her to let go.

But she had managed to wrap both her legs around his waist and to further the sickening experience she started to kiss all around his exposed neck.

'Get your smelly hands off me or I'll report you for sexy harassment!' he roared. 'You're humiliating me! Let me bloody go!' He finally sat down on a long bench, resulting in Carmel finally letting go, but not before she landed a wet sucking kiss between his neck and ear.

'Yucky, that aftershave tastes rotten' she moaned.

Christy jumped up and raced out the door, but not before noticing that he'd sat on an old wet cloth that Carmel was using for washing the floors. He rushed down the corridor towards Dr Grimes's office in a panic trying to wipe the wet patch off the arse of his jeans with one hand and with the other he used his hanky to wipe the wet saliva from his neck.

He walked at pace to a nearby staff toilet and almost vomited his breakfast up. 'For feck's sake! That's just disgusting!' he moaned as he took a few moments to compose himself.

But before he had time to catch a breath he heard a hissing noise, turning he saw it was long-term patient Frederick Bowles who had stepped out from behind one of the main pillars and peered into the toilet, wearing his usual old brown suit, white shirt and tie and covering his head was his old musty trademark 1916 Irish volunteer cap that his grandfather had left him. With his unusually strange frightened eyes peering suspiciously up, down, and all around he whispered, 'Christy, fast! Now, it's urgent!'

Christy stepped forward, trying to explain he had no time for one of their little chats.

'Hush! Don't say a word. This will only take a few seconds to explain. I need your help!' he muttered with a paranoid glance up and down the hall. 'Is there any way you can smuggle me in a semi-automatic MPA defender pistol, model 930, with a few rounds thrown in? I've a number here for an IRA man.'

Christy tried to get away, but Frederick continued. 'Don't tell me you never knew I was well in with the IRA! Oh yes, I even tried to sign up as a member. But my god, what a mission and a nightmare that turned out to be!'

'Yes, I think you told me this a dozen or more times,' gasped Christy as he checked the time.

'Well, don't you go telling stories about me, but maybe I never told you this part. I knew a friend who knew someone involved with the Ra and they contacted them on my behalf. Oh yes, you look well surprised. This man then said he'd meet me after being told I studied a bit about guns and explosives. So anyway, to cut a long story short, when I did meet this man, he told me the group was called the Continuity IRA. I paused in thought and said I never heard of them lads. 'I want to join the IRA!' He started to get annoyed and said, 'There's now four or five groups. Which bloody one are you looking for? There's us and then the Splinter IRA, the Dissident Republican IRA. Then the Real IRA.' 'Well,' I said, 'why can't there be just the one IRA? My great grandfather told my grandfather he was in the real gang, and any way are we not all supposed to be fighting together as one team for the real United Ireland?' He started to get very annoyed when I said that and yelled abuse at me across the table and then whispered he would have me shot if I continued to bullshit him. Then I said, 'Okay. I made my mind up. I'd like to join the Real IRA. That sort of sounds nearer to the real lads. Thanks I'll take another appointment to meet the real IRA lads if you have a number, and if they could send me on an application form and some literature at the earliest date and then I'll get back to them when I make up my mind about joining.' Well the abuse and threats he roared at me as he turned and charged out of the pub.

'Anyway, around that time my own nerves started to get very bad and I was sent here again. But I kept that man's number and I think he may be able to get me this gun. It's time to take one of the imposters out–'

'Right, sure,' muttered Christy as he slowly stepped away and knocked on Dr Grimes's door. 'I'll get back to you on that, Frederick.'

'It's Whelan again, you see,' Frederick continued. 'She dragged poor old Mary Howls from her sick bed by the back of the hair first thing this morning. She never leaves that poor elderly woman alone. She's suffered years of abuse from her. Furthermore, as you well know, she's always taking her little doll Kate off her, leaving her hysterical. You know,' he pointed his long thin finger at Christy. 'You know how much that little dolly means to Mary. I got an awful fright at her screams and was close to wetting myself again – me, a full-grown man. And what did I do then? Well, like the big coward that I am, I ran out of the ward and hid.' He paused to look up and down the hall again. 'I can't find ease till she leaves in the evenings. It's only then everyone can relax. And she always puts on them horrible brown glasses. Hiding the reflection of evil in her eyes to the outside world, you see, that's my opinion. Ohhh, I pray day and night that, if not me, then someone gets to blast her up to six times at close range . . .'

'Sure. I'll try and find Mary's doll and return it,' sighed Christy, trying to look interested.

The office door opened but only after the second knock, as Noel the male nurse popped his head out.

'We'll talk later, Frederick,' mumbled Christy as he ushered himself past Noel and into the office.

Christy again composed himself as he immediately noticed that Dr Grimes was seated at his desk engrossed in reading Eddie Nolan's letter for the second time.

'Sit, sit,' motioned a shock-faced Grimes as his eyes peered at the closing statements of the letter.

Christy was straight in. 'This is a misunderstanding, Dr Grimes. Eddie writes all kinds of letters, but God, I never send them.'

'Okay, relax,' muttered Grimes as he stood up and began to read some of the letter aloud.

'Dear Mary.

My name is Eddie Nolan. Can you come and visit me, it's so urgent, time is short, and this is now my 6th letter without reply. Why are you not writing back to me? WHY!'

Grimes sat back down and took a mouthful of water. 'He goes on to outline that all diseases, infections are really alien forces that were sent from another planet to kill and wipe out the entire human race. 'Wipe them all out!' he writes in block letters, underlined.

'I've studied this for many years and have come up with the only way to stop it once and for all, he continues. He goes on to state

that the reason diseases are spreading so fast is when a body is buried in the ground the alien disease that actually killed the person leaves the body and travels under the ground to nearby fields and gets into the crops, and the grass the cows eat. Then of course into the milk we drink, then he stresses that it cultivates with the likes of barley and cabbages, potatoes, etc. in a way that helps itself to grow and multiple before it enters back into our bodies. Hence the reason why diseases are so on the increase. The milk we drink.' Giggled Grimes.

'Well I've read one or two, but –' Christy went to say before Grimes laughed again and waved him not to interrupt.

He stood up again as Noel threw his eyes up to heaven for the fourth time.

This was followed by a kitchen staff member knocking on the door. 'Your tea, Doctor.'

'Yes, yes, come in, Jackie. Just leave the tray on the desk. Thank you. Bye, bye now.'

Dr Grimes poured the tea. 'And to end the letter,' he grinned, 'the answer from Eddie to the HSE and the government is they must take action. NOW! he writes. By not only burning the bodies of every person at time of death. No. We must go further than that, he suggests. We must then cordon off all graveyards, dig up every dead body that's been laid to rest and consume them by fire without delay . . . On and on he goes. Even asking for a meeting with the heads of government so that he and they can draw up a plan of action! My god, that's why he was admitted here. Digging up bodies from five separated graveyards. I just briefly read his file. And then attempting to burn them in his back garden!'

He tore the letter in half and threw it in the bin. 'Feckin' nutcase isn't the word. I cannot believe this kind of insanity actually exists. My god, I'm trying to reconstruct this hospital, but it's like trying to build a glass tower with a hammer, I don't need this kind of garbage at 8.30am in the morning,' he stressed as he poured the fresh milk into his tea.

He stopped and then lifted the cup to his mouth. He paused

as one eye gazed down at the jug containing the milk. His face froze and his eyes widened as he slowly placed the cup of tea back on the saucer. 'Maybe for now I'll just have a glass of water,' he gulped.

'Is that all for now?' asked Christy as he suddenly turned to leave.

Grimes held up his hand for Christy to remain. 'I think of late, Christy, we may have gotten off to another bad start. I admit I've been rather harsh with some insensitive comments about your appearance which I can now see you've almost fully addressed. But let's all be humble and admit you've saved a member of staff this week from certain harm. We all want this hospital to progress and I can now see what you're trying to achieve . . .'

'Well that's nice of you to say about my appearance, and yes, we all want a sane hospital. As my father said many a –'

'Well, okay,' interrupted Grimes as Noel looked completely uninterested. 'Once we agree to not go and tell tales, we can all regroup and work as a team, in harmony.' Grimes smiled. The look in his eyes suggesting he was eager to forgive and build a spirit of trust.

'Well, that's all I ever wanted,' said the surprised Christy. 'I love the patients so much and if I can just continue to help with this perfect strategy . . .'

'Yes, yes. Let's not go into all that. Your father's famous quotes again. Thanks very much for that. We'll talk again. Now go. The back gardens need cutting. Thanks very much.'

Christy paused before turning towards the door.

Suddenly Noel burst into stitches. 'What happened the arse of your jeans?' he guffawed.

Christy turned around and saw to his horror a big white stain right across the seat of his jeans.

'Ah, for feck's sake!' he fumed. 'Not my brand new jeans! I sat on feckin' bleach or something. An oul' cloth in the locker room!'

'Now, now,' smiled Grimes. 'It's just a pair of jeans. Easily replaced. You go change and have a nice day.' He ushered him out the door and closed it.

'Are you going soft in the head?' asked Noel, trying to keep his voice low.

'*Keep your friends close but your enemies closer.* Isn't that the best way to handle an old fool like Christy? Play him the old-fashioned way: good cop, bad cop. Yeah, and anyway, he's closing in on retirement, Noel. And with a bit of sweet talk I'll get him to call it a day well before then. This crazy obsession his crazy father had about a perfect Greenridge. And he's exactly the same . . .' He paused and gave Noel a strong stare. 'Come here. I want to show you something. But this goes no further. I'd get into trouble for waving this stuff around to staff members.' He pulled a file out and threw it on the table in front of an engrossed Noel. 'It's information about Christy's crazy father. 'Not to be disclosed to staff' written on the file. But go ahead. Read page six about how he really died.'

Noel read, then looked up. 'I heard a completely different story when I came to work here,' he gulped.

'I know, they kept it very hushed. Insane isn't the word for it all. I shouldn't be letting you read it,' said Grimes with a serious face. 'If the walls of this place could talk, they'd tell some dark secrets. Be very careful, Noel,' he stressed as he nervously fell into his chair. 'A place like this can creep slowly, unnoticed into parts of that mind of yours, then silently to other areas of your thought patterns, and before you have time to react you find you're unable to think the same as before. Ha, ha, ha. Oh, yes. You can be easily caged into all types of mad ideas, even of murdering people. It's happened to the best of us down the years. A kind of strange urge to inflict pain on patients can storm the mind, we all have it. It happens so easily if you don't protect yourself in a place like this.

'I myself have been having the weirdest of nightmares of late, one that I was hammering a huge six-inch nail into my leg. I could feel the pain like it was so, so real. Woke up screaming my head off. Ha, isn't that a mad one, Noel? Sure even my own marriage isn't 100 percent since taking up my post here. My wife says I've changed since I started,' he confessed with a vulnerable glance away. 'I had a very odd moment only a week ago when I found myself seated in this very chair trying for ages to think straight. Then I noticed I was humming an odd tune from some old black-and-white movie I saw when I was a kid. Back and forth, I rocked in the chair, scratching my arms like mad, then scratching at the arm of the chair. Then I started scraping at my right ear for no reason whatsoever. I stopped myself, and realised it was 530pm and I'd be sitting for nearly four hours singing to myself. It truly scared me to death, Noel. Isn't that weird?' he ended, as his glassy eyes wildly stared across the room.

'Right, Doctor, I hear you. You'd want to be very careful all right. Sounds like you're stressed out a bit. You'd want to keep a close eye on that or it will be you yourself that could end up going bloody insane. I've learned over the past ten years to remain detached and completely in control at all times. There's no way in hell will a place like Greenridge or any other hospital ever get under Noel Jennings' skin,' he assured Grimes as he made a move for the door.

'Hey, look,' said Grimes in a now saner tone. 'If I ever need to offload, is there any way we can have little open chats like this? I could do with a real strong-minded staff member like you at my side a bit more. I have to admit – and this goes no further – I'm not as fully qualified for this job as I pretend to be. I kind of forged a few exam notes to make myself look far more qualified than I was. So this feels a bit out of my league, to be perfectly honest. They were looking for a replacement fast and I saw it as my big opportunity. Money's brilliant and I am learning. I am picking up loads as I go along.'

'Of course you are,' smiled a strong-faced Noel. 'And if you need support, a chat, advice, well I'm here 24/7 if you need me.' He turned to leave.

'And Noel, that promotion job that Rex thinks he's in line for in January? It's yours, not Rex's, mate.'

Noel just winked as a big smile appeared.

'Anyway, enough said. We have work to do if we're ever going to make sure to control and contain the insanity in a place like this. You go now and make sure that Eddie Nolan has his medication changed and increased so he won't be able to write the first letter of his name, let alone a full-size letter.'

Just as Noel was heading out the door Grimes whispered in a friendly voice. 'As stated a number of times, you're my strongest staff member, Noel. We need men like you to lead by example.'

Once out in the hall Noel headed straight for the staff locker room. His hands were sweating and noticeably trembling. He waited until another staff member left before locking the door and standing alone in the centre of the room for a good three minutes without a sound. Suddenly he raced over to his locker and unlocked it with a frantic gasp.

He was breathing heavily as the sweat ran down his face. He burst out in a bizarre fit of laughing as he started pulling out boxes upon boxes of different kinds of tablets.

Big strong man Dr Grimes my arse! Just another weak link in the chain. Hammering big nails into his legs. Then crazy Eddie – aliens growing under the ground into the cow's milk! Exhuming bodies from their graves. Then to top it all off, Christy's mad father electrocuting himself in B Ward strapped to the EST table for the night. My god, what's next? My bloody head isn't able for this.

He grabbed a bottle of water from the back of the locker.

Right. Take a pink tablet first, then a little blue lad, maybe two? What's it feckin' matter? Just take the lot! He took three, maybe four. *Now a beautiful little red lad. Come on fast, Noel. Stay focused, man.*

Minutes later:

Aah. Nice thoughts . . . That's it, Noel. Breathe . . . Breathe in, out, in, out. Yessssss. Noel's normal again. You've *back in the room.*

As he closed the locker after one final swig of water there was an attempt to open the door, then a voice. 'Noel? Are you in there? It's Rex. We need the keys to the pharmacy.'

'Right . . . Just changing my trousers. Give me 30 seconds,' he gasped as he slammed the locker closed and composed himself before appearing out with eyes bulging.

'Come on, Rex, look bloody lively, for crying out loud!' he snapped as his eyes bulged further. 'Look professional, man!'

*

Christy raced back across to his flat and went about taking his jeans off. He then noticed in the mirror that the bleach had ruined his white underpants as well. 'Feckin' hell!' he moaned. He rang McFadden's clothes shop.

'Jeff? It's Christy. Yeah, from Greenridge. Listen, I'm going on a date with my lady friend. Yeah, the girl I was telling you all about. No, no. Everything's okay, Jeff. It's going great so far. Listen. Can you hear me? I'm going to need another pair of them nice jeans if you have any left in my size. I ruined the other pair.'

'You're breaking up on me, Christy. I'll put you on speaker. It's a very bad signal. What happened?'

'Ah, I destroyed them jeans. There's no way I'll ever get the stain out. Can you hear me now?'

'Yeah, just.'

'Had a bit of an accident at work. Right mess. New pair of white trunks, the lot got completely ruined.'

'I'll hand you over to Anne-Marie, Christy. I'm headin' on me break,' said Jeff as he hurried away, shaking his head.

'My god, Christy,' whispered Anne-Marie as she continued serving a customer. 'I'll have to turn up the speaker. You had an accident?'

'Went right, right through me, Anne-Marie,' he laughed.

'Sounds like a horrible bug. You must have ate sometime funny.'

There was a pause.

'Feck's sake! I didn't mean that kind of accident!' yelled Christy as he went all red-faced on the other end of the line. 'It was *bleach*. I *sat* on it, Anne-Marie. Went right through to the skin. Feck's sake, I'm a grown man, not a child, for cryin' out loud!'

'Oh god, sorry, Christy, I thought . . .'

'I know well what you thought. Now I've had a bad start already to my day so can you just tell me, have you any more of them jeans in size 38?'

'Well, of course. We always stock up.'

'Ah, that's great. I'll drop over in the morning. And Anne-Marie, I'm looking for more stylish-looking underwear, the modern ones from yer man, Cavan Climb.'

'Who? Oh . . . You mean *Calvin Klein . . .*' Anne-Marie smiled as she threw her eyes up to heaven. 'I'm sure we have, and we stock other styles as well. You can have a look when you drop in.'

Christy sat back and took the piece of paper with Wendy's phone number on it. With a deep breath he opened his laptop and went to YouTube once again. *Right. I need more information about women and dating, etc., or I'll make a complete fool of myself on this date.*

He clicked on to the same doctor who did the kissing video. *Your Wedding Night by Doctor Totty.*

Right. Here we go. he clicked *Play*.

'Hello! Welcome back to Part 2 of *Men and Women, the Wedding Night*! Let's see what we the experts have to say.' The white coat Dr Totty was wearing seemed to make him look very respectable and professional in everything he was saying. 'Moving on now from kissing, we take the next big step up,' he smiled. 'Yes, you guessed it: making love.'

Christy's eyes widened and the sweat ran down his face as the doctor went on for a good 40 minutes.

'Nothing to be embarrassed about. This is one of the most amazing, pleasurable and natural aspects of married life, part of our human enjoyment. So much to explore, and a lifetime to make it perfect for you and her.'

As the doctor ended, Christy rose up to his feet, feeling almost faint. He struggled on his feet as his mind tried to take in all the new incredible information.

He turned his eyes slowly towards the photo of his father, then to the smaller one of his mother.

Well, thanks very much for telling me the biggest load of lies ever heard on this earth, Ma. Birds and bees! And what did you tell me? 'That's only for some people to learn when they're having a little baby. Special folk. Not you, it takes just one, maybe two minutes, Christy.' Well, thanks very much for the greatest mislead of the century. Bloody hell. My heart's racing like mad here.

He sat back down, calmed himself, watched the video again several times before ringing Wendy.

'Listen, Christy! Listen to me,' she whispered before Christy could get a word in. 'I have found out some added information. Can you meet me for dinner one of the nights? Say Thursday at 8pm? Nice place in Skerries called Seasons. Lovely owner, very friendly and the food's super.'

'Yes, I'd love to,' gasped Christy. 'Sounds . . .'

'Have to go. I think I'm being watched again. I just took some photos with my phone of B Ward. Vomit, blood, and urine everywhere. Nurse Whelan has guilt written all over her. Talk later.'

The line went dead.

*

Claire arrived over to Tom's house in Mourne View, Skerries after finally getting Sue to answer her phone.

They all gathered in the back room as Tom opened the back door and lit a fag. 'Right,' he sighed as he addressed his words in the direction of Claire who stood with her back to the wall. Sue closed the hall door and sat down with both arms folded, still looking anything but happy. 'I'm not revealing everything Colm shared with me this morning as we are mates and I'm certainly not jeopardising our friendship over your relationship problems again. Remember last year I got into a row with him over something stupid you told me in confidence?'

There was a moment or two of silence as Claire kept avoiding eye contact with Sue. 'Well,' she finally said in a shaky tone, 'I wouldn't expect you, Tom, to spill the beans about your chat today, but as I'm sure you realise, it has become far more serious.'

She paused as Sue glanced up, looking edgy.

'But look, it's all sorted out,' beamed Claire, trying to look confident. 'Look, it's just Colm has insisted I say something to Amy about Rob's advances towards –'

'Oh, will you stop it, Claire!' snapped Sue as she shot out of the chair. 'Tell her, Tom, for crying out loud. Rob, after a few beers, gave you a few hugs and a friendship kiss and –'

Claire snapped back, trying hard not to mention Sue's flirting moment. 'He made a string of sexual advances towards me, okay? Is that what you want to hear, Tom? The truth of precisely what I told my Colm today. And he's convinced Rob isn't to be trusted. And he put it to me that we need to safeguard Amy. And it's me who needs to say it, as I am the victim in all this. Anyway, if I don't say it, believe me, Colm will,' she hissed.

Sue sat down, folded her legs and arms and went to say something but Tom waved at her with his hand to let him do the talking.

'Now for a start, will you both keep your voices bloody down?' He pulled up a chair and sat down and seemed to bring some calm to the tense situation. 'Now look. I'm speaking purely for myself here. I've always liked Rob. From the time I met the guy, he was bang on and always very polite and forthcoming and there's no way on earth any one can question the man's credibility and integrity. Who at the end of the day gave everything he had to save our Amy's life from a deep depression that none of us in this room could handle.'

'Well that's what I keep saying . . .' Sue went to continue.

'Hey, let me finish!' snapped Tom as he started to show signs that he was getting irritated with the whole situation. 'Yes, Colm is very upset at the way you, Claire, drool over Rob. *And you do*. And yes, he was deeply upset today in the Millstone. At the end of the day Colm is just a bit insecure, and in truth a little bit jealous of Rob's looks and charm. But my god, to go as far as branding Rob a dirty low-life on the hearsay of some guy Colm's only met once is madness! After all Rob's done for Amy? Come on, they're getting married, for crying out loud. He's paid for the whole wedding in advance. Now look at me, Claire. There is no way on earth you or Colm are going to jump in and hurt Amy and permanently ruin all our friendships over a few silly moments with drink.'

Claire was staring at the floor as Tom paced up and down,

going over and over why no one had the right to judge Rob, and how he would make sure Colm didn't open his mouth.

Claire glanced over at Sue. They were both thinking the same.

What about the fact Claire had real feelings for Rob, and not Colm?

What now?

Chapter 8

In the Blink of an Eye

Dad arrived in somewhat late and noticeably drunk from his adventures in the Gladstone pub in Skerries and seemed to have little or nothing to say.

After he struggled to eat his dinner I thought about sitting him down and giving him an earful about his drinking of late, but at the same time I didn't want to bring tension, and ruin what had been a lovely day. I strolled into the sitting room as he sat staring at a blank TV screen. I thought about just having a wee chat and feeling out the mood.

But Rob stopped me just as I was about to sit down. He gave me a nod and brought me back into the kitchen. 'Don't, Amy,' he stressed in a low, caring tone. 'He's just struggling a lot this week with the anniversary. After tomorrow he'll start getting back into a normal routine. Look at me. I promise, just leave him and I'll have a few words with him while you wash the last few dishes. How's that sound? Everything is going to be okay.' He reassured me with one of his smiles.

'Okay, thanks,' I said as he gave me a warm hug.

Rob went into him with his gentle approach as I cleaned up. He closed the door and after two minutes I could hear what sounded like Dad crying. I walked past the door and went to listen but kept going upstairs to give the impression I wasn't too close by, so as to give them more space.

'Now, now, stop this,' said Rob as he put his arm around Des. 'Don't do this to yourself. You're going to be okay, Des. Listen to me now. There's wonderful advanced treatments out there nowadays,' he assured him. 'My own father, bless him, survived it after a doctor gave him little or no hope.' *Another lie.*

Des struggled to grab onto some positives as Rob continued

to try to make him see there was hope in this seemingly dark and hopeless situation. 'No, no!' he gasped with a terrified expression on his face. 'It's feckin' after spreading to my liver. I knew the minute both doctors strolled into the room, their expressions, they were trying to hide the full reality from me, but I'm no dope. I'm riddled with it, Rob. Riddled!' he cried out, trying his best to keep his voice down.

'Hey, come here,' offered Rob as he gave him a warm squeeze. With his head turned he took a sneaky glance at his watch. *Got to get in touch with Peter,* he thought.

'I'm offloading all this stress and crap on you again. I'm so sorry.' Des paused in thought as Rob kept explaining there was definitely no way his life was nearing the end. Finally, Des appeared to slightly cheer up. 'Maybe you're right, maybe these new advanced treatments you're talking about will work,' he said as he blew his nose and composed himself.

Rob reassured him over and over as he poured him a fresh cup of tea before switching on the TV for him and heading upstairs to Amy.

'Ah, he's just really feeling the strain and worry about tomorrow,' stressed Rob as we snuggled down on the bed. He turned my face to his and took a deep breath. 'Listen, thanks once again. I know I'm sounding like a broken record, but that loan protected my future as an investor. I owe you my life.'

'You don't have to keep thanking me,' I protested as he waved a hand to continue.

'I've been just a bit worried with your Dad being upset downstairs just now. You wouldn't tell him that you loaned me so much money. It's just . . . I'd be so embarrassed and . . .'

'Hey, look at me and listen to me for the last time,' I stressed in a strong firm tone. 'That wasn't a *loan*. We're a team, a couple, almost a married couple.' I sat up on the bed. 'And no, I wouldn't dare tell a soul and bring any sense of embarrassment. You have my sworn word. Look at me, Rob. This is now *our* personal business.'

He smiled and drew my face close and gave me a prolonged

kiss before slowly pulling back with a pleasurable sigh. 'Listen, Peter rang when I was downstairs,' he said. 'He was asking how did everything go with the bank loan. He wants to meet me in an hour to go over the papers. He reckons if all goes according to plan, the deal will now go through as early as tomorrow afternoon, so I have to leg it home. But I'll be back in an hour or so.'

I picked up a pillow and threw it at him. 'Go, but hurry! And will you be so kind and pick up some chips on your way back? I'll butter some batch loaf and wait at the door for your welcome return.'

*

As soon as Rob was safely on the M1 to Swords he whipped the bank statement out of his inside pocket and again stared in amazement. . . *My god! is this really happening for me? Right. Go for it!*

He took a deep breath before whipping his phone out to ring Peter. *Stay calm and focused.*

'What is it, Rob? I'm up to me eyes,' came the impatient response.

'Well, my good man,' he tried to joke, 'first off, I have your €1,500. And will have the other half in a day or so.' He smiled before leaning over to pull the envelope containing Des's cash from the glove compartment. 'No, no, It's not a joke, Peter. I'm looking at your money as we speak. I need to see you *now*, like, in the next half hour. You're not the only one that's extremely busy. I've something to show you. This will definitely make your heart –'

'I don't mean to cut across you, I've a late meeting to catch but I'll be passing your way and will drop in for the money but that's as –'

Rob was in again. 'I put a huge investment together, Peter. I've kept it very low key! That's why I'm almost broke' He barked down the phone as his temper boiled over a tad. 'It was a well-thought-out investment,' he stressed. 'Made over a quarter million on the deal. Yeah . . . You're gone very quiet there on me. Yes, that's right, quarter of a mill. You did here me right. So come on, Peter. It's common knowledge in certain circles that you're looking for a good investor with 175k. Now listen, just listen, I'm the only man you're going to get that kind of cash from before it gets away from you. You have to be nearing a deadline.'

Peter was up out of his chair. The very mention of the possibility of securing that kind of money to seal his investment deal almost sent him into a panic. But experience kept him cool-headed as he reserved his excitement. 'First off it's none of yours or anyone else's business regarding my investments. Secondly I'd be willing to bet my life you of all people haven't got 175k sitting ready to invest. End of. I'll be over to you in a while for my 1500,' he said in a calm tone before hanging up.

'Stupid, little eejit!' screeched Rob as he threw the two grand on the passenger seat. 'This is my future and I've worked my butt off to get this cash sorted. People need to start showing me some real respect!' he moaned as he tried to calm himself down.

He finally pulled into his driveway in Jugback Green in Swords, trying his best to remain positive. He took a deep breath and sat in the car thinking, but just as he was about to grab his coat from the back seat, Peter Bradley drove up to the entrance. All business-like, he jumped from his car and hit the lock switch all in a matter of a couple of seconds.

Rob put his hand out in a welcome gesture, but Peter waved it away.

'Just give me what you owe me, Rob. I haven't got time for how's-your-father.' His tone was firm and direct.

But Rob waved him into the house for a moment as he explained that he needed to count the cash out. 'Well, I'm not counting money out in my driveway with people walking past, so if you wouldn't mind, Peter. Please.'

Peter gave him a look but waved both hands in submission. 'Make it quick.'

Once inside, Rob pulled an envelope open and began counting the €50 notes. He paused as he scrambled in his mind how best to persuade Peter to have a rethink. 'Right, there you go. 1500. It's all there. You can count it yourself. But before you do, take a look at this.' He waved the bank statement up into Peter's face, trying to make sure he saw the balance lodged and pointed out today's date in the corner. 'You're certainly not blind, so take a real close look at the amount and today's date.'

'Get that out of my bloody face! bloody hell what's wrong with you waving your business around like that,' snapped Peter as he waved the statement away with his hand without as much as throwing an eye at it. 'So you have money. Big bloody deal. So why do you want to get in with me or anyone else for that matter? If you can pull over a quarter of million on your own, why not stay on your own?'

The heated exchanges continued back and forth before Rob finally got him to sit down as he rambled on about having learned from his past mistakes, and the only reason he wanted to link back up was the fact he knew Peter was the only investor on the planet he could trust with this kind of cash.

'Please, one chance is all I'm asking,' he almost begged. 'Look at me, Peter. If at any stage you're not happy with me, you're free to drop me from your plans. I'll sign anything you want to terminate any contract at any stage. I can't be any fairer than that.'

Peter looked like he was now at last kind of listening. He took a mouthful of water and stood up and leaned against the wall as he finally took a close look at the bank statement. 'I'm going to be honest with you, Rob. There's things I hear that I don't like about you. One is, you're a little bit of a storyteller. What do I mean by that? Well, off the top of my head, here's a recent one: I was told you said we all knew each other for years; that you did investment deals with my father, lies like that. I mean, what kind of crap is that?'

'I never in my life said that! You told me yourself that your father passed some four years ago. I'd be just plain stupid to say stuff of that nature.'

'So what? It's all bullshit, yeah?'

'Yeah, of course it is,' muttered Rob, trying not to go red-faced. 'Lots of lies going around about me, spread by people who would do anything to stop us teaming up again.'

Peter sat back down and pondered while Rob sat back praying for some kind of breakthrough.

Finally Peter threw his eyes up. 'I must be out of my bloody mind. But before you dance around with excitement, listen up. There's going to be a couple of strict rules.'

'Sure, Peter, anything you –'

'Shut up and listen!' he hissed in a deadly serious tone.

'I'll do whatever you ask of me,' interrupted Rob. 'I'll even dance naked at your next party. Whatever you ask.'

'Right, whatever. Now look at me. Rule One: I am straight as an arrow in this cut-throat business and if you want to make it big you stay with me and don't dare try destroy my good reputation with greedy so-called investors like Wilson who almost ruined you in the end. You go behind my back with the next so-called big investor that dangles a red-hot deal before your greedy eyes – we're finished. Plus, I don't want to hear stories about you messing around with every fella's girlfriend. I hate that kind of crap. And don't want any unnecessary attention. You hear me now?'

'On my future kids' lives I'll never as much as look at another investor outside of you. Plus, I'm dating one girl, Peter. No, I'm not being funny. Jill Watson. And we're planning to stay together long-term. My days of messing around are well behind me. Come on. We all did a bit of that. My god, it's not my fault women adore me!' he jeered.

'Yeah, right. So what happened to what's-her-name, the one with the disabled hand?'

'She wasn't anything serious. Everyone knows that I was only helping her get over issues. We still see each other, but Jill was always going to be the one.'

'Well, you couldn't have picked a nicer-looking bird.' He paused and went to say something further, but he realised he was running late. 'Right. Sure, look. I'll be around in the morning at some stage with all the papers.'

But Rob dived in with a question of his own. 'I just can't thank you enough, but can I ask how you can be so sure that this big deal is as safe as you're saying? I mean, I'm sure the four or five other investors have asked you for a few details up front, like what kind of stocks and bonds are we actually getting involved with here. Is there any element of risk here with our money or not?' He surprised himself at how confident and tuned-in he sounded.

Peter smiled and took the last swig from his bottle of water. 'I thought you knew a bit more about me from past dealings.' He paused and thought, then laughed. 'But of course, they were just small short pants deals that we were involved in. This is big pants, suit and tie, the big expensive gold cufflinks. We're talking big league now. Best way to answer your question is to put it in the simplest of terms: I've got what they call an inside track on certain stocks and bonds. But, that's just the smaller side to this investment.

'The big central deal is this: some years back I got detailed information about a certain person who developed a treatment for a certain illness. I'm sworn not to disclose what the actual drug is, not yet anyway, but what I can tell you is, we're hoping to buy it from him if it passes a final testing. We've already had a string of advanced experiments with the drug and have approached a certain pharmaceutical company some time ago with the hope of selling it to them. Believe me, they don't want information about a remedy like this to ever see the light of day as it would lose them millions every year on two of their own products. Sounds so easy when you say it in a quick sentence like that,' he sniggered. 'But anyway, I'll run all the details by you when the meetings start next week.' He paused and let his guard down slightly. 'You have a great head on your shoulders, and that's why I picked you out from everyone else three years ago. You have talent and a certain drive for this line of work. Anyway, welcome back aboard!'

He smiled as he shook Rob's hand firmly, then turned and let himself out.

Rob thanked him for that as he closed the door and gathered his thoughts and waited a moment until Peter's car pulled away. Then he paused for a good twenty seconds as he let it sink in. Then, rather than dancing with joy, there was a dark coldness about his reaction as he clenched both fists up to his face. This was followed by an eerie, grim sense of calm as if he had just murdered a person to progress to this point in his life. He slowly pulled a bottle of red wine from the press along with a clean glass. *La Romanée-Conti 1940. Mmm . . . sweet . . .*

He heard his phone beep with a text.

Hope everything is going okay with Peter. Dad is gone to bed so it's just chips for me and you. Maybe a fresh cod. What you think? Miss you lots. Amy xxxxx

He just let out the slightest sigh, but his face revealed a sense of pure annoyance that his victory celebrations had been slightly interrupted by this unwanted reality. He paused for a moment, then hesitantly rang her.

'Ah, Rob! I was panicking like crazy about ringing you in case you were bang smack in the middle of the meeting and I interrupted you both.'

'Gosh, Amy!' came the voice so warm. 'You're fine. They're in the sitting room. The other investors were called in. I'm so, so sorry but looks like I won't be done here for hours. We're going over all the fine print. Peter wants to complete the deal here tonight. Bit scary as there are risks I wasn't aware of until minutes ago. But sure, life's a risk,' he joked, and then with an emotionless shady look in his eyes he blew the dust from inside the glass.

'So, will you be able to come back here tonight?' I sighed trying to hide my sense of disappointment.

'Don't think so, Hon. I'm so sorry, Amy. I was so looking forward to the feet up and those lovely chips. But look, I'll be around in the morning so we can all go to the graveyard to see Mammy.'

Mammy? I paused. 'To see Mammy? You never say the word *Mammy*. that's nice.'

Rob paused then laughed before ending the call with another deep apology. 'We have all day tomorrow,' he said, sounding every bit concerned. 'We'll go for that bite to eat in Seasons Café in Skerries. Okay?'

'Okay. Love you, Rob. See you in the morning.' I sat back trying to convince myself it hadn't upset me.

I then turned my attention to watching a movie in an effort to distract myself. After half an hour I started to find it hard to focus on the storyline and threw a sleepy eye across at the open fire flames flickering brighter now with the room lights off.

Don't turn around and don't look up. Everything is okay. 'This isn't real!' I screamed out in terror.

Suddenly a nest of spiders broke loose from the corner of the room and came creeping down the wall and onto my bed. I screamed my lungs out as hundreds if not thousands of them with real human faces crept under my sheets. 'Please! Nooo! Pleeease!'

'Amy! Amy!'

I woke up and flung myself off the sofa, kicking and screaming. 'Ahh! Get them away from me, Mammy!' I cried in my semi-conscious state.

'It's just one of your dreams, Amy!' shouted Dad. 'You're safe. Just a dream.' His firm words were sufficient to wake me somewhat. He held me for a moment as all my senses slowly came back to normal. 'You're okay. You're awake now. It's just one of your spider nightmares.' He paused before looking around the room. 'Where's Rob?'

*

'Ha, ha, ha!' laughed Rob down the phone as the wine kicked in. 'I'm not joking with you one jiffy, Jill. I'm that close to being set up for flippin' life,' he slurred. 'Look. Come over and have a little drink with me. I'm celebrating here on my bloody own. I'm full!' he laughed.

'I'd love to, but sorry, Rob. I'm stuck here in the nursing

home with my granny. She's 94, remember? Molly Campbell. I told you. Some of her family are here. I think she may not last the Christmas,' she sadly whispered.

The very mention of elderly people, nursing homes, was sufficient to unnerve Rob from his happy, clappy buzz. He skulled a full glass of wine in one gulp and staggered back slightly, 'Please just come over. For me. Your granny is in safe hands.' He jerked and shivered.

Jill looked back in the door at her dying granny. But then she got the nod from her mother who was sitting across on the other chair.

'Go on,' she said with a smile. 'You look love-struck. Molly would want you to meet him. Go.'

'Ah, thank you so much, Ma,' she mouthed. 'Thank you.'

'Okay, Rob. I'm on my way.' Her voice full of excitement as Rob continued to compose himself.

'Brilliant! Good girl! I'll open a fresh bottle. Stay the night, sure why not? Then, as promised, we'll go into town for a meal tomorrow evening. Love you, Jill.'

He staggered back. *Oops, nearly fell over a feckin' chair there!* He pulled a fresh bottle of wine from the press and turned off the TV as he went about opening the bottle with the corkscrew. *This is going to be one hell of a night!*

*

I awoke for the second time around 5am, this time with a pain in my head that felt very like the headaches associated with the head injury from the car accident.

'Feck, not this again,' I sighed as I crept down the stairs. On the last step I paused and felt kind of faint, then struggled into the sitting room, just managing to hit the lights before awkwardly falling onto the sofa. My head spun around, and for a moment everything went funny in my eyes and I couldn't see correctly. Then a thought. A lost thought from the past raced back to memory. A guy's face that I tried but couldn't make out.

Carrying my school books and pointing at my face. 'I love your eyes, Amy.' Before I could grasp more, the thought was gone again. *Not this,* I thought. *It's been well over six months since I got one of these dizzy spells.* I went to try get up, but then thought I heard a snoring sound from the kitchen. *Hardly!*

I opened the door slowly and there he was – Dad sitting upright with a half glass of whiskey still in hand and the bottle standing nearly empty on the table.

I hit the lights and was about to fly off the handle, but then noticed he was holding his favourite framed picture of my mother. 'Dad,' I said in a low, caring tone. 'Come on, up you get.'

He opened his eyes, but not without a struggle, as he started to giggle. 'Woooooweeee! Okay, up I get.' he tried to stand but was unable.

I kept my own emotions in check but wanted to kill him for this. I went to the press as my own dizzy spell started to ease somewhat. Taking two tablets, I washed them down with a mouthful of water. 'Right, up to bed!' I stressed. 'Up, up, up!' I pushed as he finally got to his feet, swaying backwards and forwards while still managing to hold a firm grip of Tina's photo.

I was in two minds about just leaving him on the sofa. I got him to the end of the stairs, but thought as he was now awake, he might polish off the rest of the bottle. Finally we made it to the landing.

He turned and faced me in his drunken state. 'See this photo, this was taken the day I met my Tina. Did I tell you that?' he slurred before stumbling. 'Oops-a-daisy, steady, horse, steady!' he laughed.

'You did, Dad. Now come on back to bed. You're going to have a hangover from bloody hell in the morning.'

I staggered a bit myself as my own head was still a bit light.

'Hey!' he said, now trying to look a bit more in control. 'I'm going to make sure I live to walk my beautiful daughter up that aisle and then it's down into the big hole, into the ground to rest forever with my Tina.'

'Oh, will you ever stop! That's not even one bit funny. You'll be around to mind my and Rob's babies,' I tried to joke. 'Now enough of the morbid talk.' I opened his room door and directed him in.

He looked down at the photo and then in a drunken motion kissed it, his eyes tear-filled. He turned without a word and closed the door almost in my face.

'Night, Dad,' I whispered.

'Night, Amy.'

*

Rob sat with his back to the headboard, staring intently across the room at the reflection of light from the bedroom lamp as it mirrored a odd shape on the wall.

Jill woke up and snuggled into him. 'Are you still awake?' she yawned before checking the time. 'God, it's 6.15am. Did you not go to sleep yet?' She lit up a cigarette.

'Do you believe in visions?' he finally said in an eerie tone as he took one of Jill's fags and lit it before gulping the remains of his red wine from a glass.

'What do you mean?' She turned to look him in the eye, but he wouldn't take his eyes off the wall, not even to blink.

'Em, are you in a trance from the wine?' she joked.

'Nah, this isn't a joke, Jill. I've been staring at that spot on the wall for a good hour now and it's like I saw my whole future being played out as if it was a movie on the big screen.' He took a long, pleasurable drag from his fag and continued. 'Oh, Jill, if you, if anyone just knew how close I was, so close to losing everything and ending up on the dole, maybe even being a homeless, down-and-out drunk. Now everything has dramatically changed in the blink of an eye. I feel something has opened up my inner eyes to perceive what an unbelievable and happy successful future awaits not just me, but us as a couple.'

Jill interrupted him with a warm embrace. 'Ah, you're so romantic and so cute. Me as well in the plan? I like that idea a lot!'

'You do?' he said, still staring at the wall but now smiling from ear to ear. 'Sea, sand, holidays, eating in the very best restaurants in the world, buying a bigger house, feet up, enjoying life to the max. No financial worries. That's what I keep visualising. Do you think I'm plastered on this wine or what?' he then cackled aloud.

'No, but talking about your vision, I do believe in things like that.'

'You do?' he said, sounding a tad surprised.

'Well, I hear this all the time from Granny Molly Campbell, who I was visiting tonight when you rang me,' smiled Jill as she put her fag out. 'In fact, even tonight she used those precise words *in the blink of an eye*. How odd is that? She always uses that phrase. 'In the blink of an eye the world will suddenly end!' she'd often scream out, frightening the life out of all the nurses. Oh, my god. She even goes into strange trances like you did tonight, for ages on end and then starts rambling on and on about people she says are going to have awful bad look or even die soon. My ma and all the family are well use to it. They even joke about it, calling her the Prophet of Portmarnock. Her funny ways and sayings go back 50 years or more. Some people laugh and make fun of her, saying she's wacky and delusional. But oddly enough, she's been right about a few things she said.'

'Your old Granny Molly? Right, right. Well I'm definitely not in any way like her,' he gulped with a notable change in his facial expression. 'Don't kill my moment,' he sighed as he turned off the light and punched the pillow and turned away as Jill went about apologising.

'Gosh, I wasn't meaning you were funny in the head or anything like that, Rob. Sorry!'

'I know, I know. This just means a great deal to me.' He finally said after a prolonged silence.

Moments later in the dark he turned back around and held her close and whispered, 'We're a couple now, Jill. We have the most fantastic future ahead of us. I just have to sort out an issue or two, and then we can be the couple you want us to be, and more.' He paused and held her even closer.

Jill filled up with tears and reached in and took hold of his hand and hugged him deeper. 'I love you, Rob. Since first we met.'

*

Amy woke up from a bad dream and slowly reached over and checked the time. 10:20am. *Crap.* She could hear her dad downstairs. *Hmm. He's making breakfast to say sorry for his drunken episode in the early hours.*

She grabbed her phone and then jumped when she saw a text from Rob. *Be a little later than I thought Amy. Peter here to transfer the money from my account to his. All looks good I HOPE. Hahaha. Missed you so much last night. See you at 11.30.*

Everything went according to plan when Rob finally arrived, looking a bit tired. Amy grabbed him for a long kiss in the hallway. 'Easy, easy!' he laughed.

They all headed to the cemetery for what was another very emotional moment at her ma's graveside. She and Des took a few moments together alone at the grave, as suggested by Rob. The rest of the gang, Tom and Sue, seemed edgy enough as they walked back to the cars with Rob.

As they made their way to Seasons, Amy kept checking in the mirror trying to figure out was she missing something. 'So where did Claire and Colm have to go at the last minute?' she asked again, this time sensing something was amiss.

'Oh, em, Colm wasn't feeling well so Claire headed over to his place,' said Tom. 'They said they'd ring you later.'

Sue did her best to add a similar statement, which sounded a bit more convincing.

'Ah, you know Colm. He hates the smell of graveyards,' joked Tom who seemed to undo Sue's well-spoken lies.

'Is everything okay?' Amy asked as she scanned them both again in the mirror.

'Yes, everything's okay,' offered Sue. 'Let's enjoy the bit of lunch. I'm starving!'

Rob watched and took in everything that was being said with a deep suspicious glare in his eyes. 'Won't be long to the big wedding,' he said as he waited for a reaction from the pair in the back.

'Well, the few months will fly in,' Amy said as Rob turned to eyeball Tom who dropped his eyes downward before giving Sue a giveaway side stare that Rob picked up on straight away.

'We have Christmas to look forward to as well,' added Sue with a nervous but cheerful laugh. 'Can't wait,' she stressed as they pulled up and parked the car across the street from Seasons Café.

Everything seemed okay until Amy got home and rang Claire, but no answer.

To further the tensions of the day, Rob sat her down and explained he had to meet up with Peter again in preparation for the first official meeting with the other investors.

'I thought you met them last night!' Amy asked with a confused eye.

'No, no that was just two of them last night,' Rob scrambled. 'This could take all afternoon and into the evening. But look at me, I'll stay over tomorrow evening,' he assured her. 'I do have a job now,' he warmed. 'We need cash for our future.'

'I know. I'm just being very selfish and want you all to myself. Don't I?'

*

Once in the car Rob punched the dashboard. *Something's up. I can feel it. That Tom lad knows something. He couldn't make eye contact with me all day . . .* He sat for ages, thinking. *Ah, who the hell cares! I have the money and the investment up and running. Nothing nobody can do to stop me now. But Robert, you should have definitely put more thought and preparations into how the hell to get rid of her. Think, Rob. Think . . . Right. Tell her I'm seeing the counsellor and I'm on strong anti-depressants tablets and my doctor advised me to take time out for myself. Then over a few weeks I'll just let the relationship drift. Then say my feelings have changed towards her as a result of this dark depression that I now have!*

After Peter came and left, things seemed somewhat muddled in Rob's head.

'Change of plan,' Peter had told him as he finalised the deal. 'Can't meet the other investors as they now want to remain anonymous.'

What's that all about? Rob wondered as he lit a fag. *Bloody hell. I hope this isn't something dodgy. I've just handed over 175 bleedin' grand of my future comfort to him.*

A text came from Amy. *Dad's home. Drunk again. He's asking for you. Can you ring me later? I miss you a lot. xxxx*

Ah, for feck's sake! He sat down, flung the phone on the table, and buried his face in both hands.

*

Back in Balbriggan, Colm dropped Claire home to Fancourt Heights after short but heated meeting with Tom and Sue.

'Did you really have to open your big trap about Rob trying to kiss Sue?' Claire nervously snapped as they pulled into her driveway. 'He didn't believe a word you said. I told you that in confidence.'

'*Trying to kiss*! Before, you said they *actually* kissed. No one is listening to me, stone bloody-deaf Claire. 'No one has their ears and eyes open wide enough to see this Rob lad for what he is.'

There were heated exchanges for a good twenty minutes before finally.

'Look, relax. I'll talk to Amy in the morning,' said Claire as her fear intensified. 'I promise. Okay?'

He glared at her as she jumped out of the car. 'You do it or I will,' was his final word on it as he reversed out of her driveway and sped away, wheels screeching.

Next morning at 10am, Amy's phone rang. It was Claire. 'Listen, Amy. Em . . . Is Rob there? . . . That's great . . . Look, I need to talk with you, this is really hard for me, but I need to tell you something.'

Chapter 9

The Descent

As Claire drove around to Amy's she was suddenly plagued with doubts as she nervously pondered the details of what she had to say. *Stay focused and it will run smoothly,* she told herself as she drove into Hampton Cove Drive in a sweat.

But matters were made worse when Sue rang, with Tom standing in support, listening and giving the odd shout down the phone.

'Now, listen, Sue, I –'

'No, *you* listen up, Claire!' snapped Tom as he finally boiled over and took the phone. 'My Sue never kissed Rob as you're both trying to suggest. It was nothing more than a birthday peck on the cheek. Colm is blowing this up all out of proportion with yet another personal jealousy rant!'

Claire was speechless but stayed composed.

'You're going to hurt Amy no end,' continued Tom. 'Rob has done nothing but love, support and take our Amy out of a very dark, depressing hole, and you pair of psychos are about to send her back there and destroy a perf–'

Claire hung up and threw the phone on the passenger's seat as she pulled up outside Amy's house.

*

'Listen, that's great news, Rob,' Amy smiled as she flicked her hair back. 'I'm over the moon to hear that things are moving along nicely with the deals. Now will you please hurry up and get back to me? I'm going through major withdrawals from not seeing you,' she joked before turning towards the window and spotting Claire getting out of her car.

'See you later. Love you,' said Rob in his persuasive voice. He turned around only to find Jill standing at the living room door with her makeup and hair half done.

'Love you?' 'See you feckin' later'?' she fumed as she threw the hairbrush across the room in his direction. 'I thought she was history!'

'Hey, hold up! You can't leave looking like that,' he tried to joke as she grabbed her bag and headed for the door.

'Get your hands off me now! Don't touch me!' she snapped as he grabbed her arm to try and pull her back in the door.

'We made passionate love last night and you told me we were now officially dating. And you went on and on about plans for our future, holiday in January in Lanzarote and all that, while all along you're still seeing that little bitch! You're playing mind games!' she shouted through tear-filled eyes. 'Now let go of my arm. You're hurting me!'

'Will you listen to me for one second,' he stressed in a charming tone as he tried to cool the situation down. 'Okay, you want the truth?' he said as Jill stumbled back in the door. 'Her father keeps ringing me saying shit like she's talking about killing herself over me and to please ring her. So okay, I take her calls and I'm nice down the phone to her in the warmest manner. But look at me, Jill. She means absolutely nothing to me. I got involved with her as a friend to try help her get over some issues. It was just out of pity as she was a mess. I was making good inroads helping her, but then foolishly with drink on me I got more involved and one thing led to another and I slept with her.'

'Aah, for feck's sake! What did you ever see in her? From the pictures on your phone, she's nothing to look at and . . .'

'Look, I had a few drinks on me at the time. After a few dates I came to my senses and wanted to break it off. It was at that point that she flipped the lid and started calling me up! Saying she'd kill herself if I left her.' Rob sat and dropped his head down with a look of dejection. 'I started out with the right motive, as I'm sure everyone knows, to help the girl. But there's more,' he sighed.

'What do you mean 'more'?'

'It's her father. Well, he's dying. Liver cancer. Yeah, horrible. Three years to the day after their poor mother died in that horrible car crash,' he said with a further look of sorrow as Jill put her bag down, her facial expression now changing dramatically. 'She doesn't even know he's dying. And if I don't at least be there for them, what does that make me?'

There was a pause as Jill let out a painful sigh. 'My god, I'm so sorry to hear about her dad. That's really horrible news for all involved. The poor family. But look at me, Rob,' she motioned as she bent down. 'Are you not giving her tons of false hope by being around her and saying nice things, like on the phone just now? Gosh, I feel so heartless now.'

'Come here, hon,' ushered Rob as he stood up with more than a hint of vulnerability in his tone. He took her in his arms. 'I'll find some way to break the news to her that I'm not just involved with someone else, but that I'm *in love* with someone else. Just give me a week or two max and then I'll break this news to her. And if you want to support me, then I'd ask you to pray or light a candle that she takes it the right way and we can move on with our relationship.'

*

Claire took a deep breath as she checked her phone. A text from Colm read: *Ring me when you leave Amy's. You're doing the right thing for her and our own relationship. Love you forever xxx*

She got out of the car nervously and turned to hit the lock switch. But just as she was gathering her thoughts and getting her planned speech all set in her mind the front door opened.

'Hey, come in! I've just put the kettle on,' I beamed as I threw both arms around a rather tense-looking Claire. So what's up, you sounded really freaked on th. . .'

'Look, something is actual wrong!' she cut in as she wasted no time about belting it out. Her bottom lip trembling as she unsteadily walked past me and into the sitting room. 'There's no one else home, is there?' She turned around, noticeably shaking from head to toe.

'My god, what the hell, Claire?' I asked. 'You're shivering. Sit down. For feck's sake, don't tell me it's another big row with Colm?'

'Oh, Amy, this is just killing me to say, but believe me, I'm only saying it because I care for you and your future, and don't want to see you hurt. It's nothing to do with me and Colm.'

There was an endless tense pause before she continued.

'It's Rob, Amy. Your Rob. He's been flirting and making sexual advances to both Sue and me.'

The words hung in the air as I looked intently into her face, unable to clearly take in her statement. I was ready to laugh it off, but instinctively knew by her face that she was deadly serious.

'Are you gone completely insane?' I just about managed as a strange horrible fear hit at the pit of my stomach.

Claire sat down, her eyes looking everywhere bar in my direction.

'Feck, Claire. Out with it. Rob did what? You're scaring me half to death here!'

Claire kind of jumped back up, now looking petrified. 'It's all true, Amy. I'm so, so sorry to be the one, but everyone knows about it, bar you. He's been doing it for months. While you were in the toilets in Raff's and at the Home Nightclub.' She filled up. 'Colm said we have to say this to you before it's . . .'

'Did what? What exactly are you all saying he did?' I whimpered as my head went into a dark frightening spin.

'As I said, he's been making moves on me and Sue. Flirting around. We hid it for ages but then Colm copped it all on and well, I had to say it . . .'

'Stop looking at the bloody floor, Claire, and look at me!' I cried. 'You have some bloody neck! What are you all playing at here? Why are you saying this shit? Why? Rob's well known to be a very affectionate man who hugs and gives friendship kisses to every one of his friends.' I reached over and took a firm hold of Claire's arm. 'You know how happy me and Rob are.

We're getting married and planning a family. How dare you all insinuate this kind of crap?'

'Let me go! You're hurting my arm!' said Claire as she tried to get out of my grip. 'It's all true. He made real sexual passes at me, and kissed Sue. It wasn't just friendship stuff. We're doing this out of love for *you*, Amy!' she managed as I let her go.

I stood there for a few moments trying to take in what was happening. 'Look at me, Claire,' I cried then gestured to her to look at me. 'You're lying!'

Claire panicked and moved towards the door. 'Look, I'm so sorry. I wish it wasn't true, but Colm believes Rob's been tricking everyone, tricking you and –'

I lost it completely as Claire went to open the door to leave. 'Where the hell are you going?' I shouted, jumping in between her and the door. I put my hand up to my forehead as the pressure in my skull was suddenly making it hard to remain focused. 'Okay, let's all calm down,' I somehow managed. 'Sit, sit.' We both sat. 'Now let me get this straight in my own mind,' I stressed, trying my very best to remain unruffled. 'Rob wouldn't dream of throwing an eye at anyone, let alone hurt me by doing it to my friends.' I struggled to find my stability then nervously laughed. 'I can't believe my best friend is sitting here in my house telling me this shit, and where the hell is Sue?' I snapped, pulling my phone out.

'Don't ring her!'

'Don't dare tell me what I can or can't do!' I spat out as my dizziness from the early hours returned.

'Sue here. Sorry I can't take your call. Leave a message.'

I threw the phone on the sofa and made a lightning yet unsteady move towards the kitchen to grab my medication.

Claire sat frozen as her mind began to sense an uncertainty about how this was handled. Her own phone suddenly rang, which helped her regain her own focus. It was Colm.

'Where are you? Did you tell her? Is that fool there?' His voice sounded anything but caring.

'It's going so wrong, Colm,' she gasped, as she tried her

best to keep her voice to a whisper. 'You'd be better off saying something. I'm making a bloody mess of it all.'

I charged back into the room and grabbed the phone off her as everything started to become one long dark blur. I laid into Colm for daring to come up with this kind of bullshit. 'You never liked Rob from the start!' I belted down the phone. 'Admit that much!'

But he remained calm throughout and kept trying to point out things like 'It's because we love you, Amy. He's definitely been playing games with Claire's head and mine for a long time. He tried it on with Sue a number of times, and that's not all. He once –'

'Shut your lying mouth, Colm!' I cried down the phone, trying my best to hold on to my sanity.

'Get out, get the hell out now!' I turned and said to Claire with tears streaming down my face. In a rush of blood I then quickly opened the door and fired Claire's phone into the garden.

She tried to plead with me to calm down.

'Get the hell out of my house now!'

Colm drove up the road, pulled up and jumped out of the car. With both arms open wide he tried to calm everything down.

But all I saw was this pitiful false surrendering look in his eyes and face which was sufficient to make me snap into a full-blown fit of the foulest language imaginable. Words I'd never used before. 'You're all off your heads! Now get away from me and Rob's life!' My face twisted and turned with the agonising stress of the ordeal.

A couple of the neighbours came out, looking very concerned. 'Is everything okay, Amy?' asked Mr Freeman from across the road, just as I slammed the front door closed.

I could hear Claire in a frightened voice asking Colm to do something as he ushered her into his car. I almost slid down to my knees as I made my way onto the sofa, crying my heart out as unwanted feelings of doubt now invaded my delicate mind.

Someone was knocking at the door. 'Are you okay in there?' It was Mr Freeman. 'Where's your father, Amy?'

*

Rob was pacing up and down his sitting room after getting off the phone to Peter.

He's definitely changed. Something's wrong. First it was the news that the other investors don't want to be named, now he's saying he's going straightaway, today, to the bloody USA for a week or ten days. Something to do with buying or finalising the rights to this new drug. 'There's no need to be ringing me every hour,' he keeps saying. 'I've a lot of work to do now.' Then the next bombshell – that all future investment meetings that were planned are now off until further notice! My god, maybe I shouldn't have signed all those papers without going over all the small print with a good solicitor. I rushed it! I panicked, to close the deal, he thought as his paranoia kicked in no end.

Feck's sake, what do I really know about Peter Bradley? Where is he originally from? He's never brought a family member to any drink-ups. All I know is I met him a few years ago, never said much about his past, then he got me into a few Mickey Mouse investment deals and that's it. Bloody hell, maybe there are no other investors! Or maybe there is and he's ripped them off as well! And now he's away, laughing his head off to the USA with a sack load of cash!

He sat and thought it through.

Nah, feck all this negative thinking. He never knew I had this kind of cash coming. He has a brilliant reputation. Everything is going to be just fine.

He paused, thinking things repeatedly in his mind till he finally felt settled within himself again.

Right. Don't let them feckin' evil gremlins mess with your mind again. You have 85 grand in the bank to play with. Time to relax, ring a few mates and go for a drink and get back into the habit of living.

*

Amy went into a dark uncontrollable panic. First, she rang her dad. But the call rang through to his answering machine.

'Answer it!' said Steve as he sat with Des in the small Snug Pub in Skerries.

'Nah, she'll go ballistic if she hears I'm drinking yet again. Bloody hell, I was supposed to go back to work, and here I am getting another cure! I'm drinking like a bloody fish, Steve. I just can't face this.' He sighed as the barman who overheard their conversation kindly pulled out two fresh glasses.

'This is on the house,' he smiled as he put two pints on the counter.

Steve gave him a nod to thank him, but Des never even blinked an eyelid as he continued. 'Amy is so happy. She's beaming with happiness, and if I'm being upfront, all I want is to make it to walk her up the aisle into the safe hands of Rob on their wedding day. I'd die a happy man if I make that day.' He dropped his head as a tear came to his eye.

'Hey, will you stop that right now,' snapped Steve. 'Pull yourself together, man.' He lifted Des's chin up and looked him in the eye. 'You're going to man up and stop feeling sorry for yourself and preserve your energy for winning this battle that's confronting you. I'm with you. We're all going to be with you, all the way. You hear me now?'

*

Amy, sobbing, rang Claire back in a desperate attempt to ease her growing fear. No answer. She left a message that was kind of all over the place. 'Answer your bloody phone. I swear to God I will never talk to any of you for coming around and making up a shit story like that. Now ring me!' She slurred as the tablets she had taken took full effect, leaving her more unstable.

Suddenly a sickening insecure sensation took over. *Okay! Okay!* She grabbed the phone. *Ring Rob.*

Nothing was clear in her head; all she wanted in the world was for Rob to now hold her and reassure that this was all a nasty, crazy, mixed-up lie. Her hand was shaking uncontrollably as she tried to bring herself back under some control and dial his number. *Please, God, help me.*

Rob was going through a few bills he needed to clear when the call came in.

Amy was fighting back the tears as the words stumbled out. 'Hi, Rob,' she gasped. 'Look, something awful was just said to me. It's regarding Sue and Claire.' There was a pause as she tried to catch her breath.

Rob remained silent.

'Look, this is going to sound so off the wall, Rob, but hear me out,' she mumbled. 'But did you in any way make a move on them, sexually? It's just Claire and Colm came around with this mad story and . . .'

'Hold it right there,' said Rob in a low, controlled tone. 'Back up, Amy. You're asking me did I make some kind of sexual pass on the girls.'

'Look, I'm in a state here. I got an awful shock and took tablets and . . .'

There was a lengthy, dark pause.

'You've got to be kidding me with this phone call. What the hell are you talking about?' he snapped. 'You're actually accusing me of messing around behind your back with Claire and Sue?'

'My god, I trust you with my very life,' she rushed. 'Look, this can all be sorted. All I want is you to come here now and reassure me and let's face Claire, face to face, the lot of –'

The line went dead as Rob hung up.

As the panic increased tenfold, Amy frantically went to ring him back but suddenly she glanced down at her hand, disfigured in the car crash, and every ounce of confidence that she seemed to rebuild up since meeting Rob weirdly drained away in a horrible and disturbing moment. She tried to gather her thoughts and refocus on what was unfolding.

She got his answering machine. 'Please, Rob. I wasn't accusing you. Ring me back. Please.' She begged as she saw an incoming call from *Dad*.

'Is everything okay, Amy?' he slurred. 'Mark Freeman just rang saying you were out on the path shouting abuse at one of your friends.'

'Dad, can you please get home, fast, now!' she whimpered, bursting into floods.

The room went into a spin as she seemed to lose any air to her lungs. She could hardly hear a word her dad was trying to say, as she took deep breaths. All she could hear was a faint voice. 'Stay there!' before the phone went dead.

Instinct took over as she rang Rob a number of times.

Rob sat back after picking up the bowl of freshly-washed grapes. Speechless. He popped one into his mouth as he tried to understand how the hell this could happen. He pointed at his phone that was ringing, then stopping, then ringing again.

He looked up to heaven with a dark smirk. *This is so messed up. I don't care what people say. There has to be a god up there. Has to be! I knew by Tom and Sue something was amiss yesterday in the bloody car. That was it. Right I can now play it carefully to my advantage, play the poor victim. Okay, calm down and think, then take her call and play it out sensibly.*

He finally answered his phone to a petrified Amy who, with a huge sense of relief was straight in, apologising no end.

'Oh, my god, Rob. I'm so sorry for the way I worded it earlier. I'm in shock at what Claire said but I'd never ever think you would –'

'Please Amy, don't,' Rob cut in, his voice sounding shaky but firm and direct. 'Please, I'm sitting here, devastated. I cannot believe after all I did for you, all the support and love, all the hours of wiping your tears away. Being there in your darkest hours. And never once did I ever try to play with your heart or try to hurt you in any way like other guys are in the habit of doing. I stood by you and loved you no end. And never, I mean never, ever did I as much as look at another woman.'

She tried to jump in as a horrible sick sense of guilt set in. 'But Rob, I –'

'No, listen. It's time for you to listen to me for a change. You accused me of trying to get off with not one but two of your best friends behind your back? Good god, I feel sick thinking about it.'

He paused and let that sink in before letting out a deep, painful sigh.

'The trust, Amy. The most important part of our, of any relationship is trust. Well, it's gone now, isn't it? How could you do this? To us, Amy?'

He sounded devastated, which left Amy feeling totally lost for words and at her wits' end.

She just managed a huge, deep, nervous breath and tried to think what to say. 'I can't imagine what you're feeling,' she just about managed, 'but please, Rob, come over to my place. We can sit down and work this out side by side. I'll get Claire and the rest to come over and get to the bott–'

'Will you listen to yourself?' Rob interrupted in a now angry, hurt tone that made her jump. 'Sort out what? I didn't do anything bloody wrong, Amy! My god, you're acting crazy. I'm in bits here over these allegations that you and your jealous so-called friends have made. I can't take this on right now. I'm already seeing a psychotherapist. Yes, that's right. A counsellor, Amy.'

'What do you mean you're seeing a counsellor?' Amy was shaking all over as she tried to calm the situation down.

'Ask your father. I told him about this the other day.'

The line went dead again, Amy dropped onto the sofa in shock and despair.

'Rob, Rob!' she cried while trying to redial in floods.

Rob sat down and popped another grape into his mouth. *This is just brilliant, just brilliant.* He smiled as he spat the pip from the grape out onto the table. *With a bit of luck she may crack up again.* He exhaled before popping another grape into his mouth.

I couldn't even begin to explain the state I was in or how bad the pain inside felt. The horrible realisation that I had now gone and hurt him . . . the guy who had loved me and done everything for me.

I moved anxiously into the hall towards the front door to try and open it, so I could get proper air into my lungs and get my breathing back under some control. Suddenly I stopped and turned my head slightly, catching a frightening reflection of my face in the hall mirror. *Oh my god,* I thought. The scar on my face now lay fully visible, as almost all my makeup had run down my face from the crying. My mouth looked twisted from the side-effects of the medication, my eyes reflecting back a look of pure terror.

The phone rang. I snapped back and answered it without looking at who it was. 'Rob!' I gasped in a helpless plea.

'Hi, it's me, Colm. Look, you're trying to ring Claire about this again. I know you don't think it right now, but she's as upset as you are about all this.' His voice without a hint of warmth continued about how Rob tried to make him jealous from day one. 'Me and Claire were so close to breaking up the other day over all this, but . . .'

As he rambled on and on his voice died away till I couldn't hear a single word he was saying. A flash in my head brought me back to just before I had met Rob. All the dreaded fear and the sense of hopelessness now began to creep up inside of me all over again just like one of my horrible spider dreams. Then I heard the sound of a clock ticking inside my head, followed by an eerie yet soft voice saying the words, *'Reach back in time, Amy!' Oh, Jesus. Please, not this,* I thought. I was back in that dark place as if it was yesterday, nothing to hold onto, nothing bright or colourful at all, just a greyness that slowly turns to a dark, black dense feeling that becomes responsible for the daily burning away of all my bright warm smiles and thoughts for any future hope . . .

A taxi pulled up outside. I knew instinctively it was my dad. I threw the phone onto the bottom step of the stairs with Colm still rambling on and on in his defence.

Steve was paying the driver when I opened the front door to meet Dad walking unsteadily up the driveway. His eyes met mine and once he was able to take in the enormity of the situation, he picked up pace and hobbled the last few steps and grabbed a hold of me in his arms.

'Hold me, Dad! Please, just hold me!' I grabbed on to him in a fearful attempt to try to ease the awful agony. 'I think I'm losing it again, losing my mind! I heard that voice and clock ticking again in my head!' I cried in a childlike tone.

'Jesus, Mary, and Joseph! What the hell happened to you?' he gasped as Steve raced up the pathway to offer some assistance.

'Just hold me for a sec, I think I'm going mad, Dad. I've hurt Rob! Hurt him so badly!' I cried as my eyes opened for a moment, catching a blurred, anxious glance from the taxi driver as he rolled up the window and turned his head the other way and sped away.

Dad turned my face to his and gazed into my eyes, trying his best to reassure me that everything was okay. 'Now calm down, Amy,' he said in his firm but soft voice. 'Calm down and come back into the house and tell me what actually happened here.'

Steve aided me by taking the other arm and slowly turning me around as we all went back inside. Dad closed the door but not before waving across the road to Mark Freeman who was nodding his head from his sitting room window.

Steve sat me down on the sofa and rushed off to get me a glass of water as Dad sat trying to cover over the fact that he had drink on him. He took a deep breath and looked me over to see was I even capable of talking.

'Okay, Amy, in your own words. Take all the time you need. What in God's name is going on?'

Steve arrived back with the water as I tried to compose myself and answer him.

With fresh tears welling up I told him everything from the start. 'And after Claire, I think that's when I took the two tablets, I'm not certain. Then I rang you, but no answer. Then finally I rang Rob and asked in a gentle way did he actually do it, make sexual advances towards the girls.'

I couldn't look at Dad as I knew by his face he was now fit to kill somebody.

He stood up as I explained how upset Rob sounded on the phone.

'Then he said he's seeing a counsellor, that he told you about this, something like that. I can't remember everything. Dad. Will you please ring him? Get him to come over!' I whimpered as desperation clawed mercilessly at my insides.

Des stood up as Steve tried to look anywhere bar in my direction. 'What in the name of God above were you doing listening to them pair of dopes?' Des hissed. 'Everyone down in the Milestone knows that the Colm lad is the thickest eejit in Balbriggan! Everyone up in Pinewood Green will tell you he thinks every fella that even looks across the road at his girl, every person that walks into a pub, fancies his Claire. Oh, my god, Amy. Look at me now and tell me you didn't then go and accuse Rob of anything. What exact words did you use?'

'I just told you I kind of did, in a way. It was Tom and Sue as well. Look, will you just ring him. You're good at talking to him,' I cried as Steve went off and put the kettle on.

'I'm very bloody surprised at Tom,' said Des. 'My god, Rob is the most faithful and kindest man any girl could ever meet. And you above everyone should be most conscious of this. He'd never hurt a hair on your head.'

He put both hands over his face and stood trying to think what best to do. Then he paused and looked directly at me as Steve came back into the room. 'Everyone knows Rob did everything in the world to get you where you are, and as a result, he . . .' He paused and was hesitant to continue but he did. '. . . he's had to get professional help for himself. I hate to say it, Amy, and I'm trying everything to be sensitive here to you. I love you to bits. You know that. But all your own issues dragged that man down into a very bad place within himself. He's been putting on a brave face of late. He's very sensitive behind it all. He's hid that part very well from you, me, everyone. Then in the end he poured it all out to me a few days ago. What a bleedin' mess! I swear I'll do time over this. If I see Colm or any of them in the street, I'll break all their legs! I swear I will!'

He turned and nodded to Steve to hurry up with the tea as he tried to lower his voice.

'Why didn't he tell me all this then?' I cried, burying my face in both hands. 'That just makes it way worse. We were so open about everything. How was I to know?'

Des picked his phone out of his jacket and tried to ring Rob, but it rang out.

'Rob, it's Des here. Very sorry about what's after happening. Ring me back as soon as you can. I'd appreciate it a lot.'

'Thanks, Dad. Thanks,' I sniffled.

He hung up and picked up a cup of tea Steve had just placed on the coffee table. 'Two sugars, yeah?' he smiled, trying his best to lighten the tense mood.

'Look, there has to be a way to sort –' Steve went to say before Dad in his gentlest voice so far remarked that my eyeliner and make-up were all over my face and blouse.

'Maybe a quick wash would be the best step while I try to ring Rob again?'

With a raw sense of embarrassment, I headed up the stairs and tried to hold everything together best I could. Okay, *we've never had words, not even one row, ever since we met, so this will be sorted when everything calms down a bit,* I thought before trying to put some fresh make-up and eyeliner on.

I heard the front door opening and Sue's voice. I flushed the toilet and raced down the stairs.

I was about to let rip but Tom who walked in after Sue put his hand up. 'We're on your side, Amy. We begged both of them not to do this,' he stressed in a firm tone. 'Before you say a word, we have something very important to say.'

Des, still looking fit to kill someone, stood in the centre of the room, eyeing them both up and down. 'We're here mopping up a big mess you lot started!' he barked as he waved his phone in the air. Five times I've tried to get in touch with poor Rob and . . .'

'Please, Des, I can't imagine how hurt everyone is over all this, but just give me two minutes to explain why we came around.'

'Will I put the kettle on again?' asked Steve, as he threw his eyes up in the air, now looking really irritated himself.

'No, Steve, there's no need,' said Tom as he stood with his

back to the sitting room door, looking very uncomfortable. I stood, trying my very best not to flip the lid at them both. Sue couldn't look anyone in the eye as she struggled to hold back the tears.

'Well?' shouted Dad, frightening everyone half to death. 'Out with it. What did you come around to bloody say?'

Tom sighed and nodded to Sue. 'Tell them, Sue. Tell them what you told me.'

Sue went to open her mouth, but she had to pause to keep herself from being upset. 'Okay. Rob actually never did a thing wrong, Amy.' She looked up into my eyes, looking for a glimmer of forgiveness. 'Colm believed Rob was coming on to both me and Claire. You know, when we were in the pub, he put it to Claire, and Claire said it was true, but she said it only to hide the truth.'

She paused again, her bottom lip shivering.

'Hide what truth?' I said, my heart in my mouth.

Sue sighed. 'Claire has feelings for Rob. She's maybe in love with him.'

Everyone's face dropped.

'She may never talk to me again, but I don't care. I had to say this. She blamed Rob so that she could look innocent about what she was doing herself. She's been the one trying to flirt with Rob in front of Colm all along, and to cover it up, she came up with this lie that it was Rob making the moves, when in fact it was her all along. She came around to you today to say this to look blameless and save her own relationship. God, I'm so, so sorry, Amy,' she said as the tears rolled down her cheeks. 'She even tried to convince me that Rob made passes at me, but he never did. There. That's it. That's all of it.'

*

Meanwhile, back over in Greenridge, Christy's date with Wendy was changed to 6.30pm. He stood in the bathroom after a hot shower, looking in the mirror with only his new sexy Calvin

Klein shorts on.

Something is definitely wrong with these underpants, he thought. *Bloody hell, I better ring Jeff before he closes the shop.*

Chapter 10

Benny Phillips

'Can hardly hear you. Say that again? It's a very bad connection, Christy,' sighed Jeff as he threw his eyes up to heaven again and gave Anne-Marie the stressed-out look. 'No, no, was just closing the shop, but go ahead, Christy. What's up now?'

'Sorry, I won't keep you. I'm standing here looking in the mirror with nothing but that man Calvin Klein's shorts on, and well, I think Anne-Marie may have gave me the wrong size. It says *X-Large* on the packet but there's definitely a problem. Took me a good two minutes to get them on, and without sounding personal, when I turn sideways, I'm noticing that my backside is hanging out both sides.' He laughed as his face went bright red.

'Yes,' said Jeff. 'I was standing at the counter when Anne-Marie sold them to you. She correctly pointed out that these are not the loose underpants you normally buy. They're the modern tight brand, more like swimming shorts, so even the extra-large pairs will have a very skin-tight feel to them.'

'Oh, right . . . Well, don't get me wrong. They are lovely and I love the orange spots, but don't you think they look more like women's knickers than men's underwear?' he chuckled.

Jeff checked the time and rubbed his face as the unwanted end-of-the-day stress got the better of him. 'Look, Christy. I'm tired and need to lock up here. Drop in when you're in Balbriggan next and I'll show you a few looser brands.'

He hung up and turned to Anne-Marie. 'My god, you'd need some patience. He hasn't a clue about the outside world.' He paused. 'He actually believes this blonde 21-year-old wants to date him. I mean he's very innocent and I think –'

'Well, he gives me the creeps, as did his mad father,' she stressed as he grabbed her bag and coat and headed for the door.

'I hope he doesn't harm that poor girl – that's all I'm saying.'

Christy finally got ready and did a few more checks in the mirror. *I look absolutely brilliant!* he pronounced as he did up the last button and straightened his tie and sprayed himself all over with the Hugo Boss. *Right, I'm way early,* he thought as he nervously sat down and tried to stay calm about the date. He checked he had everything. *Keys, money, the flowers and chocolates, brilliant.* He was about to get back up and head over to the canteen for a cuppa when all of a sudden, a fearful doubt invaded his thoughts. He paused for a moment then opened his laptop.

Ok, let's just see what information or advice I can find about first dates. Has never let me down so far, he thought as he came across the heading of a YouTube video called ARE YOU ABOUT TO GO ON YOUR FIRST DATE? He clicked it and saw this small, old, thin man with unshaven face, late 60s with a cigarette end in his mouth, sitting in what looked like a tiny, run-down bedsit.

At the start of the video the man coughed up into a hanky. 'Emm. Sorry about that. It's the bloody fags!' he chuckled without a hint of embarrassment.

Christy sniggered. *Well, this old withered dirtbird wouldn't have the faintest idea about dating a beautiful lady*. He went to click to another video but to his surprise he spotted that the film had a staggering three million plus views. *Bloody hell! Well he must know something if he got that many views and likes.* So he sat back and clicked to continue.

'Hi, sir,' said the man who wiped his mouth with his hanky and leaned forward to slightly adjust the camera.

The man then lit up another fag and got straight into it. 'Hi. My name's Benny Phillips,' came the Cork accent. 'I did this video in an attempt to advise men not to make the same drastic mistakes I made while dating ladies.' He paused to take his glasses off.

'I bet you're sitting there ready to go. I bet you've spent hours getting yourself all spiced up. Am I right?' he smirked before coughing again. 'Sitting there all loved up, ready for action. I can see you with that big oul' bunch of flowers and the oul' box of dark chocolates.'

Christy sat up now, becoming a tad nervous and more attentive as he looked at the flowers in his hand.

'Stop!' shouted Benny in a now high-pitched aggressive tone as he put his hands out in a pleading gesture, frightening Christy no end. 'Forget all this fancy relationship talk. That's the big mistake I made. Not once, not twice but *every bloody time* I went on a date I was straight into all this lovey-dovey romantic nonsense. Few hours later and a few glasses of wine, I was dribbling all my feelings and guts out all over the table about how in love I wanted to be with a woman, how I couldn't sleep at night thinking about it. 'Can't eat since I met you, I told one woman. 'I'm so in love with you I can't go to work,' I told another. 'All I do is sit and dream of you and want to run out and spend all my money on bunches of roses for you, my love,' I told a woman called Nancy McDermott. 'I'm a big bungling mess of soft wet tissues,' I finally admitted to another woman after our first date. Stupid little soft-hearted fool I was.'

He paused for air and lit another fag off the one he was already smoking.

'As you may figure out, I lost every woman after only a day, maybe a few days of dating. Anyway, to cut to the chase, I lost my job after one woman stayed with me for six months but then dumped me for another man. I hit the drink hard. Then finally one night in a pub this lovely man sat me down and told me the plain truth about how women want to be treated. 'In fact,' he said, 'they hate all this sloppy, whimpering way of going on. It's the worst turn-off ever,' he said.

'Well, talk about a good, firm, open-handed slap across the face. I'm now 68 years of age and foolishly I spent all them youthful years trying to plead with women to marry me, only to be told the devastating news that all my efforts were completely useless and entirely the *opposite* way to attract a woman into my life for the long term. As you can imagine, this new revelation knocked me for six. Couldn't believe how stupid I was. I won't lie, it took a long time to admit all this to myself. But over time I had to swallow my pride, and it was shortly afterwards I came up with the idea to make this video to voice the truth of what women really want, and to tell as many men as possible about the pitfalls of dating.'

Christy was now up out of his chair. Hanging intently onto Benny Phillips's every word. 'Well go on tell me!' he yelled as he threw the bunch of flowers in the direction of the bin and checked his watch.

'You need to play a game with their minds right from the start,' smirked Benny. 'Keep your wall up at all times. Play hard to get, if you get my drift. Let them think you have women pursuing you night and day. Sound confident so it makes her feel she's the weak one in the relationship. That's what these women want, my friend, to sense your power over them. Tell the lady you can't stay long on that first date as you have a very demanding schedule. Believe me, that will make them want your time all the more.' He went on and on, explaining how to win the game and control the woman in your life.

'Remember,' he ended, 'remember Benny.' He stood up and went closer to the camera and winked. 'Remember Benny Phillips has his good eye watching your back at all times. Good luck and play her smart, and let me know how it goes.'

Christy watched the 15-minute video twice. He jotted down some of the main points Benny made.

I could have blown it; he puffed as he threw the box of chocolates in the press and headed to the car park with a new game plan in mind.

Just then he heard his name being called from a nearby window. It was Carmel Barnes, puffing out of the end of a cigarette butt. She coughed, then pointed one of her tobacco-stained fingers at him. 'Mmm! Well, look who's all spiced up!' she gasped as she then wriggled her finger. 'Christy Boyle, I'm going to get my hands on you, mark my words!' she bragged with a strong air of confidence.

Christy's face turned green as his tummy heaved once again

at the sickening suggestion.

'You stop all this harassment now, Carmel Barnes. This is the fourth time in two days, and if it continues, I'll report you. Remember,' he said as a final warning, 'you're in your 70s and have passed the retirement age, so one more gross sickening comment like that and I'll report you to management.'

'Oh, I love it when you go all red-faced!' she said with a cheeky wink.

'Well, I'm already in a beautiful relationship. So there,' he blabbered out. 'Yes, it's true. With a very attractive woman, I may add,' as he started to beam. 'So I'm no longer available.' With a confident smirk he put the car in gear and began to reverse slowly out of the car park.

'I'll get you, Christy Boyle, mark my words!' she yelled in a fit of jealousy as she slammed the window shut.

'Ugh, ugh!' screeched Christy as he shivered all over at the prospect of Carmel kissing him. The awful memory of her B O alone was bad enough, not to mention anything else. 'Yucky, yuck!' he managed as he tried his best to erase the disgusting thought from his mind. *Think about kissing the lovely Wendy,* he told himself. *Now, that's it. Yummmm!* A big smile finally appeared across his face. He parked the car and pulled a page from his inside pocket. On it, he had written five main pointers from the Benny Phillips video. *Right. Close your eyes. Memorise them one by one. It's going to work. I can feel it.*

*

Sue had said her piece, finishing with the words that she was so sorry for not saying something sooner. There was an intense silence.

I couldn't move my body. It felt like I was in a terrifying lock-now.' I just sat staring at her as Steve and Des looked on in total disbelief.

'Right, enough!' said Des in an angry yet controlled tone as he strode towards the door. 'Leave now, the both of you. Leave now.'

'Jeez,' puffed Steve as he sat back dumfounded at this new revelation. 'Some bloody friends they turned out to be!'

'Steve, if you don't mind, you as well,' nodded Des in a politer tone as he threw him a look.

Tom began to say something, but Des closed him off. 'Don't! Not another word. You hear?'

'Sure, sure,' said Tom as Sue, head down and fresh tears streaming down her face, walked briskly after him out the door.

'Thanks for everything,' Des managed as Steve rang a taxi and waited outside for it to arrive.

Once the door closed Des went straight for my phone.

I just sat there still numb and sick to my soul.

He got Colm's number as the drink in his system and the anger took over.

'Go ahead, Amy,' said Colm in a stern, protective voice.

'This is Des. Have you any idea what you both just did? Are you pair on some kind of drugs? How could you claim to love Amy and be true friends and go and do something as evil as this?'

'What are you –?'

'Don't interrupt me while I'm speaking!' he hissed, 'or I'll head up to your house and break both your legs!'

'Look, Des. Don't go making threats on my life, okay?' said Colm. 'We did this for Amy's safety. The situation is –'

Des just about kept his head as he stopped Colm mid-sentence and spelled out what Sue had just told them around at his house. 'Well? All of a sudden you've gone all bloody quiet there, Colm,' he said as he paced back and forth. 'I'm going to kill the lot of ye, I swear!' he hissed.

He could hear Colm whispering and then Claire, with a convincing tone, denying it all.

'That's all a load of lies, Des,' said Colm. 'Now me and Claire have always enjoyed a healthy and trusting relationship this end.'

'God help every one of you, all of you, if Amy gets sick again. I won't be responsible for what I'll do.'

'But Rob is the one who –'

Des hung up.

Colm sat down beside Claire and put a reassuring arm around her. 'Mark my words. Everyone will wake up to Rob's ways. And then they'll all crawl back and beg us for forgiveness.'

'That's just Sue taking sides as always,' muttered Claire as she did her best to convince herself of the darkest of lies.

She then slowly took her own phone out and rang Sue. 'How bloody dare you say all that crap? I'll never talk to you or Tom again. Ever! Say something!' she screamed down the phone to a completely silent Sue on the other end of the line.

Colm stood back in the room saying nothing but intently watching Claire's body language as she filled up with tears in defence of her innocence. But he already knew there were feelings involved on Claire's side in this big mess, but in his own insecure mind, relationship survival at all costs was all that really mattered now.

He put his hand out and softly took the phone off her and hung up.

'My god, if anything goes wrong with Amy and Rob's plans,' sighed a pale-faced Tom as he told Sue not to take any more calls from the pair of them. 'We should have told Amy straightaway about all this before she rang Rob. That poor man is probably sitting at home thinking we're all involved.'

'Look,' said Sue, 'I'm going to ring in sick. There's no way I'll get my head sorted for a 12-hour shift.' She paused and poured herself a glass of water. 'I'm certain that once Rob hears the truth about Claire, everything will be sorted out and Amy will be okay.'

Tom sat down, shaking his head. 'This, as you know, Sue, is all about co-dependency. They're so self-absorbed, the pair of them, staying in a relationship just out of fear of not finding someone else. I've had ten, maybe twenty situations where I've had to pull him out of being kicked to death for going for fellas for just innocently looking at Claire in a pub or club. *'What you lookin' at me girl for?"* he mimicked. *'What you starin' at her for? Get your own girl! What, you fancy her or something?"*

'Oh, stop, Tom, stop. And what's worse, we're all supposed to be Amy's best friends. I feel so bad. Maybe she won't ever talk to me for not telling her sooner. All I keep seeing in my mind is her little face and eyes when I told her the truth. It was just beyond horrible to watch, like we'd all betrayed her. I'm actually very frightened for her,' she sighed as her face expressed deep concern.

'It'll blow over,' encouraged Tom. 'Rob's got a good smart head on his shoulders. He'll see right through all this and be up to Amy within an hour or two.'

Des walked over and bent down. 'Listen now, Amy. I'm going to talk to Rob and sort this all out once and for all. But look. Please don't get sick on me. Not now. You hear me, please? Not now.'

I leaned in and held him as if my life depended on it. My speech drawn. 'Did you hear what Sue said about Claire? Why? Why do you think she did all this to me, her friend? Why?' The tears rolled down my face. I took a painful intake of breath as flashes of holding and been loved by Rob flashed in my thoughts. My mouth shivered as the dark fear intensified. 'I feel so cold now, so, so cold. Why do I feel ice-cold, Dad? Isn't the heating on? Will you get me my quilt, please? Everything will be perfect again, won't it? Rob will listen and we'll all have the best Christmas ever.'

Des looked down over me with deep concern as I lay back on the sofa, curling my feet in and drawing my knees up to my chest. 'Sure, Amy,' he whispered. 'Everything is going to be put right.' He went upstairs and came down with a quilt and placed it over me as I started to doze off.

He went into the kitchen and was about to ring Rob but to his surprise, at that very moment, Rob rang him. There was a moment's silence before Des spoke. 'I'm so sorry about all this, Rob. Can you come up and we'll all sit and sort this out? My god, I heard what happened, every word. I'm sick to my stomach here just thinking about how you've been treated. But listen up. Sue just left and, well, she confessed that it was Claire making up stories and –'

'Please, Des, thanks, but Amy accused me of sleeping around with not one, but two of the girls,' Rob cut in in a low, hurting tone. 'Did you know that?' He popped another grape into his mouth and smoothly rolled it under his tongue and down to the side before biting into it ever so gently with a pleasurable smile, just about keeping the big act on track as his heart raced. 'I can't believe it, Des. After all I did for her, all the trust.' He went on for a good five minutes outlining added stuff to what wasn't actually said by Amy in the phone call.

'My god, she said *that*? She never told me that part!' gasped Des as he tried to listen with a sensitive ear.

'There have been a few other hurtful episodes that I won't go into, but bottom line, Des: I just can't cope anymore. As you know, my own health has suffered severely since putting all my energy into helping Amy. And now this, making up lies behind me back. Look, as my counsellor advised me ages ago, I just need some *me* time. That's what my therapist advised. Time out from all this stress, or, as he warned several times, I could well end up getting very sick if I don't take better care of myself.'

'I hear you loud and clear, Rob. So what you're saying then is, you're taking a break. Is that it? Well, it's just with Christmas only three weeks away . . .' Des said in a deep, concerned tone. 'Look, I can't blame you. You've done everything, not just for Amy but for everyone, I just feel so bad that it was her so-called bloody friends who did this. They are never, ever going to cross my door again,' he said as his temper started to boil. 'You sound very, very hurt by the accusations made and I can't blame you. But try taking on board that Amy just recov–'

'Look, Des. The trust was broken. That's the part that holds every relationship together. Plus, and I hate saying this, there's been other times in the past that Amy accused me of looking at other women. Don't say that to her, as things are bad enough. Just give me some time alone to think, will you, Des? Please.'

'Sure, sure,' sighed Des as he hung up and stood there alone wondering, feeling a sense of real desperation as to what to do next. He opened the press and pulled a half empty bottle of whiskey from behind a box of cornflakes. He poured a glass and turned the lights down and sat thinking for ages as memories of his wife Tina flashed in his thoughts . . . The day he asked her to marry him at the back of Skerries Harbour as they walked up towards the Red Island area . . . The thoughts were fresh and real as he saw himself grabbing her and swinging her around to face him as they both giggled like a pair of kids.

'I love you. You know that, don't you? Loved you from the day we met. Remember?'

'Hey, my god, why the serious face? My god!' She smiled as she pushed him away in a jokey manner as her shyness got the better of her.

'Marry me, Tina. Marry me and I'll make you the happiest woman in Balbriggan. In Dublin. In Ireland. In the world!' he yelled as he grabbed her in his arms again and swung her around full circle.

'You're serious about this, aren't you? Ha, ha, ha! Course I will!' Her eyes filling up. 'You're the only man for me!' The echo of the words repeated in his thoughts. *You're the only man . . . for me . . . for me . . .*

He poured another glass of whiskey as the tears rolled down his face.

Oh god, Tina, I can't begin to tell you how much I miss you. How much it hurts. You're so alive and real, inside of me. But I can't see you, touch you, and hold you. Talk to you. If only I could touch your face like before and tell you about the things that are bothering me. He bent down as the tears continued to stream down his face. *I feel so, so, lost without you and now I'm sick, very sick, Tina. I'm hopeless. What am I going to do with Amy? She was doing great but . . .* He paused in thought, then stood up and walked across the room and stood for a moment before pouring the glass of whiskey down the sink and emptying the contents of the bottle as well.

You'd bloody kill me yourself if you saw be wallowing in self-pity, he thought with a painful smile.

He turned, wiped the tears away and started to make the dinner.

*

Christy parked the car in Strand Street, Skerries before taking a deep breath and going over all the information he got from Benny Phillips. *Feck's sake, if I hadn't watched your video I'd have made some fool of myself.* He winked as he clicked into a positive mindset about the date. Okay, *play it real cool, be strong and full of confidence.*

Wendy rang but he let it ring out twice and waited a good five minutes before answering. 'Hi, Wendy. Couldn't take your call. Had another call from a lady friend from Rush. On the phone for ages,' he lied.

'Right, look I'm around in Paddy's Bookshop, near the Church. Drop around to me and we'll head down together to Seasons. Is that okay?' She sounded a bit anxious but Christy was on it.

'Give me five minutes. I've to ring another lady friend back. Got three missed calls from her in the past hour. Bloody hell, that's the third lady who rang me today, you being the fourth. 'Leave me alone!' I jokingly told one of them. 'My god, I haven't the time to go on another date!'' He laughed before giving himself a *You're doing a bleedin' great job* wink in the car mirror.

'Right, right, see you in a bit.' She hung up as she picked a book from the shelf. 'Is this book any good?' she asked the shop owner Paddy.

'Yes, yes,' said Paddy. '*Dublin Seven* by a local author, Frankie Gaffney. Very good reviews. He's always on TV.'

'I'll take it. Need a good read,' she smiled as she paid.

Suddenly the door opened and in walked Christy, all serious faced. He gave the owner a searching stare. 'Hi, Wendy,' he mumbled as he continued in his rather cold, detached approach. But it was hard to play the game as her attractiveness knocked him for six. His eyes dropped down to her glossy lips and back up to her beautiful eyes. He just managed to stay in control as he tried to recall more of Benny Phillips's instructions, but in the heat of the situation he almost tripped over a bundle of books that were neatly stacked on the floor.

Don't feckin' blow it, he thought.

'Be careful,' Paddy laughed. 'Place is very small. Wouldn't swing a cat in here,' he joked.

'I can bloody see that!' snapped Christy in a rather rude tone as he just managed to recover his balance and regain his focus.

'See you, Paddy,' smiled Wendy as she stared Christy up and down trying to figure out his rather odd behaviour.

Once outside, Christy put his plan back into action but emotionally it was again proving far harder than he thought. He was tripping over his words as he eyed Wendy up and down several times as they walked towards Seasons Café. He fell back on telling her a few Benny jokes, which went down a storm.

'My god, that's funny,' she laughed as she opened the door to the café. 'With everything going on, I haven't had a giggle like that in a while.'

Don't overcook it now with the jokes he remembered Benny Phillips say. *Just enough to have her think you're a bloody gas man to be around.*

The manager of Seasons, Linda, approached with a warm and sincere smile. 'Oh, Wendy it's great to see you. How are you settling into Townparks and your new job? Come this way, up the stairs. I just managed to hold you a table as there's a wonderful surprise gathering taking place here later and all but two tables were taken up by it. There's going to be a wonderful atmosphere here soon. We can't wait!' She smiled and winked. 'Can I take your coats?' She bent her head slightly to get a better look at who Wendy was accompanying.

'Thanks very much, Linda. The people in the estate are so lovely and so friendly. They couldn't do enough to make me welcome. It's even crossed my mind that I may look into buying the house,' she remarked as Christy stood behind her, taking note of her statement.

'Oh, sorry,' said Linda. 'Forgive me my manners. I didn't see this handsome man coming behind you.'

'The name's Christy,' he beamed, soaring with added confidence at the welcome remark.

'Mmmm, don't tell me now,' smiled Linda as she tried to guess who Christy was. 'Don't tell me. Yes, I know. This has to be your father.'

Christy's sunny smile was replaced with red-faced embarrassment, but Wendy stepped in.

'Ha, ha! He's not my dad!' she laughed, trying her best to recapture Christy's smile. 'This is Christy Boyle, the best and most caring man in my new job. I'd be lost without him.'

'Oh, sorry,' said Linda. 'My big mouth. Sorry.'

'Here's my coat. Did you say the table was upstairs?' said Christy through gritted teeth as he almost threw his jacket in Linda's direction.

'Yes, upstairs,' she sighed as she gave Wendy the *Sorry* gaze.

Christy settled himself down as he took his phone out and pretended to text someone. 'They'll have to hang on for me. God, I can't be in two places at the same time,' he said as he tried to throw the phone in a strong, manly manner on the table but it came across as just aggressive.

'Is everything okay?' asked Wendy as she sat back, looking a tad uncomfortable.

'Ah I've another appointment for 9pm but just changed it to 9.30. Sorry I can't stay longer,' he said in a controlled manner as a waiter poured him a full glass of red wine. His nerves got the better of him and he downed the lot in one gulp. 'Fill it again,' he told the waiter. 'No, better still, leave the bottle.'

'Right, right, okay,' said Wendy as she sipped her wine and picked up a menu. 'Shall we order?' she asked. 'Em, by the way, you look great. That shirt makes you look younger,' she whispered, trying her best to settle into the evening.

'Well, thank you very much. This is really nice,' he grinned as he sat back and stared deep into Wendy's amazing sparkly eyes. He couldn't take it in how beautiful she was. Here he was, sitting with one of the most attractive women on the planet, and try as he might, with every passing second he couldn't help falling deeper for her. He lowered another full glass of wine down in one gulp to try and stay focused. 'I won't eat a full meal. Just a starter for me,' he said. 'On a strict diet . . . So . . . have you heard from your ex-boyfriend of late?' His eyes searched hers for any hint of remaining feelings.

'Gosh,' sighed Wendy, 'No, that's history. He didn't turn out to be the man I thought he was. Anyway, I kind of like someone in the job,' she smiled but kept her head slightly downward. 'Anyway, look. Let's get into the reasons why I asked you to meet me.'

Christy sat up.

'You're the only person in the world I trust and look up to.' She pulled a notepad out of her bag and glanced around. 'Okay. As we both know, there's very serious abuse going on at Greenridge, and from the little bit of new information I've been able to squeeze out of one staff member,' she took a painful intake of breath, 'well, for one, Nurse Bridie Whelan had made it her mission to abuse a poor elderly lady of the name of Mary Howls. Apparently, over the years, if she takes a big dislike to any one patient, she gives out special painful treatment to them. But as I was told, she's very cunning not to be seen doing anything too horrible in front of the seeing eye of other staff. My god, Christy, apparently, she beats that poor lady black and blue – and that woman's in her 70s!'

She looked back at her notes as Christy looked anything but interested as he lowered another full glass of wine and refilled his glass and called for the waiter for another bottle.

'Now onto Fred Yates,' continued Wendy. 'Or *Gates* as they nicknamed the poor man. Well, from another bit of information a lady from the laundrette whispered that she had a feeling from something she heard that he was actually murdered. She wouldn't say how, as she doesn't want to get involved. No proof, she said, plus they all fear prosecution and loss of job if they go on record. Then there are all these horrible beatings in B Ward that are blamed on patients attacking one another. Well,' sighed Wendy as she sat back and folded her notepad, 'I think it's time you and I looked for some reporter from a good newspaper, or even better still, maybe contact your man David McCullough from *Primetime*. We're as bad as the likes of Nurse Whelan and that horrible, evil-faced Patricia Peters if we sit back and do nothing. Anyway, what do you think?'

Christy suddenly and unexpectedly belched. 'Oops, sorry! Em, okay. I heard everythin' you jus' said,'he slurred. 'But I have to stress that Fred Yates died of natural causes. End of.' He downed another half glass of wine and lashed into one of his jumbo chicken wings.

Wendy sat up, looking more than a little shocked at his cold and detached manner. 'You don't seem to be even listening,' she muttered as she bent over the table. 'You don't seem to be as caring as when we first chatted about this mess!'

At a nearby table a girl was sitting, waiting for her date to arrive. Her face lit up as he arrived up the stairs with the biggest bunch of red roses anyone could carry. There was a gasp from her and from a couple on the other table. Standing a little out of breath and looking a tad nervous, the young man wasted no time and dropped down on one bent knee, as with his other hand he was just about to open a small box and produce a beautiful engagement ring.

'Will you, Jenny Lyons, marr–'

'Ahh, ye big stupid dope!' interrupted Christy with a sneer. 'You're a wimp!' he slurred. 'Yuck. Gimme a bucket as I think me chicken wings and red wine are about to come up all over the floor. Hate all that silly, girly romance and flowers crap! Cop on to yourself and be a real man, for cryin' out loud!' He downed another mouthful of wine as a row of shocked faces looked on. The young guy stood stunned and now close to tears as his well-planned moment to ask the woman of his dreams to marry him was completely destroyed.

'You little fool,' continued Christy. 'Stop all that fancy relationship talk!'

Wendy's mouth hung open as she sat back completely mortified.

Linda the manager raced up the last few steps with a look of horror at Christy's loud flare-up. Behind her were both the couple's families and well-wishers who had been planning this huge, surprise banquet at Seasons to celebrate the big occasion.

The girl Jenny then started crying as Linda shot a look at Christy who was stuffing his mouth with another jumbo wing.

'Well, behind it all, women hate all that silly crap,' Christy mumbled as he downed another mouthful of wine. 'ask that man Benny Phillips. He knows it all.'

Wendy stood up. Her face said it all. 'How dare you!' She turned and tried to console the couple as best she could, but their magical moment was gone, ruined.

She turned back as Christy's over-confidence now began to dissolve slightly.

'It's all . . . garbage. Women want men to boss them about. '

Wendy let fly. 'How bloody dare you, Christy!' she hissed under her breath. 'That was the sweetest gesture ever for that girl, and it's every girl's dream come true. And you've gone and ruined their special moment, not to mention the night out with their families.'

She grabbed her bag and turned and was again all apologetic to the whole family as she stormed down the stairs.

Christy, full to the neck, was now completely muddled at the reactions, but the wine kept the reality at bay. 'Hey, what the hell! Wendy!' He tried to stand up but his head started spinning. He fell back in the chair as the families and friends headed down the stairs. He drank another glass of wine and began to try ring Wendy. Only getting her answering machine. 'Hey, fancy relationship talk never impresses anyone,' he slurred.

Linda was absolutely furious. 'Excuse me, sir. I think you've had enough drink. You have insulted my guests and ruined their whole evening, so can I ask you to please leave.'

'Heeeyy! As you can see, missy, I'm trying to get up.' He moaned as he made a further attempt to lift himself out of the chair. This time he just managed to gain his steadiness. As he was struggling to get his jacket on he held up a half bottle of wine from the table and in three gulps he downed the lot, ending with another loud belch almost into Linda's face. He staggered down the stairs as the manager stood, ready to pull all her hair out. He got more than a few angry stares from both families who were gathered outside trying to console the couple.

He looked up and down the path looking for Wendy who was well gone. 'Heeyyy!' he groaned as he fell up against a wall. 'Youse can all go back in now. I'm probably barred,' he chuckled as he headed for a side laneway to take a leak. By the time he staggered out of the laneway it was noticeable he had himself a small accident.

'Hey, what the hell!' he moaned to a passer-by, 'these feckin' shorts I got in Balbriggan. I can't seem to open them out to wee properly. They're stuck to me like superglue. Ah, noooo, feck's sake, I think I may have wet myself!' he sniggered.

He staggered into a chipper nearby and ordered fish and chips as he continued to try zip himself up.

A young couple in their early 20s, all hugs and smiles, came in all sober as the guy kissed her.

'Hey, you pair!' laughed Christy as he pointed a wet urinated finger across at them both. 'Do you know the relationship guru the Benny Phillips?'

'Sorry no, em . . . I'm not sure what you're saying. Can't make you out,' said the guy as the girl went red-faced, looking away awkwardly.

'He's all over the YouTuber. Two, or is it three million views. Sure everyone must know him by now.' He staggered as he failed to get his zip up. 'Looks like your man from TV years ago, Catweazle. Remember him?' he slurred as he staggered back into the counter. 'He was always carrying this big mad-looking frog in his pocket. Anyway, this man Benny looks like him.'

'No idea what you mean,' said the now nervous guy as Christy again almost lost his balance.

'Careful now,' said the anxious owner. 'You okay there? Do you need me to ring a taxi?' he asked as he put too much salt and vinegar on the order.

'Yeah, sure. Why not . . . Greenridge is where I live. All my life, in fact. Anyway, where was I?' He laughed as he pulled a €20 note out and paid for the fish and chips. He turned, but as he took a step, he felt extremely restricted.

'Heyyy just one jiffy, got a little problem here,' he moaned as he placed his order back on the counter and took his car keys out and went about opening a small sharp pen knife. 'Excuse me one second,' He began to slowing open his trousers belt to a row of shocked faces. 'One little cut and this little problem will be feckin' sorted.' everyone's eyes widened as a deeper sense of uneasiness descended as Christy put the blade unsteady down his jeans and seemed to be wiggling it around.

'Em, can I have a taxi, please. Macari's chip shop, Skerries. Now. right now.' Inhaled the owner as he looked on now with disgust.

'Oh my god! Get me out of here now.' gasped the horrified girl as she put her hand up to her eyes.

There was a slip of Christy's hand and a quick jerk of the wrist and with a huge sigh out came the soaking wet Calvin Klein shorts. 'Ahhh that's much better.' he breathed as he closed the knife and without a hint of embarrassment, he slapped the wet underpants shamelessly on the counter. 'Like a good man. You wouldn't mind dropping them in your nearest bin?' he drunkenly whispered as he turned and let himself out.

'Heeeyy, you dirty, rotten scumbag! Get your arse back here and clea . .' The owner yelled. However, Christy closed the door and was gone.

'The name's Dan,' smiled the taxi guy who looked grateful for the fare.

Two minutes into the journey his head was melted. 'Will you please stop eating the chips in my car? Read the sign. And no, I never heard of this man Benny, but I remember the programme *Catweazle*. Wasn't he the guy who was able to magic himself around, disappear and turn up again, like? Good laugh, that, alright.' he said, throwing his eyes up. 'Hey, please, for the third time, no eating in the back of my car!' he yelled, as Christy filled his mouth with a handful of chips and a piece of fresh cod. 'Look, if its advice you're looking for, well, every woman loves all that flowers and chocolates crack. Romance is the key to my heart. My missus pestered me with that line for years when we first dated. Your man Benny is talking through his arse by the sounds of it,' puffed Dan as he pulled up at Greenridge and took a moment to sniff the air.

'Hey, did you wet your feckin' trousers or something? If that's all over my back seat, I'll bleedin' kill ye!'

Christy, now starting to sober up a little, never said a word. He just paid Dan with a €10 tip and raced away, leaving what was left of the fish and chips stuffed under the passenger seat.

'Crazy isn't the word for you lot of smell bags!' moaned Dan as he drove fuming back out the gates at speed with all four windows down.

Christy wasted no time as he flicked open his laptop and went straight to the Benny YouTube video, his mind anything but certain. He scrolled down to the Comments, something he'd forgotten to do earlier.

You're off your bleeding head, Benny. Ha. Some head on ye!
You have no idea what us women want, you horrible freakshow!
Some buzz alright. My bird fell around laughing at this!!!
Dope!!!!
Fool….
Is this video for real like? Love the wink at the end. Headcase. Ha.

On and on it went – loads of women complaining, some laughing their heads off.

Christy's eyes widened. His face turned red as he almost lost his balance. He wobbled his way to the fridge, pulled out a cold can of Budweiser, his hands trembling as the rage began to get the better of him. 'You, Phillips!' he then roared as he tried to open the can of beer. 'This was a scam, all a scam. You're dead, you hear me, Phillips? I'm gonna wring your skinny neck!' he yelled before bouncing the unopened can of beer off the floor in temper.

Chapter 11

The Call Out

Amy awoke to find herself lying on her bed. For a moment, she tried to figure how she'd ended up there. But before she had a chance to think, the dark reality hit home. Now, without the medication in her system, the frightening events of the day raced up from the pit of her stomach. Grabbing her phone with panic, she rang Rob as she scrambled in her mind how best to resolve everything. *He'll understand,* she told herself. *Remain calm and do your utmost to explain everything clearly to him.*

Leave a message. I'll bell you back.

Hearing his soft voice only made her feel worse. She left a message, trying her best to remain positive, and again everything she said was with an apologetic plea. 'I love you so much, Rob. I'm so, so sorry. Claire and Colm have always had issues, but that's nothing to do with our relationship. I care the world for you, and would never dream of hurting you.' She rambled on and on, then realised she was repeating herself no end. She ended the message with a lump in her throat, feeling even more insecure than ever.

After she hung up she saw missed calls and a text from Tom. It read, *Ring me. I was talking to Rob. Tom x*

'What did he say?' I almost yelled down the phone. 'Look, you don't have to apologise for Sue. Just please tell me what Rob said. I'm scared out of my wits here.'

Tom went through everything Rob had said, trying his best to leave nothing out. 'He's very hurt, Amy, and asked to be left alone to try and rethink, regain his focus.'

'What did he say then? What did he mean – rethink what?' I asked, placing my hand up to my chest to try and calm myself down.

There was a pause.

'He wants to take a break, Amy. A short break to sort some personal issues out.'

I sat speechless as the tears welled up. 'But why won't he even talk to me?' I just about managed. 'My god, this isn't happening! Tell me he didn't say he was breaking it off or anything to that effect! Please, Tom. Tell me something positive.'

'God no! He never suggested anything like that. He's just burned out and is seeking some kind of help. He wouldn't go into it with me but said he told you and your dad. The call ended with him saying he can't believe how hurtful people can be in this world. Hold on – here's Sue.'

Tom handed over the phone as I sat on the bed trembling.

Sue went through everything again, from Claire telling her she had feelings for Rob and that Colm copped on to it. But to save her own relationship she twisted the facts around and blamed poor Rob. 'All lies, Amy, everything is a lie. Colm then told her she had to tell you what Rob was supposed to be up to. That's the full truth, Amy. I didn't know what to say. She told me to swear not to tell a soul. She did this to hold onto her own stupid relationship. I know, I should have had the brains to tell you sooner. But look, Amy, you and Rob will –'

'I want to see them both face to face,' I cut in. 'I want this all sorted and the truth told to Rob.'

I hung up and rang Claire. She wouldn't answer at first, but finally after ten or more attempts she answered and was straight on the defensive, saying Sue was making this all up and that it was definitely Rob who was up to no good.

'Sorry, Amy, but if you want to believe a big, mind-boggling lie that I would fall for your Rob over my Colm and then be as evil as to twist the story to lie to hurt you, my friend, well, believe all you want,' she said in a cold yet convincing tone.

Colm got on the phone and was one sentence into trying to convince me when suddenly I got too upset to continue and hung up mid-sentence.

Sue is telling the truth. Go on your first instinct, I told myself as I then tried four maybe five times to reach Rob again, but with no joy. I finally got my emotions under some control and staggered downstairs, where Dad had cleaned up the whole sitting room and had a lovely dinner prepared.

'Now don't you worry, Amy,' he said in his strong, reassuring voice. 'Sit, sit,' he motioned. 'Get a good dinner down you, and we'll get through all this. And Amy, our Rob will come around and this will all blow over in no time.'

He couldn't look me in the eye and seemed to be acting weird and somewhat nervous as he placed two plates out on the table and headed to the kitchen. I stood staring after him as he returned and placed bowls containing potatoes, peas and carrots neatly on the table and went back in and returned, this time with a freshly-cooked chicken.

'Now,' he continued, 'I got a little sign from your mother that everything is going to be just fine. I'm going to stay off the drink. Come on. Eat up before it gets cold.'

I stood staring at him. 'I can't eat,' I said, letting out a deep sigh. 'I can't even look at food. My tummy is sick. Sorry.' I turned and went to walk back towards the door.

'Sit, Amy!' he yelled, making me jump. 'And don't have me lose my temper!' He stood up and turned his face away. 'God, I wouldn't be able to bear seeing you become as sick as you were a year ago. The hospital even wanted to send you to see a doctor in that mental hospital Greenridge up the road, even proposed a little stay was worth considering. remember? Now listen to me, will you? And please, sit bloody down and eat something!' His voice was stern but with a deep sense of fatherly concern.

I sat without a word and began to just pick at the food as he kept throwing an eye across, while trying to eat his own dinner.

'I was talking to Rob,' he finally confessed. He took a mouthful of water and put his fork down as I went to get up again from the chair with a sense of new hope. 'Now don't jump up. Keep eating your dinner, and listen to me very carefully.' He went on outlining everything, choosing his words very sensibly. 'Look at me, Amy. Rob Cooper put everything he had into getting you back from the brink. And the truth is you were at that scary point of no return. Naturally it's taken a huge toll on him and not only that – and please don't start shouting at me when I say this – but ringing him suggesting what you suggested was horrific.'

'I'd never dream of accusing him of anything like that if it wasn't for –'

'Let me finish, Amy,' he said, trying his best to remain calm. 'That's water under the bridge. What we need to focus on now is allowing Rob recharge his batteries and give him time alone. That's the short and sweet of it. But rest assured he'll come around and we'll all have the best Christmas, and the wedding plans will begin to fall into place again. In the meantime, you need to establish yourself again. You hear me now?'

The very thought of not seeing Rob for a period of days, maybe weeks, had me welling up again.

'Now, now. No tears. You're going to start acting mature, start been strong again and get back into activities like walking. And maybe it'd be wise to try the gym again. That's fantastic for your overall mental wellbeing. I'll ring Platinum and I'll pay for a six months' membership. The girl Rosie knows you well and will make up a training plan for you. Now don't snap at me for saying this, but you could do with losing a few pounds.' He sighed with a determined expression. 'All I'm trying to do is get you to see that you need a little bit of your own independence back.' He sat back down.

I took up the napkin and wiped the tears away. 'Maybe you're right about being overweight,' I admitted. 'You'd wonder what Rob saw in me. I'm a bit of a mess of late,' I drank a mouthful of water and picked up a forkful of food from the plate and forced myself to chew it.

'He saw a wonderful and beautiful woman with your mother's looks,' said Dad. 'How could any man not feel honoured to be marrying a girl with your looks and personality? God, I wasn't suggesting you were fat, pet. Just a little overweight.' He paused and looked annoyed at wording it insensitively. He took a mouthful of water. 'He'll be back in a week or two. I promise.'

I ate some more before pushing my plate slightly away as a deeper sense of fear crept up inside me. There was an uncomfortable silence.

'I'd literally die if anything ever happened between us. I wouldn't want to live any longer in this world without him. That's the truth of it, Dad.' I stood up and headed back upstairs.

'He'll be back! He's mad about you, Amy,' Des anxiously called after me.

The next three or four days were an agonizing blur. I couldn't sleep right and the only comfort I found was from a shirt Rob had left behind in my room. I held it at night and prayed for a proper night's sleep, and that this hurtful nightmare would end and that Rob would get in touch soon. I then wrote two long letters and posted them to him without telling Dad. In them, I repeated how sorry I was for messing up the trust we'd shared, and hoped he'd forgive me very soon, telling him that I had him in my thoughts non-stop and it was unbearable not to be close to him, to hold him, and see his smile and hear his jokes. I went on to ask how he was and hoped he was getting back to full health as I was praying every day that he would be okay. I went on for a page and a half thanking him for all the love and support be gave me that in many ways saved my very life.

You are the greatest man in the world, Rob, I ended. *I love you so much. Come back to me soon please.*

Amy xxxxx

*

Both Tom and Sue were a huge support, but after day four I stopped taking their calls and just replied to a few of their texts. Dad I remembered looked a bit under the weather, so I kept a brave face when around him in order not to burden him any more than I had. I went for long walks on the lovely Skerries South Beach for hours on end, but to be honest it just made things worse. In my lost little world I kept seeing people whose appearance from a distance, like a hairstyle or build, even clothing, gave me a split-second glimmer of hope that it was Rob walking towards me, that he'd come back to me and we were going to be so happy again. What I didn't realise at this time was how the nature of my illness, coupled with my endless need of Rob's attention and warmth, was pushing me further into a depressed state of total blackness. I had stopped eating full meals, eating only biscuits and chocolate and drinking bottles of coke. I was taking more and more medication for the dizzy spells, and sleeping irregular hours.

One night I had a very vivid dream that I was running towards Rob in my wedding dress all smiles, a sparkling wedding ring on my finger, everyone I knew was there waving, cheering me on. When all a sudden in a white flash in my mind I stopped in my tracks and saw myself wearing a school uniform. Bag in one hand and holding this other guy's hand, whose face I couldn't see clearly.

'I love you so much, Amy . . . Remember I told you some folk are born to find places and feelings that were created only for them. Invisible spaces just for them to fit into. I read it somewhere. Remember I told you that?'

I awoke, muddled and unable to remember clearly the ending of the dream. I stumbled downstairs and took more tablets to try help get back to sleep.

By the end of the week and into the next I was sleeping during the day and then staying awake all night, which led to the next stage of my agonizing decline. I started texting Rob again and again. From there I started ringing his phone and crying into his voicemails, pouring my heart out. Everything came to a frightening climax when one of the days I took a cocktail of tablets and came to my senses with my Dad putting me into the back of the car. I had rambled around to Claire's place of work and started shouting abuse. I recalled very little, just small painful flashbacks later on of me yelling at the top of my voice: 'You don't care about the hurt you've caused Rob and me! Tell the truth! You horrible bitch!'

Later that day, after another long, drawn-out talk with Dad, I finally agreed to go back down to our family doctor. After a good twenty-minute chat about every aspect of my head injuries, Dr Bayle finally expressed some real concerns and noted from his files that on my previous visit I had high blood pressure and seemed somewhat overweight. He prescribed me a course of anti-depressants and asked if I'd return next day for a blood test and he was going to arrange a new appointment with my neurosurgeon doctor in the Mater Private.

I agreed.

'Just make sure you don't drink alcohol with these, Amy. They're new on the market and should take effect within a day or so.' He fixed me with a deep, concerned stare, then called Des back into the room as I went to use the toilet.

As we drove home I took a deep breath. 'I'm sorry, Dad, about everything. I made a show of you and myself around at Claire's job.'

Dad just looked across and gave me one of his forgiving smiles but I knew him better than that. He looked anything but happy.

Upstairs in the room I looked down at the packet of anti-depressants and let out a nervous sigh. *Jay, things must be worse than I want to admit if I'm going back on these, I* thought. *I just need to remain focused. Okay! I just have to be a little more patient and stop worrying myself sick.*

*

Rob Cooper fell around the place laughing as he drank another shot with some mates he hadn't seen in over a year. He was smart enough not to go on the rip in around the pubs of North Dublin in case he was spotted out and about in public with Jill. So he brought the gang to a small pub in Sandymount.

'Right! No one hears from you bar a few texts and the odd phone call,' said one of his old mates Ted, 'then you turn up with that self-confident smile of yours. And it wouldn't take a mastermind to see you're definitely smelling of the money and some brand-new deals again. That's our mate, never down for long!' he laughed before giving Rob a penetrating gaze, trying his best to suss him out. Ted Cummins was a thin bloke with a sunken face and a thin, pointy nose. Branded as having a nervous disposition, he avoided rows or any kind of hassle or stressful situations.

'Another round of shots to celebrate with me mates!' Rob shouted at the young barman. 'I'll be top cat in less than two years!' he grinned as the drink started to loosen his tongue. 'I always told you guys that I, Robert Cooper, would make it to the very top, and some of you here drinking with me laughed at me. Well, lads, at this moment in time, I'm one small, tiny step away from breaking into the big time!' He staggered back against the bar but regained his balance and focus in the nick of time as he recalled promising himself only days ago not to start mouthing off about his business deals with anyone. He pressed a finger up to his lips. *Sshhh! All top secret! You hear me now, Ted? This time it's cards close to chest. That was part of my downfall last time. So – no more questions about money and deals. Right, Ted? And let's just get into the buzz of another few wee drinks. Yeah!*

After the next shots went down and a huge burst of laughter, the bar door opened and in walked Jill, looking lovelier than ever and smiling from ear to ear.

'Wow! Would you look at the body on this!' gasped Ted. 'Anytime, luv. An-y-time!'

'Ha! In your dreams, Ted,' laughed the guy next to him. 'In your bloody dreams.'

'Now, lads. Get your scrutinizing eyes off my lady!' slurred Rob as he leaned back against the bar to get his own clear shot of Jill walking towards him with a glint in her eyes. 'You are looking at the woman who I just may end up with. In fact, I love her to bits. Yes, you heard me?'

Ted and the boys all laughed together.

'Am I hearing right, or am I going completely insane?' slagged Ted. 'You, Rob Cooper, sticking with the one bird? Ha, ha!'

'Laugh all you want, Teddy boy,' he slurred as he picked up his pint of beer, 'but I'm telling you all right here and now I'm going to settle down with this girl. Can any of you think of a happier ending for Rob than this beautiful woman strolling towards us. 'So – if you wouldn't mind raising your glasses to wish me a long life of happiness!'

They all raised their pints and drank as Jill walked straight into his open arms and landed him a full-on kiss, almost knocking his drink out of his hand.

'Easy!' laughed Rob as he placed the drink down.

He held her closer, to get a prolonged, intense kiss, making sure to tease the boys as they all looked on with tongues hanging out, green with envy.

*

The following morning Jill showered and raced off to work in Eason's but not before landing a kiss on Rob's lips. 'See you tomorrow night. Hate leaving you, but bills need to be paid.'

'But not for long,' he whispered in her ear. 'Not for long.'

He got up and showered and was strolling back out of the bathroom when he noticed the postman had dropped post in the letterbox. He bent down and saw Amy's handwriting. *Ah for feck's sake, not another stupid letter.* He moaned as he ripped it open.

Dear Rob,

I'm so sorry if I'm crowding you by writing you another letter. But I am truly heartbroken about all this. I can't focus on anything. I wanted to ask you in this letter, will you please forgive me and meet me for . . .

'Blah, blah, feckin' blah,' he mumbled as he tore it up and threw it into the bin and poured a fresh cup of coffee.

Have to end this. Letters, emails, then a string of bloody phone calls and texts. What if she shows up at the door while Jill's here? He sat down and thought it through very carefully. *What if she opens up and tells Des about loaning me the money? He'll hit the bloody roof for sure. Think Rob. No sure, I told Des I may encourage her to invest her money rather than her throwing it to some charity. He was delighted with that. Everything will be accounted for and she'll be paid back in full. Nothing dishonest about any of it. Can always say the deal fell apart. No way am I given a cent of that 260k back.* He thought for a good half hour. *Right. Truth is, Des hasn't got long for this world, so that's not really as big a problem as I'm making it out to be. Think, Rob, think.* Finally he stood up and drank the last mouthful of coffee.

If I want to be free to make a life with Jill, I can't keep hiding out in pubs on the southside. Jill has a razor-sharp mind and will cop on sooner than later. Right. I'll ring her in a few days. I think I know what to say.

That evening he sat alone and began to overthink everything. *What if Peter has done a bunk with the money?* Slowly he slipped into one of his increasingly paranoid states of mind. *Not even a feckin' miserable email to update me! Nothing. Something's wrong. I can feel it.* He gave in and braced himself and rang Peter.

This number is not reachable. Please try again later.

He rang several times more. As the hours ticked by his mind began to be completely overwhelmed with a sickening uncertainty. *No, no! He's legged it with all the cash. I can feckin' sense it, and I'm never bloody wrong.* He tried to eat dinner but everything got the better of him as he thought the only way he'd know for sure is to go to the house Peter was renting in Portmarnock. *I'll check and see if there are any signs that he's upped and gone. I'll ring a taxi rather than drive myself. Just to be extra safe.*

Soon he was a few corners away from the house as the taxi driver tried his best to chat away about Christmas being one big pain in the arse. 'Every bloody year it's the same. We spend like mad, and come January, we're pullin' our hair out sayin' we're never goin' to spend like that again. Then like eejits we do the same thing all ov–'

'Just pull over here,' snapped Rob, cutting across him. He pulled his black hoodie up over his head. 'Wait here. Give me ten or fifteen minutes, mate. I've just to pick up a few CDs. Here's €60.'

The driver turned around and took the money before giving Rob a searching stare. 'Hold it one second, sonny boy. Now I'm tellin' you right here and now, mate. If you're pickin' up or droppin' off drugs and thinkin' you can use my car to carry that crap, I'm tellin' you now, I'll break both your bleedin' legs and make you eat whatever drugs you're carryin'.'

'No, no, it's just a CD that I've to collect. That's it.'

'How many feckin' times have I heard that one? CD my arse! So why are we not goin' around to the actual house and parkin' outside? Do you think I'm some kind of eejit?'

'Look! Just wait for me, you can search me when I come back.' He raced off before the taxi guy had time to react again.

He looked around then up and down the road before darting into the driveway and down the side of the house to the back garden. He tried to get a look in the back windows to see if anything looked like someone had moved out for good. He was finding it harder to see as most of the curtains were fully closed over. *Maybe I should have just rang to see if the place was back up for rent,* he thought. Then slowly he made his way to the front and this time got a good look in the front window but nothing seemed out of the ordinary. *This is just crazy, Rob,* he thought. *Just get the hell out of here before you're seen and then Peter finds out and cuts you out of all future deals.* He tried to get a look in the letterbox. Then he noticed the *green bin. Maybe there's papers, documents, some sort of information that he threw out.* He used the light on his phone to help him as he rummaged through handfuls of paper. *Nothing, nothing but piles of stupid junk mail,* he gasped as he dug down deeper.

'Hey! What are you doing there? Stop right there!'

Rob lifted his head out of the bin and looked around and saw an elderly man standing at the porch of his door across the road waving a walking stick while on the phone.

'I have the Guards here. They're on the way . . . Yes, he's wearing a dark top. Tall man.'

Rob reacted at speed and tried to cover his face with one hand as he took off like a greyhound out the driveway and back down the road and around the corner, but to his horror the taxi was gone.

'Oh, my god!' he gasped.

He raced down Carrickhill Road and up Blackberry Rise, all the time his heart in his mouth, as his legs felt weak with the fear. *I'm okay, for feck's sake, it was only an oul' lad. I'm okay now,* he told himself as he reduced speed a bit. But things took a horrible turn for the worse when he arrived down another street and ran bang smack into a Garda patrol car coming towards him from the opposite direction, lights flashing.

'Oh, shit!' he gasped as he went into a crazy panic and raced towards a wall into a back garden. Once over it he jumped another two or three as he heard a cop shout after him.

'Hey, stop right now!'

But he raced on over a few more gardens till he dived over a smaller wall and stopped for breath. Holding both hands to his knees, he took a second to get air into his lungs.

Suddenly he heard what sounded like a growl. He looked up and saw a big-sized dog running towards him.

'Ahhhhhhh!' He raced for the wall but his legs wouldn't carry him fast enough. He turned as the dog took a firm hold of his right ankle.

'Ahhh no, me bleedin' leg!' he cried out, trying not to scream too loud. He saw a hurley stick yards away as he fell to the ground, kicking with his other foot to try free himself from the dog's secure grip. He just managed to clutch the hurley and swing it violently at the head of the dog. Thankfully it was sufficient to frighten the dog off. He made a huge jump over the wall again, still holding the stick in one hand in case he ran into another tricky problem. He had a quick look back and saw no one chasing him. He limped on, trying to see where he was going. He ran towards another wall and climbed it, but to his horror, he lost his footing and went tumbling down the other side into what sounded and felt like a load of flowerpots. There was a loud crashing noise. He managed to get to his feet only to realise there was something tangled around one of his hands.

He tried to shake off whatever it was best he could but suddenly without warning a spotlight at the back door of the house came on and two sliding doors flung open.

Everything seemed to go into slow motion in his head as he saw the figure of an old fat man sitting in a wheelchair. Then to seal the horror story he looked down at what he had fallen into. His body went weak, his face pale as a ghost when he saw a broken statue of the Virgin Mary lying scattered all over the grass. And tangled in the fingers of his left hand were three, maybe four sets of rosary beads and a few holy medals for good measure. In the other, he held aloft the hurley stick. It didn't take a genius to figure out that he had fallen into a well-kept travellers' shrine, dating back to their ancestors. He looked back in the direction of the man, but now standing by his wheelchair were three or four big traveller sons with faces and eyes filling with intense rage, all ready to rip Rob's heart clean out of his chest as they struggled to get past their father's wheelchair to get a hold of him.

Rob's mind was now repeatedly screaming at him to *Run! Wake up, you big clown and run for your bloody life!*

He dropped the hurley stick on the spot and made a frantic dart for the wall.

'He broke the shrine to bits!' one son repeatedly screamed at the top of his voice as they all ran in Rob's direction.

'I'll break the ugly neck off ya!' roared another as they all rushed in Rob's direction, one swinging a big iron bar.

'It's one of the dirty Connors!' shouted the father as he almost lifted himself out of the wheelchair with the swell of intense rage.

The mother rushed past the father into the unfolding saga, screaming and wailing at the top of her voice at the devastation to the shrine. She threw herself on the grass, hands in the air. 'Ahhhh, Mammy, Mammy!' she repeatedly cried out. 'Aahhh, Mammy and Mary!'

Rob made a lightning move for the wall and was just over when he felt a pain shoot up his spine as one son broke a sweeping brush across his back. Another just managed to grab one of his feet, pulling one of his Nike runners clean off, along with his sock. The terrified Rob just managed to wriggle himself loose and fell over into the next garden and was off running for his life towards another wall, hobbling, then down a back lane and across a small park to freedom. All the time he could hear the echoes of voices screaming abuse and certain death threats after him.

'Saw your ugly face!' was the last scream he thought he heard as he fled for his life.

When he stopped and got himself calmed down he cursed himself from a height. *You stupid bloody eejit! You could have been killed back there.* He looked and then realised in the tussle that he was still holding a set of rosary beads. He flung them into a ditch and thought how best to get home with just one runner on. *For feck's sake, Rob, this was the worst idea you ever came up with in your whole entire life.*

He finally rang Ted as he knew he could be trusted. And in no time Ted picked him up but was all questions.

'Don't even ask me, just drive. Ohhh,' he moaned, 'my bloody leg and back are killing me.'

'What the hell were you playing at that you have only one runner on?' giggled Ted out of nervousness.

Rob wrapped his other sock around his ankle. He told Ted half the story about the travellers' garden.

'You actually ended up in a traveller's back garden? That's got to be a joke!'

'Yes, and four big mad-looking knackers came at me and I think one of them saw my bloody face. Just drive, Ted, please. I've had enough for one night. I'm embarrassed enough about it.'

'Hey, one thing right now, Rob. Don't care who you are, don't ever call them people knackers again. You hear me now? I hate that word being used to describe them people. Hate it.'

'Feck's sake. Sorry, okay? Okay, travellers. Tinkers. Whatever.'

'Right, calm down. So tell me, enlighten me. What in the blue shit were you doing in a travelling family's back garden? You bleedin' nutcase!' Ted spoke now in a joking but supportive tone.

'Just get me home till I bandage my leg up. The bloody pain is kicking in. I was at a Christmas party, okay? And fell over a wall. Is that enough data for you? Just drive and stop asking me questions.'

'Right, relax, just concerned for you, that's all,' said Ted as he peered nosily over at Rob who was trying not to get blood all over the seats.

'I fell into some kind of statue. I think it was Mary and one of a holy angel. There. Now just get me home so I can clean myself up.'

'But that doesn't explain very much. Why if you were at a Christmas party were you jumping walls into gardens? Were you smoking the funny stuff or something?'

'Don't be the smart arse, Ted. I don't take drugs. Now enough. And will you keep your eyes on the road or we'll end up in a feckin' ditch.'

Next day Rob's phone went while he was watching RTE News with his ankle resting on a cushion. It was Peter Bradley.

Oh, my good God! He knows. He knows it was me, he gasped. *Okay, try and relax and sound completely normal.*

'Rob! Sorry for being out of touch. We may have a big problem and I need a fast favour. I got a call from the cops in Malahide. Someone was attempting to break into my house last night. Yeah, that's right. They were trying to open a window and were searching my green bin for documents. That's what it sounds like.'

'You're joking me!' whispered Rob as he gulped, trying to sound surprised but less nervous.

'Look, Rob, everything is running very smoothly over here, in fact far better than I believed. But listen. I left a feckin' laptop back at my house in the front room with files all over the table with information about our investments and my future projects. I just need you to drop around and keep an eye on the place for me. Drive by and check everything's ok. Will you do that for me? The cops checked but said there's no sign of a break-in. Just so I have peace of mind.'

'Scumbags. Bloody hell,' gulped Rob as he felt a further sense of relief. 'Look, I'm on it right now. I'll fly over and check around.' He paused. 'So how are things going? You said things are going better.' he asked, hoping to hear some positive news.

'We're almost home and dry, Rob,' stressed Peter in a thrilled voice. 'I got everything sorted and have the rights to the new drug, results and testing, everything bought and all the legal papers signed. And get this: I've to fly back to London, as the pharmaceutical company in question have at last made an offer. Just want to make sure to push them and get the best deal out of them. My legal man is in talks with them as we speak. You just keep an eye on the house for me. Please, Rob.'

'Sure, no problem.' Rob stood up with the excitement of the news. 'So what are we talking about financially?'

'Can't be certain but you're looking at 3, maybe 4 million. Breaking that down, your cut would be around 345k. Look, I've got to fly. I'm awaiting phone calls. I'll be home next Thursday at the latest. Bye.'

'Yeah. Bye, Peter. Thanks for the update. Well done, Captain.'

Rob stood, but suddenly his legs almost gave way from under him with the sheer pleasure, the shock of the unbelievable news. He had to check in his mind several times that he'd heard Peter correctly. *Almost half a bloody million … Oh my god. Even the pain in my leg is easing!* he joked to himself as he filled up with tears of pure delight. He took a kitchen tissue from the counter as he struggled to hold in the emotions.

With hands shaking as he poured himself a strong coffee and sat back down with a huge shocked face. *I'll be able to get out of this house and move to a bigger and posher house, maybe in Sutton or Howth . . . Oh yeah . . . By the sea . . . Eating delicious seafood and downing them great pints of Guinness, sitting in the sun all day long . . . Oh my god, this is actually happening for me. I'm made up for bloody life!*

Suddenly he almost dropped his cup of coffee all over his lap with the fright as he grabbed the TV control and raised the volume on the RTE News.

'What can you tell us, Paul?'

'Well, a Garda investigation is under way here in Portmarnock after Patrick Quinn and his family's shrine was smashed in a sinister attack here last night. Mr Quinn is a traveller who just three weeks ago agreed to move his family from a caravan parked in a field in the Claire Hall area to a house here in Carrickhill Heights. It was agreed Mr Quinn could bring his family shrine. But at around 8.45pm last night a man wearing a black hoodie top and blue Nike runners was seen attacking and smashing the shrine with a hurley stick. I talked earlier to one of the sons, Francie, and his mother Mary. Francie, you and your family are understandably in shock and angered at this attack. But you say you saw this man's face?'

Up stepped a half-shaved traveller built like a tank wearing tracksuit bottoms and yellow vest.

Rob stood up, his hands trembling as all his financial joy drained away, giving way to a horrible sense of dread.

'This is a call out, ya dirty *bleep bleep bleep* to meet me now, man to man, to fight me, Francie Mighty Quinn. You cowardly *bleep*, you smashed the head of Holy Mary and robbed me great granny's gold Rosary beads! We'll find ya! I saw your dirty, black rat face, you *bleep bleep*.' The swearing continued. 'You think I didn't see you? Look, I have your smelly sock and runner. I'm a man of me word!' he fumed. 'I'll find ya and I'll make ya cry your eyes out into my granny's face for mercy before beatin' ya to death with this!' He waved the hurley stick above his head. 'Ya rotten coward is what ya are!'

The old sobbing mother stepped forward, pointing her finger into the camera. Her eyes peered as Rob sank back into the sofa. 'You! I can see you watchin'. I put the gypsy curse on you now from me ancestors. Your greatest fear will pass over your doorstep. Ahhhhhhh! Mind your step . . .!'

'This is Paul Reynolds, Crime Correspondent, RTE News.'

Chapter 12

Wearing Masks

Rob felt a peculiar, crippling sensation come over him as the lasting image of the mother's eyes peered into his very soul from the TV set. He kept hearing the old gypsy's curse repeat the chilling words in his head. *What's happening?* he gasped, as the weird sensation seemed to linger. He strained to shake it from his thoughts. Her shadowy, brown, penetrating eyes, her old, wrinkled appearance added to the fright no end. *Okay, okay. Relax and pull yourself together. Regather that wonderful feeling about all the money coming your way.* He inhaled and exhaled for a good minute. Then finally, to his huge relief, everything finally seemed to return to normal. *You got a bit of a fright, that's all, Robert. It's all the excitement, that's all.*

He paused before pointing a finger at the TV set.

'I never took your stupid rosary beads, you horrible oul' wagon. They're in a ditch somewhere in the area.' He grew in confidence that he was innocent of any wrongdoing. 'It was all just a silly unfortunate accident,' he continued as he tried to recall the exact place where he had thrown the beads. 'Feck's sake, I can't remember. It was dark and . . .'

The phone rang. It was Ted. 'It was on the TV3 News as well, Rob,' he said in a deep, alarmed tone. 'What the hell have you gone and done? You never told me that you demolished the family shrine with a big bleedin' hurley stick. You lunatic!' He nervously snickered. 'I'm not being smart, Rob, when I say this, but that is by far the worst offence you can ever commit on any travelling family. No, listen to me for one second, Rob. Them Quinns are merciless enough. But my god, smashing to bits their ancient shri–'

'Will you shut your stupid mouth for a sec and listen to me? I didn't do anything on purpose!' He paused to catch his breath as his blood pressure started to soar again. 'You didn't tell anyone, did you? Tell me on your own mother's life you didn't breathe a word of this to any of your friends or family!' Rob stood up and checked out the window, trying his best to remain as calm as possible.

'Hey, Robert! You know you can trust me. But you never told me the whole truth last night, did you? I mean the night before you were all happy clappy, pulling wads of €50 notes out and splashing it around. Buying me loads of drink. Never saw you so with it and so together and happy with the new girl and all. Then next night by some unbelievable turnaround in that head of yours you pee all over your fortunes by smashing to bits the Quinns' statue of the Virgin Mary.'

'Shut the hell up! Ok look, I never told you everything. So here goes.' Rob was pacing up and down now, dragging out of a fag as his nerves started to go. He proceeded to tell Ted the bones of the story as to why he was in the area. 'Doesn't matter the investor's feckin' name. Just make sure you don't breathe a word of my business, right?' Another pull from his cigarette. 'Anyway, I was chased through gardens, got bitten by a dog and fell into that traveller's garden with the feckin' hurley stick still in my hand. That's it, so this is just one big horrible misunderstanding, Ted.' He gulped as he checked the window once again. 'Anyway, they didn't see my face. I'm sure of it. I had my black hoodie up.'

There was a moment's silence.

'I'm not calling you a liar, Rob. Please don't get all defensive and think I am. But that story sounds very, very hard to swallow. If you were telling me the god's honest truth, why then did you specifically pick out and steal the old granny's gold beads?' Ted had dropped his voice to a whisper as he himself became edgy and his own fragile mind began to weaken as he looked out his own window.

'Look, they somehow got tangled around my hand. I don't bloody know, do I! Okay? Everything happened so fast. I flung them away after running up some road and across a park.' Rob tried to sound convincing, but he was starting to realise how stupid the story sounded. 'What did the TV3 News actually say, Ted?' he gasped as he put his fag out and lit another one. 'I just caught the end of RTE News.'

'Well here goes. At first, the father was calling it a blood feud of some kind as him and one of the older sons was blaming the Connors family. Their blood was splashed over the shrine, so I think the father said something along the lines that it's a sign of a blood feud but now they think it wasn –'

'It was blood from *my bleedin' ankle,* for feck's sake!' yelled Rob.

'I'm not trying to frighten the crap out of you, Rob. I'm not. But the old mother was bawling her eyes out then started saying stuff, like putting curses on the person who was responsible for all this.'

'That's just bullshit. Oul' wives' tales.'

'No, no. I remember years ago in the big snow of 1981 or '82, an old traveller lady came begging in my mother's estate in Raheny, All Saints' Road, facing St Anne's Park. This guy abused the poor traveller and ran her from the door back into the cold of the day. She fell and split her face open and your man just laughed at her. Anyway, she turned and put a curse on him that he'd be frozen to stone just like the day that was in it. Story goes that the man continued to sneer and laugh his head off at the poor woman.

'So? And don't tell me he actually turned to stone. Is that it?' snapped Rob as his patience wore thinner.

'Wait till you hear the end of the story. People laugh and sneer at travellers who say weird shit like that, but one year later to the very day at the exact time, he was killed. No, it's no joke, yes, killed. Hit on the Howth Road near Sutton by a lorry.'

'Okay, so the man died! Big bloody deal. Nothing strange about that. He wasn't turned to stone so it's a load of codswallop. Look, I've got to –'

'Let me finish the story, will ye! Get this: the lorry that killed him was a big bloody cement lorry! Get it? Cement. Stone. Stone dead. Now, how creepy and grim and twisted is that?'

There was a silence before Rob reacted. 'Are you purposely trying to do my bloody head in and drive me right over the edge, Ted? 'Cause if you are, here's something to chew on.' He paused then smirked. 'If they did see my face, then the next thing they'll want to know is, was there anyone else involved. Like a driver, a getaway car. There's blood all over your car, isn't there?'

'Heeey, what the hell are you implying? I nev–'

'I'll buzz you later,' said Rob as he hung up and sat nervously down, picking up the tv remote to check the teletext.

Gardaí investigating a sinister attack on travelling family shrine are looking to talk to a taxi driver who was seen dropping a man off in the area of Carrick Hill at around 8.30pm, who fits description of the man they believe they want to interview . . .

Rob's eyes widened as he read on.

WHAT! That taxi guy would have my name and bloody number. Okay, I don't think I gave him my full name. Plus, if I remember, he wasn't a local taxi guy. Think he said he was from Coolock, plus he didn't pick me up at my actual address. I met him outside on the main road. No, no, I'm okay. He won't remember. He gulped as he tried to see some positives in the unfolding nightmare.

He ran his nervy fingers across his unshaven face. *I'll grow a beard. Yeah, that's it. Maybe wear dark glasses till it dies down a bit.*

His phone rang. He grabbed it off the table, trying his best to shake off the uneasiness.

Amy.

He buried his face in his hands in frustration. 'For feck's sake. that's all I need now is that yoke ringing me!' he mumbled with a face that twisted with irritation. He sat and let it ring out, then came up with one helpful idea.

He waited until Jill arrived up that evening. He sat her down and communicated the whole story about the night before. 'Yes, yes, in my head I keep repeating how stupid it was to have let this paranoid side of me creep in again, but Jill, I couldn't have visualised what unfolded in a million years. Talk about dirty rotten bad luck syndrome. I know it sounds so unbelievable a story for you or anyone to swallow, but I swear this is the God's honest truth, Jill. I don't want to start hiding things from you.'

Jill sat up, taking everything in as she gazed into his eyes, trying to comprehend all the bizarre information.

'As I keep telling you, we're a couple that's on the brink of making it to the very top. Look at me, Hon,' he gushed, as flashes of Peter's words raised his excitement above the present crisis. He showed a small gap between thumb and forefinger. 'I'm this close to being a millionaire,' he exaggerated. 'I can't believe it myself, it feels like a dream, but it's all true. I got the news directly by phone today. And there was I worrying myself into a frenzy for nothing, thinking that Peter had legged it with all my hard-earned cash. Now smile and look at me, Hon. All I'm asking of you is for you to stand by me and when we go out socialising, we'd go to the southside till this crazy disaster blows over.'

She agreed but continued to stress her annoyance at him for being so bloody careless and stupid. 'Money isn't everything in life. You may not be around to spend it,' she continued. 'There was something in the bloody *Evening Herald*. What if this taxi guy remembers? What then? You'll be murdered for sure and maybe me along with you!'

'Please! I'm going to be okay. I can feel it in my waters.'

After another few heated exchanges Jill started to calm down again.

'Look at me, Jill. Look into my eyes, love.' He thought out every word with a touch of his magic. 'I don't think you're seeing the whole picture. It's not the money. That's just a small part of this wonderful story. It's us. You and me, when we're together . . . Stop looking away and look at me,' he smiled. 'It's this amazing connection, this bond we have, and it all links into a rare kind of affectionate relationship that everyone out there can only dream about. People would give the world to have the connection we share when we make love. We're like that couple in a romantic movie.' He stood up and stretched both arms out fully. 'remember that mind-blowing scene on the bow of the ship in the movie *Titanic*? With Kate Winslet and Leonardo? Not just the scene itself, beautiful though it is, but the closeness. That's what we share, Jill. We have what the whole world is searching for. The perfect love.'

Jill was now listening intently. 'Gosh! You have a way with words,' she just about managed. 'But remember, Leonardo was frozen to death like a stone at the end of that movie.'

'Frozen like a stone? Why did you use that term frozen to death?' Uttered Rob as he thought of Ted's strange story.'

'You're the one who put the film in my head. Why?'

'Right right. Never mind.'

He slowly picked her up and held her close, looking deep into her eyes. 'I know you feel what I feel. And me falling into that tinker's garden isn't going to stop us having the best life you could ever imagine.' He convinced her with a solid argument that it was all destiny for them to meet and have this life of luxury. 'Was thinking of getting rid of this place,' he continued as he sat down and finally smiled. 'And if you agree to, it we could buy a house, maybe in your favourite town, Sutton or maybe Skerries by the sea. Can't you see it?' He smiled.

Jill paused and gathered her thoughts as she stood, still kind of scared, but in spite of the present danger she wanted to spend the rest of her life with this man.

'Okay, okay, I'm with this all the way,' she faintly smiled. 'But first off, before you ramble any further into dream world, do you think you could remember where you threw the granny's gold rosary beads? That would be a huge weight off us,' she said as she gave him another comforting hug. 'That would mean everything to those poor people and would end this manhunt and then we can plan our future. I love you so much and would die if you got yourself hurt over this stupid mess.'

Rob promised on his mother's and father's grave that he'd search the whole surrounding area when things calmed down.

'You'd look rather sexy with a beard,' Jill then beamed as the tension subsided further and she grabbed hold of his hand, pulling him close for a prolonged embrace.

That evening Ted rang in a sweat as the saga continued. 'Did you see the end of the 9 o'clock news? My head's completely fried here!' he whispered down the phone. 'My car! They now have blurred CCTV footage of me picking you bloody up. No, I'm not bloody lying. *I'm* in the middle of your big mess. Would I make a joke out of this? It's true. I'm here trying to wash your blood from my car seat. They haven't got my reg but the car model and you jumping in and me speeding off. You're going to have to go to the cops now, right now, Rob! Please. I'm scared shitless. My nerves are starting to go, they're going to track us dow–'

'Calm bloody down, Ted. You're running way ahead of yourself. My god, I didn't murder anyone. They're all making this way bigger than it actually is. No, *you* listen. How many Nissan Micras do you think there in north Dublin alone?' He turned on the TV as he continued to try cool Ted down.

'No, I'm telling you, Rob, they're going to kill us both. It's just a matter of time before they find out who we both are. It's all over YouTube as well, under *Shrine Attack*. You want to see the rage in their eyes and the threats from two of their cousins. They have loads of feckin' relations coming from as far away as Ballinasloe!'

'Okay, stop everything you're doing. No, stop, and take deep breaths. That's it. Breathe in and out slowly. That's it. Now listen to me very carefully,' said Rob as he did his best to stay calm himself. 'Take a hold of yourself. You've relentlessly struggled with this silly, stupid, nervous disposition. No one saw my face. They're bluffing to try and frighten us into panicking. Ain't gonna happen. You hear me now? They have absolutely nothing to go on. Hold the line till I check the YouTube for myself,' he gasped trying to sound less nervous than he actually was.

Up popped one huge traveller Thomas Quinn and alongside him his pint-sized brother, Mickey.

'He was wearing a black tracksuit top and jeans. The smaller brother wore a black pair of tracksuit bottoms and white vest. 'Now listen to me, snake face!' he continued after a mouthful of bad language. He stepped up to the camera of the mobile phone, fuming with a face fit to kill. 'You dirty, filthy scumbag. Patrick Quinn's son seen your ugly head. Now, I swear here today by all the Quinns from Ballinasloe, I have a headstone ready for ya, and after I beat ya to death with your own hurley stick, I'll scratch your name on the headstone with a tooth that I'll knock clean out of your face. You hear me now? Fight me like a real man, ya snakey-face coward!'

The other brother Mickey threw his shoulders back and calmly walked up to the camera, throwing a few of his own shapes. 'We want our granny's rosary beads back, rat-face!' Amazingly, that was all he said as he stood back to let Thomas in again.

Rob's confidence dissolved rapidly at the sight of the big brother firing threat after threat on his life.

Next morning the saga continued, as on page five of a newspaper was the photo of the tearful mother standing beside the smashed shrine.

FIND THE PERSON WHO DID THIS screamed *The Star* newspaper.

'The government promised us we'd be safe if we settled in a house. Now look.' quoted *The Daily Mirror* with a photo of the father in a wheelchair holding the hurley stick used in the *mindless attack*.

Rob bought both papers and was just back in the door when Ted rang.

'Mother of God, have you read the Star paper?' Ted gasped. 'They're saying you attacked a disabled man's house. I keep thinking there's maybe vanloads of them big mad travellers roaming around North Dublin looking for us. I'm half thinking of burning the car and saying it was robbed. I'm losing –'

'Calm feckin' down right now, ye nervous little whippet!' said Rob in a surprisingly calm and controlled tone. 'Get that stupid head of yours straightened out. No, no, don't say another word. If your nerves are going, then get some of your mother's Valium tablets. Bottom line, Ted: if you panic and open your big mouth about this, remember it's going to be your head on the block, as well as mine.'

Ted began to calm down somewhat as Rob stayed on the line for a good ten minutes outlining certain positives.

He hung up and let out a very nervous and desperate sigh as he read the whole story from one of the papers. *I think I'm going to have to invest in a bigger pair of dark glasses, maybe wear a hat as well,* he gulped.

He slowly walked into the bathroom and glared at his eyes in the mirror for a moment. Now for the first time he rather noticed that his eyes did look snake-like. *Jay, maybe they did see my whole face!* But he drew back from the dark thought as he began to sense or even hear the old mother's words putting the gypsy curse on him. *Ahh, that's all just a pile of cow dung. I've worked my arse off to get this far, and this little hiccup isn't going to wipe out my brilliant future! No way!*

*

Christy awoke with the hangover from hell. At first he couldn't even open his eyes with the pain in his head. Finally after a few failed attempts to lift himself up, he reached over, pulled a fresh pair of underpants from the side locker and went about putting them on.

Never wearing them stupid bloody Calvin Klein shorts again. 'Ahh!' he sighed. 'That's better.'

Suddenly the whole mess of the night before hit him. 'Up, up!' he shouted as he raced around trying to sort himself out. 'My god, have I blown my chance?' He had a quick shower and managed to get dressed while drinking cups of fresh coffee to try and kill the merciless hangover. *That witheredfool, Benny Phillips. I'll strangle him, I swear I will!* He struggled to get his socks on as flashes of the night before rushed around in his head. *I need to make up some kind of story for Wendy.*

He raced over to the hospital late for work and was met with tittering and laughing from staff members. He overheard one nurse whisper, 'Christy Boyle is in love! Ha, ha, ha!'

Everyone must bloody know, he thought as he did his shirt up.

Carmel bloody Barnes. I shouldn't have said anything to her yesterday. He went to call after the nurse but thought it would only fuel the fire, so he played the innocent as more staff gave him strange looks. He headed straight to the canteen to get another strong coffee with a plan to try and see Wendy as soon as possible. If need be he was now prepared to beg her forgiveness.

But the minute he opened the door there was more sniggering as Noel the male nurse pushed past him, laughing aloud.

'Yes, if you all want to know the truth,' Christy snapped. 'Yes, I'm in love. With a beautiful woman, as it happens. I wouldn't be the first man to fall in love with –'

'Christy!' whispered a nurse in a low tone. 'Dr Grimes would like a word in his office.'

Christy threw an angry glare at everyone in the canteen as he marched with a fresh coffee in hand back out the door and across to the main office. Brushing his hair to the side with one hand, he tried to figure out how best to explain that this wasn't some fling with a member of staff. *I'm taking no crap,* he told himself as he braced himself for the worst. *They can't stop this.*

Just as he approached the long hallway to Grimes's office the door suddenly opened and Carmel Barnes came out, dragging her bucket and mop behind her. She gave Christy just the faintest of smiles then a little wink as she passed.

Christy walked nervously up the corridor, trying his best not to give her any further encouragement. *Block her out,* he told himself as he threw her a passing glance back. It was at this point he noticed that her grey hair had tiny blonde streaks running through it. She flicked it slightly over to one side and gave him a tempting smile as he nervously walked on.

'Come in, come in,' ordered Dr Grimes as Christy gently knocked on the door. 'I haven't got all day.'

Christy almost staggered in to find Grimes spraying the whole room with air freshener. 'Eugh! The bloody bang off her is bloody horrendous. It's worse she's getting. If you ask me that whiff is close to the bang of a dead body. Sit, sit,' he motioned with his hand as he opened both windows. 'Ahh, that's better,' he sighed before turning to face a rather hung over and subdued Christy.

'Now, I'll get right to it. Rumours are flying around the canteen all morning. I mean, Christy, what in the name of God above are you playing at, trying to date a member of staff? Now we have been on good terms of late. I'm very happy with your progress. But it clearly states that all intimate relationships are discouraged and go against hospital rules. Outdated as it sounds, rules are rules.'

Christy stood up, his hands out in a surrender plea. 'What can I say? I have feelings, real feelings for a member of staff whose name I do not want been blabbered all over this or any other hospital. Furthermore, no man, woman or doctor or HSE rule book is going to stop me.' He raised his voice to get his point across as strongly as possible. 'I'll make sure it's a relationship that only goes on outside of the workplace.' He surprised himself with the confidence and determination he was showing. 'Now if that's all, I've a splitting headache and have to start work.'

Dr Grimes sat down at his desk, looking dumfounded. 'But already you've broken the rules. Two minutes ago she told me you kissed her while on duty. I was ready to throw up hearing the details. I mean, Christy, surely even you at your age, can do better than Carmel Barnes?'

Christy almost fell out of his chair. 'Whaaat? *Barnes?* It's not feckin' her I'm in love with! Who told you that?' His head went into a spin. 'Do not tell me everyone in Greenridge thinks I'm dating that oul' one!'

'Well, aren't you? You've gone as pale as a ghost, Christy. Sit back down and relax,' said Grimes as he poured Christy a glass of water but ended up drinking it himself as the saga began to amuse him no end. 'I found it very hard to believe myself, if I'm being totally upfront. I mean, I don't know what to think. She told someone in confidence. However, you know this place for gossip. Said you and her had a hot thing going on in the locker room. When I questioned her just now she said she thinks she may have feelings but would rather not say anymore but then when I pushed her she openly admitted that you've exchanged kisses, 'tongues in mouth and all-around style', as she oddly worded it. If there's any truth in it, I cringe at that thought. I mean, how you put up with the whiff off her is way beyond me.'

Christy was red with rage. 'Stop now. I have feelings for a beautiful lady, but it's certainly not Carmel bloody Barnes. We did kiss but it was . . . enforced. She forced herself on me and kind of kissed me. It was a kind of trick she played on me.' Christy wasn't sounding convincing by any stretch of the imagination.

'If you ask me it sounds like you're both playing little childish flirting games. Am I right?'

'No, no! Listen, Doctor. *She's* been pestering *me*. Sexy harassment. That's what she's been doing.'

'It's actually called *sexual* harassment,' corrected Grimes as he did his best to keep a serious face.

'Whatever! Will you at least look at me, Dr Grimes? She's trying to corner me at every turn. Nagging me, following me around the hospital of late. Even today in the hall, making little flirty gestures. You're the doctor. You can see as you said, she's completely losing all respect for herself. She should have retired years ago, as you well know. Now please, you're the one in charge. Call a meeting and inform everyone that this is a nasty rotten pack of lies. Dr Grimes, I swear on my father's gravestone, I would never go near an oul' one of that age. God, please do something and get rid of her.'

'I have to admit she's not helping advance the hospital's image with her hygiene issues. That's for sure. Hmm. So Christy, this is nothing but an impure fascination in Barnes's warped mind towards you? I've nothing to worry about?'

'Of course it bloody is!' hissed Christy as he struggled to concentrate from the pressure in his head.

'I have to say she seemed very convincing that you were the man she was going to 'nail down', to use her phrase. I then tried to joke around it all by asking did she not think in her 70s that she was way past dating. She replied with an air of confidence and remarked: 'I've bags of youthful passion that I know Christy and I can slowly venture into.' She sounded transfixed on you.'

Christy was near speechless. 'Please put me in for a holiday. Right now. I can't face everyone today. I've to pick me car up in Skerries.'

'I'll do my best to tell everyone that it's just rumours,' assured Grimes with a look of support. 'I've a meeting with staff at 12 as there seems to be medication supplies going missing of late. You wouldn't mind keeping an eye on that would –?'

But Christy was out the door and gone before he'd finished his sentence.

He spent the day trying to recover from his hangover and relieve his mounting fears that he'd lost his chance to date Wendy. He rang her and did his utmost to leave the right kind of message on her answering machine. He then watched at the window to try and catch Carmel Barnes leaving work. He looked at the Benny Phillips video a few more times, each time unleashing mouthfuls of bad language and gruesome threats. He glanced up at the photo of his father. *Yes, yes, Dad,* he admitted, *I should have requested your council on this. But I'll get a second chance. You wait and see if I don't clear up this big bloody mess.*

At around 3.30pm Wendy rang. He braced himself. *Deep breaths. In, out, in, out.*

She was furious. She wouldn't let him get a word in as she explained how she had to call back down red-faced to Linda, the manager of Seasons Café to say how sorry she was. 'Thankfully everyone went back in and they made the most of what was a ruined occasion.'

'But Wendy –'

'Don't, Christy. I'm not finished.' She slammed him about his own odd and strange ideas. Look, you go and do whatever you think your father or mother would do at Greenridge. I've another plan in mind. Anyway, there's someone else . . .'

An endless silence followed.

'Someone *else*!' gulped Christy, trying not to sound too alarmed. 'What you mean someone else?'

There was a moment's silence before she continued.

'Well, okay. Here goes. I think I know another person who may have changed and now seems very interested in linking up with me to help stop the abuse at Greenridge. Now I'm still remaining your workmate. I think Greenridge needs caring people like you. We'll still continue to have this friendly relationship at work and all that. But after last night and our conflicting ideas, I think that's as far as it goes.'

'Who is this other person?' asked Christy, trying his best not to lose his head and go into a panic.

'At this time I can't give a name. He wants it to remain confidential. For now anyway. Maybe in the next few days or so it will become obvious to you who it is. We chatted twice. He approached me. I couldn't believe how warm and understanding he now is.'

'So he's a male staff member! A nurse! Who?' Christy now sounded anything but calm as his anger boiled over a tad. 'Look, Wendy. We need to see each other again. Another meal. I can apologise to that nice lady. See, there's a man, a lunatic named Benny Phillips who plays scams, and he's the one who –'

'Look, Christy, sorry for cutting across. I have to go. We'll see each other around work. I have someone calling to the house in ten minutes, I don't mean to be rude, but I have to fly. Bye.'

The line went dead.

Someone calling? A man! Christy's head went into a dark spin. He stood, holding the phone for a good three minutes trying to take in the horrifying news.

A slow pitiful walk over to the bin. he picked up the flowers he had bought for her and started ripping and twisting them in a deadly fit of deep, green-eyed jealousy. *Someone trying to take Wendy? I'll kill him, I swear I'll kill him, strangle him with my bare hands.*

*

I had plans to go Christmas shopping early in the morning after Sue rang me for the fourth time.

'Amy, you have to get out,' she stated in a strong, firm tone.

'Okay, okay,' I slurred.

'I'm not going to lie to you, Amy. Your dad rang and asked me to buzz you and not take no for an answer. In a day or so Rob will come around with a big Christmas plan and present and things will get back on track. He's just trying to get around everything in his own head. This has certainly knocked him for six. But bottom line, he loves you and that will be the telling factor. Mark my words, Amy.'

I sat on the edge of the bed and half-smiled. Those tablets were certainly working faster than I thought. 'You're such a great friend,' I garbled. 'I was asleep there . . . What . . . what time is it?'

'It's just after 3 o'clock.'

'3 o'clock? In the afternoon?'

'Yes. Are you okay? You sound . . .'

'Oh, god, yes. Never felt better. I thought I was dreaming . . . of Rob dancing with me in the Home Nightclub. And you were there, I think. And Claire. Colm was definitely there, standing watching us dance, giggling at us from the bar. Then he started crying. I asked Rob why. 'Why is Colm crying? Do you think he's very unhappy underneath everything?' Rob smiled and said something kind of funny. 'I think most people here are very unhappy and pretending. They're wearing masks, Amy. Nearly everyone's wearing them.' Then everyone who was dancing near us turned and started taking off what looked like masks, and they all started to cry. I was the only one who didn't cry. I awoke with a strange feeling in my tummy. Do you have strange dreams that seem so real, Sue?'

There was a pause.

'Then last night I had a dream this person was following me. I started to walk faster and was terrified to look behind me. I thought he said I was in danger. I told him this wasn't a real dream. And yet it was a dream, wasn't it? Do you have weird dreams, Sue?'

'Sometimes. Sometimes I do . . . Look, Amy. I'm getting into the car and coming around now. Don't move. I'm on the way.'

Chapter 13

The Perfect Storm

Sue drove at breakneck speed around to Amy's.

Des, who himself was on the phone to his sister about his own health issues, opened the door and then indicated with his hand that Amy was upstairs in her room. 'Go on up. Thanks, Sue.' He continued with his phone conversation. 'Yes, yes. Maybe if we all meet up tomorrow, I can explain everything in detail. The plan is to start treatment.' He lowered his voice, and then closed the door to the sitting room as Sue walked quickly up the stairs and tapped gently on the bedroom door.

'Amy? It's me, Sue.'

'Ahh, Sue. Lovely to see you.' After a warm embrace Amy opened the door fully and ushered her in. Sue scanned everything and wasn't long getting a bit of a fright at the sight. Amy stood there, still in her pjs, hair tossed. There was a noticeable change in her appearance. Little or no makeup on her face coupled with that frightened stare that they were so accustomed to seeing before Rob came into her life. 'Come in, come in. It's so cold, isn't it? I can't get the heat into me. Sit, sit,' she said as Sue took another swift look around the room. There was a half packet of biscuits plus crisp bags all over the floor. 'The mess, I know,' sighed Amy as she picked up three empty coke bottles and placed them on her bedside locker.

Sue gazed at Amy's wedding dress that was lying across a chair looking like it had been tried on more than once and had what looked like chocolate stains all over the front of it.

'Do you want a sweet? I've a box of Roses that were dropped in by Mr Freeman from across the street. Hate the coffee ones.'

Sue sat on the edge of the bed trying to take in everything and conjure up something positive to say. 'No, no, you're grand. I don't want to start eating them before Christmas. I'll never stop myself,' she laughed half-heartedly. 'Anyway, Des said you haven't been out of the house in three days and it's now four days to Christmas and you need to . . .'

'Everything's great, Sue,' she cut across. 'I've been here thinking for ages and I realised that I had to get rid of all my negative feelings, even towards Claire and Colm. It's the time of good will, as my mother always said. Forgive and forget. She'd say it every year. I texted them both last night and told them it's all down to people being very confused and unhappy in their own relationships. Like that dream about wearing masks, hiding our pain from the world around us. Now I want you and Tom to forgive them as well.' She looked straight into Sue's eyes in a wild almost frantic manner. 'It's Christmas and we are all to be friends again. You hear me, Sue? Promise me now you'll do that for me.'

'Emm . . . okay. I promise,' Sue agreed reluctantly.

'Did I tell you I had this other weird dream?' rambled Amy, 'that I was in hospital again and that Dad had died, and I couldn't go to the funeral, just like when my mother died. I woke up so terrified,' she paused to try and gather her thoughts. 'So anyway . . . Oh, yeah. I need to do all my Christmas shopping. You're so right, Sue. I need to get my act together. I've been so busy in my mind picking out gifts for everyone; I have my eye on something real nice for Rob that I saw in a magazine I was reading: a sky-blue jumper, his favourite colour. Where is that magazine?' She started searching for it anxiously as Sue sat observing her nervously, trying again to find the right words to say.

'Oh, and look. Come over here. Now this is just between us?' She directed Sue's attention to the dresser after a last failed attempt to find the magazine.

Sue stood up then observed that there were two notepads on the dresser and lots of single sheets of paper tossed on the floor.

'Don't tell anyone just yet, but I'm actually writing a kind of memoir or book about my mammy and about real love. Well, it's actually about how me and Rob met and fell in love. Here. Let me read you an extract.'

She took a deep nervous scary intake of breath, then paused and gazed in a trance for a moment. Then with an unsteady hand she picked up a single page. Her tiny fingers began to shake as she started to read aloud to Sue.

'Then he looks at me and I feel my heart go all warm, and I get so nervous. He's about to kiss me, and it's the way he's smiling and then that delicate touch that follows. It's his way of telling me . . .' She stopped as Sue put her arm around her.

There was a pause. Her mouth started to quiver.

The atmosphere changed radically. She turned and put her arms sluggishly around Sue.

'Everything is going to be just fine,' Sue whispered as Amy started to moan and cry, gripping one of Sue's arms more securely.

In a sluggish but painful gasp for air, she went into a slow, dark, agonizing screech. 'Jesus Christ, help me! Help me, Sue. I don't know what's happening to me anymore. I'm so, so scared!' She let go and went down on her knees, crying like a small child.

Sue did her best as she knelt down and held her, as close as was humanly possible, trying desperately to assure her that Rob would be back.

'I just want him back, Sue! I love him so much; I can't take this pain inside anymore. It's so deep and all I do at night is pray and cry out to God or someone to take the pain away. If I could! If only I was strong enough I would.' She sniffed.' 'I keep writing him letters, ringing him and texting. Why, Sue? Why won't he forgive me. *Why?*'

'God, Amy, please stop doing this to yourself. Rob's just a little bit hurt. That's all. He'll be back.'

'I keep thinking,' she continued, 'I keep thinking crazy stuff like I'm going to die soon and I don't know why, but I keep seeing horrifying images of myself dying alone in this awful dark space or room.'

'Look at me, Amy,' Sue managed as she herself filled up with tears. 'You're not going to die. You hear me? Look at me now. Don't be talking like that. You're a brave girl and you're not going to any dark place to be alone. My god, Rob's crazy about you, as everyone keeps saying. He'll be back, I swear on my granny Frances grave he will. This is going to be the best Christmas ever. You hear me?' She stressed her words as firmly yet as sensitively as she could.

'I want Rob to hold me again. That's all I want this year. That would be the best Christmas gift ever, Sue.'

'You're going to have all that and much, much more. I even wrote a letter to Santa myself,' she joked. 'On my life, Amy, If I have to go up and drag him down and make everyone apologise and make up, I will.'

Amy half smiled as Sue's determination seemed to open a tiny ray of hope. 'So, you're that sure that everything is going to be okay?' She wiped her eyes and blew her nose and sat up straight, looking further assured.

'You're my best friend and I assure you this will all be like a bad dream, come Christmas Day.'

After a good hour encouraging Amy, Sue got into her car and thought about it for a moment. 'Ahhh, why not! Go for it!'

She drove at speed to Rob's house. *I'll beg him If I have to. Anything to make things right again for Amy.*

*

Rob was still nervously keeping the odd eye out the window in case a vanload of travellers pulled up. Dragging out of a fag, another John Player Blue, he moaned. *A week I ago I was almost off these bloody things. Now I'm gone from ten a day to feckin' twenty.*

He saw his phone go. Peter.

'Hope you're sitting your arse down for this, Rob.' He sounded anything but excited as he himself checked his boarding times for his flights from London to Dublin.

'I'm standing! What's up?' Rob nervously sighed. 'Oh, I did that favour. I checked up at your house twice a day since we last chatted. In fact, I'm not long back,' he lied. 'Nothing dodgy to report.' He took another big drag from his fag and braced himself. 'Is everything okay? You sound very apprehensive. Is everything going okay with the big deal?'

'Okay. Here goes. I'm catching the 7.40pm flight home. Are you ready for it?'

'I'm listening,' gasped Rob as his eyes widened, almost popping out of his skull.

There was a prolonged silence.

'Are you still there?'

Another silence.

'Tell me what happened! Did something go bloody wrong?' he yelled in a panic.

'Just teasing. Ha, ha, ha! . . . Mmm . . . you're now worth 4 *hundred* and 60k.' He let that news sink in.

Rob had to catch his breath. He could hardly speak as he stood trying to take in the figures. Then with a sudden burst of emotion. 'You've got to be bloody kiddin' me!' he gasped. 'I won't believe it, not till I see it in my hand. No way!' he panted as his stomach packed up with excitement.

'460k, not a cent under or over,' laughed Peter. 'And the other investments that your hard-earned cash went into are sailing a pretty calm ocean at the moment with sunny and blue clear skies all the way. I told you years back, Peter Bradley never makes a shit investment. Look, I have to leg it or I'll miss my fight. See ye in the morning. Say 10am, your place? I'll have your cheque, but it won't clear for a few days.'

The line went dead. But just as Rob went to go into a complete frenzy, he saw a car pull up outside. He saw straightaway whose motor it was and was straight into action.

Sue nervously walked up to the door, took a deep breath and rang the bell. *Stay focused,* she told herself as she saw the sitting room door open and close. No light in the hallway came on. Then the front door opened slowly just enough to allow Rob's head to stick out fractionally.

'Rob, is that you?'

There he was with a dark scruffy beard growth, dark glasses, tossed hair. 'It's not a good time. I'd ask you in, but the place is a bit of a mess.' He paused. 'Anyway, what do you all want? Who else is out in the car?' he nervously asked as he put on the performance of his life.

'Em . . . God, are you okay? . . . Sorry for springing this on you. I'm alone. I came up to see could we talk. Five minutes is all it will take. It's about Amy, Rob. She's in a bad way and I was wondering could we sort this all out before Christm–'

'Why is it that you, Colm and Claire only always think of yourselves? After the mess you all caused? I'm closing this door now. You can tell Amy I'll be ringing her tomorrow,' came the less painful sentence. 'Now if you wouldn't mind, please. I'm not very well and the heat's getting out.'

He abruptly closed the door in an unsteady manner as Sue tried to reason with him in a heartfelt plea.

'We are all so sorry,' she just managed as inside, the sitting room door closed gently.

She got back into the car and sat for a moment, thinking. *This wasn't a great idea. My god, he's in some state. Dammit!* She put the car in gear and drove off.

Nearing Balbriggan she rang Tom who was half way across the UK driving towards Scotland with a full lorry. 'Look, I'm driving as well. Now don't ask a load of questions. I drove up to Rob's place. Don't ask why. Please, Tom! He's in a terrible state. Amy said she wants all this to end and we have to try and make up with both Colm and Claire. Tell me I'm doing the right thing? I feel it's my responsibility to at least try to do something to sort this mess out before Christmas.'

Rob sat back in his chair, lit another cigarette, taking the dark shades off with a big grin. *That was just bloody brilliant. She'll report this back. She's brainless, not bad-looking though,* he muttered with another grin.

There was a dark sense in the air as he then slowly stood up and walked over and took out a well-hidden folder from under a pile of books. On the cover was a newspaper clipping of Amy coming out of court. *Crash Victim Wins Painful Court Battle* was the heading.

Under it in black marker in Rob's own handwriting was *THE STRATEGY by ROBERT COOPER.*

He took a long, slow, pleasurable drag from his cigarette and tried to get his own head around the magnitude of what he'd just pulled off. He proceeded with a touch of indescribable excitement to open the folder and read step by step how he had first devised a plan to enter Amy's life with his clinical charm. Then, next step was to groom her and gain her trust by seeming to help her with her own emotional baggage and self-esteem issues. He grinned as he read on, flicking through every newspaper clipping of the court case. He read all the delicate steps he had taken with extreme care to this point in the plan. *You are without hesitation a pure genius, Rob Cooper, nothing short of a supernatural mastermind,* he thought. *My god, who else would have pulled this off? Who would have had that level of patience and not make one slip-up along the way? Nobody.*

He smiled as he closed the folder and grinned a deep, contented leer before placing the folder neatly back in place. *Tomorrow morning it will be all over.* 'No more hiding away with Jill'. He spoke the words out aloud with a sense of finality. He then picked up his phone and booked tables for a five-course meal at the Hannigan's 5-star Restaurant in Swords. He then rang around to invite a few mates and their girlfriends to be part of this special occasion.

'Yes, a five-course meal and all the drink you want, Ted. All free, all on me. And didn't I tell ye, ye little nerd! Worrying your little arse off, over them travellers. Nothing in the papers in days. That taxi guy was wise enough not to involve himself.'

'Feck's sake,' said Ted, 'how can you remain so calm? Every time I see a van with more than two big-built lads in it I start into a panic.'

'Ah will you stop and grow feckin' up. They were bluffin' the whole time. I was right all along. They saw nothing. Everyone has now turned his or her full attention to thinking about Christmas shopping and all this is forgotten about. Now get your head into the Christmas buzz and stop with the nerve-wracking. This is going to be the best one in years. Mark my words.'

'Bloody hope you're right,' sighed Ted as he started to feel more relaxed and assured.

Rob hung up then poured a glass of red wine and braced himself with a smirk and rang his parents in London with his number blocked. 'Yes, it's really me!' he sniggered before going on to outline everything about his good fortune. 'Yes, and if he's beside you, you can tell my good-for-nothing father what his son in Ireland has accomplished, and he certainly won't blow it this time around. Oul' Doubting Thomas never believed or even once encouraged me. Isn't that the sad bloody truth of it? No, listen to me. Am I right?'

'Look,' sighed his frail-spoken mother in a low appreciative tone, 'it's Christmas. Let's not dwell on the past for now. It's so great to hear from you, great to hear you've done well for yourself. Just be very careful with the gambling. Remember the pitfalls, and learn from your past mistakes. I'm not trying to kill the moment . . .'

Suddenly his father who was listening nearby grabbed the phone.

'What're you sayin'?' he barked.

'Aah, if it's not my wonderful father. Hey, your son, who had nothing growing up as a kid, has made it. Yes, you heard me. I'm a private investor, a millionaire. Swallow that one.'

'Huh, is that all you rang to say? To mouth off again, same oul' crap talk? Ha, did you go and clean out another little old lady of her Credit Union savings? Smart arse! Get the hell out of it! You'll blow the lot in the bookies as always. Why don't you get a real job? Big private investor, my arse! You never worked an honest day in your entire life. So when are you returning what you borrowed from your cousin Declan?'

Rob laughed his head off down the phone as his fierce anger boiled over. 'Ah, and here comes the perfect role model himself, who went and stole nearly 150,000 from your place of work and gambled the lot away on the horses, then went and fiddled heaps of your friends out of their hard-earned cash to try and put the money back before it was missed. Then when the cops wanted to interview you, what did you do, ye big coward? Yeah, you legged it to London to avoid them and certain jail time. And you're preaching to *me*? Ha, ha, ha! Go away, you horrible, jealous, bitter old twisted excuse for a man. You're the laughing stock of the entire world. The feckin' cheek of ye! You, the oul' alcoholic that you are, living in a rundown flat in a council estate on state benefits. Talking like this to me, ye big scumbag loser! Now put Mother back on. I didn't ring you.'

His father roared abuse back down the phone while his mother struggled to prise the phone from his grasp.

'Son, sorry about this. You know how short-tempered he is. Look, I'm so ashamed asking. But is there any way you could send me something? I'm struggling so hard to get by and . . .'

'Ma, sorry for cuttin' across you. But not if I had twenty million would I send a penny across. No, no, listen to me. You could have done better by me yourself by making a bigger effort to stop him blowing our future wellbeing away and losing a great job, but you failed as a parent just as much as he did. No, no, mother,' he snarled. 'Spare me the excuses.'

She went into the other room, closed over the door and whispered in a heartfelt begging plea: 'Please, Robert. I tried my very best. I'm desperate; I even got a small job at the time when your dad started gambling. Remember? There were days I worked two shifts to make ends meet for you and the girls. Please, son, I wouldn't ask only he's drinking most of the welfare and my health isn't getting any . . .'

'Ah, will you stop with the begging letter speech. You're embarrassing yourself and me. Now I've something to say. Put the phone on loudspeaker so that he can hear this as well.'

She walked unsteadily back into the other room where Rob's father was now opening his fifth can of cheap beer.

'The reason I rang,' he started in a deep revengeful tone, 'was to wish you both a happy Christmas. I feel it was only fitting to ring you both with the magical news of how I made it all on my own. Oh, I've waited years to say how totally and utterly ashamed I am to be even associated with you both. So from this moment onwards I'm erasing all memory of you. You will never hear from me again. I'm moving into high living surroundings, with people of high moral standing, respectable investors. So I couldn't have them hearing that my oul' lad was a thief and a no-good conman and is now living as a down-and-out tramp in London. I couldn't have that information coming up on the radar to shame me. So from today if anyone asks me, you're both now dead, both killed in a car crash while on holiday, rotting away in your graves abroad where I arranged to bury you. So to that end we'll say our goodbyes. Bye bye now,' he sniggered.

Just as he was slowly hanging up he could catch his mother's heartfelt plea. 'Please don't, son. I love you!' were her last words as his half-drunken father stood up and roared more abuse, bouncing his half-full can of beer off the kitchen floor in temper.

With a deep, satisfied stare in his eyes, he deleted their number from his phone, poured another glass of wine and rang Jill who was just home in her mother's after a tiresome day at work.

'My god,' she complained, 'we were so busy again today. My feet are killing me from standing. Queue was out the door all day long, everyone buying the most stupid books for Christmas, or gift vouchers. What? What are you laughing at?'

'I can't stop myself tittering, I just can't, and it's not the red wine, Jill.'

You're in stitches. What's happening?' she laughed.

'Peter just rang. You better sit down to hear this.' He didn't want to sound immature but with the wine he couldn't help himself. 'I'm half-way to being a millionaire! Ha, ha, ha! Who's the top cat now? Yes, you heard me. Close to a million. Plus, my other investments are sailing pretty along the shores and rocks of fortune. Hey, and forgive me, everybody, but I can't stop bloody smiling my arse off today.'

'Great, that's just great. But you told me all this last night. Remember?'

'But it's now confirmed. I've rang Ted. I'm booking tables

for a Christmas dinner in Hannigan's. Big steak dinner and a few scoops to celebrate all this. Peter Bradley himself will be attending. He's flying in as we speak.'

'Well, sure I'm so, so glad for you. But my feet are seriously killing me,' she moaned.

Rob took another mouthful of wine. 'I don't get you, Jill Watson. I seriously don't. I'm nearly in tears here with joy; I'm getting close to a million euro in the morning. It's Christmas, life couldn't be sweeter and what? You're moaning about sore feet? Come on, honey.'

'Oh, sorry. Did I go and spoil your whole life? Wish I could go over right now and join the celebration, but I'm booked in to sit with my granny Molly. Remember, Molly Campbell in the nursing home. She's slipping in and out of consciousness a lot.'

Rob's big smile drained away in an instant.

'Portmarnock Prophet Lady. Remember her famous old saying, *In the blink of an eye*? I'm always talking about her.'

'Oh, yes, the *blink of an eye* lady. Yes, yes,' gulped Rob. 'Well, look. You'll be up tomorrow evening as planned. We'll get a takeout. I have to ring Peter back, so bye.'

Bloody hell. Nursing homes, old people. he shivered at the thought. Okay, *deep breaths and cross back into my world of youthfulness and luxury.* He poured a fresh glass of wine and lit a fag and pondered further in his darkened mind how he was going to word everything to Amy.

*

Sue arrived home to her house after an intense 40-minute meeting with Claire and Colm. She rang Tom, who had now packed the lorry and was eating a burger and chips.

'Well,' sighed Sue as she threw her jacket over a chair, 'are you going to drop the silent treatment and tell me what you think?'

'Will you give me a sec to take in all you just said,' he moaned. He took the last bite from his burger and downed it with a mouthful of coke. 'To be completely honest, this isn't going to work out. It's too emotionally confusing, too raw, and way too early. You're insane if you think you're capable of smoothing over this big mess just because it's bloody Christmas. I know the way you're thinking, *let's all do this for Amy*. But listen to me, Sue. Amy isn't in her right senses, saying she wants to forgive and forget, just like that. It's them happy clappy, anti-depressants that's clouding her judgement no end.' He continued. 'Okay, so what exactly are Colm and Claire's big Christmas plans in all this?'

'Well, he said they're both going to the Platinum Gym now! Four days a week, he said. They even started doing evening classes, both on a strict diet. 'We're going to be in top shape in no time,' he even bragged. 'We're cutting out the heavy drinking, sure I'm down to two fags a day,' he said. Claire shaking her head up and down, agreeing to it all. Not a hint of regret or sadness about this big mess.'

'Right. So that answers everything. Pair don't give a crap about any of this. Look, I have to motor on here. Ring Amy and just encourage her that Rob's going to ring her. Leave them pair to their ridiculous fantasy. Bell you later when I arrive in Scotland.'

Sue took a deep breath and rang. 'Hi, Amy. Big news. Yes, I was briefly talking to Rob. Now I don't want to get your hopes way up, but he said he's ringing you at some stage tomorrow. On my mother's life they were his words.'

'What else? My god, I'm shaking here. Tell me his exact words. Was he asking for me?'

'I have to be honest. He looked very down, like he hasn't been taking care of himself, Amy. He's unshaven. He wouldn't engage in any big conversation but just said he was ringing you tomorrow, so I didn't push it. Didn't I tell you it would turn around for the Christmas? Now just one small matter. Myself and Tom feel very strongly that you should hold off trying to make up with Colm and Claire. Just stay focused on sorting things between you and Rob. Okay?'

I raced down the stairs to tell Dad after Sue got off the phone.

He was over the moon. 'What did I tell you! I promised you, didn't I? I told you once he had a little time alone to think, he'd be back for Christmas,' smiled Des as he tried to hide a letter from the hospital.

Ok, first things first, I gasped, racing back up the stairs. *Clean my bloody room and start looking half-normal again.* For a start I hid the wedding dress and then hoovered up all the biscuits crumbs with a huge smile firmly back as the excitement spilled over.

I threw an 80s love songs CD on. A tune rang out just as I had the whole room back to normal.

Why don't you come back?
Please hurry, why don't you come back?
Please hurry,
Come back and stay for good this time.

Paul Young singing the lyrics so powerfully.

After having a warm shower, doing my hair, and putting some make-up on I almost danced back down the stairs.

'I'm back!' I laughed as Dad turned around with a shocked expression. He was wrapping some Christmas presents but stood up and burst out in a heartfelt laugh.

'Rob is ringing me in the morning!' I said. 'He's coming back to *stay for good this time,* as the song says.'

'Good god, you look incredible. Well, what are we waiting for? Let's get the spirit back into this Christmas!' he joked.

'Oh, Dad,' I smiled. 'this is going to be the best Christmas for years. Sue and I are going shopping tomorrow morning. I have loads of lovely gifts picked out for Rob, for everyone.'

'Well, make sure you get plenty of wrapping paper, as I think I just used all of yours,' he chuckled.

It was a nightmare trying to sleep, and next morning I skipped taking my tablets. *Won't need them anymore,* I assured myself as I hid the pack of anti-depressants in the back of the locker. Texting Sue, I explained I'd ring her the minute the chat with Rob was completed, and then they'd head off shopping.

Rob sat back in a state of disbelief, almost in a trance as he viewed the cheque from Peter: €460,000.

As for Peter, his barriers were unexpectedly down as he became overly-ecstatic himself, while he clarified certain aspects of the outcome of the deal. He stayed on a good hour to provide Rob with in-depth information regarding all the other pending financial deals. He spoke briefly about the drug he had bought, briefly explaining that it was actually an active ingredient that they invested in that had to undergo multiple trial tests for well over two years before he agreed to buy it as an investment. But again, he wouldn't release the name of the person on the other side of the deal, or who the other investors were. 'You don't need all the ins and outs,' Peter explained, 'but what I want to make certain is that from here onwards you remain my priority for future dealings. But some aspects about my dealings and contacts, as you can imagine, everything has to remain confidential. Only for now. Till we all build up a more permanent relationship.'

'I've no problem with that, Peter. Bloody hell, man, it's a credit to you for all the years of groundwork that must have been involved to pull this off.'

'The full truth would blow your mind.' He smiled as he checked the time.

You're a pure genius, Peter,' smiled Rob as his own excitement spilled over into a lengthy laugh. He took a moment to compose himself before reaching out with a firm open handshake. 'And let me tell you,' he grinned, 'I think this is the beginning of a long and successful partnership.'

'Yes, I believe so. But that's if we don't get complacent. We have to play it safe and avoid any pitfalls,' said Peter, now with a more sobering expression. 'But remember – never, I mean *never* disclose any of our investment deals to anyone. Not even to your pretty girlfriend. People would kill to get the inside tracks I dig up.'

'Not on my life,' promised Rob. 'Lips are sealed.'

He took a few moments to gather his thoughts after Peter left. Then he slowly stood up and went to the fridge and took out a fresh bunch of grapes. He slowly and religiously washed them and then lined them up in a straight line on the table.

He had a last change to the plan. *I won't say I'm dating Jill, not just yet. That'd be plain stupid . . . Okay, here we go.* He rolled a grape under his tongue and across to the side of his mouth. Then he picked up the phone and rang Amy.

I was texting Sue when Rob's name flashed. My God! I felt weak with nerves. Taking a really deep breath I answered.

There was an endless silence.

'Hi, Rob . . .' I just managed as my bottom lip quivered uncontrollably.

There was another endless pause.

'Hi, Amy. Sorry for taking forever to return all your calls,' came the distant yet friendly response. 'It's been an extremely difficult time.'

'Well, Sue said you looked drained and unshaven. But look. Before we get into it, I know I sent you letters, phone texts, left a load of messages, but I personally want to say how deeply sorry I am again for how careless I was with the way I worded things. You're the best and most faithful guy any girl could hope for and . . .'

'Please – we went through all that, Amy. Sorry for cutting across. Can you just please hear me out for one second, please?' He rolled another grape under his tongue and to the side with the faintest of grins.

'Please do,' I gulped as I started to recognize how unstable I was still feeling. 'Take all the time you want. I'm listening to you here, for however long it takes.' Just hearing his voice was increasingly making it even harder to remain focused. *I'm making a complete mess of this, amn't I?*

1O, maybe I5 minutes later I could hear Dad coming in the front door. He must have heard me crying upstairs and shouted something back.

'Please, Rob, don't do this to me! I'm begging you here! I'll do anything you say! Please!'

'As I keep saying, Amy, and I hate this as much as you, but I've put tons of thought into this and it's the trust. The trust is gone, Amy! And as you just admitted yourself, none of this is actually my fault. I'll repay you every cent of the money I borrowed by late next year, if and when the investments hopefully come good, if that's –'

'I don't want the stupid money!' I screeched. 'I just want everything to be the way it was! Who is this girl Jill that's helping you recover?' I sobbed down the phone as I heard Dad race up the stairs.

There was an eerie pause. 'You need to know something else.'

'What?' I appealed. 'What are you talking about?'

'Des is very sick; he's been hiding it from you. I shouldn't be the one telling you this.'

'What are you talking about? Cancer! What cancer?' I twisted in thought.

'Look at him, Amy. He's very unwell. I shouldn't have said that. Look I've to dash; I've an appointment with my own doctor. I hope, I really do hope we can still be great friends. I truly want that more than anything else.' He hung up as I was about to speak.

'Rob!' I yelled, trying frantically to redial.

'God, what's happening?' asked Dad as he walked into the room, full of concern.

I threw the phone on the bed as it rang out. 'Oh, dear God, help me!' I cried out as I stumbled back and tried to gather my thoughts. Feeling faint I fell into a sitting position on the bed, my body quivering. 'It's over, Dad. It's actually finished for good. He's on sleeping tablets. He even has this girl Jill helping him.' I paused as the reality of Rob's last statement hit. 'Are you sick, Dad? Very sick? What's he on about? What in the name of God is happening?' I stared into my father's eyes, searching for reassurance.

He couldn't eyeball me. He went to turn towards the door but suddenly he just dropped the shopping bag and put his hand up to his mouth, filling up, but then composed himself rapidly. 'Amy, I'm okay. It's nothing serious. Got a small bit of cancer on one of my lungs.'

I slowly pulled his face around to mine, heart in mouth. 'You're okay, Dad? God, tell me you're okay,' I just managed in a petrified tone.

Between wiping his eyes he managed to tell me some of the facts, mainly that he was starting treatment. 'I'm sorry, Amy. I wanted you to continue being happy. I couldn't bring myself to land this on you. It's nothing, love. They got it very early. Thanks be to God, and your mother above.'

'You're not dying, okay?' I choked. Everything started to run riot in my mind as I stood back up. 'The stress, it's all my stress that's done this to you. Just like Ma, this is my fault.'

'Don't you dare say that! You hear me, Amy? Don't you go blaming yourself over that accident, and now my health!' He stood up as I walked over and leaned my back to the wall, fresh tears rolling down my face.

I kept staring at him. My eyes rolled back and forth, my face twisted and turned, mouth quivering with a profound intense pain as everything hit me like a perfect storm.

'Say something,' said Des as he pulled a hanky from his pocket and blew his nose and wiped his tears. 'What's happening with Rob?'

There was a prolonged silence before. 'We'll what did he say?'

I started laughing in an irrational way. 'Mammy gone, Rob gone. And now . . . and now . . .'

'Now, now,' Dad cut across and went to go into one of his little father speeches, but I shouted across the room as loud as possible for him to stop.

'I killed Mammy, Dad! It was *me!*'

There was a pause.

'What are you talking about, child! It was an acc–'

'It wasn't! I was texting. Yes, on my phone.'

There was a pause as Dad looked muddled.

'I was on my phone. Open your ears. That's the real truth. I killed her! She asked me to stop texting as everyone knew she hated people using a phone while driving, but I wouldn't, I lost control of the wheel.' I whimpered as he stared at me, with a confused glare.

'Stop this now! You're out of your mind on tablets. You're

suffering from shock. You've been strangely confused about a lot of things since the head injury. That's why we have to go back to see your doctor in the Mater Private Hosp–'

'No, Dad, everything is a lie! The whole court case was a lie. I lied under oath about the roadworks. It was me, your little princess. I'm responsible for killing Ma!' I slid down the wall as Dad slowly strode over, now looking traumatised.

'I talked to you in the hospital! You're not making any sense. You were very clear about what you remembered when the Gardaí interviewed you. I was there when they asked the questions.'

'I wanted to tell you the truth,' I sobbed, hardly able now to get the words out clearly. 'But remember what you said to me? Remember, Daddy, what you said when I woke up? Remember?' I shouted the last word, almost spitting the words in his face.

He stood looking still astonished as he tried to remember and take in everything being said.

'You told me as I wasn't able to attend the funeral you put a photo of me into the coffin with Mammy. Remember now? Yeah, I bet you feckin' do.' I felt my face burning up as I choked and shivered through the dark tears.

Des sat back on the bed. 'Yes, yes, I remember my words. And so, what's this got to do with anything? You're making no sense.' He slowly went to take his phone out. 'I'm ringing the doctor. You're unwell, Amy.'

'I thought,' I yelled, frightening him to the point that he dropped the phone to the ground, 'I thought and believed you wished it was *me* who was in that coffin and not Mammy. That's why you put my picture in with her. Isn't that all true? Isn't that what you meant that day in the hospital? There was I, feeling it was supposed to me who died. So how could I tell you the truth about the crash? And so I hid it all. I played it so well, didn't I, Daddy? Now as a result of my actions and your loss and the stress of the past three years, you've got cancer. Don't you see, Daddy?' I sobbed, trying to wipe my tears and nose with my sleeve.

He couldn't speak. He just stared with an unbearable expression of pain in his eyes, unable to respond.

'That's the horrible truth.' Now with my face buried in hands I muttered out the final statement. 'I killed Ma, and now you. I killed Rob. I killed everything good in my life!'

Chapter 14

The Financial Assassin

'Say something, Dad! Say something!' I howled at the top of my voice as he just sat staring at me with an expression of utter confusion and disbelief. 'Stop staring at me like that!'

'You're having a breakdown, Amy,' he muttered. 'I'm calling Doctor Bayle.' He picked up his phone and headed for the door and went to dial a number.

Now like a crazy person, I grabbed his arm in a violent, aggressive manner.

But he turned fast and twisted around to free himself.

'That's why I tried to take my life after the court case, Dad,' I stressed. 'That's why it took me three long painful years to visit the grave. Can't you see? Can't you hear me properly? I was responsible for the accident!' another horrible slur as I went dizzy and stumbled out of my standing enough for Dad to free himself from the grip. He gently pushed me back without a word and walked swiftly out the door and down the stairs. I just about regained my balance to avoid going down awkwardly on the floor. Now standing in the centre of the room, still repeatedly screaming how sorry I was and for him to forgive me.

Then everything went very strange and frightening. Amy remembered little else as everything went silent. A chilling flash went off in her head, she picked the book up that she was writing and started ripping pages out and flinging them around the room in hysterics, tossing the contents of make-up and perfume off the dresser. From that point, everything became a blur until hours passed and she saw herself under the covers in the bed, trying everything to remain perfectly quiet. She thought she heard what sounded like voices, police or detectives talking as if they were at a crime scene, taking notes.

Low whispers. 'The mirrors smashed. Watch where you're walking, Mark. There's blood on the carpet. Carefully bag up all the evidence.'

A younger male voice spoke with sympathy. 'Poor Rob Cooper put his heart and soul into this chaos.'

'You know she crashed the car herself and concealed the facts for three years,' muttered another.

'Yes, texting while driving,' said a female in a low, undoubted tone.

'There will have to be a new trial.'

'She may face a jail term.'

Confident agreements followed before everything when silent.

Amy was too petrified to pull back the covers to even peep. *Surely they know I'm under the covers. Surely. Maybe not. Maybe if I just stay so, so quiet . . .* she thought as she became increasingly terrified to even breathe. She slowly prayed her heart and soul out that they wouldn't find her.

Suddenly she looked to her right in the darkness and saw what looked like the inside of a clock or watch. Springs and small gadgets and arms all working in harmony as she slowly reached across.

It was then she heard a soft voice beside her as a flicker of sunlight entered from a small gap under the covers. 'Hey, why don't we skip school just for today and stay here a while more!' came the warm, friendly laugh as a guy tried to put his hand up the front of her jumper for the second time.

It was Jason Boland from 6th year.

'Sshh! Will you stop! My mother will hear us and come up the stairs!' She giggled as she looked down into his gentle, caring eyes. 'We have our Irish exam at 11am, remember? We have to go now, Jason. Right now!' She tried to see the time on her watch. 'It's 10.25,' she said in a light-hearted whisper before looking back down into his eyes. 'What? What?' She asked as his dilated eyes stared intently up and directly into hers.

His facial expression now surprisingly altered.

There was a pause.

'God, Amy,' his voice trembled, 'I love you so much.' His words, so real, so powerful and straight from somewhere new.

There was a strange, almost frightening, emotional silence.

'My God, Jason!' she gulped with a huge lump in her throat, 'where did that come from? You never talk like that. Never, ever.'

'Amy! Amy!' She heard a voice calling. It was Des. He was at the bedside as she came out of a deep coma-like sleep. 'Amy, everything's okay. How are you feeling?'

She felt so drowsy and hardly able to lift her head off the pillow. With great difficulty she just managed to open her eyes and saw a figure of a girl standing beside her dad. It was Sue.

'Don't try to get up, Amy. Rest. You need to rest. Try not to move your right hand. There's a dressing on it. You have a few small stitches from a cut. The doctor was here yesterday. He gave you something, an injection.'

Amy slowly looked across to the other side of the room and thought she could see that the full-size mirror had been smashed. Even some wallpaper around the dressing table was torn and scratched. Her mouth was dry as she tried to lick her lips.

Des gave her a small drink of cold water. 'Gently does it,' he said with a half-smile.

'Jason Boland. I saw him,' she began, as the tears welled. 'He was here, Sue. In this room. He said, he said he . . .' The memory now seemed not as real but as she started to doze, a few more odd recollections that had been wiped clean from her memory flooded in and imposed themselves back into her mind.

'I wrote you a letter, but don't read it till you're up in your room.' Jason smiled as he threw his schoolbag over his shoulder and put his hand out to stop the 33 bus to Skerries. He leaned back and grabbed her to give her one last warm kiss.

'You're amazing and I love you, Amy,' he winked.

I couldn't wait. I opened the letter there and then in full excitement. *Gosh!* I gasped as he clearly poured his feelings out to me in a three-pager.

. . . Isn't it the connection that we have? Amy, I woke up Saturday night, 2.15am, and as true as you know me, I could feel your presence

here with me in my room. There's times when I'm with you, and we're just chatting about nothing and I feel something I can't put into words in this letter but I know you know what this is, but being honest, Amy, it scares me to think of it for too long. So strange, yeah. So what's this we have, Amy? This connection, this magic, this closeness . . . time with you means everything to me . . . Sure let us just travel with this. Will we? . . .

I stopped reading to keep the rest for home as his bus pulled away. His eyes sparkled as he mouthed to me that he loved me. Only me.

I waved and waved with such excitement . . .

Sue sat on the bed as I came back from the warm memory. I felt a little more alert but whatever was in the injection, the pain of the whole situation seemed to have disappeared.

Sue took my hand firmly and looked intently at me. 'Jason Boland went away to Canada, remember? Years back. You dated him for a long time but then spli–'

Des interrupted and threw an eye at Sue as he came over and sat on the other side of the bed, looking very concerned.

'I'll leave you both to chat and I'll make a nice pot of tea,' smiled Sue as she gave me a huge hug and headed out the door and down the stairs.

I sat up and gave the room another glance before directing my eyes intently at my dad who seemed to be preparing for a lengthy speech.

'Okay, Amy. I've to keep to the doctor's strict terms,' he finally said in the deepest caring tone ever. 'This isn't easy to say, but here goes. You were close to a full-on breakdown here yesterday. Yes, very close. There's too much happening emotionally and your mind isn't able for any more of this stress. So okay, it's three days to Christmas, and you have to do nothing stressful at all. Nothing! You hear me, pet? No reading, texting, ringing. Nothing but rest for at least two full weeks. You hear me now? Rest, that's it. And loads of walking was the doctor's advice. Sue and Tom are going to help. When we get the Christmas out of the way and you're feeling back to yourself, we're going to sit down and talk about everything in full. But not now.'

He didn't look angry, just deeply concerned, as I nervously looked away. He turned my face back.

'You think you know all the facts but you . . .'

'*You* think you do,' I went to correct him, but he stopped me.

'Not another word till after Christmas and you're back on your feet. Now before you jump in, I had my own first treatment this morning and everything isn't as bad as even I thought. I've a few years left, the doctor assured me.' He smiled with a strong air of confidence.

There was a pause as he handed me my anti-depression tablet with a fresh glass of water.

'I haven't got any more tears left, Dad. That's the God's honest truth of it.'

He put his arm around and held me and reassured that everything was going to work out fine.

I said nothing else, as my energy levels were so low. I shuffled different thoughts in my head: *Dad's health; the truth about the accident; and Rob.*

I lay back and kind of gave Dad a confused, funny look and gently asked, 'Did you ring the guards or detectives? Were they in my room?'

He gave me a searching stare. 'No! But if you get out of that bed and don't rest, I'll get a few Balbriggan Gardaí up here in a flash. I'll even ask that great detective Pat Marry himself to have a word with you,' he chuckled. He looked at me with a gentle gaze. 'We're going to be all okay. You hear me now?'

After Sue came back up, Dad left the room.

I started to ramble and ask her about Jill Watson and did she remember ever seeing her or what she looked like. 'And what about Rob? I mean, what's going to –?'

'No more till after Christmas, Amy. No more stress till you're well enough to talk about it. We have to get you back firmly on your feet again. So,' she smiled, 'now do you want to start telling me what gifts I can pick up for you later today? Let's make out a small list.'

*

Christy spent the whole day off trying to come up with a way to get Wendy back into his way of thinking and find out who this other scumbag male worker was who was moving in on his patch.

He got one huge relief to his growing problems when Dr Grimes rang him late that afternoon. 'Just wanted to inform you that at the staff meeting today I informed everyone that this supposed relationship that's going on, that it was nothing but an ugly rumour, that there wasn't any kind of hanky panky going on between you and the young Carmel Barnes,' he joked. 'I had them inform every staff member of this fact and there was to be no more whispering. Or they'll have to answer to the big dog. Me.'

'Oh, Dr Grimes, I cannot thank you enough for this. Thank you so much. The embarrassment alone that I, Christy Boyle, would stoop as low as that. My god, the sick pestering and advances I've been subject to . . .'

'Yes, yes, we went through it all today, so let that be the end of it. Now, as was asked today, will you keep a close eye on the medication distribution? Certain treatments are unaccounted for.'

'Oh yes, I'll make it my business to do a full check on everyone's medication charts when I return to work in the morning. Thanks again, Dr Grimes, it's a huge weight off my mind and I –'

Grimes hung up mid-sentence.

Next morning Christy sneaked around the place, following Wendy from the time she arrived for work. He kept his head down and did his jobs, keeping well out of sight. But the tension was unbearable. He ducked and dived down one hallway after another watching and making note of every man she spoke with. *Wonder if it's him . . . No, he's too stupid and plain ugly,* he jeered under his breath as his jealous eyes scanned everyone. *Maybe it's*

Noel feckin' Jennings! No . . . wouldn't be the Wendy type.

Finally, the breakthrough came late afternoon when he spotted Wendy slipping away on her own, looking nervously behind her as she checked her phone again and again, walking hurriedly away up the long stairway. He followed behind. *Don't let her see you, you big idiot!'* he breathed, diving to the ground just in time.

She headed to one of the old bathrooms at the back of the hospital and closed the door anxiously behind her.

Christy crept forward almost on his tippy toes. *Feck's sake, did you have to wear these big oul' working steel-cap boots!* he hissed under his breath. *You sound like a bloody big farmer's horse!* He just made it across the noisy floor without making any huge amount of noise and put his ear to the door. He could hear a man talking but couldn't recognise the voice or make out what was being said, one to the other.

He then hid himself behind a large stack of fresh bed sheets at top of the stairway and waited to see who emerged from the room.

A good ten minutes passed and then, out walked Wendy doing her blouse up. Behind her, male nurse Rex Read strolled out, all smiles.

Christy's chin dropped. His face went from half normal to intense red to green with a murderous jealousy. *'YOU!'* he mouthed and then inhaled.

Rex grabbed Wendy's hand, pulled her back into his arms and gave her a prolonged kiss as they both giggled.

'Stop, will you, Rex!' she gasped. 'Not here. Okay? I'll meet you for a chat outside working hours, but in the meantime will you take in all I'm saying, and think hard about my plan? We need to move fast before another poor helpless patient is beaten up or maybe even worse.'

'Of course I will,' smirked Rex, looking anything but sincere. 'But let's take it *real* slow,' he grinned. 'It may be very dangerous exposing people too fast. If individuals high up the ladder get wind of our plan to expose them, it may end up with us both being fired. So let's be extra careful. And in the meantime, let's just have ourselves a little drinkie-drink. Mmm? You look so stunning wearing that uniform. What do you think?' he smiled as he tried for another kiss.

Christy had both fists clenched, his eyes bulging out of his head. He just about held it together as he trailed back to the locker room, closed the door and let all the hellish jealousy spill out. He kicked the toilet door, then repeatedly punched a locker door, leaving huge dents. He held his right hand as he saw a swelling appearing across his knuckles. *Big shithead Rex Read kissing my Wendy!* The torment deepened as he screamed. 'Ahhhhhhh!' He punched out again, this time breaking open a locker door with the force. *This is a nightmare I don't want! Please tell me this isn't happening to me.* His head started to go completely before he took a deep breath. *Okay, calm down. Relax. Deep intake of breath and a drink of water.* He opened his locker and downed a mouthful from a plastic Ballygowan bottle.

As he started to calm slightly down he suddenly noticed someone had placed an envelope under the door of his locker. He wiped his mouth slowly with his sleeve and saw it was just addressed to *Christy xx*. He ripped it open and unfolded the single page.

It started:

Dear Christy,

Would you consider a trial date?

He glanced to the bottom of the page.

Carmel feckin' Barnes? I do not believe this! He ripped the letter before reading another sentence and tossed it across the locker room. Putting his now sore knuckles up to his mouth to nurse them, he screeched. *Rex Read, you're one dead man. I promise on me father's grave, you won't do this to me and get away with it!*

He waited till 5.30pm till he saw Rex heading to the locker room himself, all smiles and whistling the tune,

'You've got me, babe,
And I've got you, babe,
La, la, la.'

Christy walked in as Rex did a small dance then a whirl move while changing out of his uniform. Christy with clinched fists and sweat running down his forehead waited until a staff member left. Then he closed the door with a loud bang.

'Can I have a small word with you, Rex?' he asked, now in a polite tone. His anger seemed well concealed, but his red, puffed-up face gave it away.

'Sure, fire away, Christy. But make it short. I'm in a mad hurry.'

'Well, there's no easy way to say this, so here goes. What are you playing at with Wendy Collins? What's your involvement with her? No, don't give me that surprised stare. Don't! You were seen today upstairs, playing the flirty-flirty, and kissing the woman. Now let me give you some sound advice, a warning in fact.' He upped his tone to a yell. 'Back the hell away, Rex! She isn't interested in you and your little drinkie-drink games!'

Rex looked astonished. 'Hey, hey, Christy!' he finally smirked as he flexed his chest out. 'Don't you bloody dare question me about my personal life. Who I can and can't date, etc. The bleedin' cheek of ye! Now get the hell out of me face!' he fumed as Christy's head started to go.

'Now listen to me, Read. I know your type. We all do. You always go for the new nurse on the block till you get your wicked way. Then you always dump them for the next. I see everything around here and Wendy Collins is a decent, respectable young lady from a good home, and you're preying on her vulnerabilities. And I'm not sitting back keeping my mouth shut and allowing it to happen.' He clenched his fists and gave Rex the eye.

Rex stood further back and looked Christy up and down almost in astonishment.

Christy was in again. 'You're telling her you're going to help her with the Greenridge abuse? Ha! A big lie if ever I heard one. You're no more interested than the man up there in the moon. I have you sussed out. You're a lying, good-for-nothing, two-faced womaniser!' he yelled as he started to lose it further and moved closer to Rex.

'The bleedin' cheek of ye, butting your big red-veined nose into my personal life. This is none of yours or anyone else's damn business!' He paused, then stood further back before bursting into a fit of uncontrollable laughter, slapping his leg with his hand.

'Stop laughing! What are you laughing for!' yelled Christy as Rex caught his breath.

'You! You feckin' fancy her yourself! That's it, isn't it? It's written all over your bleedin' face. You, an oul' lad, into Wendy Collins! Ha, ha, ha!'

Christy snapped, lost it and tackled him. They both fell to the ground with a loud crashing noise and began to roll over and back awkwardly around the floor.

'Get your bloody hands off me, ye big fool!' gasped Rex as he tried to free himself.

'Stay away from my Wendy, you hear me!' gasped a breathless Christy as they rolled around some more like a pair of children in a schoolyard. 'I'm the better man; you just want to hurt her!'

Rex finally got the better of the childish tussle and got to his feet as male nurse Noel Jennings barged in the door.

'What the hell are you pair playing at?' he yelled as Christy struggled to his feet, trying to pick up his shirt buttons that had popped out in the struggle.

'I'm out of here,' snarled Rex. 'You'd want to get that head of yours seen to fast!' he yelled as he grabbed his jacket and marched out, fixing his own shirt back into his trousers as he walked.

Christy never opened his mouth. He just fixed his hair, brushed himself down and marched out, blood boiling.

Noel shouted after the two of them. 'Be a little more professional, the pair of ye!' He then bolted the door, took a deep intake of breath before opening his locker and proceeding to take more stolen medication. He placed his hand into his side pocket and carefully placed two more boxes of stolen tablets, placing them at the very back of the locker.

Staff goin' bananas as well. Lovely. Just lovely. Thanks, lads. Just what I need. Hell's bells instead of Christmas bells this year. Pains in my head are getting' way worse. Haven't been able to sleep. Maybe I should go back to work in London before I have a huge breakdown. Someone is watching this hospital. Secret cameras all set up. I sense it. My god, we're all going to be caught beating patients up. Jailed for 15 big ones. Okay – three yellow tablets, down you go. Maybe one blue lad. Down you go as well. He swallowed.

I can't take much more. He looked at his reflection in the mirror. *Oh, my good god, the weight's falling off my face from all the tablets. I'm takin' far too many. I have to try and wean myself off them before I get hooked again.*

He waited a good ten minutes. *Ah, that's it. My god, stop with this worry. Ahhhhh, yes, feel much better. Much better now.*

*

Christy, now back home, pacing up and down, absolutely freaking it, images of Rex kissing Wendy still fresh in his mind. *Dirty, rat-face scumbag, trying to take her away from me! That will NOT transpire! That you can be sure of.*

He went to the curtain to try and eagle-eye Wendy leaving for home. He took a quick glance up at the photo of his father. *Don't you start at me! One stupid mistake! It was the drink – and that fool, Benny feckin' Phillips.*

Suddenly he heard female voices outside in the car park, approaching.

'Wendy, can I have a small word?' he pleaded in a low, friendly tone.

But she put both hands out to stop him in his tracks. 'Nothing to say to you, Christy.'

'The rules state you can't be hugging with staff and . . .'

'Nothing to say. Bye.'

'Rex cares nothing for Greenridge,' he uttered in a low tone. But Wendy was already in her car. She turned the key, reversed back and drove away.

'He's no bloody good, Wendy! He's nothing but a flirt, a

user!' he yelled after her.

He sat back down later than night and stated writing a long letter.

Dear Wendy . . .

On and on he wrote until he was on page five, pouring out his undying love to her.

Then later that night he woke with a strict order from his father. He got up and headed to the locker room, picked up his boxing gloves and medal along with a wet towel. The plan was to leave no visual facial marks on any of his unfortunate victims. *Just body blows I hear you dad.* With a dark glare, he paced unnoticed back down to B Ward. Again, Paddy Blake who had held the knife to the nurse's throat was again his main unfortunate victim as Christy handed out extra punishment to him alone.

'Everything went horribly wrong today!' he shouted as he let all his frustrations out on the poor defenceless man. 'You're showing little or no signs of improving. You're a waste of oxygen, is what you are!'

Christy boxed him around the ribs a number of times before walking away, giving off one of his warp-minded victory salutes.

Mel Flynn once again had the closing words. With one eye pressed up to the small window in his cell, he repeated his familiar sentence.

'Once you don't tell,

No one goes to hell!'

Christy couldn't sleep. He twisted and turned, Wendy's beautiful face and smile turning over and over in his mind.

He got up and started to think seriously. *If it's the last bloody thing I ever do in this life of mine, I'm going to win her back to me. Speedy feckin' Read needs to have himself a little accident. That's it, take him out of the picture for a while, that's it. Something that will hospitalise him for a good six months. But think, Christy, think, how, what way can I hurt the little scumbag. How?*

Next morning at around 11am while patients were having their Christmas visits, Noel Jennings' beeper went.

It was Dr Grimes in a serious panic. 'Get your head in gear, Noel,' he gasped. 'Two top inspectors are heading to inspect the hospital.'

'You're joking!'

'Of course I'm not bloody joking!' he yelled. 'We have half an hour to forty minutes to get everything looking half normal. Go, go, go!'

'Calm down! My god, why does everything have to be a panic around here?' yelled Noel. 'I'm on it!' he said in a dead calm tone.

Noel spread the word calmly to as many nurses and kitchen staff as possible as Rex Read dragged himself into action from tittering around in the canteen, drinking coffee with Wendy. Christy was starting to rewrite his letter to Wendy when the call from Grimes came in.

'Two top HSE inspectors, I think! Do I have to spell it all out?' seethed Grimes.

Christy's head went into a spin. 'Oh my god! Wendy, she's after spilling her guts to the authorities!' he slurred as he stood up and threw the letter to one side. 'What have you gone and done now?'

Noel Jennings gave final instructions to a number of staff before slipping away to the locker room for a top-up on the tablets. *My god, I was right, they know something about me! The rat Christy rang them! No, no, calm down. They're just doing a small Christmas inspection. Routine-like. Get your head in gear fast.*

He took four, maybe five tablets in one go before slamming the locker in frustration and racing out, looking full of confidence. 'Right, everyone. Smile and look smart and professional.'

Dr Grimes raced into the main hall with Nurse Whelan and Peters on either side, looking anything but calm. 'They're here! A man and woman just pulled up! Noel, come with us. The rest, look busy! And you,' he pointed at Carmel Barnes. 'Stay out of sight.'

Two tense hours later.

'Yes, yes,' remarked Inspector Aiden O'Sullivan, as his

assistant Miss Paula Carroll took the last few notes. 'I'm very impressed. Just make sure for my return that you have the CCTV cameras in the main hall fixed immediately. And I want to look into getting some of the smaller wards fitted with extra ones as this complies with new rules. Place looks great and all your report sheets are up to date.'

'Well,' said Dr Grimes with a broad smile, 'as always we give it one hundred and ten per cent. We care deeply for all the patients as if they were family – as you both clearly sensed.' He gave a sigh of relief, followed by a little sly wink to Nurse Whelan. 'I'm so glad you like the new improvements to our health and safety and once the CCTV is installed it will be the complete hospital. You know, some accuse me of being a perfectionist, but as I'm not afraid to stress, I want to take the responsibility to improve and raise every area of the wellbeing of both staff and patients to a new level.'

'Your staff awareness and professionalism are one of the best I've seen in any hospital,' Mr O'Sullivan continued.

Miss Carroll was observing everything and taken notes. For the first time she spoke further words of tribute to the work being done. 'Massive changes since we were here last year, massive!' she stressed as they walked towards the main hall to say their goodbyes.

Suddenly just across to the left sitting outside the washroom waiting to be brought in sat a little old man, crying as an elderly woman sat in the queue beside him, smiling then laughing, playing in a world of her own with a small comfort blanket.

'Okay, moving on,' stressed Dr Grimes as Noel Jennings swayed a little from the effects of the intake of tablets.

But Miss Carroll stopped and with a hint of sadness asked, 'What's wrong with that poor man?'

Whelan tried to brush it off and usher everyone on towards the main doors. But Grimes stepped in to make sure the inspection ended on an even higher note.

'Let me ask,' he smiled, bending down and in a gentle tone. 'Now what's all this? And don't tell me there's nothing wrong.'

He checked with a sly nod to Nurse Whelan for a name.

'Mr Alan Galvin. She whispered.

'Now, now, what's the matter, Alan? Tell me. Mmm? Tell me why you're upset like this. It's Christmas. Did your mammy not come in to see you today? Ahhhh!' he guessed.

The man looked up with a frightened glare at all the faces looking down at him. 'She . . .' – pointing at the old lady next to him – 'She took . . . She took my glasses,' he snuffled.

'Ohhhh, okay,' smiled Dr Grimes. 'we can fix that. You just dry those little tears and let me get them for you.' He turned to everyone. 'This happens all the time. Should have remembered it was only days ago she did this to him and I had to intervene on that occasion.' He placed his hand on her shoulder. 'Now, now, Miss Fray isn't it. These are Mr Galvin's glasses . . . Yes . . . He just wants them back . . . Gently does it . . . You know, this is the third time you've done this in a week. Remember? Come now, off they come. Now . . . That wasn't hard, was it?'

He gently gave them back to Mr Galvin before turning to everyone. 'Easy as that!'

'I can't see, I can't see!' howled Miss Fray. 'My glasses! My glasses! Who took my glasses?'

'Now, now, Miss Fray, they're not yours,' stressed Dr Grimes as Mr Galvin stood up beaming, waving and doing a few dance steps in a victory celebration.

'I have glasses! Look at me, everyone! I have glasses!' He grabbed Miss Carroll who nervously pulled back, trying to remain all smiles.

'Yes, yes, you have your glasses back.'

'I have glasses,' he took Dr Grimes's hand, then Mr O'Sullivan's. 'I was blind but now I have glasses!'

The door opened and Nurse Jeffries stepped out as Miss Fray had to be held down as she continued to cry out, 'My glasses!'

The nurse stepped forward and grabbed the glasses off Galvin. 'Now, now, you don't wear glasses!' she announced. 'Here's your glasses back, Miss Fray. Now come on, Mr Galvin. You're next for a wash.'

Everyone slowly turned their heads and stared at Grimes as he stood red-faced and speechless. Mr O'Sullivan's warm smile was now changed to a look of serious doubt.

But before the embarrassment had time to settle, a small group of patients, some coming from their family Christmas visits, arrived into the main hall.

One small chubby man with wild eyes appeared, holding a small banjo. 'Look what my granny bring me,' he beamed. 'Can I sing now?' he said as he directed his words towards Miss Carroll and O'Sullivan with a hint of excitement appearing.

'Now, now, all back to the recreation room,' ordered Grimes in a warm friendly tone as he gave Whelan a face to help end this saga. 'Now I'll walk you both to your car. Shall I?'

However, both Miss Carroll and O'Sullivan at the same time asked if they could hear the man play.

Nurse Whelan, now trying to keep her own irritation under wraps, politely stepped forward. 'This is poor Mr Tony Morris. He imagines in his mind he's part of an Irish folk band. Poor man hasn't a note in his head. Now can we move out to the car park?' she suggested.

'Me sing for you!' Tony fearlessly stepped forward in a confident stance demanding the attention mainly of Miss Carroll.

'Oh, it's Christmas. Sure why not let him have a bash!' said Mr O'Sullivan with enthusiasm. 'Isn't this a part of the rehabilitation? To encourage, to embrace, as we were stressing earlier?' he pointed out with the first signs of irritation at their now lack of encouragement.

'Well of course,' stepped in Grimes recovering the situation best he could. 'Let Tony have his little moment. Sure why not!'

His face beaming brightly, Tony stepped into the middle of the hall and got ready, as his excitement was clear for all to see. He hit one note, stopped, then did a little fine-tuning.

'Sorry!' he said as a few more patients assembled and even a few staff took a moment to listen.

'The Dubliners. Yeah . . . and it's one, two, three.

As down the glen came McAlpine's men

With their shovels slung behind them.
'Twas in the pub they drank the sub
And up in the spike you'll find them.
They sweated blood and they washed down mud
With pints and quarts of beer
And now we're on the road again
With McAlpine's Fusiliers.

He continued to a line of absolutely stunned faces.

'My good god,' gasped Mr O'Sullivan, 'I can't believe what I'm hearing! Close your eyes and you'd bet your life's savings it was Ronnie Drew himself. He gave Whelan a look. 'Not a note in his head? Get your ears checked!'

Miss Carroll was in full agreement as she then even began to clap her hands and encourage some of the standing staff and patients to join in with the encouragement.

Tony now in full swing from the encouraging words stripped off his shirt, showing off his sweaty hairy chest as the place went mad.

'Up the Real I.R.A.!' yelled Fredrick Bowles from behind one of the pillars.

I stripped to the skin with the Darky Flynn
Way down upon the Isle of Grain.
With the Horseface Toole I knew the rule
No money if you stop for rain . . .

Nurse Whelan was fit to murder when Miss Carroll nudged her and Noel Jennings to clap along. Noel wasn't fazed as he clapped along in his own happy buzz.

'No bother, Miss! Wooooooo!' he clapped as Grimes started clapping away, all smiles. 'It's wonderful alright!' he gasped, trying to seem completely in on the thrill.

Suddenly Mary Howls came in, bearing her fading facial bruising from a blow from Whelan. She kicked off both slippers without a moment's hesitation and was away, dancing to the tune.

'Wow! Go, girl!' clapped Miss Carroll.

Nurse Whelan's blood boiled at the sight of Mary dancing so

well and getting the warm praise.

I remember the day that Bear O'Shea
Fell into a concrete stairs . . .

continued Tony as he gave it his all. Nearly every patient now watched with entertained faces, some clapping.

A second song was allowed that almost lifted the roof off Greenridge. Yes, a rare and wonderful magical moment in an otherwise dark and painful dwelling which ended with a huge roar of thankfulness for the two talented patients.

'Bravo! Bravo!' shouted everyone.

'My god, what a hidden bit of talent!' shouted Miss Carroll as she turned to shake hands with Mary Howls who was beaming more from the fact she overcame her fear just this once in front of Nurse Whelan. 'Has anyone a gift? Anything we can give Mary for her wonderful performance? What a brilliant bit of Irish dancing!' she stressed. She looked to Grimes, not wanting to sound like she was overstepping the line. 'Oh, maybe I'm getting carried away . . .'

'Kate!' said Mary. 'My Kate. That's all I want in the whole world. Please!' she gasped in a now terrified tone as she glanced in the direction of Nurse Whelan whose face went bright red.

'Kate who?' asked Mr O'Sullivan before Miss Carroll had a chance.

'Her little baby, Mary's little doll,' came the voice of Fredrick Bowles who was still watching the proceedings from just out of sight, near the main doors. He ran off before anyone's head had time to turn.

'Oh, we had to take it off her as the other patients were taking it from her,' Nurse Whelan was in with a lie and a smile. 'Sure we'll get it for her, for Christmas.'

A nurse came back after fetching it.

'Well, great. Here you go,' smiled Miss Carroll.

Mary's hands were trembling. Tears filled her sad eyes as she almost grabbed it before feeling, then smelling and then hugging, kissing the small doll as if it was her own child. Suddenly she broke down completely. 'Ahhhh, Kate, my baby, my little, little baby girl. I missed you so, so much.' She hugged it as if her life depended on it.

Miss Carroll filled up. She walked away up the hall sobbing as Grimes stepped in with a low whisper. 'Her three-year-old child Kate was hit with a car right in front of her some 42, maybe 45 years ago. The report read that she stopped to talk to a lady friend and let the child's hand go for a second. Shattered her mind completely,' explained Grimes as he walked both O'Sullivan and Miss Carroll to their car.

Once back in the office Grimes stared out the window with Noel. 'They're still sitting in the car, and they don't seem so happy now. They're writing further notes,' he hissed. 'Writing more stuff about me I bet,' he turned, fuming. 'All over a stupid pair of glasses. Can you believe that, Noel? Say something! I had them both eating out of my hands till this happened. Over a pair of silly glasses I was made to look a compete liar. Can you believe it, Noel?'

'Wasn't that big a deal. Look at the positives. We covered everything else. They could have asked what happened to Frank Crosby. You jumped in nicely saying he had a fall while at home for the weekend.'

'Yes, and what if they check and find he has no bloody family! Another big fat lie by me to add to the glasses. Not to mention Whelan saying Tony couldn't sing to save his life. My god, that man even blew me away, and I don't like ballads.'

Nurse Whelan locked the washroom door behind her as she approached Mary Howls who was singing a song while carefully drying her doll Kate after a small wash in the sink.

'All clean and ready for little afternoon sleep?' Mary whispered softly.

'Turn around,' muttered Nurse Whelan in a low, cold tone. With arms folded she laughed. 'You think you're a wonderful dancer now, ha? Making a full show of yourself is what you did. Well you can keep Kate. For a little while, till I say it's time to take her away again. Remember you're the one that let go her hand. Remember?' she sniggered.

She stood continuing to sneer as Mary held Kate, terrified to even look up. Then suddenly Whelan lifted her big fat leg without warning and slammed the heel of her shoe full weight down on one of Mary's bare feet. The pain shot up her leg as she collapsed to the floor, still holding Kate but not a scream from the pain as the shock kept everything at bay for a few moments.

'You'll hardly be able to dance again now, will you?'

She unlocked the door and signalled to a nurse in the hall that was passing. 'Mary had herself a little fall. Take her over to the hospital wing immediately. I'll write the report.'

*

I sat trying to get the heat into myself as I tried to settle alone on the sofa. Two days to Christmas. The doctor gave me something different, a stronger tablet to take when he called that morning, which left me feeling weird. I kept seeing Rob's face and smile, constantly playing out over and over in my head but the reality of the situation was kept at bay. Just.

Sue had bought me a jumper close to the one I wanted to get from the magazine, and it was all wrapped neatly under the tree while I continued to live in the hope that he'd click back into his old self and appear at the door. Every car that passed the house I was up off the sofa and pulling the curtain in hope. Each time disappointed.

Dad was planning to go out with the workmates for a Christmas drink but was ready to call it off but I wouldn't let him, telling him I was grand that Sue was calling around. Never in a million years did I imagine what was to unfold in my life. Never. As I stared at my phone that evening, I was tempted to ring Rob or even text him. But then as the clock ticked 5pm I threw the TV control to one side, got dressed and thought, *That's it. I have to see him, face him. I can't do this anymore. I can't leave it like this. Don't know what I'll say but I'm sure when we see each other, things will be different.*

I remember clearly throwing the wrapped jumper onto the

passenger seat of the car feeling more nervous than at any time in my life. Turning the key, then texting Sue to say I was going to try get some sleep and would buzz her in the morning.

The journey was filled with extreme anxiety as I kept looking at my reflection in the mirror.

You're okay, I tried to convince myself when in truth I looked terrible. *Gosh, hurry. If Dad comes home and sees I'm out driving he'll go mental.*

As I drove nervously into his estate I noticed two taxis pulled up outside his house. Or was it the house next door? I wasn't sure. However, after parking up the road, I turned off the engine, took a few deep breaths, turned and grabbed the wrapped jumper. As I was opening, the car door I noticed Rob's door was now open and a few people going in, all talking, some laughing loudly. I stepped out of the car to get a better look and saw a well-dressed girl get out of the second taxi and walk up Rob's driveway.

Then unexpectedly, Rob appeared looking out of this world, holding a glass of drink. He burst into a big smile and clearly said the words, 'Hey, baby! You look stunning! The big night to celebrate our future awaits. I'm full!' he laughed as he staggered a bit. 'Everyone's here to celebrate!'

He romantically grabbed her, then kissed her. 'I love you, you hear me, Jill? We're going to have some Christmas. You and me forever, baby. You hear me?' He staggered a little more as she responded by saying something, but I didn't catch it. 'Table's booked for 8. Come in, come in. I've never been so existed. I can't feckin' breathe!' he giggled.

'Hey!' he said just before he closed the door as I stood feeling as if my insides were about to come up. 'Teddy has an unbelievable new nickname for me. I'm *The Financial Assassin*. Ha, ha, ha! That's exactly what I said. 'Where did you get that saying from? I love it!'

The door closed.

Chapter 15

Once You Don't Tell . . .

I stood frozen to the path for more than a few moments, trying to take in what I had just witnessed. Astoundingly there wasn't a burst of rage or desire to race over and bang down his door, screaming out for an explanation. Nothing but a horrible sense of being slowly engulfed by a strong merciless ache.

After about a minute, maybe longer, still holding the wrapped Christmas gift, I sauntered unsteadily into the garden and up to the front window. The curtains were pulled but his voice was easy to pick from the celebrating voices as he cheered and boasted about being in the form of his life.

I came back to my senses somewhat and wandered out the gate now at a pace, fumbling to get the keys out of my pocket. I purposely dropped the wrapped jumper as everything started spinning in my mind. Stopping I took a moment to try re-focus, but then turned rapidly and leaned over a wall and vomited violently into his neighbour's garden. My legs felt as weak as jelly. I struggled again to regain concentration and get the hell out of that estate.

Trying to focus on the road was a nightmare as horrifying lying statements flashed into my mind of him saying on the phone that he was devastated and depressed and hardly able to talk or go outside the door. *The bank won't give me the loan* raced over and over in my tormented mind as I tried to reject the thoughts that everything was a scheme. Then all the stuff Colm was saying. *He can't be trusted, Amy. I heard stuff about him.* Sue telling me that Claire had feelings for him. Then all the smiling comments that we were becoming soulmates as one charming deceitful lie after another became painfully real . . .

When I managed to get home, I sat for a while in the car,

bewildered. Then once inside I was able to half-think straight. Dad rang me from the pub just as I was about to sit down. I was incredibly calm and assured him everything was okay and to watch the amount of drink he was having. Sitting on the sofa in the dark alone, I tried my best to find a way to deny the clear facts. *Jesus above, this can't be it!*

An hour slowly passed as I sat staring into the open fire.

I managed to get up and foolishly I proceeded to open a bottle of vodka that was bought for Christmas and just sat drinking one glass after another straight as memories of him kissing me, making love to me, created dark feelings that I was violated, even raped. A horrible flash of him going to my mother's grave, all sympathetic, when it was only the money that interested him from the very beginning.

'Oh . . . my . . . god . . .' I slurred as I stood up and went about taking two of my anti-depression tablets as the drink deadened the horrible reality somewhat. My eyes then slowly looked up to the mantelpiece at the receipt for the wedding reception that Rob had booked for the Bracken Court Hotel. The slip of paper was still neatly placed beside my mother's framed picture.

'Yes. Can you hold the line, Miss Watts? . . . No, there's nothing booked under that name . . . Rob Cooper . . .? No . . . Sorry. Can you hold the line while I just check with the manager?'

Forever passed before the manager came on the line. 'I'm afraid there must be some mistake. There's no record of a booking under a Rob Cooper. And if there was, I would have been working with him as part of the early arrangements. And your name is again?'

'Oh, it must be the Carnegie Hotel in Swords,' I just managed and hung up.

Now stunned, I sat for ages, staring into space. I started to drink straight from the bottle, holding it to myself as I stumbled upstairs and sat down to look at my pitiful remains in the bedroom mirror.

Everything was now flashing fast in my brain. *Lies, lies, all of it was a lie!* I slurred. Placing the bottle down after two, more gulps. Everything was becoming a blur. One minute I was aware of everything, then it all went blank. Then I just picked up the scissors and waited a moment. After a moment's hesitation I let out a sigh and started cutting my own hair, first at the sides, then bits off the top. Then I applied the makeup, not noticing that I was making a complete mess of it. I picked out a sky-blue dress and put a white jacket on over it. Two more gulps and I had polished off the rest of the vodka.

Time to ring a taxi. 'Swords. Thank youuu,' I slurred.

As we drove out of Balbriggan the streetlights seemed so bright.

'Off to a fancy dress, are ye, love?' joked the taxi driver Dave.

I never replied.

'Are you okay back there?' he then asked in a concerned tone.

'I'm okay,' came the slur as he turned around and gave me a quick searching glance.

'Are you meeting friends?' he then asked as they drove up the Swords main street past the Star pub.

'Here, drop me off here,' I mumbled.

He sat staring in the rear-view mirror ready to say something but then just sped away after I gave him the fare.

I walked into the nearest pub as it lightly started to rain.

'Double vodka,' I garbled as I tried to push past a few people to get to the bar.

'You okay, love?' asked the young barman with a look of alarm.

'Thanks, yes, I'm fine, really.' I fumbled to get the money before the barman closed my hand. 'Merry Christmas. That's on the house,' he smiled.

'Take the bloody money,' I growled. 'I can pay my way!'

He took it, then bent over as he put the change softly into my hand. Then bent further and whispered. 'That's your first and last drink. I can ring you a taxi. You're out of your head, love.'

I staggered back and downed the drink in one go, turning to a sea of faces. Loads of good-looking girls with boyfriends, done up to the nines, all whispering to each other.

'Look at your woman!'

'Out of her face!'

'God, is she okay?' muttered a concerned guy. 'Someone should get her home.'

'What happened to her hair?' one girl sneered, before laughing with her friends. 'Edward Scissorhands. Hahahaha'

But I just passed everyone and made my way out. 'I managed to get two further drinks in another pub before stumbling out the door again.

One girl raced out the door with two of her friends calling her back.

'She's gone,' they moaned. 'Let's go back in. It's raining.'

'No! I'm telling ye both, that was Amy Watts from Balbriggan. She's doesn't be well. I'm going to ring one of her friends now.'

I tripped along as the rain got heavier. Everything was somewhat blank one moment then crystal clear the next as I swung my way into Hannigan's Restaurant past two huge bouncers. One of them gave me a funny searching look up and down but said nothing. I managed to secure a seat up in a corner close to the bar as an older barman served me and then enquired was everything okay.

I paid but never answered him. People were now maybe too drunk to notice me as the Christmas spirit and laughter passed back and forth with people swigging out of their pints and glasses of wine.

I drank a mouthful from my vodka and turned a searching face towards the restaurant part of the pub. With a double-take I thought I could see the top of Rob's head. *It couldn't be. It was?* I changed seats to get a better view. And there he was, almost out of sight, next to him was the girl Jill, sitting all smiles along with a small group of people I'd never seen before. He smiled with an air of happiness as he had everyone laughing at whatever he was saying. Not a single care in the world he showed as he tucked into a big steak.

'More onion rings. And hey, two extra portions of mushrooms,' he greedily requested from the waiter. 'And a fresh jug of gravy.'

I moved my chair slightly, almost falling over as one of the bouncers eyed me up but went back talking to a girl at the bar that seemed to have lost her coat or bag. I held myself back up and sat back and narrowed my eyes and studied him.

He looked totally different, nothing like the kind, caring, loving Rob that had charmed me no end. Then it started to painfully hit me. As he wiped gravy off his chin it came home to me that this was the real Rob I was observing. The guy he presented for a year was a fabrication, an act, a cunning game played out to near perfection. I knocked back a half glass of vodka and made the move to leave but that blurred thought was suddenly swung another way in my head as out of nowhere I recalled clearly him holding my disabled hand and asking did I want to have children. The delight in his eyes as he smiled and said he was thinking yes, maybe two.

I got up and slowly pushed past some people and staggered towards the table.

'Where the hell is Peter?' moaned Rob as he lashed another slice of steak into his mouth, washing it down with a mouthful of beer. 'He's missing everything.'

Ted nudged him with his elbow, throwing an eye in my direction. 'Who's your woman looking at you?'

Rob threw his eye across to the right where I stood staring straight at him.

I started blanking out slightly but tried to remain focused and think of something to say.

'What's the story?' asked one of his mates. 'Who is she?'

'Well, hi, Amy,' he asked as he kept a remarkable sense of calm. 'Is the gang with you?'

'Who is . . .?' Jill went to ask before Rob waved his hand to stop her mid-sentence. A line of confused faces looked on. Placing both knife and fork neatly down, he folded both arms and sat up straight and in the politest manner imaginable said, 'You need to go home, Amy. Let me ring you a taxi. I'll call you tomorrow morning first thing.'

I scanned his face, seeing past his phony politeness into his dark, conceited eyes that mirrored a sickening, self-gratifying evil.

'What? Amy, please,' he continued in a composed tone. 'I did my best, as you know. Now I'm trying to rebuild my life after everything that happened with us and your friends. So would you mind allowing me to finish my steak? Please?' He turned to apologize to his friends, who all looked extremely embarrassed.

I plunged forward in a moment of pure rage, picked up the steak knife and rammed it downwards into his chest.

There was an eerie silence before Rob with a horrified expression and both arms up in the air screeched in terror. 'I've been knifed!' His right foot shot up as he fell backwards, turning over the whole table. Drinks, food, the lot crashed to the floor before Jill went into hysterics.

'Robert! Someone! She's after stabbing Rob!'

All hell broke out as people started screaming and panicking, some heading for the door. The two bouncers rushed forward. One raced to aid Rob who was sitting upright, trying to scream out, but now total shock.

'I'm dying!' he finally cried out in fear as his eyes rolled up into his head.

'Help him!' yelled a pale-faced Ted. 'Get a bloody doctor! An ambulance!'

The other bouncer tackled me as I stood motionless, holding my face up to a wall with one arm gripped behind my back. 'Easy now, easy!' he whispered into my ear.

I could hear nothing but unnatural screams as Jill sobbed and roared and kicked. 'You evil crazy bitch!'

From the corner of my eye I could see blood all over the other bouncer's white shirt as he attempted to stop the bleeding. Another guy had to use all his strength to stop Jill attacking me.

'You horrible crazy freak . . .!' she hissed.

I looked behind to the other side as my face remained pressed up to a wall. Everything started to go peculiar inside my head.

I saw what looked like the back of a clock, or watch, it opened up again, all the small parts were so clear to see, as if I was in the clock myself and every part was alive and moving in such beautiful harmony. Straight away I reached over and touched it.

Then I thought I could see this magical stunning ocean spreading out as far as the eye could see. Just out of reach I saw the figure of a person calling, waving one hand. I looked closer and thought it looked like a very young version of my mother. But I couldn't be sure. *Push out, Amy, push out,* the calm voice counselled. In a split second, all the loud voices started to fade into the background. *You'll be safe now, swim, swim, and just keep swimming, Amy.*

I could still see the lights from the pub windows and the streetlights diminish as I pushed out into the warm water and away from the scuffles and screams. *Don't look back, no matter what,* I told myself as I drifted further out.

I stopped and gazed sideways and thought I saw a flash of Sue's face, crying, and the lights of an ambulance blinking.

The cop closed the back door of the car after jumping in to aid me as I finally came back into some focus. 'Relax,' he stressed with a look of alarm. Then as the other cop turned around from the front seat I noticed I was handcuffed. Placing his hat back on he said, 'We've to take her to Greenridge.'

'Right, right. Go, go!' stressed the cop. 'Go!'

*

Peter Bradley arrived late. Pushing past people almost in a panic, without hesitation he raced to Rob's side. 'What the hell!' he yelled as two paramedics worked frantically on him. 'I'm his business partner,' he explained.

'Don't care who you are! Stand well back and let them do their job,' stressed one of the bouncers as he stood back himself.

Rob, just barely able to open his eyes, muttered a faint gasp. 'Peter, God, Peter! I think. . . I can't breathe,' he managed. 'I'm scared.'

'You're going to be okay,' Peter assured him. 'Save your energy, mate.'

He turned to Jill who was still inconsolable and just shook his head. 'What the hell happened?' he asked Ted who was standing with two others trying to calm Jill down.

'Some crazy bitch out of her head on drugs stabbed him,' he just about managed before filling up himself.

Peter put his arm around Jill and drew her close and into both arms. 'Hey Jill everything is going to be okay. I'm here now. I'll take care of you.'

*

I barely managed to open my eyes as I found myself being led down a long, brightly-lit corridor. I remember thinking I saw Dad crying as the younger of the two cops talked intently to him. He walked away holding his hands to his face as two caring nurses took my hands as a cop placed his hat back on and with a distraught look on his face turned and calmly walked back down the long hallway.

'Come this way now,' ordered a nurse. I saw her badge: Bridie Whelan. 'Now, now easy does it,' she stressed, her warm smile vanishing fast.

I was brought into a cream-coloured room as Nurse Whelan opened a press, and another nurse took a firm hold of both my arms. 'Now, now, easy does it,' she said as she turned, holding a syringe.

'No,' I said as the panic increased no end. 'Get my dad back in, please!'

'Now, now, don't talk,' said the nurse holding me. 'Easy, Amy, easy.'

Unexpectedly I just freaked out and kicked out and started screaming for her to let me go. 'I want to go home!' I shrieked. 'I'm starting to feel a bit better now!'

'Hold her down!' yelled Nurse Whelan as she tried to hold me with her free hand.

In the tussle I threw both legs up and out, hitting and sending her flying almost to the other side of the room. She lost her footing and fell face first against the side of a radiator. There was a pause before she screeched in pain. She struggled to get on her feet as the blood poured through her fingers from a cut to the right side of her face just below her eye. She wiped the blood away with a tissue as best she could, her hands, her body now shaking with rage and a sense of disbelief that anyone would dare hit her.

'By God, you're going to pay with what remains of your decrepit life for that violent attack on me!' she said through gritted teeth as she tried to regain her focus. She grabbed my arm with force this time as the other nurse held my other arm and body from behind. 'Hold the little bitch!' she hissed.

'I'm really sor– . . .' I went to say as they administered the injection with force. Everything went blurry, then seconds later, I must have passed out.

I remember trying to wake up and feeling horrible beyond belief. My head was thumping with the pain of a rotten hangover. Then I kind of remembered being given something, an injection of something that made me feel so out of it. Both my arms were bruised and swollen. I was wearing a type of gown. But for the life of me, I couldn't recollect very much else about what took place the night before, just small flashes that made little or no sense.

I then realised that the room I was in was almost pitch dark. I tried to figure out where I was as I slowly felt around for the light switch. To complete my horror scenario I realised everything was padded. *My god.* I gulped as I saw there was only one small window on the door that gave the dimmest of light from the outside in.

Panic that you couldn't humanly describe gripped me as I screamed out for someone to come and open the door. 'Is there anyone there? Help me get my father now!' I slurred as I tried to stand up, but the drowsy effects of the drink and the injection made me fall back to the floor. My speech slurred, as I felt so weak and sleepy. I just managed to screech 'Hello? . . . Is there anyone there? . . .'

A male voice came from . . . from somewhere . . .

'Once you don't tell
No one goes to hell.'

To be continued . . .